Sun was sinking, even so far north and high summer, so late I was on the road; tide was ebbing as I came at last to the last bridge over the last river and saw the glow of my city right ahead. Mud flats below me, glistening darkly and striped with shadow; council flats before me, grey concrete towers tinged pink and striped with light. Catch me living in one of those: I had a pretty good idea how much the constructors had paid my family for the contract, which meant I could make a pretty good guess just how pre-stressed that concrete was. They had to make their profit some-where, after all . . .

Light Errant

Chaz Brenchley

NEW ENGLISH LIBRARY
Hodder and Stoughton

First published in Great Britain in 1997 by Hodder and Stoughton
First published in paperback in 1998 by Hodder and Stoughton
A division of Hodder Headline PLC

A New English Library Paperback

10 9 8 7 6 5 4 3 2 1

A CIP catalogue record is available
from the British Library

ISBN 0 340 68557 3

Printed and bound in Great Britain by
Clays Ltd, St Ives plc

Hodder and Stoughton
A division of Hodder Headline PLC
338 Euston Road
London NW1 3BH

This is for Carolyn:
shortest, longest, cattiest of editors.
Prrr, prrr . . .

ONE

FAIR SPANISH LADIES

Summer in Spain: beach sports, sex and slaughter in the sun.

Well, actually the slaughter was from someone else's schedule. Some malign god (if gods there be) had scribbled it down on the list with a bloody finger, my punishment for not paying attention.

Me, I was wholly occupied with what came first on that list, and what I'd planned for later. And why not, what else should a young man be doing or planning to do in the heat and freedom of a Spanish summer Sunday?

The sky was clear, the sea was cool and calm, as we were not: a dozen lads laughing, gasping, sweating in the hot light as we chased a plastic ball, tackled and shoulder-charged and tried to foul each other monstrously with bare feet in soft sand.

I was wearing swim-shorts and nothing, my regular outfit these baking, undemanding days. And shorts and skin both might be sticky and crusted now but skin could be showered and soaped clean, shorts could be shed – *soon, soon* – and meanwhile my blood fizzed and sparkled under the sun's lash and I could do anything on such a day, no limits.

And this was a grudge match, staff against students, and we were trailing by a single much-disputed goal; and the repugnant cheat Luis who'd claimed that score had the ball again and was all too certainly going to pass it to his equally-vile kid brother Ramon to share the honours around the family; and what chance our corpulent, sand-blind and chickenhearted goalkeeper making a heroic dive to snatch the ball from the boy's disgusting feet . . . ?

Precisely zero chance, I reckoned. Which meant it was up to me, last line of defence and no way, no *way* were these two monoglot morons going to waltz past me this time in arrogant defiance of the offside law and my infinitely superior status . . .

I watched Luis's eyes, made pretence to back off, listened for the thud of feet on sand behind me; and *mirabile dictu*, it really did work. I saw his intention a moment before he moved to make it so, nor was he selling me a dummy. His eyes flickered to find his brother, his foot slid the ball across the bumping sand – and I was already stretching to intercept, catching it atop the arch of my foot and sending it almost straight up into the air. And taking it on the chest as it came down, and momentum carrying us both forward together, me and the ball, so that it looked for all the world as though I had trapped it neatly and brought it under instant control.

And now I was running, dribbling, dodging tackles with phenomenal skill or laughable ease, depending; and my team-mates' cries filled the air from left and right of me, screaming for a pass; but this was my moment, I could feel it, and I wasn't sharing it with anyone. Luis and Ramon had an elder sister, and I hadn't looked to find her but she should be here by now, she should be watching . . .

So I skittered and dodged and somehow – for the first, the only time in my life – came through all the traffic with the ball still at my feet, and now it was *mano a mano*, just me and their goalie and oh God, surely, *surely* I couldn't screw this now . . . ?

No more than ours was he a dive-at-their-feet hero; he scuttled forward crouching, spreading arms and legs as wide as possible, hoping mostly that I would miss, I guess. And I grinned and toe-poked a shot straight forward, straight between his legs, sweetly nutmegged him and was already punching the air in triumph as I saw the ball falter in its rolling, as I saw it die a foot short of the excavated goal-line, just not enough power to carry it over this soft, sucking sand.

Only a moment I had, before the twisting, sprawling goalie's hand would reach it; only a moment to cheat, to break at least the implicit rules of the game, and in doing that also to betray myself and my honour, two years'-worth of oaths sworn and clung to. But, hell, they'd cheated too, their goal had been blatantly offside and they knew it; the rest was my own concern, and what did my honour mean against the crucial matter of Staff vs Students?

Sun on my back, on my shoulders and legs, doing far more to my blood than just warm it: my eyes on the ball, I reached mentally for a long-neglected skill, I gripped the world and nudged it, just a touch . . .

And the ball kicked, a fraction ahead of the goalie's desperate fingers; it skipped, slowed, trickled to another halt, this time a sweet foot's length the yonder side of the line.

And I whooped, heedless and happy, and spun on my heel to dance my celebration under the eyes of Marina, beautiful big sister of my two star students. I could hear her voice already, crying applause from the sidelines. I hoped I could hear her thoughts too, I hoped she was thinking *siesta* as I was, thinking of a wide bed in a shuttered room, a cool bottle of rosada and a long hot afternoon, soft voices and hard breaths . . .

And my eyes found Marina in her gold-brown skin, and plenty of it; her tumbling hair, plenty of that too and only a couple of shades darker; her shades, her baggy sleeveless T-shirt, her tormenting shorts. And her long arms were waving to salute me, and like a print-boy she had armpits like chalices, if chalices are hairy; and her longer legs were swinging where she sat on the wall above the beach; and right beside her and also slightly, tightly waving was Sallah. So much shorter, so much darker, so very much not supposed to be there . . .

My feet faltered on the sand, my throat stifled my delight. *Forget the siesta, Ben.* Forget the bed, the rosada, the slow sex in fugitive bars of sunlight. These girls, I thought, were not here to offer me a threesome.

These girls, I remembered, were not supposed to know each other at all. Certainly not to know about each other and me. Ach, and I'd been looking forward so much to what was left of the summer. I'd even had a line fit for a postcard home, *I'm a well-loved man, and I'm carrying the bruises to prove it.*

I'd been so keen to use that, good lines come so rarely: more rarely even than my postcards home. Little enough chance of it now, I was afraid. Little chance of its being honest, at least; I might use it regardless. I had more reasons than one for wanting to send that card, and the important ones didn't require honesty.

At my back the game was going on, but I was still standing rooted, seeming to have stepped without moving into something totally else. Another game? Perhaps; but my understanding of girls – based on limited experience, and a lot of listening to cousins – suggested that when they got together this way, when they ganged up, all the points would be scored on their side and the only goal was retribution.

Might as well get it over, Ben boy. Someone behind me

yelled my name, calling me back to help in a desperate defence; I barely glanced around, waved an apologetic hand and abandoned them. Walked off the field of play and poked my toes into sandals half-buried in the sand, kicked at nothing to work them free of the clinging beach and trotted up concrete steps to face my fate.

Briefly, it didn't seem so bad. Marina kissed me where we met, leaping from the wall she sat on and showing a lot more enthusiasm than I could manage in the circumstances. Lips to lips and tongue to tongue she greeted me, much as I'd pictured this moment in anticipation; and only I was spoiling my own picture, almost flinching away from this tall, tender, teasing girl where I should have been wrapping my arms around her, knocking heads with her, setting my eyes against her shades to squint the best I could through to the dark heart of her . . .

Not Sallah kissed me, no. When Marina untangled at last her fingers from my hair and let me look, I saw her dark companion – hers? Mine, had been and should have been, mine only and shouldn't have been anywhere near me this day – on her feet and silent like a shadow but making no shadow-moves else, not moving to shadow Marina's pleasure in me.

So I went to her, bravely to one lover under the watchful eyes of another I went, put my hands on her narrow shoulders and kissed her in greeting as the Spanish do, chastely on the cheeks; and felt more than heard her sigh, felt the bone-deep tension in her, read something close to panic in her eyes; and *sod it*, I did the arm-wrapping thing regardless of its being the wrong girl I wrapped. I held her close and tight, what mute comfort I could offer in my confusion, and saw Marina's approval as I did it and understood nothing except that this was not after all retribution.

Sallah's head in my shoulder, and me too muddled to

move: it was Marina again who broke the tableau at last, gripping one of my wrists, one of Sallah's. I startled at her touch, like a guilty thing not at all surprised; but she only smiled, and peeled us gently apart.

"Sallah has troubles," she said, in the English I was teaching her: no longer broken but not fluent either, not yet a seamless whole. Patchwork, I suppose. "We can go and talk now?"

"Yes, of course." I had troubles also, these two together still troubled me greatly; but there are troubles and troubles, and as I looked at Sallah the phrase 'hill of beans' attached itself inexorably to mine. I should count myself lucky, probably, to be apparently getting out of this with a whole skin and the privilege of someone else's burden. If my plans for the summer – my tipsy and delicious plans, slip-sliding from one girl to the other, from happy tumbling to soul-shaking erotic intensity – if those plans were the only victim here, likely we would all be getting off lightly. "Where do you want to go?"

"To your room, please. Where we are private."

"Um, I came down on the bike . . ."

A shrug, a smile, "So we go back on the bike. Sallah is little, we will – accommodate ourselves?"

"Fit," I suggested.

"*Si*. We will fit. Sallah in between, so my hair does not bite her face."

"Sting."

"Sting is a singer."

"Sure, Sting is a singer; but sting is what your hair does, not bite. It hasn't got teeth," though it felt sometimes as though it had, whipping in the bike's wind. When I let her drive, I took the helmet for protection: put it on her head if she'd wear it, or on my own with the visor down if she wouldn't.

That day I drove, with both girls stacked behind me.

Short-haired Sallah was the meat in our sandwich, and actually I thought Marina's hair only the excuse, not the reason. There were hugs inherent here: Sallah was cosseted by definition, with someone to hold to and someone holding her, the pressure of bodies fore and aft, no danger of feeling alone even for five minutes, even in transit.

Glad of that she was or seemed to be, the way she clung. Me, I was glad of it also, and not for the feel of her fingers on my bare and cooling skin, not that, not now; rather for the extra weight changing the bike's balance as we swung around the curve of the bay. No one could challenge my right to this bike. It was registered, taxed and insured, all in my name, and many thousands of miles it had carried me, the last two years; but still I was always neurotically glad of passengers. One was good, two I thought was better: this bike was *full*. No room for anyone or anything to ride my back, ride my mind, rowel me with memory.

No room for my sister's ghost to reclaim what had been hers. Sometimes I felt her there despite all the years and all the miles I'd laid down between us now; sometimes there were hard fingers laid over mine, cold breath on my neck and an indomitable will set against me, hissing *mine!*

Only if I were alone, though, never with company riding pillion. If I were feeling fatuous, I might claim hence the two girlfriends: to double my chances of escaping a haunting, each time I drove. I seldom went anywhere on the bike these days, after all, without one girl or the other; and *quod erat demonstrandum*, the effect obviously explained the cause, the end justified the means. Of course it did.

No doubt I also ate garlic only to keep the vampires away. It worked, after all; the vampires were keeping many leagues away from me, lurking back in Transylvania. I knew, I'd interviewed a couple of their victims . . .

Actually, of course, I believed in ghosts no more than I did

in vampires, and my sister did not, did *not* ride at my back
even when no other girl did. It only felt that way when my
mind slipped a gear, when I forgot to remember that I was
a free spirit these days, not at all bound to the past or to
the sad, fucked-up boy I used to be. Born a twin, I was
a singleton now, all alone in a wide, wide world; and if I
chose to double up on lovers, it was a choice I'd made and
a risk I'd taken for reasons that had nothing whatsoever to
do with what lay so far behind me.

A risk come home to roost now, seemingly; but not
seemingly with malevolent intent. Only because there was
a need, Sallah had a problem and Marina thought maybe I
could help, though God alone knew why or how. Sallah I
guessed had demurred, Marina insisted; and I knew myself,
Marina's insistence was not a thing to be lightly put aside.
Nor, though, was Sallah's ordinarily-strict demurral; hence
the two of them here together, Marina making sure of an
uncertain victory. Otherwise no doubt they'd have kept apart
and let me go on dating each in turn, thinking in my naïvety
that neither one knew about the other . . .

Had they been going in for comparative studies, I wondered: dark head and darkly golden bent gigglingly close in
a café, murmuring about my misdeeds and making wicked
recommendations, each to the other?

Maybe they had, but it didn't matter. What mattered was
here and now, both girls on the bike behind me, Sallah in
trouble and something perhaps that I could do to help. Never
mind about the past – *never ever* – nor the future either,
which of the girls if either one would keep me. Their choice,
I thought it would be, and me no more than an acquiescent;
I hoped it wouldn't matter too much to me, which way they
chose. Doubted that, but hoped none the less. Best I could
manage; but what more can anyone proffer to the future,
what more convincing than hope?

*   *   *

Home – where we were heading, this risk realised, with roosting on its mind – was a room in the centre of town, ten minutes' walk from anywhere that counted, ten minutes' drive from work. Six months I'd been there now, or a little longer. The house actually belonged to a senior lecturer at the college; he usually let the room to a student, but I'd landed lucky with this as with the job: a contract not honoured, an unexpected vacancy after Christmas and suddenly there I was, free, capable and willing. I hadn't signed up for the next year's teaching yet, but I thought that probably I would. I liked it here: great food, great people, north coast so no tourists but sun enough for anyone, even sun enough for me who fizzed and sparkled in the light but lost it all at nightfall . . .

Even with my quiet deceits exposed, I still thought I might stay. If the girls would let me.

In all truth, my landlord probably hadn't noticed too much difference between letting to me and letting to a student. The college boys puttered around on mopeds for the most part, where I thundered on a big BMW; that aside, young men are young men, and I still had some catching-up to do. I played music at antisocial hours, I had rowdy room-parties, I brought girls home for the night or more often for the siesta (it made for less trouble at home, they said; privately I suspected they preferred it, for the tingle they could catch off my skin even in broken sunlight, that just wasn't the same after dark) and I came into school sometimes looking more bedraggled and hung over than my charges. No one had complained, though – yet – and they had at least offered me that second year, so I had to be doing something right.

The town filled a headland with bays on either side. Deep water to the west gave it a harbour for the fishing fleet, a massive freezing-plant, other industries throwing muck into the heavy, sweaty air; to the east was the long curve of the beach with the promenade above it, open-air stalls and a funfair at the end, also the college campus just beyond.

Squeezed between the two, the old town was all narrow streets and high stone walls, dark shopfronts and no pavements, unexpected corners and sudden surprises.

As where I lived, which might not surprise the locals but still got me every time, known and anticipated and none the less startling. On a street like all the others, tight-arsed and dingy and unforthcoming, making no promises, there was a jeweller and a baker and a gloomy ungated arch to separate them. I turned the bike under the arch, saw the light at the end of the tunnel; eight, ten yards of murk and dazzle and we came out the other side into a courtyard bright with flowers in earthenware tubs, hard with light and shadow on the whitewashed walls.

The girls slipped off as I held the bike steady for them, each of them knew this routine; then I parked in the cool, or the best approximation I could find, the corner that would get no more sun today. Gave the bike a little rub on its petrol tank, not so much a polish as a caress or a touch for luck; and it still seemed strange to me sometimes that I'd never thought to give it a name, we were that close, we'd been so far together.

I stood in the shadow, the girls were waiting in the sun; and as I came back to them both reached for a hand to hold, and this too was routine, only that there were two of them here today and barely enough hands to go around. Even Sallah's mouth twitched into something of a smile as she caught Marina's eye, as they sorted out silently between them who went left and who went right.

Sensitised to it now, I felt the little kick in each of them as they touched and clung, as my sundizzy blood passed on its charge. Sometimes I could feel maybe a little resentful, that they loved me for my side-effects and not myself; but *smarten up, Macallan,* what's personality if it isn't the sum of our side-effects? And besides, they didn't love me at all, and it really didn't matter. I didn't love them either. We were just good bunkmates, nothing more . . .

Had been just good bunkmates, or so I'd thought. So I'd thought I wanted. Today, obviously, was nothing to do with bunking. Something more there was, then, after all; I had an uncomfortable feeling in my gut that they were about to call in a presumptive debt, and what could I do but pay up?

My room in the house had its own entrance, at the top of an iron staircase that spiralled up one corner of the courtyard. There were geraniums in pots on every step, which made climbing it a hazard in the drunken dark, and an exercise in strict single file even now. We went up hand in hand, though, Marina leading: and this was how it always was with either girl individually, we went up linked but she led me and always I led Sallah.

Barely space for three of us on the little landing at the top, and here too an established routine played itself out. I wasn't allowed to let go of either girl's hand; it was Marina who grinned with an extra wickedness today as she slipped her fingers into my pocket and fished for the keys, as she worked the door open one-handed and tugged us all inside.

Routine said we should cross the threshold kissing; at least she didn't insist on that. Instead she let me go and took Sallah from me also, took both her hands and pulled her over to the bed. Marina sprawled, Sallah sat neatly, tightly on the edge, her small feet barely reaching the floor. They talked in soft Spanish, too fast for me to follow. Figuring that meant my attention was not immediately required, I went over to the corner of the room, where forethought had laid a bottle of rosada in my washbasin, keeping cool in water. Sighing one more time for the afternoon that wasn't going to happen, I fished it out and fetched three glasses from a cupboard.

Observant little creature of virtue that she was, Sallah hardly ever drank anything stronger than coffee, and never where she might be seen by another believer. The occasional glass of wine, though, with an infidel or two, that didn't seem to be a problem: like other things forbidden to her – like the conjunction of bodies on a shuttered afternoon, an animal act without benefit of law or blessing – she would give it as much solemn attention as she gave to her prayers or her cooking or her English lessons, and take as much pleasure from the doing of it as she did from the taste or the touch or the tingle. And as much pleasure again from doing it not, back in the bosom of her family. It wasn't a Catholic-style guilt thing, she didn't sin the better to repent after; I thought it was a control thing mostly, Sallah demonstrating to herself that she did govern her own life, that even her religion was of her choosing and its rules subject to her willing acceptance, not she to their arbitrary diktat.

Here in my room, a little light or sometimes concentrated sinning was second nature to us both. Today I didn't even ask, I just poured her a glass along with Marina and myself. I thought she needed it; if she disagreed, the steely gears of her mind would lock that decision into place, and she'd set the glass aside and never think more about it.

Ordinarily, at least. That was my expectation, but I'm good at getting things wrong. Scary sometimes how firm she could be, how certain in what seemed to me a highly debatable world: scary today how doubtful she seemed, how hesitant, how needful. There was a tremble in her fingers when I passed her the wine; I cupped my own hands around hers for a moment and pressed gently, warm palms against cold fingers against cool beaded glass. Her smile was unconvincing, her eyes were not. Ridiculously big always in her small, fine-boned face, today they were to die in, deep dark pools of danger rimmed with red where she'd spent half the night crying by the look of her. Crying silently, I was sure, crying face-down into her pillow not to wake anyone else, not to worry her family . . .

I kissed her fleetingly, squeezed her hands again and went to fetch Marina's wine, and my own. *Autre temps, autre moeurs*: if this had panned out the way I'd planned it, I might have been sinking to the floor at her feet right now in one of those deliberate, delicious moments of delay, resting my head against her thigh, feeling her long fingers in my hair teasing and twisting, starting to tug . . .

But the two girls filled the bed: space enough for three, perhaps, but emotional room there was not. I retreated to the window, and perched there.

"Come on, then," I said softly. "Who's going to tell me about it?"

Actually, I already knew the answer to that. Sallah came to me for private tuition, and she worked hard, but her English wasn't strong enough to hold against such tension as I could see in her now; nor could my Spanish keep up anywhere off the phrase-book paths of dalliance, even if it could have handled her immigrant accent.

One mute glance she gave, towards Marina; but that was for form only, and quite redundant. They'd worked this out already. They might even have rehearsed.

"Ben," Marina began, "you know Sallah's family, that they are not lawful here?"

Yes, I did know that. A little I'd had from Sallah, what exchanges of confidence we could manage in alien tongues; more I'd picked up from gossip with staff and students at the college. Sallah's parents had come here from Morocco years ago, and long outstayed their visas. They didn't hide, they sold leatherwork from a stall right on the promenade; and they had a longstanding and easy relationship with the chief of police, I'd heard, paying a gentle bribe every month to be sure he continued to overlook their lack of official papers.

But that complaisant policeman had retired, Marina told

me, his pension no doubt comfortably swollen by all those backhanders; and, "The new man," she said, "he is not so convenient."

"He can't want to deport them, surely?" I demanded; then, when she frowned, "Not to send them back, Marina? After so long?"

"No," she said slowly. "But he threats this, yes? Unless . . ."

Threatens, but I didn't say it. There are times to worry about a pupil's grammar, and times definitely not. "Unless what?"

Now she was awkward, she was embarrassed – for Sallah, not for herself: I read that in the glance aside, in the hand that reached for her friend's – and she didn't want to answer. And that reluctance was answer enough, I could read the truth also, I wasn't that naïve.

"*Jesus . . .!*"

Marina the sometimes-good Catholic girl scowled at me for the blasphemy, but nodded also. "He has seen Sallah, and he says, he says he will not take money, but . . ."

He would take her instead, a tribute to his new-won authority. Regularly, no doubt; monthly, perhaps, his own version of a mensal bribe; very much against her will, it went without saying. Sallah would do a great deal for her family, that I knew. I had thought before that she might even marry according to their choice and not her own, though it would be her own choice to do so. This, though – no. Or I thought not; or that was my first thought, at least. But for her parents' livelihood, for her parents' *life* – and what was it, after all? The conjunction of bodies, only an animal act, and no more than she did with me already, and sweetly, fiercely more than once a month . . .

The impossibility of decision, she couldn't and yet she must: this, then, was the thing too great even for her mind to encompass, what had forced her gears out of mesh.

"Does your brother know?" I asked her directly. She

shook her head, mute and appealing, *don't tell him*; I nodded
my understanding. Her brother Mahmout was at the college,
though she was not. I knew him by sight, and by reputation:
a hothead, too streetwise too young, a charmer with a ready
smile and a knife just as ready, or so rumour said.

"Mahmout would kill him," Marina murmured. I believed
that, as absolutely as they did. For his family's honour,
he would kill; and with that killing his family would be
destroyed, himself jailed and perhaps his parents also, for
a year or two before they were deported.

So no, Mahmout was not to know. They had come to me
instead, with or more likely without her parents' consent or
knowledge. What was I? Publicly, Sallah's English tutor;
privately, her lover; more private still, I was a young man
who knew too much about bribes and blackmail and all
the excesses of power. My own family was expert in such
practices.

Marina knew something of that, if Sallah didn't. This must
have been her idea; she'd be looking to me for a solution, a
way out of a brutal maze.

And yes, I could give them that, I had it in me. There
would be a price, of course, and it would be mine to pay;
and yes, I owed them. I owed them both, more than they
knew; so what matter if they were asking more than they
could possibly know?

Besides, I was angry. Coldly, furiously angry, sick with
anger in a way I'd not felt for years. I knew vileness, I was
an old hand at recognising the stink of it; and oh, this was
vile, this was worthy of a Macallan.

"What's his name?" I demanded; and almost wouldn't
have been surprised if they'd said *Macallan*.

I left the girls in my room, with instructions to finish the
wine and sleep after if they wanted, share the bed, they
were welcome to it; then go, I said, go out to the beach,

enjoy the sun, have a coffee, have dinner, have fun. Lock
up when you leave, I said, stick the key under one of the
geraniums.

Where was I going? Never mind, I said. And don't worry,
I said that too. I'll sort this out, I said.

Hot and eager the bike was, under my hard hands; hot and
ready I was, even in the chill blast of wind it made as I
devilrode it. Bareback under the sun's lash, I could never
be anything else.

The police station was a modern concrete block on the
outskirts of town, the ugly side, appropriately wreathed as
often as not with a thick yellow hellsmoke, the downfall
from a gross of industrial chimneys. I gave it a glance as
I drove past, only hoping that Inspector de Policía Mañuel
Garcia de Ramos found himself on duty and available this
fine afternoon. If he was there, he would make himself
available, I thought. If not, I thought I could get a message
to him regardless. Good policemen – ambitious, promotable
policemen – always stay in touch; and he would declare himself on special duty when that message arrived, I thought,
whatever private pleasure he might previously have been
pursuing.

Past the police station and a long way past, past the fac-
tories and the processing plant, through the burnt-chemicals-
and-fishguts fug and at last out to where I could breathe
again; and now the road was increasingly rough, breaking
up for lack of use or care, as I came to the next headland.
No town here, no usable harbour so no village, even, no
human habitation. Just a ness, rocks and shale and grass
like wire and a far fall down to the sea; God alone knew
why they'd built a road this far in the first place, no blame
that they hadn't bothered to maintain it. At night, I knew,
teenagers came out here in their fathers' cars, wrecking the
suspension with the potholes and the jig-a-jig. You could see

all the headlights from town sometimes, lighting the place like a carnival, beaming like a signal out to sea. There was little action in daylight, though, and none at all right now, in the muggy heart of the day.

I checked that, then turned and retraced my tracks for half a mile, to the last of the industrial estates. Here were bus-stops, and here also public phones; in my head, the number Sallah had given me.

"Inspector Ramos, please?" No trouble to sound like a young English traveller, tense and nervous and a little excited; I pretty much was all of those, for real.

"*Si.*"

"Er, do you speak English?"

"A little. You speak, I understand."

"Okay, good. Great. Listen, there's a girl, out on the Munchial? You know where I mean?"

"*Si.* Yes, I know. What girl?"

"She's standing right on the edge there, and she says she's going to jump. She says she wants to talk to you. No one else, she said, only you . . ."

"Her name?"

"Sallah, she said. That's all, she said you'd know . . ."

"Yes. Your name, please?"

I gave him a false one and said I was just passing through, not staying in town, I'd only stopped for the view and a doze in the sun. Better hurry, I said, the girl looked desperate . . .

He said thank you and goodbye, told me not to go back to the headland, not to go near the girl; then he hung up. I drove a couple of hundred metres down the road and then pulled off it, parked in the shade of a high wall and waited.

Ten minutes, twenty, and here he came. Not in a jam sandwich, a *coche-patrulla*, a police car with sirens blaring and lights aflare (the Mexican kids at college just called

them *coches*, with a particular twist of the lip to tell you they
weren't talking about ordinary cars but they did indeed mean
pigs, which the word also meant to them): fast but quiet he
came in what was probably his private car, unmarked and
unremarkable, barely breaking the speed limit. But he was
still in uniform, he'd had no time or chance to change that.
I was certain of him.

I gave him a fifty-metre start, and followed. It occurred
to me then, briefly, that I didn't actually know why he had
come, though I'd been absolutely sure that he would. To
gloat? To bully or persuade or entice Sallah back from the
edge – or else to push her over, literally or metaphorically,
to cut his small losses and be assured of silence?

I couldn't say, I didn't know the man. I knew only the
one thing about him, indeed, that he was spiritually flesh of
my flesh, all my family incarnate in one man when I thought
I'd left them a thousand miles behind.

Dangerous as a Macallan, ugly inside and no main beauty
on the surface either; and stupid with it, stupid with arrogance, that was another trait shared between my kin and
him. One phone-call from a stranger had fetched him, alone
and unquestioning; he wasn't even watching for a tail.

I drove behind him, hating him, all the way back to the
point. A heavy-set man, mid-thirties, glossy black hair and a
five o'clock shadow; that much I'd registered, even through
the windscreen and his hurry. The interior view concerned
me more, though. Whatever he was hurrying towards, it was
meant to be his own benefit and none of Sallah's. Already
he'd broken what had seemed so strong in her, the absolute
conviction that the world worked, that what was right was
clear to be seen and engaging with it simply a matter of
choice. She was wrong, of course, but admirably so and I'd
loved her for it; and that was gone now, shattered like the
movement of a sprung clock and probably irreparable.

Irreparable from his side also, his fault unredeemable.

Anger had worked this ambush, my anger had fetched him to me; now, now was the time to unleash it.

Second time today I'd broken all the vows in the world, reclaimed my heritage, made myself monstrous. On the football sand it had been a momentary inspiration, pure ego, weakness disguised; here it was cold and deliberate, and for cause. This I could live with, and its consequences also.

Actually, I could live with the other also. Being weak was not a worry, it was an old and half-forgotten habit that felt like coming home.

The road here hugged the cliff-edge, before petering out among rocks and grass. The sun was bright in my eyes, hot on my skin but my blood was hotter beneath, remembering the chill on Sallah's face.

All I needed to do, all I did was to focus, to reach out with my mind's hidden strength, to allow my fury a moment's release.

As God is my witness, was my only witness that day – if there is a God, which I doubt, which I usually deny – all I meant to do was bring pain and ruin to a vile man, to destroy his life and his career, to save Sallah by putting him in hospital and on the pension list. The rocks were my targets, not the sea. A tumbling wreck I wanted, and I was ready to nudge, to push, to bend steel if necessary to make it happen.

All I did was use my talent to set his tyres alight. No more than that. Just a touch, just a thought of pale flame in sunlight and there it was, a fierce shimmer in the car's shadow and soft explosions after.

Not my fault, surely not my fault that he was stupid or unlucky or just surprised and not thinking straight: that when he lost control, when he felt the car veer he turned the wheel left instead of right.

Nothing I could do then, nothing but watch as the car

skirred the wrong way, left the road to hit air and not rocks, seemed to hang like a cartoon joke for a moment before it plunged out of my sight.

Nothing to do but slam on the brakes and skid a little myself, fight the Beemer to a halt on the bad road and sit still for a breathless second before I kicked the stand down and set reluctant sandals to the tarmac, walked slowly and shakily to where blackened tracks marked a fatal take-off.

I stood and looked, looked down; saw a crushed chaos of metal and presumptive flesh, saw it tip and roll in the tidal suck, saw it sucked under.

Not wanting to count, but that made two policemen I'd killed in my life, and neither one intentionally. This should have been easier to live with than the other, but not then was it, nor later. Still not. Among other lacks, I don't have my family's traditional insouciance.

A few minutes I guess I stood there, not really thinking, only tasting defeat and acceptance, not justice but a just return for arrogance. Mine, as much as his. Then I mounted the bike again and drove slowly back to town with a sense of finality riding my shoulders all the way, a barrier between the sun and me.

This much at least I had expected and planned for, that I would be packed and gone by sunset. Even if my designs had worked as they were meant to, I couldn't have stayed. Room and job both were sacrifices to the day's necessity; Marina and Sallah both, and all my easy pleasures. A bad man's unintended death didn't even add urgency, only bitterness.

I parked in the courtyard, in the shade; trotted up the stairs, bent to find the key beneath a geranium pot, let myself in. Shoved armfuls of clothes into a rucksack, carried the rest of my gear down – little enough: a few books, a few folders, a few precious mementos – to stow in the bike's panniers; went back up for one last look round, nostalgia and practicality mixed, then locked the door, dropped the key through my landlord's letterbox and drove away with no more farewell than that.

Hit the road as so often before, but no longer pretending I was rootless, or a free spirit, or young and alone in a wide and wonderful world. Comes a time when running and hiding can't cut it any more, even for a craven soul like mine.

Where was I going? I was going home.

· TWO ·

ILL-LIT BY MOONLIGHT

Go slowly, come back quickly.

That hadn't been the plan, actually, neither part of it: I'd left home, left town, left friends and family and life behind me in a roar and a *hurry, hurry* fury, and I hadn't planned to come back at all.

But once gone, once irrevocably somewhere else – Manchester as it had happened, but it might have been anywhere: I'd simply driven until I wanted to stop, not looking ahead at all, only making a trailer for the road-movie of my future life – the air and the tarmac and everything I touched had been suddenly gluey, and my toes were growing roots. I wasn't finished with the going yet, I knew that, I might be gone but I wasn't gone nearly far enough; but it was suddenly impossibly hard to go further. Once stopped, I couldn't get started again. Took me months to get me out of the country, though I'd known all along I had to go. Things to do and people to see, I had, people to *find*: and there couldn't be many of them and the world was broad, and I was damn sure they were none of them on this small archipelago with me. With us.

If they had been, my Uncle Allan would have found them, long since . . .

Two years ago, that was: me with my eyes wide and all my antennae outstretched, gazing at the far horizons. Looking and looking but too stupid scared to leap, perhaps; clinging, at any rate, finding excuses, finding months'-worth of things to do, people to see, anything that would keep me yonder side of the Channel a week or two longer.

And here I was now, most reluctant of prodigal kids returning, in no kind of hurry to see the old homestead one more time but hurrying none the less. A slow going I'd made of it to be sure, but the coming back was manic, taken at a sprint, longest possible distance in the shortest possible time.

Always is the longest in distance, this particular journey. Count it, measure it. Name it. Heaven to hell? Freedom to slavery, fantasy to reality, there to here? They say you can't go home again, you can't step twice into the same river; sometimes I say that you have to. And it's one mother of a slog getting back there, so much ground to cover and the roads not built for returning traffic.

Hard work also, swimming against the rush of your life. I was tired after just the run up the coast to Santander, which was always going to be the easiest stretch of the journey. Tired but not sleepy, no question of sleeping: I caught the overnight ferry but never for a moment thought of joining the crashed-out backpackers on the banquettes. I munched a cheap burger – no BSE scare for me, I *knew* how bad my blood was, what madness I carried in my veins – and chugged my way slowly through a giant bottle of Coke for the caffeine kick of it; spent a lot of time up on deck, watching lights define the darkness on the water; finally found my way to the video lounge for the in float entertainment and watched *The Dirty Dozen* for what might have been the dozenth time in a world that liked to round things off nicely, but almost certainly wasn't.

I'd never noticed the world do that, not of its own accord. Neat endings, patterns and symmetries, things coming together at the last: we say it's so, *what goes around comes around* we say, and *history repeats* and all of that, but that we say it doesn't make it true.

We make it true, sometimes. Not history, but we repeat. We go around, and we come around; and occasionally, very occasionally – fighting hard, driving hard – we go away and then we come home again. We draw our own line in the sand, and drag it round in a circle before the sucking tide can break it.

Or we lose our metaphor entirely, scrape it deeper and call it a moat, wait for the tide to fill it and hope we can hide inside. All the world's a wooden O, and O is for oyster and it had I thought been mine, or so I'd been pretending, but I was maybe discovering a disaffinity with shellfish.

You can run, but you really can't hide.

Go slowly, come back quickly. We disembarked at Plymouth, the bike and I, and the bike was full of cheap Spanish petrol and I was virtuously empty of cheap Spanish wine but sloshingly full of Coke, dizzy only with a night's sleeplessness and a caffeine kick and the soul's wrack of the day before, and maybe a little dizzy with setting my feet one more time on good English concrete, with all that that implied.

Customs was a breeze, there was no one there even to wave me through, let alone to check me, check my papers, tell me I was a deeply undesirable citizen and lock me away in darkness, out of the sun's potent glare.

It was sunlight that kept me going, kept me quick. If I'd landed in the dark I might have stopped for the night, sought out some cheap boarding-house and slept, been sensible. And then I might have lost my nerve, or at least recovered my wits and taken my time, gone slow and careful.

But no, I came out onto the road in bright morning, and my blood sang in the light and it was like drinking pure energy, my mind might be exhausted but my body was up for this, no question. Four hundred miles, four-fifty? Not a problem . . .

So I drove, all day I drove north and east, stopping only to refuel my belly and my bike.

So I was stupid, and what's new?

Sun was sinking, even so far north and high summer, so late I was on the road; tide was ebbing as I came at last to the last bridge over the last river and saw the glow of my city right ahead. Mud flats below me, glistening darkly and striped with shadow; council flats before me, grey concrete towers tinged pink and striped with light. Catch me living in one of those: I had a pretty good idea how much the constructors had paid my family for the contract, which meant I could make a pretty good guess just how pre-stressed that concrete was. They had to make their profit somewhere, after all . . .

The girders of the bridge sang to me as I crossed, high and strange and ethereal. They always did at sunset. Something to do with temperature differentials, Jamie said; me, tonight, I thought they were singing me a welcome. *Welcome home Benedict, black sheep Macallan.* Or a white sheep, I thought myself, from a family flock of black; but that was old imagery, a teenage habit and utterly redundant now. Bleached or blackened, I thought I was. Parade me with my peers, my kin; count the cops I'd killed and my other victim also, a life claimed not in heat or clumsiness but in cold, deliberate justice or revenge, if there's a difference; look from my family's faces to my own, and see if there's a difference . . .

*   *   *

I came back into town like a bat into hell, quick no more: coasting on the updraught, very circumspect, very cautious of my widespread wings, not to flurry the sulphurous smoke and draw eyes upward, not to show my silhouette against the flames.

Something like that, at least. If I'd gone roaring through the streets, boy in black leathers on a big black bike, even two years on someone would have whispered, the whisper would have spread, there would have been phone-calls made and "*Benedict?* Are you sure? No? Well, check it out anyway . . ."

I did not, I very emphatically did not want to meet any member of my clan tonight, nor tomorrow either. I suppose that's what I'd come back for ultimately, to face the family and exorcise some ghosts, but I'd been haunted a long time and a few days more wouldn't hurt. I wanted to ease myself back, slip in under the skin unfelt, spend a little quality time with the bones of this city and my history.

Put it bluntly, I wanted to put it off, all the hard stuff I was here for. *Still running, Ben?* I asked myself, sneering; and yes, still running I was, but at least I was running on the spot now. The right spot.

Actually I felt like a ghost myself, like my own ghost or my sister's; and I could have been taken for either as I slid the murmuring bike through quiet streets no louder for our passing, up unlit alleys where I could.

Where was I going, exactly? I didn't know, I hadn't thought; I should do that now, of course, I should make some decisions. But I felt stranded on a time-lag, Rip van Winkle in miniature. Rip van Tiddleywinks, perhaps. I'd kept in touch with no one, this time I'd been away – or almost so: I'd sent the occasional postcard, but never a return address – and I might have no friends left here now, or none that I could find. Students move, some students graduate and move away. I might be forced to my family after all . . .

No. Sooner than that, I'd try the boarding-house option, even in my own home town; sooner than either, I put it off again. Just for an hour, just for a breath of familiar air and the touch of known ground beneath my feet.

Gravity sucked me downhill, back to the slow dark of the river. The town seemed grave-quiet; not so odd, perhaps, with the students away, though I remembered it as showing more life than this even in the long vac.

They'd greened a stretch of the quayside since I'd left, made a little park of it with grass and saplings, swings and a seesaw for the kids, benches for their parents. I parked the bike on some hardstanding and stripped off rucksack, helmet, jacket; stretched and twisted for a minute against the aches and weariness of a full day in the saddle after a night of no sleep, and then walked slowly along by the bollards and chains that marked the river's edge.

Walked, and saw that I was not after all alone. There was a man on the furthest bench, there were sodium lights and a bright moon to show him to me: a man running to fat in middle age, losing a little of his hair, sitting huddled with his face in his hands. Not so rare in this town, fear and depression were common currency. I checked, thought perhaps I should walk the other way, not to disturb a stranger in his misery; but too late for that, he'd heard my footsteps on the flags, he lowered his hands and lifted his head and turned his eyes to find me.

One of those moments it was, when the world stills on its axis. Even in this most silent of nights, a greater silence fell; I lost the sounds of the river and the distant sounds of traffic to the south, even the sounds of my own breathing and the blood in my body. Lost the will to motion, any grip on good sense.

Got my breath back first, a slow, juddering draw of air, just enough to speak with.

"Dad?"

He didn't speak. No *Benedict, son, how are you?* or *Where did you spring from, what are you doing home again, why didn't you tell us you were coming?* Not even *Where've you been, your mother's missed you, boy, she's been worried as hell . . .*

No, he only stirred, stood, walked heavily towards me. Like his body, his face was puffing out, losing the definition of my childhood years; his skin glistened, and briefly I thought his flesh was all dissolving on his bones. I'd seen it happen. But no, that was only mind and memory and the night, the being back; he was sweating, that was all, surely, it was a warm night and fat men sweat. I'm not fat and I was sweating myself, I could feel my skin sticky with it under my leathers and under my hair . . .

But the first noise he made was a sniff – nothing neat or disdainful, this was a wet and raucous snot-sucking mother of a sniff – and the first gesture was a dash of his hand across his face, and maybe that wasn't sweat after all. But why would my father, my *father* be sitting out in the city, in the night – his time, the night – and crying? It made no sense. Couldn't be, that was all. Couldn't be. I was misunderstanding.

He didn't speak, he didn't touch me, or not yet. Not with his hands or his heart, no silent hugging welcome for the strayed sheep straying home, the prodigal son unwashed, unclean but wanted none the less.

He stood there in the moonlight, my loving father, three, maybe four metres away – close enough to be sure of me, not close enough to touch – and he didn't lift a finger, but he hit me.

Something hit me, at least; or nothing did, but I was hit regardless. There was nothing there: no shape or shadow glimpsed in the corner of my eye, no breath of displaced air, but some intangible force slapped furiously against the side of my head and sent me reeling. The right way, thank God, away from the river, or there might have been a young man drowned that night.

As it was, I staggered and stopped, gasped in confusion, lifted a hand to my pounding skull and was struck again, a thudding blow into my belly.

All doubled up now, breathless and desperate and utterly muddled, I lifted my head to find my father, to look for help. Stupidly, I looked to him to help me; and saw the savage contentment on his face a moment before a brutal sideswipe against my jaw had me sprawling on my back.

Then he really went to work on me.

Do what thou wilt, but not against blood kin. That was pretty much the whole of the law, any law that my family would recognise: that all things were open to them, except to use their talent on each other. That was a universal, it was Medes and Persians stuff, ineradicable from the fabric of what we were; except that it seemed to fall into utter disuse around me. All my life I'd been my sister's soft target, until she died; and then Uncle James had done it, taken control of my body from me and tugged my strings like a malevolent puppeteer; Uncle Allan had been the great exception, acknowledging no laws nor common practice; and now it was my father's turn, third and slowest of the brothers but he hurt me most, inside and out.

I lay on the ground, on the grass and he loomed above me with that dangerous moon hanging over his shoulder, feeding his intent. Nothing, but nothing I could do in the dark, no sun to work with; nothing but roll and grunt and suffer, yell and bleed.

I did yell a lot, more than I needed to, even, but no one came. Of course no one came, what was I thinking? No one in this town would go near a Macallan in his wrath.

And anyone in trouble, anyone yelling in the night, likely
there'd be a Macallan making him yell . . .

No, the good citizenry would be drawing their curtains
tighter, turning the television up, trying so hard not to hear
me. See no evil, hear no evil: it was a survival trait, and
this town was full of survivors. By definition, no one else
could take it.

Ach, and I was a survivor myself, again by definition; I
was here, wasn't I? And he wasn't going to kill me, my own
father, he might do me some damage but he'd stop, for sure
he'd stop, he'd have to . . .

And he did at last, though he went on for a while with
his feet after he let his talent rest. He kicked me and
walked away, and hesitated, and came back to kick me
again. Several times he did this; and even in the dark and
through the blood and mess that was clagging up my eyes,
that my tears couldn't wash away, I could see that I wasn't
the only one here who was crying. His face was twisted
with it, and his nose was running.

Didn't stop him kicking me, though.

Exhausted and shocked and soaking up pain like tissue-
paper soaks up blood, I just lay there and let him do it to
me, didn't try to evade it or escape it or fight back. He
kicked me in the back and the ribs and the head, kicked
me in the kidneys and the gut like he wanted to kick me
out of the family, out of the city, out of his life and the
world altogether.

But that he didn't do, he did stop in the end, whatever he
wanted. For a minute longer he stood above me, breathing
heavily, noisily, like some animal barely checked; and then
he turned and blundered away across the grass and out of
my hearing, well out of my wet sight.

And I lay breathing shallowly, breathing softly like some
animal barely alive; and I tried, I did my best to draw my
soul together in my battered body and be me again. But

oh! it was hard, it was cruel. My body was no shelter for
a wounded spirit then, and my spirit was bleeding more than
my body was.

Didn't try to move, not for a while. Not for a long time.
Breathing was movement enough, and almost too much for
me. Air had never been so hard-won nor hurt so badly, going
in and coming out. If I tried anything more adventurous –
shifting a hand, say, laying it flat to earth, only thinking
about taking a little weight onto it in a minute or two –
all my muscles went into spasm, and then I couldn't even
breathe.

   Strange thoughts found me, as I lay in stasis. I thought
the grass was tangling around me, drawing me down under;
I thought I was sinking through soil and gravel and ancient
pipe to a prisoned, poisoned stream that fed the river; I
thought I was flowing against the stream's flow, swimming
up to the buried heart of the city, all its hidden history. I
thought I found a time before my family came, before the
Macallan tribe twisted this place out of true, and I thought
I could be happy there. I could lie still and listen to lost
voices, forgotten lives, a freedom long gone from here. Only
a dream, perhaps, only a mind dissociating, detaching itself
from what was too terrible to be borne; but it seemed real
enough for a while, it seemed enough.

   Only another chance to run away, I realised at last.

Strange thoughts found me, but no person did. No policeman
passed that way that night, no romancing teenagers drifted
down to play on the swings or each other's budding bodies,
no good Samaritan came to offer rescue. I was on my own,
and nothing new there.

   Time passed, more slowly than I was used to. A time came
when I could move my fingers, move hand and arm without
those paralysing cramps; when I could roll over and push

myself cautiously onto all fours. I could hold that, though my bones ached and my flesh trembled and my breath came in racking sobs and that was the best of it, there was blood also and stabbing pains and under it all the constant droning, deadening chorus, *my father, my own father it was did this to me, and took a pleasure in it* . . .

Go so far, I could go further. Of course I could. I could stand up. If I concentrated, if I focused . . .

Did that, feeling my face twist with intent, feeling the blood run. And made it, shaking and giddy and hurting dreadfully but on my feet and stumbling, taking steps. Leaving a dark trail, I was sure, over grass and flagstones and staggering dangerously close to the drop into darker water; wouldn't take a dog's nose or a hunter's skills to track me in the betraying moonlight if my father chose to come back, or if he told anyone else who might come looking.

I didn't, I did *not* want to be found again tonight. Once was more than enough. Only one way to get safe, to break the trail: I headed back to the horsepower, my international rescue, my beautiful Beemer. Snails famously carried their homes on their backs; mine carried me. Not this city was my home any more, though I longed for it and loathed it in equal measure, though I thought of it that way from old habit. Home was speed and balance, those times when I hung my helmet on my head.

Could I drive? Not fast, for sure, and not safely; not seeingly, with blood and water in my eyes and the constant vision of my father's face behind them. But I knew the roads, at least, and there was no traffic. I could try.

Awkwardly and painfully on with the jacket, and then with the rucksack, which was worse. I jammed the helmet down over sticky hair, hoping the weight of it might act like a compress, maybe stop the bleeding for a while; I sat for a while sidesaddle and then astride, feeling the

strength and solidity of the machine against my own frailty,
thinking that it should be making the decisions here, it
should do the driving; finally I turned the key and pressed
the switch, felt the responsive rumble beneath me, shivered
against the vibration that set all my nerves once more
ajangle.

Kicked the stand up, worked clutch and gears, went
slowly and a little wobblingly away from there.

Knew the roads, yes; didn't know, didn't have the first
clue where I was going. Up the hill, yes, away from
the river, so much was easy. The quayside had become
my father's territory, and he might yet be back for more
kicking. Besides, quayside housing was all grand Victorian
sandstone stuff, shipping-company offices and warehouses
converted; nice flats they made, to be sure, big rooms and
many of them, but not for the likes of me or my friends.
Collaborators, councillors, clever and unscrupulous men
made their homes on the river front. You had to be clever
and unscrupulous both, to stay rich in this town; you had
to make my family like you. QED.

So up the hill I went, blinking and squinting and trying
to fight through the dizziness that was kicking in now,
brain-damage or a haemorrhage or just the after-effects
of being well kicked by my father, just the shock and the
pain and a deeper level of distress spilling over. Could've
been any of them, could've been all; privately, though, I
suspected that the brain-damage had happened earlier. I
accused myself. Lack of oxygen at birth, maybe, or too
many drugs as a teenager. Something, anyway. I mean,
even given my inheritance, my genetic tendency towards
it, just how stupid could I get?

Driving into town at sunset, when they became strong and
I lost it, I became a target, a victim, nothing more . . . Okay,
so I couldn't have predicted or anticipated this, no one could;

but that my family might be unsure of me at best, that they might have wanted me restrained and perhaps softened up a little, as a warning or just as a habit – that I should have been prepared for. The last they knew of me bar the postcards, the last sign they'd seen to say *Benedict was here*, I'd left my favourite uncle splattered and defunct in his hospital bed, and was it any wonder that I wasn't getting the prodigal welcome the prodigal son had never really deserved?

I should have stopped out of town tonight, come in with the daylight, if I really had to come in at all.

Ah, hindsight. Wonderful thing. I might not be seeing so clearly just then when I looked ahead, but my hindsight was as sharp as ever.

Where to go? I didn't know, I couldn't think. Keeping upright, keeping moving, kicking myself in the only bit my father hadn't kicked, that black hole I called my mind: those took all that I had of strength, of energy, of reserve. Nothing spare for thinking with, for making any of those tough decisions, *left or right at the junction? west or east?*, where best to look for shelter.

Disconnect the brain, and muscle-memory takes over. Some cellular imitation of intellect, maybe it's what we had before we had a brain, a kind of genetic preamp that just boosts your chances of survival a wee bit above the chaotic mush of instinct. Whatever, it boosted mine that night. I drove unthinkingly, and my body or maybe my bike took me left and right and along and up, till at last we came to what had been my own front door, last time I saw it.

Not my parents': I wasn't going anywhere near there, or no nearer than this, at least. This was a sight too near for my entire liking. And a foolish place to come, O my foolish muscles. What was the point? I used to share this flat with Jacko, but I had no keys now and no right of entry. He'd have finished his course a year ago, and students are a motile population; the betting was heavy against his still being here. I could knock, sure, but it'd only be some stranger answered the door. Some kid nervous anyway in this neighbourhood this time of night, opening up on demand to find a man unknown bleeding and hurting, close to fainting on their doorstep: not a kind act, Ben, to put them through that. Engage your brain, engage your gears, get yourself away from here . . .

But something held me, as I gazed at the window of the flat. The light was on behind the familiar ill-hung, ill-fitting curtains, but it was more than that. No sure sign of occupancy anyway, a burning light, and I'd already worked out that any occupant would likely be a stranger. So why were we sitting here, the bike and me, both rumbling in neutral, going nowhere?

It was the cheeseplant, was what it was. Taller than me, taller than Jacko, almost taller than that high-ceilinged room despite all the twists and kinks in its pale trunk, vast leaves like fingered fans, it had probably also had more character than either me or Jacko, certainly more than the room. Jacko's pride and joy, that plant. He'd raised it from a cutting or a seed or whatever you do with cheeseplants, however they're propagated by barely-teenage kids; he'd hired a van to move it when we moved in, though the rest of his stuff would hardly have made one load for a small car; he loved it almost as much as his instruments, or possibly more. Instruments he'd sell, he'd trade, he'd upgrade, but the cheeseplant was forever.

So he'd said, at any rate, more than one drunk or stoned evening in, lying on the carpet with his head almost in its water-tray, gazing up at it in barely-exaggerated worship. Drunk or stoned myself, I'd believed him, and I believed him still; some things you cling to, you just have to. Hell, I was still riding my sister's bike, wasn't I? Still wearing her helmet?

And the cheeseplant was still in the alcove, still getting in the way of those faded, fraying curtains, a leaf or two thrusting through, reaching for the streetlight. Harbouring ambitions, maybe, *I know I'm supposed to be a daylight creature, but if I slurp up all this heavy yellow stuff, can I get to be as tall as you?*

I was surprised but confident now, not a question in my head beyond would I be welcome or would this be truly bad timing, would he just have his hand up some sweet boy's T-shirt or down his jeans? I dismounted, gave my steed an approving pat for finding me a refuge – well, actually I leaned for a moment for support but I did it one-handed, just to pretend – and walked up to the door, trying not to stagger as I went.

Made a fist and made a noise, flesh on wood; and waited, listened, heard footsteps and thanked a God I gave no credence to. Tried to ready a smile, didn't do so well at that to judge by the feel of it on my sticky face, lost it altogether when the door was opened and all my logical, inarguable assumptions were proved false.

I'd been looking for fizzy red hair and a scant red beard, and didn't see either one of them. Looking for my former flatmate, I emphatically didn't see him; and for a moment, seeing no more than that failure, I assumed I was seeing a stranger. A young lad he was, cropped bleached hair just showing dark at the roots, an earring and uncertainty fading into something more anxious, and no wonder. What was he seeing? A stranger again, surely: a figure of menace, black leathers and black helmet, tinted visor shoved up to show a face pale with distress and streaked dark with blood . . .

But after a second he said my name, he said, *"Ben . . . ?"* on a rising note, startlement mixed with concern; and then I knew him, despite the change of style. Not Jacko, no, but the next best thing, perhaps.

"Jonathan . . ." Hard to credit, two years on and the same boyfriend; but I supposed stranger things had happened. Leopards could after all change their spots, I knew that from my own life-story. "Is Jacko in?"

"No. No, Tim doesn't live here any more. But listen, Christ, come in, what happened to you? You don't . . ."

I didn't look so good, I knew that. I might have demurred, but he'd already slipped an arm around my waist, and there was nothing left in me to resist with. He guided, I leaned on him more than I wanted but no more than I needed, and we crabbed awkwardly together down the hall. Not into the front room – my assumptions again and again confounded, he pulled against me when I twitched that way, so I just went with the flow – but around the corner and straight to the bathroom. He helped me peel off rucksack and jacket in a single hissing motion, knocked the toilet cover down and settled me on top of it, then lifted the helmet carefully off my head when my shaking hands couldn't manage the thing.

"Jesus, you're a mess. Just sit still, okay? Let me . . ."

Actually, I didn't have much choice in the matter. A friendly voice and firm, helpful fingers had sapped the last of my will; all I could do suddenly was slump, and give myself over to whatever amateur nursing he could provide.

He didn't do so badly. A clean J-cloth soaked in cold water, he used it to mop up the worst of the blood and then pressed it against what must have been an open cut above my eye. The water dribbled down over my cheek and eventually under the collar of my T-shirt, but that was cool and welcome. The cut stung a bit, briefly, and I didn't mind that either.

"Look, can you hold this?" he asked, lifting my hand for me and touching my fingers into place. "Just till it stops bleeding?"

I could, I did.

"Good." His fingers searched hurriedly through bottles and jars in the cabinet, came up with nothing. "I thought we had plasters, but maybe it'll just scab by itself. So what else, where are you hurting?"

Everywhere. I couldn't even shrug without flinching. I shrugged, I flinched, I said, "Ribs, stomach. Legs and arms. Back. Nothing else is bleeding, though."

"How do you know, have you looked?"

"No." I didn't want to look, and I didn't want him looking either. Didn't want to put it on show, what harm my father wished me. "I'm pretty sure, though. I think I'd feel it. The leather looked after me, pretty much. That's what it's for, you know? Second skin . . ."

"Uh-huh. Came off your bike, then, did you?" he asked neutrally. He knew damn well I hadn't come off my bike – not a scratch on the helmet, lots of damage underneath – but he was giving me the chance to be discreet, if I chose to take it.

"No, Jon. I just met someone with a score to settle," though I hadn't realised and still didn't understand how deep it had gouged him, how acid it burned. "Um, I'll tell you in the morning, okay?" Couldn't face it now, didn't want to shape my mouth around the words though I didn't want to lie or hide the truth either. And then I realised what I'd said, the implications of it; and here I was making easy assumptions again, and, "Oh, fuck. I'm sorry, Jon, landing you with my troubles again. Would you mind, if I just crashed the night on your floor somewhere?"

"Well, you're not going anywhere else," he said, "that's for sure. You can have my bed."

"No, I don't want to—" though I did, bed sounded heaven the way I felt, set against a sleeping-bag and a couple of sofa cushions.

"Doesn't matter what you want, that's the way it'll be. It's not a problem, I'll just double up with my flatmate."

"Oh. I didn't realise," though I should have thought. "I'm sorry, have I been interrupting . . . ?"

"No, not at all," he said, grinning. "She's been in bed the last two hours. First to crash, last to get up, always."

"*She?* Jonathan, are you losing your grip?"

"Flatmate, I said. That's all. Share the rent, share the cooking. Share a bed sometimes, when we've got visitors. No big deal, we're very sisterly. I do her ironing. Chances are she won't even notice, she'll be well away by now. Sleeping's a religion with her. Are you sure you don't want me to check you over for broken bones or whatever, before you go to bed?"

"I'm sure. What could you do, if you found any?"

"Get you to hospital, of course. You should probably go anyway, just for a check-over, just to be safe . . ."

I shook my head. "No hospital. Nothing is broken, I'd know if it was." A rib or two might be cracked, I thought, breathing was such a hard and painful business; but cracked ribs would heal without attention, without fuss or strapping, without taking me through the doors of the hospital where I'd last seen my uncle. Splattered and defunct . . . "Tell you what you could do, though. You could bring the bike inside. You'll need the keys, here, there's a steering lock. It'll jam the hall up, but . . ." *But I don't want it sitting outside all night, telling everyone I'm home.*

"How's about if I take it round the back, stick it in the yard? No one'll see, with the gate closed."

"Even better. Don't rev her too loud when you start her up, she doesn't need it and you don't want to wake the street." *Don't want to wake the street to the sound of a bike the neighbours know, if there are any of the old neighbours left and I bet there are . . .*

"Can't drive," he said cheerfully, quite unfazed. "I'll push. Back in three minutes, you just sit there."

I wasn't planning on doing much else. From the angle I

was sitting, though, I could see a couple of prescription-looking plastic tubs in the cabinet; so I did stand cautiously up and edge a couple of steps across, grabbing at cistern and wall en route to keep from keeling over – having finally quit moving, it was hellish hard to get going again, and the floor was bucking beneath me – and modified joy, one of them said 'Ibuprofen' on the label and wasn't empty. Might not be Ibuprofen inside, of course, but the odds were in my favour; and while it's not my favourite treatment for a headache or other hurts (I'm a bedtime Co-Co man myself), I knew it to be punchy stuff, and oh, my head and other parts did hurt.

So I took three for now with a glass of water, and kept a couple for later in case I couldn't hang on to sleep. Perched myself on the edge of the bath to wait for Jonathan, the toilet seemed too far away; showed him what I'd found when he came back – "Look," I said, "treasure . . ." – and I carried more water through to the bedroom while he all but carried me.

Same old room, unredecorated except for a change of posters; same old bed also, and it felt pretty close to coming home as I collapsed onto it. Jon helped me undress, rolled me under the covers and tucked me in like a boy much practised at nursing sick young men, which I dared swear that he was. And he kissed me goodnight chastely on the cheek, took a baggy T-shirt and shorts to sleep in, not to shock his flatmate too much when she woke, and turned the light off and left me; and I sighed, groaned a little as I tried to settle sore bones in sore flesh, and spun into the darkness like I was drunk or stoned or both.

· THREE ·

NOT THE SAME RIVER

Woke by degrees, feeling my way reluctantly back into a world that had left me battered and bewildered, headsore and heartsore and humiliated. No, worse than humiliated: being his victim of anyone's, being so thoroughly done over by my own father made me feel craven, self-pitying, pathetic. Logically I knew there had been absolutely no defence, nothing at all that I could have done; even so, my mind-set had slipped back years overnight. I felt like cattle again, like one of the contemptible herd, despite sunlight and memories and all available evidence . . .

God. One night back and already I was thinking Macallan-style once more, dividing all of humanity into us and them and only we counted. No great surprise, though, and no real blame either: this town really was a Manichaean universe in miniature, where there was only light and darkness, good and evil, no shading in between. White hats and black hats, and my family wore the black. Except for me. Never any use on either side but hating the night and its uses – and to be honest my inability to use it, my freakishness – I'd chosen to live among the much-abused townsfolk though I could never truly be one of them either, my blood and my smiling, contemptuous relatives had lent me too much immunity. And then when I did at last discover my own talent, it wasn't the needs of the ordinary people that drove me to use it. Blood called to blood, and cousins of mine were being killed; it was to defend my abominable family that I finally turned assassin in my turn.

If there was any grey at all in this black-and-white city, I thought it was myself. Ambiguous and uncertain, not knowing where I belonged and finally needing to find out, I thought I was a loose cannon with its fuse already lit, charged and unpredictable and deadly.

Had thought so, at least. That had been one of the pictures in my head on yesterday's long road up, one of the arguments not to come. And I'd come regardless, dangerous though I was; and first thing that happened, first human contact, I got beaten up by my dad and I didn't know why.

This did not feel good. This felt worse than my body felt, and my body felt bad indeed.

I was lying on my belly, and my legs, I thought, felt worst. Impossibly heavy they felt, as well as aching throughout, all the way from hip to heel.

Impossibly heavy was right, actually; but it took me a while, took me an embarrassing time to figure out that some of the weight was extrinsic. Something was sitting on the back of my knees.

Also impossible, surely. What was I suggesting here, had Jon brought me a breakfast-tray and confused me with the bedside table, left it carefully balanced just where I couldn't get at it? Let's not be foolish, folks . . .

But yet, there wasn't any real doubt about it: something heavy was lying on top of the duvet on top of me, pressing me deeper into the mattress. *Check it out, Macallan*; I lifted my head from the pillow to see what gave, apart from my knees and the bedsprings.

Tried to, at least. I lifted my head and the pillow came also, rising two or three inches before it peeled away stingingly from my face, like sticking-plaster ripped off too soon; and when I gazed, gaped down I saw dried blood on the pillowcase, a glue that had failed but a stain that would stay, bugger it.

I worked one hand out from under the duvet to touch my brow with tentative fingers. No new bleeding, that I could feel; but I should've thought last night, I should've made Jon search harder. There's rarely very much in a young man's medical arsenal, but he can usually run to Elastoplast.

Elastoplast and pills for a headache, that last guaranteed. And I had pills and a glass of water ready by the bed, and I had the mother — no, the father of all headaches pounding away inside my skull, and all I had to do was reach . . .

Turn over, and reach. And I couldn't turn over, not till I knew what was making my legs so heavy. So okay, try the head thing again, now the pillow's made its bid for freedom. Lift head and never mind the throbbing, twist neck and never mind those sharp stabbing pains, this too shall pass; raise eyes and squinny into the light, where it's falling blindingly in between the curtains . . .

Where it was falling in a line that bisected the bed, that bisected also a large black amorphous mass before it dazzled me. Some kind of pelt, I thought. Discarded bearskin, one previous owner, not wanted on voyage? I shifted my legs beneath it, pulled myself up onto one elbow; it opened two yellow-green eyes and gazed at me. Thoughtfully, I thought, though God alone knew what it was thinking.

"Sorry, kitten," I said, croaking slightly. "You've got to move, I'm losing circulation here . . ."

Move it did, as I rolled over. Very measured, its movements, quite unhurried. It stood up neatly on the duvet, absolutely not a kitten, one big cat; waited patiently while I settled on my back, heaping pillows awkwardly behind my head and grunting as I rediscovered all the separate pains in my body; then it paced slowly up the bed, stared into my eyes from an inch's distance, and stepped onto my chest. Sat there for a moment, rumbling a greeting, then curled up tidily, rested its massive head on its paws and lay there with its eyes narrowed now to contemplative slits, seemingly considering my place in the natural order of things.

Okay, I could handle this. Not any too impressed by myself, I didn't mind being judged by a cat. Nor did I mind lying still and serving as furniture, though it did feel somewhat like having a medicine ball balanced on my ribs, which was not maybe the best thing for me at that time. Lying still was still better than moving, though; breathing I could manage, apparently, even against the cat's weight. And the bed was warm and I was dozy yet, my head was suffering badly but that I could live with, treat it like a hangover and ride it out. I needed a piss but not badly, not enough to dispute the cat's comfort or my own more questionable compromise. I gave it a grin, though grinning hurt where it pulled on torn skin, and let my head topple back into the pillows and my eyes close, cherishing the feel of that bar of sunlight laid like a brand across my face from stubbled chin to bruised scalp. Sleep again I wouldn't, dozy or not, but flopping was very much on the agenda.

So we lay there in comparative content; the cat at least seemed contented, to judge by its constant purring – more vibration than sound, I felt it in my bones; but it soothed and not irritated, and maybe I didn't have any broken edges in there after all – and that contented me. Eventually there were noises in the flat around us, footsteps to and fro and soft voices, doors opening and closing, hot water banging in the pipes and the flush of the toilet, once and then again a few minutes after. The cat twitched its ears a time or two, I would undoubtedly have twitched mine more if I'd had the twitching ability, but neither one of us moved more than that.

*   *   *

The bedroom door moved at last, and we both moved our eyes to meet it.

Jonathan came in, with a mug of something steaming in his hand. We both sniffed; didn't smell like coffee.

"Oh, Fizzy. Are you being a nuisance?"

"Not at all," I said, quick in defence of my new friend.

"He's a ton weight, and you're sick. How are you feeling this morning?"

"Not sick," I said, not true. I was sick at heart, and that is all-pervasive. "Just sore."

"I brought you some tea," he said, laying it on the bedside table, graphic evidence of how little he knew me. "No hurry, you don't have to get up; this isn't a hint or anything. You take your time. We're not going anywhere."

The cat was, though, seemingly; Jonathan hoicked it up two-handed, ducked his head between its legs, spread it across his shoulders. The unquesting beast made no demur, it just lay passive and comfortable and by the smug look on its face didn't even falter in that subsonic purring.

With its weight lifted off me, I felt I was floating suddenly, inches above the bed. Nor did my head seem so bad, now that I could reach the pills. I took them anyway, though, on general principles; left the mug of tea severely alone, washing them down with last night's stale water, and said, "Jon?"

"Yes?"

"Why's the cat called Fizzy?"

"It's short for Malfeasance," he said. "Go back to sleep. I was just testing the water, and you're not half cooked yet."

If there's one thing guaranteed to keep me awake, it's a mixed metaphor. Five minutes later I was headed for the bathroom with my toothbrush in my hand and jeans pulled on for decency, refusing to be more body-conscious than that in what used to be my own flat and was now my friend's; and of course I met the flatmate in the hall, that was written, that was inevitable. If I hadn't bothered with the jeans, she'd have had her mother with her.

"Er, hullo . . ."

"Hi," she said. And she was checking me over with her eyes and quite unashamed about it – well, of course she was, what else was she going to do with a half-naked stranger in what was her flat now and no longer mine, and the state I was in only adding piquancy to it? – so I did the same, while the conversation lulled between us.

She was tall, lean and not overdressed herself, in a loose faded-purple singlet over old frayed leggings and feet as bare as mine. Her hair was dark and raggedy, hanging in strands over her shoulders, and she had a tattoo on one shoulder and a smoking rollie between her fingers.

"Janice," she said, holding out her other hand. I smiled, we shook politely, I told her what she surely already knew, that I was Benedict, Ben.

"Nice set of bruises, Ben," she said, still looking. There was a light Scottish burr in her voice: east coast, I thought, but not Edinburgh. Borders maybe, maybe Fife.

"Yeah. I, um, I come from a very dysfunctional family . . ."

"Mmm. Jon told me."

Clever old Jon. I hadn't told him where the damage had originated. Probably wasn't so hard to figure out, though, not in this town. Not after dark.

"Well, I'll just . . ." I waved the toothbrush vaguely, in lieu of words. Now I was on my feet and moving, that piss was more of a priority.

"Sure. Anything you need?"

"Squeeze of toothpaste, if that's okay. A rub of soap."

"I meant witch-hazel, arnica. TCP. Bandages, doctor, that sort of thing?"

"No, really. I'm fine." And I was, really, almost

miraculously: a night's sleep and the first shock worn off, I was stiff and sore but no worse than that. Even the ribs were doing their thing with no more than a muted protest. Not cracked after all, I thought maybe, only bruised bone-deep.

"Okay. Do you do breakfast?"

Sometimes, often, but not today. "I do coffee," I said hopefully, fearful that maybe in this house they might only do tea.

"Nescaff?"

"Whatever." I'd been spoiled for two years, travelling in foreign lands where instant coffee was a foreign concept; have to get over that. Or go away again . . .

"No worries, then. It'll be waiting."

And it was waiting, as was she; nor was she alone.

Here is Janice, here is Jon. Here is their cat Fizzy. They are in the kitchen. Here comes their friend Ben. Ben is carrying the cup of tea that Jon made him, that he doesn't want to drink. Ben isn't expecting to find Jon in the kitchen. See Ben blush . . .

But at least I'd covered up under a baggy peasant shirt (Marina's favourite, that had been: it had ties instead of buttons, and she liked to play), I wasn't showing so many souvenirs any more. My face was badly marked, though, and I couldn't hide that. Stubble didn't do it.

I put the mug of cooling tea on the drainer, and accepted coffee from Janice. Gave Jon a rueful glance, but he just shrugged, smiled, not bothered.

"Sit down," he said, "you look wobbly."

"Yeah." It was true, I did still feel shaky on my legs. There had only ever been room for one chair, in this small kitchen; they'd left it for me, bless them, and I took it gratefully.

It was strange to sit at that table, to look around at that dirty paintwork, that chipped enamel on the cooker and the sink, so much that my eyes knew the look and my fingers the feel of, and to see other people's things everywhere. Familiarity and change, both at once: there was an eerie sense of slippage here, of no longer belonging in a place that had once been my own.

I thought that might become a theme, for the duration.

"Better now?" Jon asked.

"A bit. I will be." A little better for five minutes in the bathroom, for a tentative wash and a vigorous session on my teeth; I'd have liked a shave too, I never felt truly clean without, but there hadn't been any question of that. Too sore, too many cuts and bruises on my face. *Thanks, Dad* . . .

Fizzy the cat had been nosing indignantly at a food-bowl on the floor, apparently outraged by its emptiness. Now he lifted his head, turned sharply, focused in on me. Leaped easily from floor to table and paced towards me, met me nose-to-nose and sniffing – and suddenly snogged me without invitation, serious french-kissing and in public too.

I jerked back, coughing, wiping my mouth on the back of my hand – his breath was *disgusting* – while the other two hugged each other with delight, their crowing laughter echoing in my skull like some smart electronic effect, setting my headache off again.

"Jon," I groaned, "is your cat a pouf or what?"

"Don't blame me, he's not my cat."

"It's the toothpaste," Janice said, still giggling. "You used the spearmint, didn't you?"

"Yes?" I'd used the fuller of the two tubes on the shelf above the sink. Good manners, I'd thought I was using, taking a little of what they could best spare . . .

"He's got a passion for it. Any kind of mint. You can't even suck a Polo around Fizzy, he'll be down your throat for his share. We have to use herbal toothpaste, it's just too gross else, or too much like hard work fighting him off. Someone left the spearmint. We ought to give it away, I suppose, but . . ."

"But you like to watch your visitors being orally raped?" I suggested.

She grinned, nodded. "Something like that. It'd be such a shame to spoil Fizzy's fun altogether."

I glowered at her, took a mouthful of coffee and swilled it around my teeth, gave Fizzy the benefit of that; breathed out fiercely in his direction, and watched him recoil across the table. And then of course coaxed him back and tickled his ears until he jumped heavily down into my lap, pawed my groin for a few seconds in a way that I really wished he wouldn't, and finally nestled into a warm furry, purry heap with occasional sharp bits.

Fun over, his and mine both. I sipped coffee, waited for the questions. Here they came.

"Who was it, then? Beat you up like that?"

"My father." Easy one, for starters; easy now, at least, in the clear fluorescent light of a kitchen morning. Though I'd expected it to be Jon doing the interrogating. It was still pretty easy, saying it to a stranger. I even managed a romantically-twisted smile to go with.

"Jesus. What for?"

"I don't know, he didn't say. We're not on speaking terms."

"Don't be flippant, Ben. That's pretty serious, what he's done to you."

"Yeah, well. I'm hardly going to sue him for assault, am I?"

A quirk of her head acknowledged the point, though I don't think either one of us knew quite which I meant, that I wouldn't sue him because he was my father or that I couldn't sue him because he was a Macallan and legal remedy was not a viable option in this town.

"Do you really not know why he did it?"

"Not really. I mean, something I did before I left," *I killed his brother, the family's main man*, "he's not going to be happy about that; but he must know by now, why I did it. This was, what, a fairly extreme reaction? After so long, I mean . . ." And he'd been in tears when I found him, or I thought so, and that didn't fit either with my long-held image of my father. Okay, all kids expect their parents to be adult all the time, to cope with anything; but something drastic must have happened to bring him to this, weeping in a public place, even where he thought he was alone. I couldn't get my head around it.

"There've been a lot of changes here," Jon said, his first contribution. "It's not the same town any more."

No. On one level that was hard to believe, for anyone who grew up in the place; tyranny enforced by absolute power makes for stable government, by and large. Things don't tend to change. But what I'd done must have shaken my family to its roots, hence by definition the city to its foundations; I should never have expected to find it just as it had been.

"What's different?" I asked; and was answered by Janice, with one final question of her own.

"Have you got any plans for the day?"

"No."

"All right, then. We'll show you."

Jonathan twitched at that, like he wasn't sure of the wisdom. Fair enough. I was in no position to take offence. Even if people didn't remember me, they'd know me for what I was, a full-blooded Macallan with the face to prove it; if they did remember me, they might know that I wasn't after all the harmless sport I'd thought and advertised myself and tried so hard to be. In either case, being seen out and about with me might be good protection if Jon or Janice ever needed it, might accord them a little influence if they ever chose to use it, but it wouldn't be conducive to making friends.

*   *   *

It was a hot day, they said, though it felt fresh to me after the heavy humidity of the Spanish coast. Not a day for leathers, though; it was a change, a pleasure to feel too cool in loose shirt and shorts, so that was what I did.

How many times had I walked this way, this exact route down the hill into town? I couldn't say; but I'd lived the best part of a year in that flat, while my studies and my social life were both focused around the town centre. Hundreds of times, then, for sure. Given the way I used to dash around, hectically determined to be so much a student, so involved – and given that I never caught buses, every penny saved had been crucial and I could save pounds in a week by walking everywhere – it might be pushing a thousand.

The same streets a thousand times, and not so long ago: too recent for my feet to forget, at any rate. Sore muscle-memory took over again, following tracks I'd laid in my head more than on the pavement. I let it get on with things, never gave a thought to turning left or right at corners; my eyes and mind were busy searching, scanning, trying to spot what was different.

Not much seemed to be the early answer. A few shopfronts on the long hill were boarded up, or dark behind their locked security grilles; but this had always been the shady side of town, businesses came and went overnight almost, empty properties simply emphasised the status quo. Or seemed to. People used to open unannounced and not bother with fixtures and fittings, or signage outside; they'd fill the window with gear that was dodgy or hot or usually both, sell cheap and buy cheaper and hope to get in two or three weeks' trading before the police or the Macallans came to call. Either one would put them out of business. No slack in the turnover, nothing spare to pay bribes or fines or protection money.

It didn't matter, seemingly to anyone. Even the traders themselves didn't noticeably worry. A mayfly trade it was:

live for a day here, a day there. Follow a shop with a market stall, a stall with a van, each progressively more mobile, better able to keep ahead of the chase; when the van dies, run an insurance scam on the carcase and rent a shop again with the proceeds. They made a living, and never seriously troubled anybody.

So I'd have expected changes, departures and new arrivals on that stretch. Even right in the heart of the city, where we came ten minutes later, it was no great surprise to find a couple of what had been major retail sites shuttered and for rent. It was ever thus. Long-time businessmen would tire eventually of the peculiar economy here, the extra overheads imposed by my family's demands and the failures of the police; they'd find some gullible entrepreneur – usually from outside, often from a long way outside – to sell up to, and make tracks rapidly for a less interesting environment. The new boy would often last no more than a year or two, before selling on usually at a loss; and so it would go, fly-by-nights and failures following each other in ever-decreasing circles until at last some cousin of mine (or Uncle James, often Uncle James but never, ever my father, he had no eye for this) would pick the place up for a song or else – more likely – seize it in lieu of unpaid debts that might or might not be genuine or legitimate. They'd install their own man, there were always plenty of collaborators in the queue for Macallan backing; and that was the *status quo ante* comfortably restored, for the next decade or the next generation or however long it took before constant friction broke it down again.

So a couple of dead sites, yes, but only a couple that I passed, that I saw. That was pretty much average, for any time these twenty years. No mass exodus, then, no stampede or cattle-drive; and I'd half expected one or the other. With Uncle James head of the family now, I'd thought greed might finally unbalance what had always teetered on a very fine edge. I'd thought disaster was all but guaranteed, and one of my favourite scenarios would have brought me back to a ghost town, with all the civilians fled or chased away and Macallans taking in each other's washing for lack of anyone else to do the work . . .

Not so, the streets were heaving. Serious contrast to the night before, when my father had been apparently the one, the only, the odd man out.

But this was where the difference lay, in the people, in their faces and the way they carried themselves. Not for nothing had my family named them cattle, all these years; and not for arrogance either, or not entirely. Arrogant it was, to be sure, but perceptive also. Generations of repression left their mark: when I left this city, the citizenry had been subdued, passive, a people long defeated and only making what poor best of life they could manage beneath a tyrannical heel. Oh, there had been hotheads, of course, there had been rebels; but never many at once, and never for long. Few indeed, among those born here. They learned young, in the cradle maybe, maybe even in the womb, picking up vibes from the amniotic fluid. Trouble usually came in from outside, and never lasted.

Now, though: now shoulders that had been perennially slumped were tense instead, faces were drawn and watchful. When they saw me – when they saw my big nose, my heritage blazoned on my features – eyes didn't look down or flicker away. They stared, they watched me, the people that owned the eyes stiffened and turned towards me, sometimes took half a step to follow. Voices muttered, there were even fingers that pointed.

No one would have said that these people were doing well, that they were comfortable in their lives, in their city; but they were not the cowed folk that I had abandoned to a predictable fate. Undoubtedly, things had changed here.

Changed so much, indeed, that I was grateful not to be

alone. Not my presence that offered protection to Janice and Jon; the world had turned on its axis, everything was reversed, and I was very glad to have company.

Glad also to be walking in sunshine, to have that tingle on my skin that said my own talent was active, on a hair-trigger, there to be reached for if tension and watchfulness resolved into genuine threat.

My face was my fortune, as it always had been on these streets; and for the first time in my life, that fortune felt dangerously uncertain.

A man coming towards me, glowering behind shades: as he passed his shoulder jarred mine, and there was nothing accidental about it. I whipped round, anger doing its traditional thing and overriding good sense and discomfort both. He likely heard me gasp as my bones jarred, but all the acknowledgement I got was to see him turn his head and spit aggressively into the gutter.

And this no crop-headed yob, no tattooed youth with a fatal dose of bravado; he was a man in his forties, in a suit. In danger of his life, though he might not have known that.

A hand closed on my arm in warning, but it wasn't Jonathan's, and it wasn't saying *don't do it, Ben, don't roast him, a little jostle isn't worth a death sentence whatever your pride is demanding* . . .

Janice it was who was gripping me, tugging at me, hissing, "Don't, Ben. Don't get involved. Start trouble here, you'll have a dozen of them on you as soon as they raise the yell, that there's a Macallan caught out in daylight . . ."

Maybe Jon hadn't told her everything after all, what I could do in daylight; or maybe she was only trying to forestall my having to, fearful of a dozen human torches blazing my way through the city. Whichever, I didn't want a showdown either; and true enough, a wee shove on a sore shoulder didn't merit the sort of punishment my swift flare of anger might have sent after the man. I nodded, turned again, walked on

with one of them on either side of me now, working in mute
concert here to prevent the same thing happening again.

"Can we get off the street, then?" I murmured. "If my
face makes me a target, then some idiot's going to go
for it eventually. Last thing I want is a confrontation."
Actually, the last thing I wanted was a bloodbath. Never
mind what it did to her, even assuming that she really was
seeing it; that image of human torches scared the hell out
of me. Spontaneous human combustion was not quite so
spontaneous in my ambit, and my score was too high already.
I could make it happen, and knew I would if I had to, to save
my own life; and hated myself for the knowledge, and wanted
never to hate myself for anything more substantial, the fact
of it, knowledge made history.

"Right. Good idea. Anywhere special you want to go?"

"No. Coffee-shop. Not a caff." Enough of instant: I wanted
the bitter tang of strong fresh coffee, and the kick of it in
my blood to supplement the sunshine. Also I wanted to
talk, and it wasn't possible out here, on the move, with
my eyes jittering constantly from face to face to track the
ever-swelling sense of risk I felt. It was so odd, such an
incredible change: resentment I'd been used to all my life,
I was a Macallan, but all I knew of resentment was that it
was twinned to fear, and fear was the stronger. Resentment
sulked, it didn't throw stones. But now suddenly I was
resented and hated, and fear was subsumed or so it seemed,
unless that was my own fear rising to mask it; because I was
afraid, where I'd never expected to be afraid again, and I was
afraid too of my own reactions to that. Even if they literally
started throwing stones, I had ways to protect myself and
those around me; no call to torch the stonethrowers. But I
was still afraid that that might happen, I had the strength to
do it and I might not have the strength to stop myself. Power
without responsibility, that had always been the family curse
and I had it, full measure.

"Morry's Deli, then?" from Jon; and it was flashback time
for me, just at the name. Memories of being thrown out of
Morry's Deli for my face, for my name, for the crime of
my inheritance; and then allowed back in again, but only
to be shown what my sweet late sister had done to poor
Aunt Bella.

"No," I said. A bad time, that, and building up to worse;
nostalgia's thorns lay everywhere, I couldn't hope to escape
them, but that didn't mean I had to throw myself onto the
spikes. Besides, "Morry might not be so pleased to see me,
actually." If strangers had taken to staring Macallans down
and shoulder-barging them for fun, then I for one was not
walking into Morry's. He had better cause than many, to
hold a grudge against my blood; and his deli was down below
ground-level, almost a basement, only a couple of high windows and precious little sunlight to work with. I was going
to be cautious, at least until I knew what was going on.

Jon and Janice pulled faces at each other, looking for
inspiration.

"Some of the pubs do coffee in the mornings . . ."

"Or there's that new place, the bistro thing down by the
station . . ."

"That'll do," I said quickly. Anything that end of town
would take us out of the crush, though it did mean pushing
our way through it first.

"All right. We'll go the back way," Janice said firmly,
tucking her arm through mine. "Less chance of trouble, in
the alleys."

Less chance of rescue also if trouble came regardless; but
by the collective look of them, there was precious little rescue
to be had in any case from the people thronging the streets
today. Not when the young man needing rescue carried the
Macallan imprint on his face as deeply as I did. Old friends
and strangers both knew me for what I was, no disguising it.

*   *   *

'The bistro thing down by the station' turned out to be a tapas bar. I couldn't believe it; Mediterranean culture, come this far? To my little insular pocket of the north?

There it was, though, and looking legitimately Spanish, too: cheap and a little sordid, very basic, nothing spent on the decor. No Costa glitz, but this place could have been lifted whole from any town in the hinterland. Even the menu in the window was authentic, hand-written on a dirty piece of paper that had been there so long it was fraying at the edges. Tortillas and salads, *mejillones* and *calamares* and *gambas*, or if you wanted meat rather than seafood there was *chorizo picante*, *jamon serrano*, *albondigas diablo* . . .

"Okay?" Jon asked.

"Terrific, so far." Except that you had to buy food if you wanted to drink, I'd forgotten Britain's extraordinary licensing laws; but then, why go to a tapas bar if you didn't want to eat tapas?

Because you want to drink decent coffee, I reminded myself, with a brief prayer offered up that there too this place might seem reasonably authentic.

Inside, the image took something of a hammering. The TV on the wall was right enough, tuned to Eurosport, though the English commentary took the gloss off it; but the owners were a couple of Geordies, the business presumably a hangover from years of package holidays at Torremolinos or Benidorm.

I didn't want to sit in the window, though I'd have liked the promise of sunlight on my skin. It was a case of balancing one insecurity against another, and in the end caution won out over strength: better not to precipitate a problem, than to be ready to meet it. We took a table at the back, ordered tea and coffee for now with a thought towards maybe beer and tapas later, and waited almost without speaking until we had steaming cups in front of us and the privacy to talk undisturbed.

"Come on, then," I said, getting straight down to it against the temptation to prevaricate. "What the hell is going on?"

They looked at each other; Janice made a gesture. "It's your town, not mine. I'm an incomer, what do I know?" Her smile said that actually she knew a lot, or she thought she did, but she was holding back here for reasons of her own. Sort of smile I'd seen before, usually on girls; learned 'em in girlschool, I guess, or from each other. Sometimes they were even justified, but I thought likely not here. However quick to pick things up you might be, understanding the soul of this city was genetic, I thought; you had to be born here. Unless it was environmental but you still had to be born here, it had to soak like a stain into your soft baby bones, it had to come to you like a taint in your mother's milk. I thought.

Jonathan was native, Janice was not; Jon said, "Things changed, right after you went away, I suppose it was. That's when it started. Your Uncle James was in charge suddenly, he was running the place; and boy, did he let everyone know it."

My Uncle James was a bully and a bastard. Nothing new there, nothing to make him stand out much among my male relations; but Uncle James with the power, with the dominance he'd always been denied before and with a major grudge to work out of his system – yes, I'd pretty much predicted this, that under his charge the hand of the Macallans would fall more heavily than ever on the shoulders of their victims.

"Even my dad," Jon said, "he had his little business, cleaning windows round about, clearing gutters, a bit of housepainting on the side. One-man show it was, there wasn't enough work for me to join him, yeah? But they put the sting on him, even. And he couldn't pay it, of course he couldn't, not so much of his take. When he told them, they just came round at night and trashed all his gear. Burnt his van out, and wrecked the garage where he kept his ladders and stuff."

"Jesus, Jon, I'm sorry," and I was; though I'd spent a lifetime being sorry for what my family did, I still felt it fresh every time. "What happened after, what did he do?"

"Well, he really couldn't pay them then, could he? He tried to find a job, but there just weren't any; so him and my mam, they left in the end. Went to Liverpool, he's working for a garage over there, doing resprays."

Yeah, right. That was an old story, often retold; people ran into the brick wall that was the Macallans' inflexible greed, they packed their bags and departed. A desert of dreams, this city could be, under my family's rule. They never used to bother before with the really small beer, but the principle was painfully familiar.

"You stayed, though," I said, looking to find some good in the dreary waste of lives, some hint of a silver lining.

He smiled. "That was Tim. He said I could move in with him, only I had to stop dossing around and try for college. I did a year's foundation course, and they let me in to do art. It's brilliant," the smile stretching to a grin now, an expression of absolute content. "Even with Tim gone, even with all the shit that's going on, it's still brilliant."

"So tell me about the shit," I said, sighing inside. "My uncle got heavy, okay, that's not a surprise. He never did have any sense of proportion. There's more than that, though. Isn't there?"

"Well, yes. People stood it for a while, but in the end it got too much. There were so many businesses going under, a lot worse than my dad. They had meetings in the town hall, they talked a lot, but no one thought anything would happen . . ."

No. Again, this was nothing new. Uncle James wouldn't have been worried by a few town meetings, he thought he was invulnerable, him and all his kind. He probably wouldn't even bother to send spies along. "But?"

"But there must have been some group having meetings in secret too, making plans. Don't know who, I don't think anyone does know; only one day, about a month ago this was, the last week of term, we all got sent home from college and told to keep our heads down, not to go out that night. There were all kinds of rumours, no one knew anything for sure, only that it was something to do with Macallans and they were going to be out for trouble. It was dead scary. We locked the doors and turned all the lights off, went to bed and listened to local radio all night, didn't we?"

He glanced at Janice, she nodded; I pictured them huddled together for comfort, in the dark with the curtains pulled against any stray intrusion of starlight. But he was doing that deliberately, I thought, giving me pictures to avoid giving me the truth.

"What was the radio saying?" I asked, thinking myself ready for anything; expecting news of another cousin murdered, some futile rebellion.

"More than usual," he said. "You know what it's like, Macallans aren't news usually, the station doesn't dare; but this time it did. They'd taken hostages, it said," he said, and I wasn't anything like ready for that, and he knew it. "Half a dozen, women and girls. They'd snatched them all from their homes, all at the same time, all over the city. It was really organised . . ."

"Hang on. *Macallan* women?"

"Yeah."

"Oh, Christ." That was clever, it was wickedly clever. Except for my freaky twin sister – my freaky *dead* sister, culled by my late Uncle Allan – the family talent had never run down the distaff side. Macallan women would be no threat to their kidnappers. "Who?"

"Wives and sisters," Janice said.

Jonathan nodded. "Sorry, Ben, I don't know their names. I don't think it was ever on the news, even. I mean, who are the reporters going to ask?"

Not Macallans, that was for sure. They'd ask the police; but the police were an instrument of the family, pretty much, or else second-rate competition. They'd give out precious little more than the family.

"Okay, doesn't matter. I can find out. So what happened then?"

"There was, I guess you'd call it an ultimatum. Your uncle had to lay off the town, or the hostages would suffer . . ."

Obviously. And what followed, I thought, was equally obvious. "He didn't, though. Right?"

"Well, no. The guy who'd been leading the public protests, he'd been really brave," *really stupid*, I thought, "making himself a target, almost; he had this big warehouse out of town, and it burned down that night. The fire brigade wouldn't even go out till the morning. But when they did, they found his body in the ashes."

That was typical, that was how Uncle James thought: meet a threat with overmastering force, cow the cattle into submission. It had worked for years, for centuries maybe; no reason why it shouldn't work now. Except that patently it hadn't. I sat waiting, very still, very contained; at last Jonathan gave me the really bad news.

"That same day they found one of the hostages dumped by the road, out by your uncle's house. She'd had her throat cut."

I nodded slowly. A life for a life: that was inevitable, the kidnappers wouldn't have started this if they hadn't meant business, and they must have known from the start that they'd have to prove they did indeed mean it.

Any man's death diminishes me, and any woman's too; and more, far more when that death was in the family, when it was my own blood that had run. I'd lost another cousin, and it didn't matter that I couldn't yet put a name or a face to her; no matter whether I'd loved her or loathed her, she was mine, she was a part of me and she'd been ripped away from me, not innocent perhaps – hard to say that any Macallan was innocent, we were all tainted by association – but terrified and helpless, powerless, absolutely a victim of this war . . .

I felt lethally angry. For a moment I wanted to run to my uncle, offer my unique services unconditionally to his support; but only for a moment. I still despised my uncle, he presumably would still despise me, and there were better places to run that were still not running away.

"Thanks, Jon," I said; and drained my coffee, pushed my chair back, ready to stand up and go. "Can one of you give us a key to the flat? Don't bother to come back, I'll just pick my stuff up, get the bike and go . . ."

"Go where?" Janice demanded.

"There's someone I've got to see." Someone I had to find, first; and I'd try a long shot to start with, keep as far as I could from Uncle James. "It'll be better if I don't come back to you, after. Unless there's more you haven't told me?"

Another glance between them, and two heads shook as one. "It's been a stalemate since then," Jon said. "As far as we know, at least. There's been no news. You don't see Macallans out by day much, that's why you were getting stared at; and everyone stays home at night. God knows what's going to happen . . ."

Maybe so; but I knew one thing that was going to happen, if any macho fool bastard did anything more than stare at me this morning. I had pictures in my head, five caged cousins and one murdered. I was not feeling temperate, and there were no clouds to mask the sun.

"You shouldn't go out there alone," Janice said.

"You shouldn't come with," I retaliated. "Trust me, you don't want to be anywhere near." I didn't want them seen with me too much, either. There could so easily be a backlash against collaborators; I wouldn't willingly put my friends in danger. Then, a late thought, "Is there a phone at the flat now?"

."Yes," from Janice, "I had one put in. Want the number?"

"Please."

She wrote it on my hand, though there was paper in plenty lying around the bar. Then she gave me her keys, and said to lock up behind me and drop them back through the letter-box. I told them to stay where they were, enjoy their day, not to worry about me. Call us, she said, and I said I would, of course, soonest. Trust me, I said. And I walked out into hard hot sunshine on a hard hot city and felt no less hard and hot myself, steel-hard and furnace-hot; and had walked no more than a dozen paces past the bar's big window before I heard a quick mutter from down the street behind me and then a single voice, yelling.

"Oy, you!"

I stopped, turned; saw half a dozen youths some distance back but already up on their toes and spreading out, making room for a rumble.

"You a fucking Macallan, are you? You look like one . . ."

Well spotted, I thought, they could only have had a moment of my profile; but the profile of course was famous, and recognition probably again genetic. *Know thine enemy*; always useful, in this town it was essential.

I gave them an answer, quick, before they could come a step closer. Raging I was, but there was still something in control inside me, something that wanted to see no more blood on my hands. *No more than is necessary*, I qualified. I'd have no qualms with the throat-cutters, but these were just stroppy kids. Not innocent – you didn't get to be shaven and scarred and innocent, not around here – but near enough. Guilt not proven, at any rate. They didn't look like any subtle, brutal kidnappers to me. One out of the three, perhaps. Not enough.

So I kept the genie in the bottle, more or less. Gave them just a glimpse: enough to startle and scare, enough to spread the word, *it's not true what they say, Macallans aren't harmless in daylight*. That might help, somewhere, sometime; might even help my captive cousins, make the kidnappers think twice before they slaughtered another . . .

What I did, I stood there in their sight, hands by my sides and ultimately relaxed; and between us, the bar's big plate glass window suddenly exploded.

Punching it in would have been easy, but my friends were in there, and others closer to the window. Sucking it outward was harder, needed a mental twist; but I gripped and jerked and it came like a sweetheart, splintering into great shards and spears of glass that shattered the windows of parked cars and ruined their paintwork, smashed against the opposite wall, scattered a million glints of light across the road.

Right before those lads' feet, the glass danced and skittered, but I don't think one of them got cut.

I do think one of them pissed himself, I swear I saw the dark stain spreading on his jeans just before they turned and sprinted off.

I couldn't even enjoy it. This was nothing set against a cousin – *who?* – with her throat cut, an uncle out of control, a father in tears in public and what did that mean?

Janice and Jonathan were coming out of the bar, treading warily, calling my name; I turned my back and started to run myself, forcing reluctant flesh, desperate not to have them catch me now.

• FOUR •

BIKE A HILL AND WALK A SHORE

Never had I felt that my family was worth much, that they had any real value in the world; occasionally I was truly surprised, just how much they were worth to me.

Perhaps I shouldn't have been surprised. Even a snail might be admirable to a slug, say, a cockroach to a beetle; and I'd never felt I was worth anything at all. With that as a baseline, perhaps it's no great wonder that I would lay my life on the line, to protect people whose lives and morals I deplored.

What they thought of me I had already had graphic, gripping evidence of, in the touch of my father's talent, the touches of his boot. I still thought that they needed me; I could give them the one thing that they lacked, protection in daylight. And I wanted to, perhaps I needed to, to win acceptance even this late in my giddy career from weakling to parricide to runaway to returnee. Prodigal-time, and I blushed to wish for the fatted calf, and wished for it none the less.

And doubted its delivery, with my father weeping and denying me, my cold Uncle James remembering my now even colder Uncle Allan, both living brothers with their faces for sure set against me: pride, I thought, would lock their gates and keep me out.

Pride, I thought, might not be enough to keep the town out for ever, now that fear seemed to be losing its grip. And hence I thought they needed me, and hence I would offer myself as security guard for the daylight shift.

But not to the brothers, to my father and uncle, no. I was going where I could at least get a hearing, where my questions might receive an answer; or more honestly, perhaps, I was going to look for someone who might just possibly smile when he saw me.

Longest shot first: I was heading for where I'd seen him last, where I thought he was least likely to be now. It was also where I least wanted to find him, which is maybe another reason I was doing this at a run, *get it over with, before you lose your nerve. He won't be there, of course he won't, but all doubts resolved, that's the way, be sure . . .*

So past the station and up the hill and pushing it all the way, a quick glance or two over my shoulder to be sure the other two weren't following. Running from them, I guess I was, as well as running to enlist; equivocal they might be but family they were not, and there could only ever be two sides in this war, in this city. I didn't want to see them compromised with either side. Neither did I want them compromising me, more than I was already.

I ran hard, sweating and gasping and feeling sick with the effort, reawakening memories of all the night's pains though not thank God the pains themselves, only an ache like an echo in each pain's place. Healing fast, I was, unless I'd just been a drama queen last evening, hurt more in the soul – or, let's face it, in the *amour propre* – than in the flesh. A man could exaggerate his wounds even to himself, perhaps, when it was his own father doing the wounding . . .

Whatever. I ran, I sweated, I ached; and it was uphill all the way and Christ, I remembered doing this for *fun* a time or two when I was a student. Doing it drunk, too, I remembered that. Just the once, but I was fizzing with elation and I couldn't have walked. Laura had kissed me; what more did a boy need?

As it turned out, a boy had needed a whole lot more than one kiss, and Laura wouldn't supply it; but I wasn't so hot on foresight, then or ever. She kissed me, I fizzed, I ran home. Easy.

Today the same run but no alcohol in me, no kisses burning on my lips, no wings on my heels as gifted by Laura to a younger and more foolish me. Fizz there was, though, albeit of a very different sort. I ran in sunshine, and no matter how weary or how hard-pressed, no matter how much the running hurt, I wasn't going to stop. Heavy legs wouldn't drag me to a walk, to a halt, to the unforgiving ground. Sun on my shoulders, I could run forever. Sobbing, sure; screaming inside, maybe, and maybe doing untold harm; but I could run.

And did, and came to the flat at last, at long last. Better locks it had now, than of yore; either we were cocky then, or my name had some influence even where I didn't, or we thought so. Whichever, I thought I detected Janice in the change, as I deChubbed the door and let myself in.

And lost the light's support in the shadowy hall, and slumped against the wall and sank to my haunches, to my knees; almost lay flat out on the floor, my legs were so rubber suddenly. Painful rubber, and worse when I stretched them out across the carpet and Fizzy the cat came to sit on them.

The phone was right there, I noticed, just an arm's stretch away; and I could do that instead, I could reach out and punch a number that was graven still in my memory, I didn't need to go round in person.

I could do that, and one of five things would happen. He would answer, or she would answer; or a total stranger would answer; or else no one at all would answer, or else the number would be dead, redundant, out of service, gone. Five possibilities, and I couldn't handle any one of them.

So no, *stick to plan A, Ben boy*. A knock on the door would at least reduce the possibilities to four. Unless the flat was boarded up and obviously empty, that was possible also. Still five, then. But they seemed preferable, somehow, though I couldn't have said why.

So. I needed to get my breath back, get my legs working, get up on my feet and moving. Get my things together, get out of here, go . . .

The thought was easy; acting on it, not. But I managed, shakily, glad not to be witnessed as I shambled around the flat, clinging to the furniture while I collected jacket and rucksack, remembered my toothbrush from the bathroom, tripped more than once over the curious, following cat.

I talked to him, I remember, all the way round. Better than talking to myself, which I might well have been doing else. It felt better, at any rate, and I felt better for it.

Then there were all the complications of letting myself out of the back door without letting Fizzy out too, unbolting the gate in the yard, wheeling the bike out and driving round to the front, making the most of the energy-giving sun before I went back in to rebolt the gate and then the back door, be sure the flat was secure before I carried my things out and Chubbed up again.

And posted the keys as promised, donned my jacket despite the heat and then the heavy rucksack. The helmet last, and lo! I was ready, or as ready as I ever would be.

Here was another route that was utterly familiar, branded so deep in my brain I didn't need to think about it.

On the other hand, not thinking about the route left me with nothing to think about bar what I might find at the end of it, which of those possibilities would turn out true. Each carried its own anxiety, each threatened its own distress; I could make a case both for wanting and for not wanting any and all of them.

To travel hopefully may be better than to arrive, but to travel in a state of panic-driven muddle when you don't know what you're hoping to find when you get there is no way to see the world, even when it's one you've seen before. So I did choose to think about the route after all, in preference; I concerned myself with left and right turns, with mini-roundabouts and correct behaviour at the lights, and was searingly glad when I took the last right-hander and found myself there, on the street where she lived.

Where she used to live. Where it was quite unlikely that she lived now, only that she wouldn't have graduated yet, medics go on forever; and she might play the wild girl sometimes but underneath she liked settlement, she liked stability, she'd probably stay unless she had a good reason to move.

And by the same token she might like settlement and stability in her boyfriends, she might keep hold of someone she loved unless and until she had a good reason to let them go.

She might. How would I know?

I turned the corner, not knowing; I glanced up the street towards what had always been her door to me, not knowing; and then I knew.

Some questions are easy answered. There was Laura's door, and there was Jamie's beloved jeep parked in front of it. What I'd hoped to see, what an antique yearning inside me had dreaded to see, *oh Laura*; I had no idea how I was truly going to deal with this, whether there would be anything more than nostalgia to deal with, but at least I knew where all three of us stood now, I knew what there was to find out.

There was my cousin, my adoptive brother Jamie, best of

all my relations; there was my everlost Laura, the girl who loved the wrong Macallan lad; there was me, the refugee, the wanderer returned. Three points, one triangle; three people joined by a complex web, and my return could only put more stress on it, and who knew what strands were strong enough to cope and what would tear under the strain?

Not I. I just parked the bike, took off the helmet, pressed the bell without a single solid thought in my head. Walking on memories, I was here, and it felt like floating; it felt like the start of a trip, almost, when you know you're going somewhere and you're not clear yet whether it's up or down.

There were footsteps on stairs, the other side of the door; there was the sound of the latch unlocking, a slight hint of creak and squeak in the hinges; there was Laura's face big in my vision, her eyes big with the sight of me.

"Holy fuck," she said softly. "Benedict Macallan, you bastard. Lose the number, did you?"

"I wanted to see you," I muttered, "face to face, it's better, I thought you wouldn't mind . . ."

"Mind? Who's talking about minding? I meant for the last two years, fool. Why didn't you phone?"

"I sent postcards."

"Sure, you sent postcards. Sometimes. With no address, no way we could get back to you. That's short rations for old friends, Ben. But never mind, you're here now." And then she reached for a hug, or started to, or I thought she did, putting my helmet down on the wall to make room for it; but she checked, visibly making connections, though not with the marks on my face, and asked another slow question instead. "Did your family send for you?"

I shook my head. "They didn't get an address either, nobody did. What, I'd tell Uncle James but not Jamie? Do me a favour . . ."

"You might have told your mother," and sure enough, I

might have; but that was the same thing. I told Mum, I told Dad, by definition; I told Dad, I told Uncle James. Also by definition. The long grass whispered, in those unElysian fields; the trees always found out.

I said all that with a shrug; and then I did get my hug, though it was a little awkward with the rucksack and sympathy now as much as welcome that inspired it, *poor boy, can't even talk to his mum* . . .

Fuck that, I thought, and cast my arms around her, lifted her off her feet and hugged her bigger and bolder than ever I had when I lived for and around but never with her, when I loved her against her denial.

Putting on weight, was Laura; but then, weren't we all? In my case it was mostly due to an acquired habit of gyms, always a place to go when you're alone in foreign towns, as I had been perhaps too often in the last couple of years. Gyms are great, for that condition: you can focus on yourself without feeling lonely, you can work out all the tensions in sweat, and they're good for meeting people also.

It wasn't so much muscle that Laura had added, only a little softness, flesh on her bones. Age, I supposed, just a little more living that she'd done without me; or else contentment, perhaps, as she grew more comfortable with the choices that she'd made?

I put her down, anyway, and she laughed up at me and said, "Are you coming in, then, or what?"

"Yeah. Uh, is Jamie here . . . ?" I did have to ask, to be ready to meet him if the answer was yes, just those few seconds of warning I wanted; but even as I asked I had a moment of doubt, *what if they're not together, what if he gave her the jeep as a farewell present, what then?*

But she only shook her head, dark hair tossing cheerfully across her face as she said, "You've just missed him, he slipped off somewhere on his bike. Why, did you come to see him?" All sorts of undercurrents there: a playful pout, *didn't you come to see me, you dog?* but a serious question beneath it, *do you know what's going on, is that why you're here, looking for your blood-brother?*

Yes. "No," I said, "both of you," I said, and that seemed to be good enough. She grunted disbelievingly, *I know what you boys are like*, but she grabbed my hand and tugged me inside, hauled me up the stairs and into Lauraland.

I used to love this flat, because I used to love her. That past-tense feeling would be a good thing to hang on to, I thought. Just to be clear about things. Maybe there'd be some help upstairs, new furniture, rearrangements. I wanted unfamiliarity, to kill any nostalgic welling in me for the sufferings of yesteryear; I was even looking forward – sort of – to seeing Jamie's things around, blokeish touches to temper the subtle but positive femininity I remembered, that had been totally Laura.

Blokeish touches there were aplenty, from the bass guitar on the landing to the auto mags piled by the sofa in the living-room to the collection of serious beers in racks below the hi-fi, Jamie's version of a wine-cellar; and there had been redecoration also, plain shades of paint over all the various wallpapers of a classic student flat. But the furniture remained the same, as it was in my own— no, in Jon's place now, Jon's and Janice's; the flat smelled the same as it ever had, of flowers and fresh air and nothing nasty lurking in any corner; and there was an indefinable sense of order that I associated still with a female hand, and here with no one but Laura. That guitar wasn't just dumped on the landing for want of anywhere else to put it, or – even more laddishly – want of the enthusiasm to find or carry it anywhere else; that was its place and it seemed to belong there, to have a statement to make as you came up the stairs. The magazines weren't exactly tidy in their pile, but neither were they strewn across the floor or scattered through the flat. Might have been Jamie who had stacked them there, maybe even without Laura's standing over him to insist; but it was still her mind-set that was in charge here, it was still very much her flat.

The furniture surprised me, a little. Cheap and manky as it was, I'd have thought it would be long gone from here. Jamie too had his standards, derived from a lifetime in clover, second and only surviving son of my only surviving uncle; used to mahogany and oak and fine leather beneath his arse, he seemed unlikely to have stuck this stuff so long. Maybe they didn't spend much time here, but even so I'd have expected him to sweep it all out and refit completely.

But then, really I'd have expected him to sweep Laura out of here and set up home for the two of them in an area very much smarter than this. Rented accommodation just wasn't Jamie's style; rented furniture was almost funny. Perhaps this was Laura's hand again, though, her stubborn feet digging in, *no, I won't be your kept woman, Jamie, and I won't touch your family's filthy money. You want me, you share my life, woodworm and wet rot and all . . .*

Yes, that made sense. I was pleased with myself, sorting it out so fast; but then I saw her watching me, much amused, and realised I'd been stood in the middle of the living-room gazing around me, logging everything, practically working it out on my fingers while she no doubt followed all the workings on my face . . .

"Ben, love. Put the helmet down, take the backpack off, take the jacket off, sit down. What can I get you?"

This was still morning; did she need to ask?

"Coffee, of course. Strongest, blackest. See if I can outchew you . . ."

Stunningly, amazingly, she shook her head. "I don't think we've got any real. I'm off it at the moment, and Jamie doesn't care, he drinks the most disgusting muck. I can do you a mug of disgusting muck, if you want one?"

That meant instant, and if she'd had anything to do with
the shopping it'd be good instant, or as good as instant gets;
but this was still not a credible position. "Hang on. Run that
past me again. You're *off coffee?*"

The Cappuccino Kid, we used to call her; Elle Espressa, in
the evenings. Limitless capacity for caffeine in all its forms,
endless enjoyment thereof.

She shrugged, smiled. "Makes me feel sick. Hormones,
I suppose. Nasty girly stuff, you don't want to know."

Damn right I didn't, but it was too late for that. This was
suddenly, achingly, unbearably familiar. Good hot Catholic
country, Spain, full of bad hot Catholic kids. Lots of sex,
little contraception. "Laura, are you pregnant?"

"Clever boy. Do you think it shows?" She flattened her
hands, her clothes across her stomach, peering down at it,
exaggerating everything. Trying hard, doing no good at all.

No, I didn't think it showed. She'd put on weight all over;
there might be a little extra swelling, a little hardening of
the belly to talk of the alien within, but I couldn't tell
without touching and I wasn't going to touch. Even with
an invitation, I wouldn't have wanted to touch.

Thinking *alien* (though it wasn't, not really, it was only
part and part of two people I loved), thinking of foreign
bodies stirring into life within concealing flesh, I felt something not at all foreign but bitterly unwelcome stirring in
my own guts, a sudden sharp twist of a long-buried blade.
The echo of an old cry, *it should have been me!* – and
the echo returning brought all the old pain with it, cruelly
renewed.

I'd thought – or no, maybe not that, but at least I'd
vaguely hoped – that I might have been past this by
now. Older and wiser, I'd thought myself (don't *laugh*),
infinitely more experienced: Marina and Sallah, a dozen
girls in a dozen cities, more than. So cosmopolitan, I'd
thought myself, so sophisticated, how could I possibly still

be carrying a torch for a girl who'd never so much as kissed me with her mouth open?

I guess I had my mouth open, just then. Laura was smiling at me, reaching to run her fingers through my hair, *sorry, I shouldn't have tried to be smart, you needed it breaking more gently*, still doing what she could to make this easy: anxious for me perhaps, but not at all for herself or anything that came with her. Totally comfortable with that she seemed, with being pregnant and Jamie's girlfriend and all that that implied; and I think that's what flipped me over in the end. Pregnant – okay, that happened, though she was a medic, for God's sake, she should have known better. Pregnant by Jamie – well, again okay, sort of. Somehow. I could find a way to handle that. He was always a careless bastard; the only real surprise was that it hadn't happened before, that I knew of. But pregnant by Jamie and utterly content, all the weight of clan history hanging over her like the darkest of thunderclouds about to break and her still unfazed, blithely unheeding: I could never have wished her unhappy, but this was too much. This was a wedding-ring and more, this was *I'll take on all his cursed family, all their evil, past and future both; it's worth it to me, so long as I can have him.*

Grief enough to me that she had found him sexy, desirable, acceptable two years ago, and me not. The time between had changed me not enough, seemingly, and her too much, if she could make such a commitment; Laura had a solemn soul under her wild skin, she'd never make a baby without making promises to go with. Making and demanding, and just how changed must Jamie be, that they could make this work?

Didn't matter. It was just a stray thought spinning through a mind sick and dizzy, hurting, reeling. What did matter, what could possibly matter? Answer, not a lot. Certainly not my own behaviour, that clearly didn't matter a damn to her, she was only trying to be nice because she was a nice girl and it was the nice thing to do.

If it didn't matter to her, it didn't matter. Not a problem then that I was on my feet in a surge and blundering mutely for the door, jerking free of her staying hand and not listening, only distantly aware that she was talking, following, pleading with me almost as I took the stairs two and three at a time. Couldn't hear a word, against the hiss and suck of a dark tide pulling at me that I had no will to fight.

To get out of there, that was all I wanted; not to see that radiant calm in her, not to look and look for any hint of a bulge in her waistline, not above all to wait for Jamie and see him, see him and her together. Been there, seen that already. I'd been carrying those pictures in my head all this time, wondering, imagining; didn't want the truth of them acted out now before me, where it couldn't be denied or dismissed as not important any more. The real truth was in me, impelling me through the door and slamming it behind me.

Onto the bike, and only realising then that I'd left jacket, helmet, rucksack behind me. Too late to worry, I wasn't going back. Keys were in my pocket, that was all that counted.

I blasted away from her door like all the demons of hell were behind me, and I thought they were. Looking back was a no-no, whether she came or not; she might be standing there in the street screaming my name, but I couldn't hear and I didn't want to know.

Where to go? Again it was a question, and likely the answer eventually would be back to Jon's, but not yet. I wanted speed, I wanted to stare open-eyed into the wind to drive incipient tears back into my skull. Only one route to take, then, the same way I'd always gone when this fierce need was on me; once more it didn't need thinking about, it didn't require decision.

*   *   *

Adolescence famously has its agonies; adolescents famously try to run away from them, into drink or drugs or whatever mind-blasting high can numb the pain awhile. Me, I'd tried and used them all, but driving at speed was always the fall-back position, if only because it did the thing twice: it gave you an experience to escape into and at the same time it actually took you away from there, it brought you physical escape. Whatever shit I took with me in my head, I always reckoned geographical distance had a lot to recommend it.

Which I guess is why I'd gone eventually to Europe, looking for escape on the grand scale; I might have picked America or Australia, only that there would have been problems getting the bike across and I never would have left it.

And now I'd come back, thinking myself so grown-up, grown out at last of those teenage clothes, albeit a few years late; and here I was doing it all again, racing shadows of the past down a long straight road, trying to outrun what I carried with me . . .

Ten miles the road ran with hardly a kink in it, thanks to the Romans who built it first. Never mind what else they'd ever done for me, Latin classes and toga parties and walks along the wall, this was enough to earn and keep my gratitude. This was plenty.

Jamie and I used to race this road; sometimes I used to race this road alone, when the need to get away was stronger. Later, after I left the family home in my first weak rebellion, I used to yearn for it; loving and losing Laura, never truly having Laura to lose, could have driven me this way a dozen times a month, except that then I had no bike.

And now here I was and there was Laura and she'd done it to me again, or I'd done it to myself because of her; and I did have the bike, and I did crouch over the handlebars and gun

the engine to the max, and pity any poor fool who got in my
way because I was truly in no condition to be driving at all,
let alone driving like this, but oh, I was going to drive.

And did; and nobody did get in my way, because actually
there was a dual carriageway now from city to coast, had
been the best part of my life, and that tracked the river and
took most of the traffic. The old Military Road didn't really
go anywhere any more, only past a defunct industrial estate
and a lot of farms to the site of a Roman camp long since
buried under sand-dunes. Good beaches beyond, and a very
good hill just before the sea came in sight: boy racers loved
this road, but no one else used it much.

So I wasn't really a danger to anyone but myself, once I
got past the city limits. That was fine, that was just the way I
wanted it. I cooled down fast, in the chill of the drive; didn't
take long before it was only myself I was hating here.

Or so I thought, slacking off on the speed at last; but
suddenly there was another wheel nosing into sight, catching
at the corner of my eye, another bike unexpectedly keeping
pace with me. I glanced across, scowling, wanting no
competitor – and all but lost control of the BMW as I found
myself staring at Jamie from only a metre's distance.

Oh, *fuck* it! My head jerked forward again, I squeezed
another kick of power out of my bike, and still couldn't
leave him behind. Virtuously helmeted, he was riding a
stripped-down Japanese scrambler that shouldn't have been
able to match me this way on a clear road. He must have
tweaked the engine for racing; racing me on tarmac was
going to knack his tyres, but that was small comfort.

Jamie my cousin, my blood-brother, always my rival and
always the victor, now more than ever so: right then hating
him was no problem, no burden at all.

We screamed along that road, wheel to wheel and head
to head, no advantage except that he always did have the

advantage over me; and it can't have been more than a minute or so but it seemed like an age before at last we came to the gravelled lay-by that was the turning onto Hob's Hill.

I twitched left and slammed on the brakes, coming to a savage halt on the rough ground. He did the same, and again we glared at each other. No words needed: he gestured up at the track and the scrubby slopes, I nodded, and we were off again.

I had to stick to the track on my heavy roadster, he didn't; we might be racing again, but at least we weren't side by side any more.

I took stupid risks on the climb, hauling my machine around the sharp zigzags, perilously close to losing it altogether and sliding off, broken bones and a broken bike guaranteed if I let it happen. Even so, all I saw of him was his dust as he ploughed straight up the hillside, and when I got to the top he was there already, his bike on its stand and the helmet off his head, himself standing waiting for me.

Well, that was written, that was inherent, both in the bikes and in us. Of course he won, didn't he always?

I switched off my engine, kicked my stand down, stood up to meet him. Walked across, even, with no thought in my head, what I should or could or wanted to say to him; and then it didn't matter anyway, because he didn't want to talk at all, he just hit me.

A hard round-arm slap it was, the hand cupped for added impact, plenty of time to see it coming if I'd only had the wit to duck. I didn't, and he made sweet contact with my cheek, jarred all my teeth and the bones that held them. And I still wasn't thinking, I just felt a hot spur of relief underlying the shock of it. And reacted a second late, perhaps, but still too fast for him as I swung my fist in return.

Caught him right on the chin, knuckle-crunchingly hard. I don't believe I'd ever knocked anyone down before, in all the fights of my youth; but he went over like a target on a trip, straight down he went without even a stagger to try to catch himself. He lay still in the shadow of his bike, and I felt a moment's panic as my head cleared.

"*Jamie . . . ?*"

I crouched over him and saw the glitter of his open eyes, slitting against the sun; huffed with relief as he brought a cautious hand up to touch his jaw, where his skin was already staining red.

"Jesus," he whispered. "Was that all you?"

I had to stop and work it out, but, "Yes," I said. "I think so. Unless just being in the sun gives me something . . ." If there'd been any talent in that punch, it wasn't deliberate; or not conscious, at any rate. I couldn't speak for my id.

"Fuck. You been working out, or what?"

All those gyms, in all those separate cities: I knew I'd put on weight, I knew I had more muscle to show the girls, I'd never known till now that I could actually use it.

"Are you getting up," I said, "or what?"

"Think I'll stay here, thanks. You might hit me again . . ."

I grinned and lay down to join him, side by side and easy touching distance. All passion spent, it seemed, in one blow each.

"Was that male bonding, d'you reckon?"

"No." I had my eyes closed, sunlight heavy on the lids, tingling everywhere it touched. "Didn't go on long enough. You want to try again?"

"No." I heard him breathing deeply, working up to something, waiting till his head felt straight enough to handle it; and then, "Brother, thou hast my Laura much offended."

"Brother," coming straight back at him, "you have *my* Laura much offended."

A pause, while he did me the grace to consider that; and there was nothing challenging in his tone, only strict neutrality when he said, "Do you really think so?"

"No," *damn it*, "of course I don't. She isn't, never has been," *not my Laura* . . . "It's her choice, who the hell am I to criticise? I just acted like a shit, that's all. I'm sorry."

"Good," he said, sounding oddly cheerful. "That's what I thought, what I told her."

"What, that I was a shit?"

"A sorry shit. Don't worry."

That was stupid; how could I not worry? "She seems happy," I said tentatively. "About the baby, I mean . . ." Meaning, *how about you, are you happy?*

"Yeah. Mad cow. Too many burgers, I reckon," but there was a grin in his voice that seemed to be an answer.

I heard him move then, beside me; cracked my eyes open, and saw him take a mobile phone out of a pouch on his belt. He flipped it open, punched a number, waited, winked at me when he saw me watching; and then said, "Hi, it's me. Told you I'd find him . . . Yeah, he's fine. He says he's a sorry shit. I'll bring him back later, okay? You can kiss and make up then . . . No. No can do. We've got to go and play first. It's a boy thang. See you . . ."

He switched off and put the phone away, then grinned down at me and said, "Come on, we'll go to the Island."

Pirate's Island had been a part of our lives for as long as I could remember. Ditto for my older cousins, ditto maybe for my parents' generation too, though I'd never asked. Neither one of my uncles, perhaps, but I could see my dad there: demanding as a kid, drunk and sweating and demanding as a teenager, fumbling at girls and cheating clumsily with the air-rifles and getting away with it because of who he was.

Pretty much like us, really . . .

Well, like we used to be. The Island was a semi-permanent funfair with cheap rides and tacky stalls, open from Easter to August Bank Holiday; it was an easy place for parents to take their children, and easy too for lads to take their

girls, individually or en masse. Two totally separate sets
of memories it had given me: ten years of candy floss
and roundabouts, dodgem cars and toffee-apples, goldfish
in plastic bags and being sick with sweets and excitement;
then another ten years of warm lager and the roller coaster,
sweet cider and would-she-or-wouldn't-she, finding out in
shadows and being sick with alcohol and excitement.

In winter it was a skeleton, everywhere closed and dead
and dusty, again an easy place to come for kids or adolescents. Climb the gates and you could roller-blade or
skateboard in and out of the attractions (or actually on the
attractions, if you broke a lock or a shutter to get through;
no one bothered, no one watched the place in winter, they
just trusted us not to burn it down and patched up lesser
damage come the spring), you could take your best girl or
any willing girl into some dark and quiet corner and do all
those things you didn't dare try at home. If it was raining,
not to worry, there was plenty of shelter; if it was snowing,
so what? You'd keep each other warm . . .

Actually that last was more Jamie's story than mine: he'd
been lucky with girls as with everything, where I'd had too
many hang-ups even to keep up with the average family
score. Even before Laura. But that was the Island's reputation, and it was more than an urban myth; even I'd copped
the odd snog and feel, usually with someone provided for
that purpose by Jamie or his big bastard brother Marty or
else some other cousin taking pity, showing concern.

The Island wasn't really quite an island, except at the top
of the tide. It was only a few hundred metres offshore and
there was a causeway exposed at low water, a tarmac'd
road with a sort of watchtower affair in the middle, a
walled platform on high stilts that had a ladder up and a
roof above, for the convenience of anyone stupid enough
to get caught by the incoming sea when they were only

halfway across. That was another place good for girling, according to Jamie, if you could only time it right: take them up for a fag and a cuddle and a look at the view, and before you know it the tide's come in and you can't leave, all you can do is watch the water cover the road and giggle a lot, find a quarter-bottle of vodka in your pocket, share that between you and suggest some friendly way to kill the next few hours . . .

There's a road, but there's no great point in driving along it. Not in a car, at least, and not even on a bike in high summer. Too many pedestrians coming and going, and nowhere to park once you've crossed. Acres of free parking on the mainland, though, so we left the bikes there as so often before, locked his helmet in my box and walked past the anxious knot of visitors reading the tide tables on the noticeboard, *better safe than sorry, dear, we don't want to get stranded, now do we?* and onto and over the causeway. Going with the flow, just two young men in a crowd, nothing to mark us out . . .

Except our faces, of course. Jamie didn't carry the family features so forcefully marked as mine, but in my company there wasn't any question, his genetic inheritance was there to be seen. Maybe people just weren't looking for it, though, not here. This was still very much Macallan territory but there wasn't the same edge, the same sense of tension unresolved. I supposed the Island had always been a refuge, a place to forget your troubles for a while; which in this area meant a place to forget my family for a while. Maybe recognition just got left on the mainland, with the car . . .

Whatever. I took what precautions I could, weaving a fine web of sunlight like a halo around us, gossamer-thin and utterly immaterial, just so that anyone who glanced at us casually was going to be a little dazzled by the light, would have to blink water from their eyes before they could see clearly again. It wouldn't fool a concentrated glare, but why should we invite one?

Jamie twigged what I was doing, after a minute or two. "Neat idea," he murmured. "Where'd you learn that?"

"Made it up." I'd taught myself a lot of new tricks in the first month or two after I left home, before I forswore the talent. Now I was forsworn they were all available to me again; and Christ, I'd missed them so much . . .

"Ben," Jamie said, "I think you are going to be a revelation. Could be just what this family needs . . ."

Could be, perhaps. Could be just the opposite. I couldn't tell.

The Island was a place for having fun, reunions are a time for fun and laughter, for boyish folly and childish excess; but not that day. There was just too much other stuff around: behind us, between us, ahead of us. Inhibitions were in, exhibitions out. Despite what he'd said on the phone, we didn't really play at all. The half-hearted capture of a fluffy rhinoceros at a darts stall to take back for Laura – and bless him, he didn't say *for the baby* and showed no signs that he was even thinking it – satisfied us both, though Jamie had been throwing the arrows.

It was a big rhino; he slung it across his shoulders – *like a child*, and I could only hope my face wasn't saying so – and said, "Oy. Were you nudging those darts?"

"Might have been," I said neutrally. "Maybe you're a better player than you think you are."

"Ben, *nobody* could be better than I think I am. It's just that I don't often prove it."

"Well. Does it matter? Laura deserves rhinos."

He frowned at me, then shrugged beneath his burden. "No, you're right. It doesn't matter."

It would matter to her, of course, we both knew that; but she wasn't here, and neither one of us was about to tell her.

*   *   *

We looked at some of the rides with a nostalgic eye, but indecision was a killer; nothing tempted, nothing was strong enough to tug against the gravity of what we knew, what we weren't yet talking about, what we had to come to.

In the end it was Jamie as ever who took the lead, who sighed and said, "I'm hungry."

"Yeah."

Hungry on the Island meant fish and chips in a cone of newspaper, lager from a can to wash it down; it meant a scramble over seaweed-slippery rocks to get away from the noise and crush of the crowds, to sit with our feet dangling over grey-green depths too unchancy even for us to swim in; above all, it meant talking quietly and seriously, tackling the big issues, facing the facts. We used to do that all through our teenage years, I'd tell him my problems and he'd tell me his triumphs. What goes around, comes around; here we were again, we had to talk, of course we'd talk like this.

I bought the food, he bought a four-pack, we headed for our private ground. Others had come this way before us, trespassers, intruders; but they'd peeled off left or right, looking for the rock-pools or the caves. We slipped and slithered around the great rock we called Greenbeard for the long tangles of weed that clung to its chin, and there was the boulder we always used to sit on, and there was the long view out with nothing to interrupt it bar the odd container vessel keeping her distance from our shore. This could have been ten years ago, easy, except that ten years ago my family was ever on the up and I was sinking, and right here, right now neither part of that was true.

My turn to lead off, then. Tang of salt in the air, salt and vinegar both on hot food in damp paper heavy in my hands; I chewed, swallowed, breathed, said, "Who was it, Jamie?"

"Who was it what?"

"Died. Which cousin?"

"Christ. Don't you even know that?"

"If I knew, I wouldn't be bloody asking, would I?"

The antagonism was all seeming, all defensive, both of us recognised that. He broke off a chunk of fish and threw it at a seagull, the bird dodged it in missile mode then came up beneath to catch it falling, treat it as a treat; Jamie said, "It was Karen. They cut her fucking *throat* . . ."

That much I knew; but, Karen? Karen Macallan . . . A moment's searching, and then I had her. Pale blonde, bit of a damp dishcloth to look at though that had not been her reputation, but I didn't know if her reputation was accurate because, "Jesus, Jamie, she was only a bloody kid . . ."

"Seventeen last birthday," he said bleakly. "I saw her body, and her head was hanging off, nearly. There wasn't any blood in her at all. Father Hamish reckoned they'd maybe hung her upside down, to drain it all out. There were marks on her ankles, which might have been the rope. That meant they did it living, Hamish said."

Oh, sweet. It had to be symbolic, draining her of Macallan blood; never mind that hers would have had no spark of magic in it, except the background buzz to mark her as a carrier. All our women had that, at least, but nothing else. Nothing of benefit, if talent was a benefit; and there were times – *like when they're hanging you upside down, bleeding you to death, maybe?* – when yes, for sure it was.

Though they'd have done it in daylight, I guessed, to be doubly sure.

I only wished they'd try it in daylight with me . . .

Last time I'd seen Karen was the day they held the wake for Jamie's brother Marty, first victim of Uncle Allan's cull. The day I'd been brought back into the family, my rebellion crushed under the dominant will of my twin Hazel, who'd been victim number three. Death was haunting us, hounding us, in this generation; but Karen was the closest a Macallan could get to a blameless innocent where the others had not been, and that did make a difference, I thought.

Uncle James had been using her as a servant that day, to take coats, to fetch and carry. All the use he'd ever seen for her, most likely; but, "Jamie, what's your father doing about it?" Surely to God he had to be doing something.

"I don't know. I haven't got an inside track any more."

"How come?"

"Dad's not talking to me. I've taken on your mantle, bro, I'm the new black sheep. Living with cattle, making a baby outside the family, I'm a disgrace . . ."

He didn't sound too distressed about it; but it must have been harder for him than it had been for me, even, and I'd found it hard enough. Too hard, at the last. And Jamie had always belonged, always had a place right at the heart, which hadn't been true for me since I was sixteen or so, and showing definite signs of no talent. With Uncle James chief of the clan now, losing his father's approval must be like losing the family altogether, being sent into exile; and I knew how that had felt for me, and for him it must be worse, and I didn't believe his smile and I didn't know what to say.

So of course I said nothing, only chewed and swallowed and lobbed chips at gulls in lieu of hugging him; and at last it was Jamie who said, "Christ, Ben, what are we going to do?"

"Dunno. Not much we can do, is there?" I was still burning to avenge Karen, but less inclined than ever to sign up with Uncle James to do so. Jamie had been my route back into the family circle, and that route was blocked, it seemed; and what could two lads do alone? "Let's go for a walk."

Always a solution, short-term; always another aspect to a trip to the Island. A walk on the beach might come first, before we crossed the causeway, if we were meeting friends or girls; if we were just the two of us it usually came after, a

slow saunter in the dark to look at the stars and dream aloud
a while before we headed home.

Midday sun and beach parties changed the ritual, but
not dramatically. Kids were paddling, all along the water's
edge; Jamie had boots and jeans on, so we couldn't join in
properly, but I kicked my deck-shoes off and went barefoot
just where the incoming tide seethed onto dry sand. He
scuffed along parallel with me, a couple of metres higher
up the beach: easy talking distance, but we didn't really
talk. As far as I remember, the only things he said were
said to the rhino that still lay across his shoulders.

We'd done half the length of the beach, and it's a long
beach; I suggested turning back.

"Not yet," Jamie said. "I want to watch the kites."

Fair enough. I sat down and put my shoes on again,
and we both watched the kites that dipped and soared
overhead, guided expertly by a bunch of thirtysomethings
who'd probably been doing this since they were teens and
hadn't grown out of it yet. After a minute my neck got
cricked, so I turned to watch the water instead, where a
couple of jet-skiers were bumping and bouncing and falling
off in the surf while their machines gently screamed.

Only one thing out there making more noise, another
engine. I searched for it, found it: a low black Zodiac, the
twin propellors of its outboard threshing the water, occasionally threshing the air as it skipped like a thrown pebble
over the waves. It was heading inshore, racing or chasing
shadows, and I wondered if it was going to drive right up
onto the beach. Looked like it. I nudged Jamie, nodded my
head without taking my eyes away from the inflatable.

"I got it," he murmured. Of course he'd got it. Everyone
on the beach had got it by now, you couldn't ignore the
noise or the hurtling turtle shape of the thing, or its manic
rush towards land.

At the last moment, the Zodiac swung across the face of a wave and its engine cut. It lost momentum quickly in the heavy swell, but the tide would still bring it in if it just sat there . . .

Just sit there it did not. There were two men in the boat, I could see that now, though I couldn't see their faces; they seemed to be wearing hoods or masks, balaclavas maybe. They bent and lifted something, something long and black and plastic, gleaming in the light; and they threw it over the side.

It floated, or I thought it did, just about. It was hard to see, so low in the water.

The engine howled again, the Zodiac sped off out to sea; already a crowd was forming at the water's edge, a couple of boys in trunks were wading out to fetch in this strange sea-gift.

"Come on," Jamie said abruptly, urgently. "I want that."

He dropped the rhino, and ran. I wasn't on his wavelength, quite, but this had to be important to make him abandon Laura's present.

It's hard to run on soft sand, but we ran hard; and after a few seconds I cheated. Grabbed a bit of sunlight and helped us out, leaned a little on the beach ahead to compact it and give our feet something to push against. That wasn't easy either on the fly, on the run, on the instant; but I managed after a fashion, though the result wasn't the straight true path I was reaching for.

I don't think Jamie even noticed.

We pushed our way through the mill when we got there, and found the boys just hauling their burden out of the water, leaving a slug's trail for the waves to wash away.

Black plastic sheeting, sealed and roped and knotted tight around its secret contents; and already I think we knew and every adult there knew and most of the kids most likely knew too what that contents was.

We knew who it was meant for also, we didn't really need the direction spray-painted on the plastic, *Deliver to James Macallan*.

Only thing we didn't know, we didn't know who it was inside. Jamie wasn't going to wait for his father, to find out; he was tearing at that plastic with his bare hands, before he realised the nail-breaking futility of that and pulled a knife from his pocket.

Snapped the blade open, hacked through the sheeting; people were already covering their children's eyes or leading them away.

Ripped the wrapping open and it was Cousin Josie, a hard bastard I'd wished in hell a dozen times or more, but I would never have wished her this.

• FIVE •

LIVERISH ALLSORTS

How did I know it was Josie? God knows, perhaps; I don't.
You wouldn't have thought there were enough clues there
even for her nearest and dearest to name her, and I must
have been pretty much her furthest away, her least dear.

Somehow, though, I knew her. Not from her peach-blonde
hair, distinctive enough in life but clagged and matted now,
dark not with seawater that hadn't had a chance to get at
it, dark only where it was clotted with her blood. Certainly
not from her face, which had once been a work of careful
art but had become a jigsaw, torn into scraps and flaps of
skin that clung to what was red and black beneath. In places
– on her forehead, on her chin, on the bridge of her nose
– there hadn't been enough red stuff for the skin to cling
to, so it was gone, and what there was instead was stained
bone. Like Webster I saw the skull beneath the skin, where
before I'd never seen the skin even for all the foundation and
blusher and shader and such that it routinely wore; unlike
Webster I wasn't looking for it and didn't want to see it,
didn't relish this too-close confrontation with the ultimate
memento mori.

Cover her face, I thought, *mine eyes dazzle: she died
young.*

Jamie wasn't listening. No telepathic touch between us, not just now. Far from putting her back into a decent darkness, he was still chopping at the plastic, cutting the ropes away, exposing more and more of Cousin Josie.

No new sight to him, I suddenly remembered, or not in her original condition, cold and stiff and living. He was one of the few who would have seen her adult face uncovered, *au naturel*. She'd been one of his conquests when we were sixteen or so and she must have been twenty, and none of us lesser lads could understand why; he was smiling and mysterious, not faithful by any means but seeing her, sleeping with her for months before she called it off. His first older woman, I suppose, with many tricks to teach him; and his parents' presumptive approval for it too, keeping it in the family, very proper . . .

So yes, I thought, Jamie had a particular reason to be so cold and stiff himself now, dragging silently at ropes and sheeting, his face focused on her cold stiff body. At least she wasn't naked, they hadn't done that to her, though she wore only knickers and a skimpy blouse and that brutal mask of blood. Made it easier to see the damage she'd taken, with no extra layers in the way. Assuming you wanted to see the damage, of course, which I didn't and Jamie apparently – no, definitely – did. He'd have to, no reason else to peel back the plastic and give her, us, nowhere to hide.

Not only her face had been chewed up – and yes, I thought, that's what it was, even her skull had been channelled by a grating tooth. Like she'd been tossed to the pigs for a titbit, and snatched back too soon for them but too late, much too late for her . . .

Her face destroyed, that was all she'd ever cared about: medically speaking, that was the least of it. Trust me, no one ever died of being ugly. That particular jigsaw could have been reassembled and patched where pieces were missing, though they could never have sewn her looks back on.

Her hands were a ruin also, almost worse. Raw red pulp, both, with fingers missing. I saw unwelcome pictures in my mind, how she'd tried to protect herself, her face, same thing: how she'd wrapped her arms about her head, perhaps – and yes, there were bite-marks on her elbows too, I could see them now – and then how she'd pushed and scrabbled at whatever-it-was, the hound from hell, from the Baskervilles, wherever; how it had been monstrously undeterred, and snacked on her fingers before it came through to her face.

Face and hands gone, all three; and her throat was gone too, only a hole dark and deep enough to dive through, to come up God knew where, what lies beyond a black hole? That's what had killed her, the rest was cruel cosmetics and I wondered if there was art in that too, did they know her? Did they know about her make-up and her manicures, was this *irony* they'd practised here?

Jamie was kneeling over her now, rocking slightly, making no noise. We were entirely alone, the crowd melted and the beach almost empty behind us, and I was utterly certain not one of them had gone to phone for the police or an ambulance or anyone.

Which made it my job, though I really, really didn't want it.

I crouched beside Jamie, talking against his silence, just in case some hidden part of him might be listening.

"I just need your phone, Jamie, okay? We need to call someone, this isn't for us to handle . . ."

Someone I'd said, as if there was a choice. Big joke. Times of crisis, you go to the top, of course you do, you yell for the big cheese to come get you out of this. Used to be Uncle Allan, but I'd killed him. Now . . .

Now I unclipped the pouch on Jamie's belt and took the phone out, and he reacted not at all. I stood up, stepped back, puzzled over the keypad for a moment before I worked out how to work it; then punched a number that was no puzzle at all, that came readily to my mind, utterly unready as I was to use it.

It rang once, a few times, many times; I was set to give up when at last someone answered. "James Macallan," he said.

It was, it was himself, gruff and abrupt and charmless as ever. My least-favourite relative, even still, even knowing everything that Uncle Allan had done to us.

What, no butler? I thought, startled beyond words; I'd expected a minute's grace while the menial fetched the man. It marked a change indeed, if Uncle James was answering his own phone. The former uncle never would, though he were sitting right beside it.

"Yes? Hullo?"

"Hullo, Uncle James," I said, with an effort. "This is Benedict."

"What? What in the world do you want?"

Nothing in the world that he could offer me, that was for sure. "I'm on North Sands with Jamie," I said. "You'd better come."

"Why?"

"It's Josie," I said, and stalled unexpectedly. *She's been killed*, I wanted to say, *her body's here*, but I couldn't get the words out.

Didn't need to. He knew of course that she was among the missing; my awkwardness told him the rest. "Dead?" he asked.

"Yes."

He grunted, said, "Wait," hung up.

I folded the phone up neatly, reached to hand it back to Jamie, saw that he still wasn't seeing me or anything I did, and hunkered down again to put it back in its pouch, on his belt, without his noticing at all.

Three Macallans on a beach, utterly alone: and only one of

us was easy. Josie had had it easy all her life, she was the epitome of a full-blooded female cousin, taking what she wanted, tyranny her birthright. She'd have paid her dues to the family too, I was sure of that, married inside the clan and done her best to produce sons, if she'd lived so long.

Her death now, her death had not been easy, and there would be those – probably many, probably everyone else in town, all the citizenry, all the cattle with but a single voice – who would say that it was no more than she deserved. But that was over, and this was the aftermath; and she could RIP from here to eternity, quite untroubled. The rest of us, not so. Or not yet, though we'd catch up later . . .

Three Macallans waiting on a beach, and then there were many.

When they came, they came in a cavalcade, a slow procession of four-wheel-drives rolling over the dunes and down onto the beach.

I'd have called it a cortège only that it became clear very quickly that the focus, the intent of all these vehicles was not to mourn Cousin Josie. They had come here to collect her, granted; but even that was not the sole purpose behind their arrival. The cars, all those Macallans were there to protect Uncle James; and Uncle James was there at least partly to collect me.

They parked their cars all around us, and a dozen men stepped out watchfully and took up classic bodyguard positions – watching us, watching the lone and level sands, watching the sea – before ever Uncle James set foot to beach and walked across to join us.

All those men were carrying guns, quite openly. Rifles, shotguns, handguns. Macallans, with *guns?*

Macallans in daylight, I reminded myself. And no longer assured of the protection of their name, that not cutting the

mustard any more; and centuries of seething resentment
banked up, the dam that had held it back so long starting
to crumble at last . . .

No, I couldn't blame them for the guns; but Christ, it
was frightening. Not that anyone was pointing guns at me.
Jamie's presence beside me was enough guarantee even for
a rebel son, perhaps; or else they'd just been well briefed
beforehand, *yes, it's only Benedict; but remember, what we
do in the dark he does in sunshine.* Suited me, either way.
Though if they were this twitchy already and they hadn't
even seen Josie's body yet, then what followed could get
very bad indeed.

The guns might only be for show, of course, an ego-
massage for the troops, a way to make them feel better.
*Look, we're not vulnerable, we're dangerous by daylight
also* . . .

I didn't believe that, though. Macallans weren't used to
doing things for show, unless it was making a serious
example of someone *pour encourager les autres.* I thought
they were carrying this much firepower because Uncle
James had told them to, because he was afraid to go out
in daylight without heavyweight protection; I thought he
saw serious risk of a shoot-out, the cattle finally rising up
against the ranchers, *kill them quick and we needn't fear the
night* . . .

I also thought that guns made men cocky and confident, where doubt was far the better life-choice. I thought
Macallan egos shaken by an unheard-of stand-off, shaken
too perhaps by the need to carry guns, might be hazardously
bolstered by the guns themselves. The weight of blued
steel in their hands, the smell of oil, the sense of power
independent of the light: I couldn't imagine anything more
volatile than this, armed Macallans out on the streets and
angry in the daytime.

Uncle James walked ponderously across the sand towards

us. He'd put on weight these last years, but it hadn't given him *gravitas*, though I'm sure he thought that it had. He just looked like a seriously, unhealthily fat man in a suit, with a grim scowl on his face. *Fat and deadly*, I reminded myself quickly. Never mind what he looked like, it was the inside that mattered, and he was dark and dank and rotting under the skin. The seed, the potential for that was in his blood and in his upbringing, nature and nurture both, as it was in Jamie's and in mine, as it had been in Josie's; and we were none of us innocent, we all stood condemned. But we were not all of us psychopaths, either. Jamie not, myself I thought not; Josie yes, perhaps, though she'd reaped what she'd sown in appalling measure.

Of Uncle James, there was simply no question. In him the blood turned bad, the seed had taken root and fruited richly; his soul was as black as all my family was painted.

He gazed at me from behind heavy-framed spectacles, and his silence seemed to blame me for all of this, as my father's violence had blamed me the night before. He looked at his son and there was blame there also, the blame of betrayal. Lastly he looked down at what lay between us, what lay between us all, Josie's body reduced to a symbol.

For a long minute he stood above her, saying nothing; then he looked beyond us, to summon a couple of his heavies with a gesture.

His heavies, my relations: but I felt no sing of blood between us, for all that I knew their names, their histories and their childhood secrets. In this at least I had grown, it seemed, that I could look past familiar features and see them as strangers where it mattered, in their hearts.

"Take her up," said Uncle James; and the sound of his voice was a cold bite on the back of my neck, no hope of outgrowing that. Him I still couldn't deny. "For this," he said, "there must be an accounting."

For this, I thought, *there must be a reason*; and again I

remembered my father last night, and that also was a chill
I couldn't shrug away. I give little credence to instinct or
prescience, it was unadulterated knowledge that drew a
connection here, between my father in tears in a public
place, my father blindly attacking me, and the death of a
hostage held against my family's behaviour. I didn't know
what that connection might be, I lacked the information, but
I would have been willing to bet that it existed. That my
father had gambled also – with Josie's life, yet – and had
lost . . .

The men my cousins wrapped the dead woman my cousin
in her plastic shroud again, and carried her away. Not even
my eyes followed them with their burden; Uncle James had
me in his sight, in his sights.

"Why did you come back?" he asked, every word a difficulty, as though even so much recognition was somehow
a betrayal of himself.

For him I had no true answer, I hadn't come back for him.
I could lie, I supposed; but he wasn't the only one who could
taste the gall of incipient betrayal in the air. There had been
a death here, or at least a body delivered. I could find some
distance, perhaps, but not enough, and Jamie none at all; I
thought my own father might be involved, might be directly
responsible for it; and indirectly, sure, Uncle James was
right. It all came back to me, to what I'd done to unbalance
the family and the town. All of that lay on my shoulders,
and to lie would be to betray Josie, Jamie, myself.

I shrugged, said nothing.

"Well." He breathed heavily a time or two, working
himself up to it; and said, "You are not welcome, but I
suppose we can use you. Come back with me now. Both
of you," tossed over his shoulder to his errant son.

He was already walking. Whether we glanced at each
other and made a mutual decision, I've never been able to
sort out in my head; maybe we made individual decisions

and then came the glance, surprise or relief or whatever to find that we weren't each of us alone, that blood-brotherhood was thicker than a watery will.

Took Uncle James a second to realise he didn't have two obedient dogs at his tail. He stopped, looked back, saw us standing; and when we still didn't jump under the lash of his gaze, he turned and came back a couple of paces.

"Well?" Speaking to me, assuming perhaps that Jamie was standing guard over a disobedient cousin, watching me for his father's sake.

"You said you could use me. Use me how?" I temporised, knowing full well but needing a moment longer to muster argument, determination, both.

"Your – *inversion*," he said, though *perversion* he meant and we both knew it, "will be convenient. Better than these," and a flap of his hand covered all the guns that covered us, "to remind the cattle that we still govern here. Day and night."

"That's what I thought you meant," I said, "and the answer's no."

"I beg your pardon?"

"Whatever I came back for, Uncle James, it wasn't to be your hired executioner."

His nostrils flared. "You had few qualms about executing my brother Allan."

Fuck. "He killed your son," I said, hoping I didn't sound desperate, or desperately short of any sustaining logic here, "and my sister, and the others . . ."

"Yes. And these scum have killed your cousins."

Yes, and I'd run out of the tapas bar to find my family and enlist. But not this way, I wouldn't be conscripted into Uncle James' private and vindictive army.

I would sign up with Jamie, though; and Jamie was standing firm at my side, and his body language said that he'd sign up with me.

"I'll fight them," I said, "but not your way."

His face twisted with fury. *Not under your command*, he was hearing; and sure, I was saying that too. But I actually meant it the way that I'd said it, and that he wouldn't understand. He wouldn't think there was another way. Demands enforced by terror, that was all he understood; and with me in his arsenal he could terrorise twenty-four hours a day, and even hostages could buy them no respite from that.

So no, I wouldn't march under his banner, even to save my own relatively guiltless kin, who were not ultimately responsible for what they'd been born or married into. And beside me Jamie said, "That goes for me too, Dad. We'll do what we can, we both will; but we're not going to hurt civilians. No eye-for-an-eye stuff, no chain reactions. We'll get nowhere that way, we'll only end up with more dead cousins . . ."

Uncle James looked like he couldn't believe what he was hearing. I was having trouble enough myself. Jamie said it all as if it was a pact signed and sealed between us, as if we'd discussed nothing else while we'd been waiting. *Blood-brother, can you read my mind?* I wanted to ask him; only I knew the answer already, it was *sometimes*, but not this time. This was all Jamie, unless it was Jamie mediated by two years of Laura. Except that that was the same thing, of course, Jamie was mediated by Laura now, there wasn't any other version of him . . .

"It'd be more useful," I suggested as quietly as I could manage, not to seem confrontational, "if you could find out why they did this. They must have had a reason, no one kills hostages for fun." *Ask my father*. I didn't add that, but I didn't need to. Dad would have a voice in my uncle's counsels, if not one that would be listened to. His birth entitled him to so much, and Uncle James was big on birthright. So long as they paused at all to consider why

this had happened, before they risked any more lives –
before someone said or whispered or implied *they're only
women, they don't have talent, they barely count against
what we have to lose here* – I thought my father would
give himself away. Uncle James wasn't exactly stupid,
only tunnel-minded and the tunnel lit only by his own
self-interest. Right now his antennae would be as sensitive
as ever they got, with that interest so very threatened.

He stared at me, at us both, trying to dominate us with
his weight and age as he used to when we were kids. Almost
it worked, too, I thought Jamie was very close to caving.
Whatever practice he'd had in standing up to his father, I
didn't think it would prove to be enough in such a crisis.
Head to head, eyeball to eyeball, will pitted against will: no,
Uncle James was immovable, and Jamie not. So I thought, at
least. For all our sakes – his, Laura's, our kidnapped cousins'
and my own – I thought he needed rescuing.

"Look," I said, "what we will do, we'll sniff around in the
town, okay? We've got friends, we can ask people, find out
who's behind it, maybe we'll find out where they're being
held . . ."

Actually, as a serious proposal that was only pissing into
the wind: we were known Macallans, Jamie and me, and
easily identifiable to anyone who didn't know. We might
have been accepted on sufferance, but nobody was going
to talk to us now. All I wanted to do was take the heat off
Jamie, even if that only brought it onto me. I thought I was
scorch-proof.

Apparently I was beneath withering; he waved a loose
hand to silence me, didn't so much as glance in my direction.
The full force of his glare was held on Jamie, and my best
coz, my bro, for many years my idol was going to wilt under
it, any second now . . .

My uncle was speaking, saying something soft and men-
acing that certainly I could have heard if I'd tuned in. But I

was casting around desperately for a way to lead Jamie out
of this, or failing that for a distraction, for anything . . .

All I saw was men with guns, and empty sand, and sea.

Guns, sand, sea. No gun ever hurt the sand, no bullet
could harm the sea . . .

I focused, frowning just a tad. Cousin Duquesne, the Duke
was one of Uncle James' entourage; he was the nearest, the
easiest target, and I had to be both quick and subtle. He held
a shotgun under his arm, closed up and ready for action,
typically Macallan where there was clearly no action to
be had.

Nightfire, that all my male relations had in their gift:
nightfire burns cold, but it can make bangable things go
pop none the less. My own opposing talent gave me what
inevitably I had to call dayfire, as well as a great deal
more besides; and that I knew could make rubber melt or
a petrol-tank explode. I'd even set a flame on water, and
made it hot.

No trouble then to heat the barrel of a gun, from this
distance; and I could control it, I thought, I wouldn't twist
the metal. But I couldn't cool it after, and even the Duke
would notice, and say, and Uncle James would understand.
A distraction exposed for what it was, what use was that?
Some, maybe; not enough, perhaps.

So no, nothing so clumsy; but I liked the idea, and I
worked it. I reached out to take a feather-light grip on
that shotgun, so gently that the Duke never noticed the
tug. I gripped and I squeezed just where it was balanced
across his elbow, not even he being stupid enough to
keep his finger on the trigger all the time; I squeezed
that trigger in my mind, and the gun cracked and leaped
in my grip and his, kicking so hard that the barrel shot
up and caught him on the cheek before I let it go and he
dropped it.

There was a faint spray of dry sand before his feet,

where a cartridgeload of pellets had just buried themselves in the beach.

Everyone spun round, of course, at the sudden noise and the movement, his yelp of pain after and the thud of the shotgun's falling. I thought of firing off the other barrel then, but once was enough; I didn't want to sting anyone's ankles.

Uncle James had turned with the rest, and his face was livid. I wished him a heart attack, choleric angina; he looked ripe for it, fat and purple and ripe he looked.

No such luck, alas; but I'd got what I really wanted, his determination deflected, if only for a moment or two. I nudged Jamie's elbow, murmured, "Wanna go back to Laura, talk this through with her?"

He nodded slowly.

"But nothing," I said, against the thought I could see on his face. "Trust me, okay? Follow me . . ."

Not often, I'd said that to Jamie; not often he'd said yes, when I did. But he said yes that day, and I think perhaps that all things sprang from there.

My uncle his father was scathing the poor Duke, who stammered and blushed like a child though he was well past thirty now, must have thought himself well hard, well past a public scolding.

"Cousin James, I never . . . I swear . . ."

"Oh, it went off by itself, did it?" And without pausing to consider the merits of that, "You fool, you could have killed any one of us, you're not safe with such a weapon."

Which really was a joke, said to a Macallan; but Uncle James wasn't laughing, and nor was anyone else. Not even I, especially when I saw him stoop to pick up the shotgun himself. Now if I'd gone for the heat treatment and the Duke had somehow missed noticing pale flames licking around the barrel where it broke, Uncle James for sure would not have missed noticing the residual heat, and his accountant's mind would have gone click click, and I'd be in serious trouble . . .

Thanking my lucky stars for my own good sense – and that was a rarity also, usually I did the other thing, cursed my own stupidity – I stood still and signed for Jamie to do the same, to wait. This was a diversion, yes, but I had no plans to run away. In a room with a door, perhaps, anywhere there was a fast exit to be made; but on a wide beach, where they had four-bys and we had nothing but feet? Thanks, but no thanks.

We stood still, stood like patient captives in defeat, or a decent imitation thereof. When Uncle James finally came back towards us, with the shotgun under his arm now and properly broken open, with his men our cousins already scattering to their various vehicles and a *this is it, you boys, no more prevarication* look on his face, I met him with the best I could manage in the way of sullen surrender.

"We left our bikes in the car park up at the end of the beach. They can't sit there all night, they'll be pinched . . ."

He'd heard that tone from me all my life, the stubbornness that always tried to find some minor victory in capitulation. That must have seduced him, or else he simply didn't believe either one of us could sustain our defiance for long.

At any rate, he nodded brusquely. "All right." *Don't want to leave good Macallan property for the cattle to steal.* "We'll take you that far, then you can drive back with us. Get into the Range Rover."

The Ranger was his own, of course. Everything a status-symbol, because status was everything. Even his sandals would have been Timberland, if he'd only worn sandals to the beach.

He sat in the front, we in the back, and his driver another cousin took us down the beach, with all the cavalcade in attendance behind. When we came to the car park, our

two bikes were standing side by side in utter emptiness:
the whole place had been deserted, else. We were lucky, I
suppose. If they'd linked the bikes to us and us to the swarm-
ing Macallans, some brave punter might have ploughed his
pick-up over our darlings before he headed off.

Uncle James had his driver stop reasonably if not con-
siderately close to the bikes – a careful or a casual distance:
I thought a distance precisely measured in his mind – and
waited while we powered up, no doubt waited for us to fall
into formation behind.

That we didn't do. I drove boldly to the head of the parade,
in front of the Ranger yet; I drove and Jamie followed as
he'd promised, and that was lèse majesté if ever anything
had been. Except that he could always pretend we were
outriders, of course, such as any sovereign might command.
Could and would, no doubt, but oh, he would be scowling in
his car there, he'd be adding this to the burden of grievance
charged against us both. Jamie gave me an anxious glance;
I winked, and mouthed, *Trust me* . . .

Not far from the seafront we came to a roundabout, where
the road that hugged the coast met the Coast Road, the main
dual carriageway from town. Not a massive roundabout, but
not mini either: just perfect for my needs just now. We pulled
up like good boys at the white line, giving way to the right;
and I called across, "Jamie, stick with me! What I do . . ."

What I do, you do. Other kids called the game follow-
my-leader, but we always had to be different from other
kids. They were cattle, we were family; and this game
we'd played not only as children on foot or on furniture,
but also as teenagers on bikes. He nodded, found a grin
from somewhere. Tight and challenging, that was: *make it
good*, it said.

What in fact I did or seemed to do was make it funny,
make a joke of it, make Uncle James madder than hell. I

drove onto the roundabout when traffic permitted, Jamie
beside me and all the parade behind; and all I did was not
select an exit, I just kept going round. The Ranger followed
us, everyone else followed the Ranger, and as I'd hoped, as
I'd figured there were just enough cars in the line to bring us
up neatly to the rear of the last. We made a traffic-choking
daisy-chain, bringing the whole junction to a halt.

After a lap and a half I looked innocently back over my
shoulder, and pulled a *where-do-you-want-us-to-go?* face at
Uncle James. He gestured furiously, and the Ranger peeled
off onto the Coast Road. I waved obedience; the other
cars all followed him, and we tagged on behind, the pack
reshuffled to put us at the bottom of the deck. He would
never have let us set off this way, he'd have stopped in the
car park to put us somewhere in the middle, but it would be
beneath his dignity to pull up on the hard shoulder now.

He'd be checking the wing-mirror, though, or having his
driver do it; so I drove a mile or so practically in the gutter,
where I was sure he could see me. Then I drifted a little
wider, tucking in behind the last car in line, where I was sure
he couldn't. Jamie joined me, yelling something I couldn't
hear; I pulled a face to say so, and held up three fingers.

As we passed the next junction, a slip road leading off
to another roundabout, I held up two. He nodded.

The next junction, one finger; another nod, and a thumbs-
up in reply.

We knew this road, as we knew them all. When the junction
came, we were ready. *Wait for it, wait for it* – I waited until
the car ahead had passed the hatchings on the road, too
late for them to follow even if they were watching for this
and I very much hoped they weren't. Then a twitch of the
handlebars and a squeeze of the throttle and I was away, my
tyres scraping the kerb that divided the main carriageway
from the slip road; just a second behind me, Jamie had to

bump over the grass to make it, but his bike was designed for rougher rides than that and he wasn't about to be jolted off, not my bro.

Up the slip road to the inevitable roundabout, three-quarters of the way around that and over the bridge that spanned the highway; I didn't look down but I could hear blaring horns below me, the rear car trying to warn my uncle up front that we were gone. Well, nothing they could do now even if the message got through. No chance of a U-turn on the dual carriageway, or no legal chance; if they did double back, we'd still be well away before they got here.

Not run away, no, there'd been no point in trying it; but race away, sure, there was nothing in my philosophy to stop me doing that.

One fast mile through a housing estate, to be certain sure they'd lose us; then Jamie overtook me, made a slow-down gesture, and pulled up in a lay-by.

I drew up beside him, wondering what the problem was; he already had his phone out, and was punching numbers.

"Sweets? Me again . . . No, listen. Grab a jacket and get out of there, right now. Move, move . . . Well, turn it off. My dad's on his way, and he won't be happy when he gets there. You shift, I'll explain later. Meet us at the Blue Boar, yes? . . . Good girl. I love you . . ."

He switched off and put the phone away; I was seriously proud of myself when all I said and all I thought was, "Good thinking, Batman."

"Did you know, all the Blue Boars in the country used to be white? The White Boar, they used to be. That was Richard of Gloucester's badge, Richard the Third, and he was a popular man. Besides, it was good policy. So they all named their inns sort of in tribute, yeah? Only then he gets killed at Bosworth, there's a new king, Henry the wossname,

Seventh? Yeah, Seventh, and suddenly the White Boar is not
such a good idea, right? So they all change overnight. But it's
easy, because the white paint they used then, it was pretty
much blue anyway; so you call yourself the Blue Boar, you
don't even need to repaint the sign, see? Easy . . ."

"Ben."

"Yeah?"

"Shut up."

Okay. You can race, but you still can't hide. I wasn't even
that drunk; actually I wasn't drunk at all, I only wanted to
be, no more than that. I shut up.

We were sitting in what had been a favourite pub once,
bloodied by the years but stubbornly unbowed: bad décor
and lousy turnover but good music, good beer and a pretty
good clientèle also. Hell, we went there, didn't we? So
by definition, good clientèle. Also the landlady used to
supplement her income by selling dope and dancing drugs
pretty much across the counter, which endeared her to us
no end. Poppers she actually kept literally on the counter,
right there on the bar-top in their little bottles. Figured she'd
wait a long time for the Royal Pharmaceutical Society to
sue her for selling medicines without a licence; and right
she was, too.

But that was then and this was now, and as usual things
were different now. The place had been bought up and
done out, they'd wrecked a genuinely old pub to create an
artificial version: lino was out and polished boards were in,
the traditional lounge and public bar had been knocked into
one big room and then divided into nooks and alcoves and
booths with many wooden partitions.

I hated it like this, we all did. But it did have two
advantages, which had made it Jamie's first thought for
a rendezvous. It was a sensible bus-ride from Laura's flat
and a lengthy drive from anywhere in town, a three-in-one
advantage: no one was going to be looking for us out

here; we weren't likely to run into any chance-met family member or fellow-traveller so far from the power-base, so dangerously close to the border where the real world overlapped; similarly we weren't likely to run into the opposite kind of trouble, the radical rebels who'd stir up a riot at the sight of a Macallan nose dipping into a pint glass.

The second advantage was provided by that web of partitions. Loathe them we might and did, but no denying they did make for private conversation and easy plotting.

Jamie and I had had to loop right around the town to get here, and we'd probably stretched the journey further than we needed to, being extra careful not to attract any beady and curious eye. As a consequence Laura had been here already when we arrived; and that she'd moved so fast on Jamie's word said a lot, I thought, about her relationship with her, what, her father-in-common-law?

Smart girl, she'd clearly got to know him well.

She wasn't showing so smart just now, though. She'd had time to stew, obviously, sitting flustered and sweaty watching the door for our arrival. There'd been no kiss for Jamie though he took one anyway, no smile for either one of us. She'd sat and listened a mite frostily, if someone so visibly hot and bothered can be frosty also, and I thought she could; and now that we'd told her the tale, from cousin's death to uncle-and-father's confusion, our triumph on the roads, she was fidgeting with the glass of blackcurrant-and-lemonade that seemed to please her no better than our story, and she was asking foolish questions.

"What, and you had to go and do that, did you? You just had to piss him off that way?"

"I think so, yes." Jamie glanced at me for support in this, got a nod and a shrug in return, *of course we did, what's her problem?* He went on more gently than I thought he wanted to, more sharply than ever I could have spoken to Laura: "I suppose you'd rather I was back in his pocket and out on the streets tonight with the lads, taking revenge? Is that what you want? It's what he wants."

"No, that's not what I want. You know that." That's what she'd taken him away from. Me and her between us, perhaps – but no fooling, it had mostly been her. She'd had most opportunity, after all. "But I'd rather you didn't go out of your way to fight with him, either. Not now."

My lip twitched, and she was onto me like a shot. "Well, what? What's funny?"

Actually, I'd just experienced a moment of unadulterated happiness, finding that Jamie and I did still have a telepathic link after all. We'd been so close just then, the two of us, to catching each other's eye and sharing a single indivisible thought, *ah, it's a baby thang*; and I'd felt the stillness in him that said he wasn't going to do it, and I'd known he was feeling the same in me, and so I'd smiled.

Fortunately a second thought had ridden in on the back of the first, *I was wrong, she doesn't know him so well after all*; and I could justify myself with that, and let her feel only a little patronised. "You don't have to go out of your way," I said, "to fight with Uncle James. He's very biblical on that score. He that is not with me is against me, yeah? You either knuckle under and do just what he wants when he wants it, or you're in opposition and he'll do anything he can to screw you. You can't be neutral, and you can't come to an understanding with him. He wouldn't understand." I smirked a little, pleased with that; Jamie applauded, Laura scowled.

"You don't have to wind him up, though," she said, dragging us back from the general to the specific. "That's just childish, it's stupid. If you didn't want to go with him, why couldn't you just say so?"

"We did, but . . ." But I'd thought Jamie was weakening,

only I couldn't say so, I couldn't betray him that way. Not to her. "He doesn't listen," I went on, a little lamely. "He's a bully, you know that."

She snorted. "He just needs standing up to." Meaning, *If I'd been there, I'd have stood up to him. I'd have said no, and meant it.* Which she would have done, she admitted no more compromise than my uncle; but if she'd been there, he'd have had his men pick her up and carry her to his car, and then Jamie and I would have had no choice but to go along. I wasn't going to say that either, though. Which of course left me with nothing to say.

"Anyway," from Jamie, "we did it, it's done now . . ."

"And we can't go home, as a result."

"No, we can't."

Not tonight, at any rate. There'd be someone watching for us. And Jamie wouldn't use his talent against family, that went without saying; and probably whoever his father sent would have no such inhibitions, he'd be under orders to do so if necessary, to bring us in. Uncle James hated to be defied.

"So what do we do now?" Laura demanded.

Camp out with friends was the obvious answer, but the way they were looking at each other, I had a sudden doubt. There was an unspoken question between them, *who can we go to?*, and neither one of them was coming up with a solution.

My heart ached briefly, for them and for myself. I'd seen this before with couples, how they could turn inward to each other so strongly that they let old friendships, sometimes all their friendships drift and ultimately die of neglect. Jamie of course had suffered from the usual Macallan complaint, too few friends outside the family. Laura had been the compleat student, a social animal *par excellence*; but that was a picture two years old, and from the uncertain face of her I guessed that it no longer applied. She hadn't mixed with medics much, to be sure, and the others would have graduated by now and likely moved on.

"Keep away from your own circle," I said, more to help them out with an excuse than by way of genuine advice. "Just to be safe. He may have been keeping tabs on who you hang out with, especially if you've been in his bad books recently. He never lets anyone go."

"Who, then?"

I looked down at my hand and said, "Give us your phone, Jamie."

He passed it across; I called the number that was scribbled on my skin. It rang half a dozen times, and I was just getting anxious when the phone was picked up at the other end.

"Yes, hullo?"

"Hi, is that Janice?"

"Uh-huh."

"Um, this is Ben. Sorry I ran out on you like that . . ."

"That's okay." For someone who'd tasted what was likely her first experience of Macallan magic that morning, when I'd smashed the bar window, she sounded admirably cool. "How's it going, are you all right? We've been worried about you . . ."

"I'm fine. Only, we've got a problem. Can I impose on you again tonight?"

"Of course. The bed's there, it's not an imposition."

"It may be, this time. There's three of us . . ."

"Three in a bed?" she suggested sweetly.

Ouch. And double ouch, as I realised how inevitable the sleeping arrangements were. "I'll take the sofa," I said. "If you don't mind . . ."

"Ben, we don't mind. You come. Have you eaten?"

Lunch was a long time ago now. "We'll pick something up on the way. For you, too. For you two too. Indian, or Chinese?"

"Indian," definitely. "Please," added just for form's sake.

And "Veggie, though," with no hesitation, no anxiety about being awkward.

Laura rode pillion behind Jamie, though she'd have been a lot more comfortable with me. She and I were helmetless, in defiance of good law and good sense; I looked in my mirror more often than I needed to as I led them by devious ways through the dusk light, saw how her hair was being blown into rats' tails, and saw in my head how she'd sit on the floor at Jamie's feet and curse his clumsiness while he gently teased it out with fingers and comb . . .

Food came first, though, geographically and chronologically and otherwise also. I thought this was a hopeful sign, that I could watch them together and imagine them at play and still feel hungry; I never used to eat, when I was grieving over Laura. Not unless she was watching, when I would eat and eat, not to let her know that I was grieving.

The city had changed, but not this much: not that I should drive down a certain cobbled alley in a certain shady quarter and fail to find the Hole. Technically *Al-Halal*, we knew it by many names, *Halalujah* and *Halal on Earth* and *The Black Halal of Calcutta*, but mostly it was just the Hole. It was dark, it was dingy, you descended many steps to find it and you didn't like the look of it when you got there, what little of it you could see; but it produced the best Kashmiri takeaway this or any other side of the Karakorams.

High summer, few students, no queue. In twenty minutes we left with a warm, steaming and remarkably heavy box – well, there would be five of us, and we were catering for veggies and carnivores both; and besides, Jamie had paid – which Laura had to balance across her knees because my panniers were still full of my junk and it wouldn't balance itself across the queen seat behind me.

On to the flat, and to the welcome due anyone bearing such

gifts. Myself I thought it might be a poisoned chalice we carried in with such pomp, we might be playing the Greeks here, *beware of us*; but I was weary of being a Jeremiah. I could worry later about antidotes. Right now I made brisk introductions – "Jon, did you meet Jamie or Laura? I don't remember. If not, these are they; and this is Janice, you two" – while the others ran around clearing space on the floor, finding plates and forks and pickles and chutneys, while Jamie cursed and slipped out again, up to the offie to fetch the essential cans.

We made a little ceremony of opening and unwrapping and passing around, I guess we always had. And with that ceremony came a renewal of the old unspoken law, *no shop in the mess*; it seemed to follow naturally, that you didn't spoil ritual and good food and self-indulgence with conversation that dug too deep or turned up sour flavours.

So while we ate I did most of the talking, because I had the most to talk about that wasn't to do with the town. I told them about taking a TEFL course and teaching my way across Europe; and to give them a giggle I told them what else I'd been doing, though I didn't tell them why.

"Bit of journalism on the side," I said.

"Oh, yes? Who for?"

"Oh, *Fortean Times*," very casually. "*International Enquirer*, that sort of stuff. Any paper with a weird-and-wacky column."

"What," from Laura, breathlessly because I knew by her expression she didn't dare breathe, she'd only explode and she didn't want to do that to me, bless her, "alien abductions and my-dog-made-me-pregnant, like that?"

"Actually, that was 'my husband's ghost took possession of the dog and made me pregnant'," I said sternly. "Very important ground-breaking story."

"Hey, I *read* that!" She looked delighted, but I wasn't at all surprised. We used to read them all the time but she was the most addicted, it was usually Laura who paid out for them. She loved the medical stories.

"Ben?"

"Jamie?"

"*Why?*"

Of all of them, he should have been able to answer that himself. He wasn't thinking; and *no shop in the mess*, I couldn't answer him. Not truthfully, at least.

"Pocket money," I said. "Something fun to do, when you haven't really got a home to go to. And I met the *best* people. Vampires? I can do you vampires. And a were-bear, and *three* women who take musical dictation from Mozart, don't know why they're always women but they always are, and any number of poltergeist babies . . ."

I kept them going with stories like that for a while. Then when I was tired of talking and wanted a chance to eat, I said, "Jamie, I know you've still got the jeep, I saw that; but what happened to the sports jobs?"

He'd had two or three that I remembered, one to drive and the others to store in a barn in a kind of serial monogamy; but it was his father's barn, and Uncle James was good at grudges.

"Sold 'em," he said. "What do you think bought dinner?"

"We're living off the proceeds," Laura confirmed. "Carefully." Which was what I'd really been asking, and here it came. "Looks good on the bank statements, but I've got to take a year out from school for the baby, so we can't go wild. It's capital, really; I want Jamie to go into business. If we can figure out anything he can do . . ."

He flicked a piece of poppadum at her for that, but it would be a problem. Macallans were the next best thing to unemployable, I knew that from my own experience, especially when my uncle was being vindictive; and that was before things changed. I guessed it would be even harder now.

That took the conversation on to college courses and future careers, which gave me the opportunity to catch up on feasting; they knew about me now, and no one thought to ask if I wanted a change. Janice was studying law, apparently. Jon – like all the art students I'd ever known – didn't have a clue what he'd do when he graduated.

At last the foil containers were all empty, most wiped as clean as the plates with fingers or final shreds of naan. We sprawled, on furniture or carpet; Laura leaned back against Jamie's knees, and he fingered her hair as I'd known he would; and Jon dropped the bombshell that our mutual intent had held back this long.

Whether he knew its significance I wasn't sure, but it was a fair bet that he did.

"There was a man killed last night," he said, "the whole street's been buzzing with it. It was only just over the hill, on Laurel Drive, you know it?"

Oh yes, I knew it. My parents lived on Laurel Drive, and last night my father had been out in the dark on his own, and crying.

SIX

GROLSCH AND VOMIT™

What a piece of work is my dad! How base in reason! how limited in faculty! in form, in moving, how lumbering and contemptible! in action how like a demon! in apprehension how like a stone! the foulness of the world! the debasement of animals . . .!

Well, actually – at the time – I just thought, *how like my dad, to shit in his own back yard*. Comparisons came later. As did confession: of the four friends here, new and old, only Jamie knew my old address, and he was keeping mum. All but his speaking eyes, and I wasn't listening to them, they were saying nothing I was not already telling myself.

What I wanted – no, what I didn't want, but what I needed most, I had to ask from Jon.

"Killed how?"

He might not know my father's house, but he knew the hand of my family well enough, or else the rumours had been more explicit than he was saying. He flinched, he glanced at Janice, he didn't want to tell me.

"Jon? Killed how?"

It was Janice who said, in the end.

"He had his head bashed in. On the bricks, on the corner of his house. That's what they're saying. They found him this morning, they say, just lying on the ground there with his skull crushed, and blood all over the walls . . ."

Just as if some irresistibly-strong hand had gripped the back of his neck, as I pictured it from her words, and pounded his head – no, his face, it would for sure have been his face – against the sharp angle, the bricks already red before his blood reddened them. Except that this would have been in the dark, of course, and the streetlights were sodium orange, that would have fucked up the colour as much as one man with a fucked-up head was fucking up the head of another . . .

Ah, shit.

It might even have been my fault, I supposed vaguely. Say my father had been crying only with the frustration of his new life, his family reduced and his pride trampled underfoot, sneered at by cattle; say that I chance along to find him so, and even he knows that this is all my fault *ab origine*; say he kicks seven kinds of shit out of me and is still not satisfied, he's lost control now and he can't get a grip again, blood has slicked his hands but not yet slaked his thirst . . .

Say this, say that, say anything you like. I tried to blame myself twice over, but I couldn't make it stick. Many things I could accuse myself of and with justice, with conviction; but not this.

"Ben? Do you want to go round?"

That was Jamie not keeping mum any longer, letting mum and dad too right out of the bag. Though the others weren't seeing them yet, I guess they were just seeing us as a couple of ghouls, wanting to ogle.

"No," I said, already pushing up onto my feet, spotting an awkward but manageable path between bodies and discarded plates. Every journey begins with but a single step: this was a route that would take me to my parents' door, the world's most reluctant prodigal.

"What's with him?" That was Laura, and this might have been the first time in my life I heard her voice and didn't turn to find her.

"It's his dad. Laurel Drive? Got to be . . ."

"They wouldn't. Would they? Not at night? They couldn't. And we'd have heard . . ." The flow of her words died slowly, as she understood him at last, too late. I almost expected her to go on then, *Well, so what's he so upset about? It's hardly the first time. Macallan men kill people as a puberty rite, and then they just keep on going. Wankers all their lives. So his dad's added another to his list, so what?*

She wouldn't have been that callous, of course; she'd have cared too much about the victim. But the question was still there, albeit unspoken and kinder put. I could have said, *because this time his killing killed one of ours also, and he knew it would, and he did it anyway*; or I could have said, *because I've been away, and I came back looking for a miracle, a family I could love*. But neither would have earned me what I needed, her empathy, her understanding. No point fishing for it, so I said nothing to her. I stood in the doorway and looked back, looked at Jamie, said, "You coming?"

Please?

"Yeah, I'm coming."

Actually he was one stage short of coming, still disentangling Laura from his legs and making room to stand.

"I'm not going in, mind. I just . . ." *I just have to be there for a bit*, I just had to stand there on the street where they lived, Lerner and Loewe and the Hon Freddie twisting to destruction in my head while my eyes scanned the walls to find the bloodstain. *Very like a ghoul*, I thought, and walked out.

Fizzy the cat sneaked between my legs as I opened the front door. I felt a moment's anxiety, but it would have been too too bathetic to have gone back to enquire, *is it okay if the cat goes out?*

Besides, he was gone now; and not in any sense seeming like a truant, pausing in the middle of the pavement to wash himself briskly before sniffing the air and positively sauntering down the hill, very much king of the road. *Should've called him Ozymandias*, I thought, and wondered if cats understood the concept of hubris, and decided not. Of course not. Nothing to do with intellect, it's a matter of genetics. Some creatures are simply born superior, and that's that.

Must be why I felt such a kinship, I thought bitterly. And then out to join me came the guy for whom I felt so much more than a kinship, call it a twinship, a truer sharing than ever I'd had with my twin; and off we went up the hill, and not sauntering at all.

This was one route not embedded in my muscle-memories, one I'd hardly walked at all although the way was obvious, short and easy. When I left home I did so in disgrace and in disgust, and for three years I had no willing contact with my family. I'd been as careful as I could manage, even to avoid accidental runnings-into each other; that most particularly included keeping well away from my father's house. I used to go so far as not to go to parties, if they were inside a quarter-mile radius of Laurel Drive.

Still. Up the hill, over the main road (look left, look right, look left again: don't look ahead, never anticipate) and carry straight on, take a left and then a right and here we were, just where we didn't want to be, and what was new?

Well, it must still be something of a new experience for Jamie, to find himself so much the outsider where he always used to be the heart, the new generation, the smart young hopeful boy. I thought he was coping pretty well, from what I'd seen: better than ever I had, at any rate.

Right now he was coping brilliantly, walking shoulder-to-shoulder with me, saying nothing. Attaching himself to someone even more outcast from his father's favour,

demanding nothing except the right to go with me, being
his cousin's keeper. *Whither thou goest I will go, because
thou art my bro*.

On his face, even in the harsh chiaroscuro of the streetlights, I could see the mark where I'd hit him because he'd
made his girlfriend pregnant. I had also earlier seen Laura
touching it with questioning fingers; hadn't been able to hear
or read what he'd said in reply, but I guessed that my name
had been no part of it. She hadn't turned to find me, to stare
or glare or come across in fury. *Fell off my bike*, he might
have said, or something like it.

I reached out to touch him in my turn, gripped his arm
in lieu of words; he misunderstood entirely, grunting softly
and coming to a halt with his eyes fixed firmly on the other
side of the road, seeing what we'd come to see.

Reluctantly, I followed his gaze.

There was my father's house, with all lights burning; and
there beside it was my father's neighbour's house, with no
lights burning and broad tape stretched across the gateway.
There were words printed on the tape, but I didn't need to
cross the road to read them. POLICE LINE – DO NOT CROSS
those words would say, or something like it. The police had
little enough to do in this town, but here was something
they'd dared to get involved in.

In my father's drive was my father's car, the old Ford
that he loved and cared for very much more, it had always
seemed, than he loved and cared for us. But the windscreen
was smashed, the bonnet was buckled and bent, the roof
looked like someone had been dancing on it in boots.

This was easy, alas, this was a story written in such big
letters than no one would need to cross a road to read them.
Not a popular man, my father. Especially on this street,
where he liked to throw his weight around with all the
weight of his name behind it. His neighbour in particular
had many reasons, many years'-worth of reasons to hate

him. And *the Macallans are weak* they must have been whispering, all up and down the street, *the Macallans are on the run at last*; and not quite daring to face down the man himself – my father would have a gun for sure, if guns were on the family agenda now – he must have come out in broad daylight, picked a time when Dad was out without his car, and trashed the thing. Petty vindictiveness, small change set against so long and strong a resentment, but it must have been irresistible.

And Dad, dear Dad, what did he do? He waited, of course, for the dark. When the moon was high, when his skin tingled with his strength, he must have called or forced or dragged his neighbour out, never mind how. Perhaps the neighbour came willingly, perhaps he came laughing, bragging, knowing that Macallan women were hostage against my father's good behaviour.

But my raging father had not behaved well. That corner there, between the front door and the garage set back: that would be where the neighbour's head had met the neighbour's bricks, full frontal and in-your-face . . .

A shadow moved in a lighted window. I stiffened, and even as my eyes jerked to be sure of it I was wondering, *can he see us, are we standing exposed here, or has good luck found us a shadow?*

But it wasn't my father's, that slender silhouette. Of course it wouldn't be my father's. He would be at Uncle James' mansion just now, there would be a family council, they would all be preaching war. *Someone will have had to pick him up*, I thought, and grinned almost at the humiliation of that, how much he would have hated it. Someone I hoped would be interrogating him right now, forcing a confession from him, *yes, it was me, it's all my fault, I good as killed her myself*. He'd hate that worse, and my grin only stretched the wider for it. My bones might have forgotten the beating he'd given me, but my mind not, my mind not at all.

No, not Dad; that was my mother up there on the landing, gazing out. Lurking behind locked doors, I imagined, abandoned without a thought: frightened for herself but probably frightened more for the future, for the terror that would surely come.

My mother, my only relative whom I could love without reservation, and pity likewise.

Almost I waved to catch her eye, if it wasn't caught already; almost I went to her, to bring what poor comfort I could.

Almost, but not quite. Once over that threshold, I knew I wouldn't leave again. I couldn't desert her as my father had, on such a night. I'd have to wait at least till he returned, which would likely not be till near dawn; and call me chicken, as I called myself, but I couldn't face either part of that, neither the long hours of waiting for the inevitable nor the inevitable that must inevitably follow.

My mother also, I told myself firmly, couldn't be asked or expected to confront that. She wouldn't want to see it, when Dad came home to find me there. Love her as I did, I couldn't put her through it. She'd lost one child already, to the cold evaluation of her husband's brother, *tried and found wanting, Hazel dear; and cui bono, who benefits but me? Did Uncle Allan no good at all, that much is for sure* . . . How could I ask her to witness the hot uncalculating rage of her husband against her surviving son? He'd pulp me, I thought, as he had by the river only harder, longer, more lastingly. Everlastingly, maybe. He wasn't good on control at the best of times, and right then would be pretty much the opposite of that. Him brought home shamed and sulking, guilty and desperate; him finding me there, the onlie begetter of his misery; and the sun not far from rising, him in his power but knowing he would lose it soon, while I would wax and grow strong in the light he hid from?

No, I could die in such a story, and my mother do nothing but watch. I should let this happen to her? I thought not. Better to leave her as she was, alone and unprotected, a duck among geese. For her own sake, better to see her ignored and sorrowing than for her to see me murdered . . .

Ach, I sicken myself sometimes, so pharisaical I can be. But even the self-disgust rising like gorge in my throat was not enough to drive me over that road like a threshold and into my mother's loving arms.

"What do you want to do?" Jamie asked at last.

Not share my thoughts with you, bro, though I wondered how far he had tracked them anyway. Enough to build the same story in his head, I was sure; enough to understand why I didn't cross the street to see my mother, after so long a parting and so fraught a return? Maybe, maybe even that. He knew me well, did Jamie.

"Let's go back," I said, with difficulty. "Dunno why we came, anyway. What's to see? Couple of ghouls . . ."

Your dad's car is there to see, and your mother's shadow, but bless him, he said none of that. He tucked his arm through mine and all but dragged me away from there, against the tug of my unresponsive feet that didn't after all want to move.

Up on the main road, on the corner was a pharmacy still open. Jamie steered us inside and bought three toothbrushes, thinking ahead on a scale I couldn't manage. On the opposite corner was the off-licence, an old friend of mine. Jamie had been in there once tonight already, and come back with a couple of four-packs to wash our dinner down; now he took me in for a second visit, stood me in the middle of the floor and waved an expansive arm at all those bottles, all those cans.

"What would you like?" And when I just looked at him, "I think we should drink our way through at least one of my poor cars tonight. Don't you?"

"Laura won't like it."

"Laura's not getting it," he said, grinning. "She's off alcohol, remember?"

Yes, I remembered; and no, I wasn't going to argue any more. I turned my gaze back to the tempting, glittering displays. Forgetfulness lay there, perhaps, or standing here we could pretend that it did; and never mind the experience of a hundred other such binges that had never, ever produced a moment of much-desired amnesia. Didn't matter, anyway. I was back with my best buddy after a long time gone, and what more excuse did we need?

"Whisky?" Jamie suggested. "Brandy?"

I shook my head. Laura had ruled herself out, but the other two not; and Jon was young and Janice was female, and in my experience either condition could apparently provoke a dislike of spirits. On the other hand, I knew they both drank lager. I'd watched them do it, earlier.

So. Cans, bottles . . . Ah.

"Grolsch," I said.

"Okay. How much?"

"How much can we carry?"

"In our arms, or in our heads?"

"Whichever."

"Lots, then. Whichever."

So we bought all the bottles they had and a giant Coke for Laura, and carried the haul home in bags whose stretching handles cut deep red grooves in our palms. We were welcomed back quietly, almost without questions, to a room cleared and lit by candles now; they must have been talking while we were gone, figuring out the facts and deciding discretion was the better part of valuing your friends.

Laura was on tea already, but Jon and Janice were happy to drink with us. For a while, that's all we really did. We talked a little about subjects carefully chosen not to matter; and we listened to music by bands I'd never heard of, so out of touch you can get in a couple of years abroad, hearing nothing but the major British hits; but mostly, we just drank.

Up to me, I thought, to make us cost what truly counted. I drained a bottle, fetched another round from the fridge where they were cooling nicely, and said, "Maybe you should've gone with your dad, Jamie."

"No," from Laura, instantly; from him a slightly more considered, "Why?"

"Just so's we'd know what's going on. We could use a spy."

"Well, there are people I can phone. Some of the cousins still talk to me. But I can tell you what's going on anyway, I don't need to be there. Nor do you, you know as well as I do. They're having a wake, over Josie's body. My dad demands action, he wants a fight; so does everyone else, more or less. Give or take. Only someone's going to be sensible, they're going to ask why this happened; and they'll know about," a gesture, "about Laurel Drive, they're bound to by now. So your dad gets the third degree, and he confesses—"

"Well, actually he blusters," I said, "but yeah, it's the same thing."

"Right. So in the end nothing happens, because nothing's really changed. It's still a life for a life, and there's nothing anyone there can do about it."

When justice meets brutality, he was saying, *brutality wins. On both sides.* And, *the sleep of reason breeds monsters*, he was saying that too.

Me, I could say that in Spanish, only that now was not the time.

"Us neither," I said instead.

"Unh?"

"Well, what can we do about it?"

Jamie considered that, or seemed to, cocking his head on one side and gazing deep into the soul of his bottle; which he then waggled at me gently, and the stopper rattled against the neck with a quiet chinking doom-laden sound, like Death's bone bracelets chiming on his bony wrist.

"Drink?" Jamie suggested.

"Yeah."

We clinked our bottles together, mouth to mouth and base to base and mouth to mouth again in an old, rapid, crafty salute I'd thought I'd long forgotten; and he said, "Here's to Josie," and I said, "Yeah," again though I'd hated her much of my life, thought the world well rid of her now.

"Is that a private toast," Janice murmured behind me, "or can anyone join in?"

Strictly private, actually, but we'd done it now. The world had moved on from there, spinning giddily through dusty space, and who says there's no such thing as progress? It was an utterly separate event when I turned to her, touched my bottle to hers, didn't say a word.

She considered me, or my silence, much as Jamie had considered his bottle: head askance on a long neck, dark eyes narrowed and thoughtful. Disturbingly close, she was, and disturbingly sober: not even trying to keep pace with the lads here, sipping where we swallowed and listening where we talked.

Now she said, "Want to tell us about Josie, then?"

"No," I said instantly. Why spoil a good drunk? If we were going to be helpless, we might as well be happy with it.

"She was a cow," Jamie said. "Ben hated her. Hell, everyone hated her, except me. I loved her."

"No, you didn't."

"Once I did."

"No, you just shagged her. Not the same thing," and it

wasn't planned, it wasn't at all deliberate or intended, but my eyes inevitably drifted to find Laura's as I said that; and if I meant anything at all I only meant, *see how crude I can be when I'm drunk, what a hard shell I've grown under my soft exterior, not at all the sweet sad Benedict you remember?* But I realised suddenly what it might look like to her, to Jamie, to any or all of them: those words, that movement, disaster!

I felt myself redden furiously, and only hoped the candle-light would hide it, and had little enough hope of that. I tried to look away from all of them at once, not easy in a circle without utterly turning my back; there was up or there was down, and down was a confession of guilt where up would be only a confession of drunkenness, so that's what I did. I dropped back onto my elbows and lifted my eyes to the ceiling, from whence cometh no help at all, but I could at least find there a blanket of dark to hide my gaze therein.

Someone's fingers closed around my wrist. Cool, slender fingers, left wrist: Janice. Okay. Other people's gestures I could live with. Made them feel good, didn't hurt me.

Didn't help me either, but I was well used to that. Had been, at least, before I left this place, and it wasn't only muscles that fell into familiar, unthinking habits. Memory is a sticky, sucking thing; break nostalgia down to its root meanings, and it means the pain of returning. This was it, I guessed: cruelly dead cousins, loyalties twisted beyond bearing, Laura like an open wound and me slipping a dagger in and twisting every now and then, to be sure I was bleeding right.

Felt like I'd never been away.

Time passed, moods shifted, as they do; we talked about other things. They talked, mostly, while I hovered between self-pity and self-disgust, and tried to drown them both. Not good at doing two things at once, me, I never had

been. *Stick to drinking, Ben, it's what you're best qualified for*.

More time passed. Janice stopped drinking alcohol, moved
on to orange juice, and I remember hoping that she wouldn't
drink it all, thinking there would be a need in the morning.
Jon put down a half-finished bottle and glug-glugged his own
share of juice, straight from the carton; *traitor*, I remember
thinking, *you're young, what's the matter with you?*

Too young, was the matter with him; Janice was just too
sleepy. To be fair, they did have to share a bed. Hosts with
poor endurance, they failed and left us, squabbling vaguely
over who got to use the bathroom first.

Jamie and I shared a grin, affectionately mocking, but we
didn't have long to enjoy it. As if that first retreat was a
signal, Laura gave us no more than ten minutes, no more
time than it needed for two people to swap use of a bathroom
and be done with it. Then she collected toothbrushes from
Jamie's pocket and Jamie from the armchair, and took him
away to share toothpaste and toilet and bed. *My bed*,
I thought vaguely, trying to summon up some level of
resentment, or else to see potent symbolism in it.

And failed, and popped another bottle open in lieu. In
lieu of what? Work it backwards: symbols, resentment,
company. Cousin Josie. A plan to avenge her, any plan
for tomorrow, any plan for the rest of my life . . .

I could, I suppose, have gone to bed. To sofa, rather. There
was a sheet, there was a sleeping-bag though it was surely
too warm a night to need it, there were cushions; and I had
in fact slept on the sofa before, when I lived here and we
had guests. Not a problem.

Except that sleeping, just the idea of sleeping was a
serious problem. I couldn't get my head around it. I lay
down somewhat, stretched out for comfort's sake – but no,
no way was I going to sleep.

My books were in the panniers of my bike, and my pocket chess-set also, but I didn't want to be banging about out there, fumbling with keys in the dark. The only books I could see in this flat were legal texts, no fun at all; I didn't dare switch on the telly or the radio, for fear of waking sleepers, damaging their luck.

Once again, then, it came down to this: that there was nothing to do but drink. Well, there at least I was able, I could certainly get my head around that.

I fetched all the remaining bottles from the fridge, not to have to thump to and fro all night disturbing people; I lined them up conveniently to hand, along the unravelling fringe of the sofa's shabby cover; I pursed my lips around chill brown glass, and tilted.

If this was a wake, I thought, it was not for Cousin Josie. For the new me, perhaps: for the confident, cured young man I'd thought I was bringing back from the continent. All laid out on the sofa here, dead to everything except the world.

Except the world, except my world. The world sucks, I thought, and grinned savagely in the flickering light. *There ain't no such thing as gravity, the earth sucks*; and what went around came around, including me. I'd been sucked in a vicious, vicious circle, and here I was, right back where I'd started: weak and ineffectual, bereft, and drinking because I could think of no better thing to do.

At some point during that long procession of liquid down my throat, I started to worry about Fizzy. Malfeasance, and there was a right lawyerly name to give a cat. But I'd let him out, perhaps in defiance of house law, I hadn't checked; and if he'd been let in again I hadn't noticed, I certainly hadn't seen him in the flat.

Perhaps he was out there now, sitting on the doorstep or the windowsill, piteously wailing, hopelessly waiting . . .

I gave my worry a drink to settle it, but it didn't go away. Gave it a bottle, two bottles, and it only got sharper.

Somewhere during the second of those bottles the last candle burned out and left me in the dark, but my worry didn't leave me. Teeth and claws, my worry had, and it scratched and bit at me so that I couldn't be comfortable, I had to go see.

Not such a bad thing anyway, I thought. I could stand in the doorway, get some air, look at the street and the stars . . .

Poor thinking, that was. Moving was a big mistake. I jerked myself upright, and the room spun around me; I stood up and was already swaying before I took a step, my stomach lurched inside me and an acid burning rose in my throat.

I staggered and caught myself against the wall, and even that seemed to lurch and fall away from me. Now there was an urgency stronger than all my worry: front door or bathroom, either one but quickly. Front door was closer and I could find it more easily, moving flat-handed along those untrustworthy walls, with my jaw clenched and all my skin sweating and my feet stumbling on the treacherous, tripping carpet . . .

Door: found it with my eyes, then with my hands. Yale lock: turned it, pulled. Fresh air, cool breeze: unlocked my mouth and breathed in, good and deep.

That was the big mistake, the *coup de grâce*; or else it was the signal my desperate body had been waiting for, *safe now, relax, let go* . . .

Let go I did, violently, spectacularly. All that had gone down came up again, dinner and drinking both; I doubled over and spewed heroically, couldn't even make it to the gutter. My eyes blurred, my body spasmed, a foul stream gushed from my mouth and pooled below the doorstep where I stood.

Gush drained to dribble, I dribbled and spat against the vile taste, the bile taste that cloyed in my skinned mouth. And had to sit down, and did, on the low wall that was handy there; and hunched over with my hands in my sweat-sodden hair, still retching empty, and groaning wretchedly between the retches.

And then there were fingers other than mine in my hair; my head startled upward and my eyes found Janice standing beside me, shadowed face framed by tousled hair, legs bare to the breeze, a short gown belted tight between face and legs.

"You okay, Ben?" she asked, her voice hoarse with broken sleep; and then she chuckled at the absurdity, and answered for me. "No, you're not okay, are you?"

"Sorry," I said awkwardly, painfully, sorry for many things tonight. "I'll be fine . . ."

Sure I would. In a year or two, maybe a decade or so: when the stench of my puking and the embarrassment of drinking myself sick in someone else's home had faded at least a little from my memory, when dead cousins were history, when Laura's and Jamie's child was out in the world and growing, maybe full-grown and gone from them and from me also . . .

"Uh-huh," she said. "Now," dismissing all of that, dragging me back to the immediate, where I was sitting with the rising stink all about me, dribble on my chin and nothing fixed or fated, "are you okay to stand up?"

"In a bit." Her hand moved down to my neck and I liked that, I leaned against it like a cat, and remembered. "I was, I was looking for Fizzy, I thought maybe he was shut out and wanted in . . ."

She laughed. "You won't find Fizzy. He's off doing big butch tom-cat things, he won't be home till breakfast now. Don't worry about him, we always leave a window open."

All right, I wouldn't worry about Fizzy. No teeth, no claws: only my own humiliation to shred me now.

"And you're not to worry about this, either."

"Mind-reader."

Again the laughter, and, "You're an open book, Benjamin."

"Benedict."

"Benedict. Right. But honestly, everybody barfs some-time; and at least you made it to the door. I've cleaned it up off carpets before now, and washed people's jeans for them, everything. Had to put a boy in a shower once. With all his clothes on, it was the less disgusting option."

"I'll clean this up," I said. "Got a bucket?"

"In the morning. Now, are you ready to move?"

"Sure," I said, not sure at all. "Where are we going?"

"Bathroom."

"Shower?"

"If you want. I was thinking you might like to clean your teeth, but . . ."

But a shower sounded great; but there was no shower, so why was she offering one? Never had been, at least. The landlord could have put one in since I left, but herds of flying pigs were more likely. Besides, I'd have noticed, wouldn't I? When I'd had a piss, earlier? I thought back. Not easy, but I did it. No, no proper shower: only a flexible hosepipe in the bath, tap attachments and a shower head. And the plumbing made a hell of a din, I remembered, and people were sleeping.

"Teeth'll be fine. Sounds good . . ." My tongue indeed was checking out my teeth, acid-etched and slimy; brushing was suddenly mandatory.

She slipped a hand under my arm, and helped me up. Funny thing about puking, it always clears your head; I was glad of her support, but only because I was weak and shaky, not because I was reeling drunk still. Still drunk I was, surely, but I didn't feel it.

Into the flat, close the door, crab along the passage not wide enough for two abreast; I had a quick flashback to last night, when I was doing the same thing with Jon to hold me up. Another day, another trouble, another helping hand. At least I hadn't much aggravated yesterday's healing damage; my ribs were sore once more after all that heaving, but no worse than that.

Halfway there and my stomach turned again, threatening disaster.

"All right?"

"Yeah," swallowing hard against a rush of sour saliva. "Maybe. Don't stop . . ."

Hurry, I was really saying. We hurried, and we made it, though barely; I shoved her away at the door, fell to my knees before the loo, felt my innards twist and my throat fill, saw a thin brown spatter on the white porcelain.

And felt her arm around my shoulders, her hand on my head again. "It's all right, Ben. Take your time."

Well, I wasn't planning to move. I hugged that bowl, my eyes watered, somehow I managed a choking laugh. "This is not," I gasped, "how it's supposed to be. You get this close to Macallans, it's supposed to be you that's sick . . ."

"You don't make me feel sick," she said. "Just sort of tingly, when I touch you. I like it."

Yeah, right. The girls' delight, we Macallan boys. Individually, at least. "Even with the two of us?" I asked her. "Me and Jamie, together?" I hadn't been thinking, all evening; but it was a blessing now, to have a puzzle to focus on. More than one of us in a room, traditionally that was hard for ordinary mortals to bear.

"We talked about that, while you were out. Laura reckons that the two of you cancel each other out. Yin and yang, you fit together. Matter and antimatter."

That made sense, I supposed. Except, "You put matter and antimatter together, you're supposed to get an explosion."

"Something else, then. Things that neutralise each other. Teeth?"

"Teeth."

The washbasin wobbled when I leaned on it, but it always had. I cleaned my teeth, she stayed to watch; but the running tap was causing me other problems.

"Um, would you mind . . . ? I need a wazz."

She chuckled, but left me delicately alone. I drained my bladder, flushed the toilet, caught sudden sight of my reflection in the mirror and was puzzling distractedly over the lack of bruises on my face when she opened the door and distracted me altogether.

"I've decided, you're not fit to be left tonight. We're rearranging."

What did that mean? That meant that Jon came shuffling down the passage in sleeping-shorts, glancing in to give me a wicked smile as he passed; it meant that Janice tucked her shoulder under mine and took me to her bedroom, to her bed; it meant that I was not offered any choice in the matter, nor given a chance to argue.

It meant also that she helped me get undressed, and offered me no sleeping-shorts nor any other nod towards modesty; and that once I was in and under the sheet she walked around to the other side and slipped her robe off before she turned the light out, just to keep us equal.

The bed creaked and dipped a little, as she joined me. She slid across to lie cosily, contentedly against me, so close her head shared my pillow though she had one of her own; and she said, "So does you being hung up over Laura mean you don't sleep with other girls, Ben? Benedict?"

After a silence, her hand touched my chest, light-fingered and dangerous. "Okay, two alternatives. You can pass out on me, if you like; or you can talk to me. You can't just lie there and stew, that's not an option."

"Who told you I was, was hung up over Laura?"

"You all did, all three of you. I said, I can read you like a book."

Oh, fuck . . .

I said nothing; she said, "Does it, though?"

"No. It doesn't . . ." At least it didn't, hundreds of miles from here. Left to myself, I'd have made no moves on anyone in this town; not now, emphatically, not tonight.

But I hadn't been left to myself, she wouldn't have it so. "Don't feel threatened," she said, nestling, shifting an arm across my chest and touching my cheek with her fingers. "No means no, in this bed. But just think, I've been two nights now in here with a boy who doesn't love me for my body. Jon doesn't even have to say no, it's not a question. Have you got any idea how frustrating that is? And now there's you, and I know you have your priorities the right way round, and that's only going to make it worse if you just lie there and snore for what's left of the night . . ."

I'm no fool, I can spot a serious invitation wrapped up in facetiousness. I wasn't prepared to play, though, not on that level; so, "That's it, is it? You just want me to, what, service your needs? Like some fucking stud bull?"

I felt her chuckle, felt her suppress it sternly; heard not a trace of it in her voice as she said, "No, that's not it. Not just it. It's a good sleepy-time remedy for you, too. Better than lying there stewing, with a snoring girl on your shoulder. Besides, it's a good offer, and they're never that common. No one really gets enough. Why waste the chance?"

Janice: I've just puked my guts up, I must still be dizzy-drunk even if I don't feel it, it's only twenty-four hours since I was beaten up by my dad even if I have recovered bloody quick, I've seen another of my cousins butchered this afternoon, I've just found out today that I'm still obsessed with the girl who's pregnant by my blood-brother; do you really think this is the ideal time to make a pass at me?

It was like a message in my head, I wanted to send it Western Union. But she was lying half on top of me, her breath moist on my neck and her skin sticky-warm on this hot night, and all the scents and touches of her were unexpected but for sure very much better than the couch and the bottles and the long long night; and everything in the message might be true but it seemed to me suddenly that it didn't after all necessarily demand the answer no. Maybe this was a perfect time, maybe I could lose it all for an hour; and then for a few hours more, sleeping as she'd said the sleep of the damned lucky . . .

I was dreadfully uncertain, though, about many things, and her motives were top of the list. Was this generosity, or curiosity, or what? There was gossip, I knew, about the benefits and revelations of sleeping with a Macallan man. Not to boast, but the experience was irrefutably different. Maybe that's what she was after; or just another scalp and it didn't matter whose? Jon had said sleeping was a religion with her; maybe he'd been unnecessarily delicate, maybe he meant sleeping around?

Questions not voiced, impossible of asking. I went the other way instead, questioned my own potency. "Janice, I'm drunk, I don't feel good, I don't know if I can . . ."

Her fingers drummed a warning tattoo on my ribs. "I'll pretend I didn't hear that. You can say no, but you can't wimp out on me."

"No threats, you said."

"Merely an observation," and she proved it, skin slipping over skin, hers over mine; and no, there wouldn't be a problem there, she wouldn't be left frustrated. "You going to turn me down, then?" she asked sweetly, pulling away with delicious timing; my arm moved way ahead of my thoughts, reaching to draw her close again.

"Janice . . ."

"Yes?"

". . . Oh, fuck. I don't know." More doubts, more unaskable questions: *is this kindness or pursuit of kudos, or do you really fancy me, or what?* was what they all boiled down to. I'd forgotten the terrors of insecurity, the years I'd been away; now here I was, home for barely more than twenty-four hours and pulling on discarded attitudes like a boy caught naked in a public place, grabbing at anything to cover his bits.

"You know," she said, "a girl could begin to think you didn't fancy her."

An echo of my own thought, except that she blatantly didn't mean it; no craven self-doubting for her. Even so the suggestion needed dealing with, it demanded a response. Actually, I thought, fancying someone was never much of an issue once you'd got or been brought this far, into bed in the dark; but that was not the point.

As she knew damn well, and she wasn't really offering me any choice at all. No might mean no, but there were ways and ways to gag a man from saying it.

Whatever. *What the hell*, I thought, and turned my head and kissed her. She tasted smoky from the thin fags she made herself, tight twists of paper round a pinch of tobacco; that was no hardship, I was well used to it. Continental girls smoke like crematoria and taste like Lapsang, like Laphroaig. Eventually. Once you've trained your tongue to think that way, think positive . . .

"If we roll around," I said, "I'm going to be sick again."

"No rolling," she promised, and already her leg was slithering over mine, implicit instructions, *you lie still and leave the active stuff to me.*

"And I might pass out yet," I added, deliberately a beat too late. "You said I could, that was one of the alternatives . . ." Which this was not, but I decided not to point that out.

"Not any more, boy."

And she had fingers and fingernails, muscles and teeth to ensure it; but she was gentle, mostly, laughingly respectful of my invalid status for as long as I remembered it, which was not long at all.

And afterwards we lay tightly tangled in the sweat-sodden sheet, lightly tangled with each other; and I think I murmured, "Fuck," and I think she whispered, "What, again?" and I might even have managed a breath of "Later," before I slid willingly into a thoughtless, dreamless dark.

I woke to daylight, a monstrous headache and a tugging sensation, which was Janice trying to unknot herself from the sheet and me. I did my best to help, but my leg was still sleeping where the rest of me was not; in the end she had to lift it for me, to work herself out from under.

"Sorry," she said, laughing, hitching herself over to the far side of the bed.

"Doesn't matter. Where are you going?" The words were slurred, my mouth was furred and foul. "Come back."

"I need a pee."

"Unh." So did I, but I wasn't doing anything about it. I stretched and groaned, feeling an ache in the hollows of my bones. "Come back after?"

"Maybe," she said, picking up her robe and slipping her arms into the sleeves, wrapping it around her. When she opened the door, though, we both heard voices, the clink of empty bottles being collected; and she said, "Maybe not, though," which was fair enough in the circs. "Coffee?" she suggested in lieu.

"I guess. Yeah . . ."

The voices had been male, Jon and Jamie; I roused myself more quickly than I wanted to, carrying my hangover and a half-drunk mug through to the kitchen, hoping desperately that Laura would still be sleeping.

No such luck. She was there, with Janice, with the lads; and they were laddish and conspiratorial, slipping me winks

I didn't want, while she watched me neutrally from behind the shelter of a steaming cup of tea and talked exclusively to Janice, exclusively about being pregnant.

Coffee and Ibuprofen, juice and coffee and toast; we ran out of bread, inevitably. Jon went to buy more and came back to say that there was no news, no gossip on the street, nothing had happened overnight.

"So what do we do now?" Janice asked, looking at me.

It was Jamie who answered her. "Sort things out," he said, also looking at me, as if I was some kind of hero *ex machina*, brought back to the city to do just that. "We've done it before."

Yeah, right. *Thanks, Jamie.*

To be sure, we'd done it before; and last time it had cost us all so much, and no way would it be any cheaper this time around. *Someone else's turn*, I wanted to shout at him; actually I wanted to get on my bike and leave again, I wished I'd never come back in the first place.

But of course there wasn't anyone else, only we few, we happy few, we band of siblings. Heirs and graces, I thought we were; and the three graces could choose for themselves and I hoped they'd choose sensibly and stay the hell out of it, though that didn't seem likely, but Jamie and I were doomed by our blood as we always had been, and there could be no running away for either one of us.

· SEVEN ·

GANGSTERS' MOLES

How have you done it before? was the question Janice conspicuously didn't ask, nor would I have expected her to. This was home, and not everything had changed. Gossip was currency, Macallan gossip was sterling; she'd have been brought well up to speed her first term here, her first week of her first term. And this last year of course she'd had Jonathan, with all his added kudos of knowing me; he'd have filled in the gaps for her, if any gaps there were.

But the only other question anyone could ask was, *how do we do it this time?* That one had us all stymied, we were all asking it of ourselves and no one brave enough to lay it on the table, for fear of getting no answer. So we sat and crunched yet more toast as Jon made it and laid it before us, in lieu of questions; I nursed my head just as Laura nursed her hidden baby, as Janice nursed her loudly-purring cat, each of us cupping gentle hands around our personal concerns; it was Jamie, perhaps for lack of anything to do with his big competent hands, who finally found a positive suggestion to offer. That it ran contrary to my own private hopes and probably his also was just the way things worked, the entirely contrary way the world was put together. *Life's a beach*, I thought bleakly, my mind spinning back only a couple of days to Spain, to sea and sand and a wholly different life. *Life's a beach*, I thought, *then you get melanoma*.

"What we need," Jamie said, "is information. Somebody's got to know where the hostages are being held. A lot of people, not just the ones who took them. The town's not that big, that you can hide half a dozen prisoners and not have anyone guess. We need to be out there sniffing around, asking questions. Only . . ."

Only Jamie and I, the two of us who were really involved here, we couldn't do that. We were known, we were the enemy; and even those who didn't know us would see easily what we were. A suntan and a couple of years' absence was no disguise for me, I carried my heritage too plainly stamped on my face, bred in my bone. Which left it to the others to be our spies, Laura and Janice and Jon; and I couldn't ask them to risk that, and I was amazed that Jamie apparently could.

Not easily, he couldn't, that was clear; but Laura made it as easy as she could.

"Only you need us," she said for him when he failed to say it for himself. "Of course you do. I'll go sniff around at the hospital, everybody knows my face there but I'm only another student, they don't know who I'm shacked up with. And they'll all be talking, with another body turned up. I'll just put on a white coat and listen in, no bother."

"Okay, good. I'll come with, though, I'll sit in the jeep and wait for you . . ."

"No, me," I said instantly. "Daylight out there, remember?"

He glared at me, for the suggestion that I could protect his girl and his unborn child where he could not. I did my best to look neutral, and Laura just laughed at us both, the kind of laugh that's only one stage short of throwing things.

"Don't be stupid," she said. "Neither one of you's coming, and we're certainly not taking the jeep. For one thing, it's back at the flat and one of your moron cousins will be watching it; for another, I said, I'm trying to be anonymous here. And one of you wants to sit outside the door in a jeep that you've been driving all your life, Jamie, with your big nose sticking over the windscreen sniffing for trouble? Do me a favour . . ."

Actually Jamie's nose was not so large by family standards, but this really wasn't the time for either one of us to point it out.

"You shouldn't go alone," he said almost sulkily. "You're not that anonymous. 'Specially if you start asking questions . . ."

"She's not going alone," Janice said. "I'll be with her. You and me, Laura, right? We'll do the hospital first, then try the police. I've got friends at court," winking or possibly wincing at the pun, "they'll tell me if there's any rumours round the cells."

"See?" Laura said to Jamie, triumphant. "All fixed, not a problem. And you two don't go playing boy racers while we're gone. You stay right here, where we can get you. You're our liaison. If there's a phone. Is there a phone?" She glanced at Janice, got a nod of confirmation. "Good. You stay, we call you."

"You could call the mobile," Jamie pointed out.

"Nuts. We're *taking* the mobile. Then you can call us too, if you need to."

And she did, unclipping it from Jamie's belt without waiting for permission; and he just sat there and let her, and I didn't even try to keep myself from grinning.

So that was it, they had their plans and we not our marching but our sitting-still orders; and an onlooker might have thought we'd all forgotten that there were five of us in the room, Jonathan had been so thoroughly left out.

He'd been neither invited along with the girls nor told

to stay with us, and both of those omissions were right, I thought, proactive and sensible; he'd only be in the way, on either side. But what else could we ask him to do? An art student, an ex-window cleaner, he had nothing to offer that I could see, and I couldn't think how to tell him.

And didn't need to, because he made a move himself, and this time not to bring us toast. We all of us watched him, with more or less guilty eyes, all of us more or less relieved that he wasn't waiting to be told; and when he reached the door he glanced back – right at me, it seemed, which hardly seemed fair to me – and said, "I'll ask around too, some of my old friends. If there's any word on the street, they'll know."

Who, I wanted to ask him, nastily, *the window cleaners, the street sweepers? The housewives you dunned for coins?*

And perhaps he read the thought on my face, or else I was broadcasting so loud he picked it up mind-to-mind, perhaps I was shouting at him as silently, as clearly as my sister used to shout at me; because he was, he was definitely looking straight at me as he went on, "I wasn't just a windler, not all the time. There wasn't the work. I did other things, when I really needed money."

To my shame, I couldn't figure what he meant.

He left, though, before I could ask. Perhaps he didn't want to tell, I thought; or else he thought I ought to know, it ought to be easy. Perhaps it was, and I was stupid.

He left, at any rate, and the girls left too. Which left Jamie and me on our own again as so often before, and this wasn't like any of the other times that I could remember. A lifetime – no, two, his and mine both – of being alone with each other, being bloodbrothers and cousins, friends often and occasionally great foes; and still there were surprises, there were new ways for two young men to be together. There was a feeling of impotence, of being utterly in other people's hands now, that was endlessly familiar to me, but I couldn't conceive how Jamie would begin to handle it.

He stretched his legs under the table, cocked his head to one side and smiled self-mockingly, said, "You know, if they hadn't taken the mobile, I could have phoned my father."

"Why?"

"Find out what he's up to, of course. He's got to be doing something."

Sure. Frowning momentously and uttering threats, if I knew Uncle James. Waiting for the dark, when his threats might have some value. But, "There's a phone in the hall," I said.

"If I use that, he can trace the call. Dial 1471, and some helpful machine will give him this number; and he's got friends enough, even now, someone'll find the address for him. There's another code you can dial first to stop 1471 from working, only I can't remember what it is; and I wouldn't trust it anyway. He's probably got someone at the exchange who'll cough regardless."

That was all new since my day, all except the last bit. Never mind machines, my family always had people just where they wanted them. I shrugged. "He wouldn't tell you anything useful. You've signed up with the enemy, remember?"

"Yeah. I guess."

There's nothing useful you can do, Jamie, was on the tip of my tongue to say, *nothing useful for either one of us to do, till Laura phones*. But then I remembered a promise from last night, and didn't say a word; I just got to my feet and rummaged till I found a bucket and a J-cloth. Filled the bucket with steaming water, and carried it and the cloth to the front door.

Jamie followed curiously, just what I didn't want him to do. But I opened the door regardless, and yes, there below the step was the wide pool of my vomit, dried at the edges now and crusted all over. One heelmark had broken the crust and skidded a little; Jon's, most likely. I could see Janice clearly in my head, remembering and skipping over it, with Laura shadowing her and both girls laughing, perhaps, as they headed off down the street, Janice perhaps telling her about how she'd found me, not needing to say what she'd done with me thereafter . . .

The same sunlight that had baked that broken crust was working its familiar magic on my skin, but there was no magic to fix this. Only me to get down on my knees with cloth and water while Jamie watched; and I didn't need to look up to see his smile, and not himself the subject of his mockery now. *Poor Ben, can't take his liquor . . .*

I heard him walk away, didn't look up even to see the back of him; but he came back a minute later, while I was still dabbing with the cloth and thinking I needed another, maybe several more, the way this one was abrading on the concrete and still not shifting the stain.

"Not like that, Ben," he said, above my head. "Like this. You slosh, I'll scrub."

And he dangled a stiff broom before my eyes, and he was so obviously right I tried to swear in disgust at myself and ended up laughing instead. And standing up and hurling the remains of the J-cloth into the gutter, and sloshing water while Jamie scrubbed with all the energy of conspicuous virtue, *I didn't even make this particular puddle and here I am doing the hard part*, and fetching fresh water and sloshing and swilling to be certain of pristine purity of pavement; and by the time we were done his boots and my deck-shoes were splattered and soaked respectively, I hoped only with cleanish water, and we'd sloshed and scrubbed a path from door to gutter that you could have seen from the end of the street.

We kicked off our footwear and left it to dry in the sun on the step, though I could have done that in a moment with a weave of light and fire; I might be home but I still wasn't thinking Macallan, thought it likely I never would. And we went inside grinning and matey, fetched a couple of glasses and what was left of Laura's Coke from last night, and kicked bedding off the sofa to make slumping space for two in the living-room.

"Aah. That's better. That's *good*. Coke was invented as a hangover cure, did you know? Think about it, it's got everything you need: caffeine, sugar. Cocaine. Well, it used to have cocaine. And it's carbonated, so it gets into your bloodstream quicker . . ."

"Yes, of course I know, moron. It was me told you."

"Never was. Was it?"

"'Course it was. I taught you all you know."

"Ah, right. They keep telling me I'm ignorant, that'll be why, then . . ."

And actually I'd been wrong before, this was just like a hundred other mornings tasted and tested and tried again, ten years ago: I'd forgotten the aimlessness of teenagers without an immediate target, nothing to fill the next hour's awful void. There might be an added tension underlying us today, a sense of waiting for something more crucial than lunch, but you'd never have known from watching and even I had to jerk myself consciously into remembering. Too easy to forget, to let the years slip, to be suddenly fifteen again and so much closer to something that I used to think of as happy . . .

Jamie picked up a remote control, and thumbed buttons. Daytime TV, *morning* TV – it was like being back in Spain again, any time, day or night. Colours too bright, volume too loud and I simply didn't see the point. Why would people want to watch cookery competitions or asinine quizzes all day, or listen to ineffectual strangers exposing their fascist opinions or else their most intimate problems?

"Why do people do that?" Jamie demanded, seizing the

other end of the stick as so often, right or wrong. "I mean, sitting in front of a camera and saying how you can't get it up without a roll of clingfilm – why do they want to *do* that?"

"Why do you want to watch?" I countered.

"You're watching too."

"Only because you turned it on. I wouldn't have."

He looked at me then, not the screen; and after a second he said, "No, you wouldn't, would you?" Which obviously meant something, and I was still trying to work out what when he danced through the channels again, found some adverts and decided those were easier.

And he chuckled after a minute, and said, "Hey, Ben, you ever known a girl menstruate blue?"

"No."

"Because they all do in the ads, have you noticed? Tampons, pads, they always show 'em soaking up blue. Maybe we just don't sleep with the right quality of girl, did you ever consider that?"

And when I didn't answer he glanced at me again, and grunted, and said, "What, then, shall I turn it off before we get one about nappies? 'Cos we will, it's daytime, they reckon it's all women watching . . ."

Always sharp, our Jamie; often a mind-reader, with me. Right now, that wasn't fair. It was like having my sister back, riding inside my head, leaving me nowhere to hide.

Because he was right, of course he was right; menstruating led automatically for me to its opposite, to not menstruating, which was what Laura was doing right now because she was pregnant. By him. And I'd known for hours now, for a full day, and I still couldn't get past it or round it or over it. Too big a fact, too big a bump, too too big a baby . . .

Nothing I could say except *I'm sorry*, and if he was tracking me that closely he knew that much already. So I went on saying nothing, sipping sweet fizz and staring at the telly, and yes, here came a nappy ad right on cue. Unfair of me perhaps, but I left it to him to do the hard stuff, the talking.

So he did, he said, "Christ, Ben, what are we going to do with you?"

That was cheating, I thought, asking questions; worse, he made it non-rhetorical, he played Brutus and paused for a reply.

"Same as last time," I said eventually, when he didn't relent.

"What, you mean wait till we've sorted the shit out here and then let you bugger off, watch you drive into the sunset like some homeless fucking drifter, is that what you mean?"

"Yeah, that's what I mean." I couldn't see any other hope for me. Much, *much* too big a baby.

"Like fuck we will. You know your trouble? You don't know family when it kicks you in the teeth."

Actually that was all my experience of family, my definition; but Laura had said something much the same to me two years before in the crisis, in the church, and it was too heartbreakingly strange to hear her words come back at me from his mouth. It said too much about them both, again I was stranded, I couldn't reply.

So he said, "I've got a different plan, mate. You're godfather to the baby and best man at the wedding too if we have one, that's my idea . . ."

And Father Hamish would preside at both ceremonies, no doubt, and the pews would be full of scowling Macallans making the air spit and crackle. My parents and his, all the uncles and aunts and cousins. What joy. And me, no doubt I'd be praying that he wouldn't turn up for the wedding; I might even fix it so that he didn't, so I could do the traditional thing and take his place, marry her in lieu, I was sad enough to settle for that.

Not Laura, though. She'd say *I don't* instead of *I do*, she'd fight me off with her bouquet and storm off big-bellied to find what had happened to him; and the image of that in my mind had me giggling despite myself, shaking my head and reaching for my glass, trying to swallow against the rising laughter and snorting bubbles out through my nose like some incompetent kid.

Jamie pounded me on the back till I could breathe again, then he grabbed me round the throat and squeezed until I couldn't, and growled, "What, you don't think she'd marry me, is that it?"

Actually no, that wasn't it at all, he was way off track now; but I said it was, of course, I croaked, "Yeah, that's it. No chance. Do me a favour . . ."

He grinned, pressed his stubbly cheek against my own and whispered, "Just you watch. You *stay* and watch, you'll see."

And then he let me go. I massaged my throat gently, coughed a little, reached for my voice and found it. "Seriously, Jamie. How can I? I'm sorry, I'm not proud of it but it guts me, seeing the two of you together. And now she's pregnant, and I can't bear it. I *love* her . . ."

"No, you don't," he said. Not the first to say that, either. "You only think you do. Just grow up a bit, can't you? There are other girls. Some of them even want you, for God's sake. What about Janice?"

I didn't know what about Janice. Whether she wanted me or not, whether she'd have done the same for Jamie or any other drunk boy in her bed last night. All I knew was that she occupied a totally separate part of my head, her and every girl I'd slept with since I'd met Laura; and yes, I knew how I felt about Laura wasn't safe or sensible, wasn't even sane maybe, but it was the thing I'd labelled 'love' a long time ago and it hadn't faded with the years and hadn't changed, it was still sharp as wire and cutting deep, still making me bleed.

"I'd swap," I said bleakly.

"She wouldn't."

She Laura, or she Janice? Didn't matter. Swapping was not on anybody's agenda, not even mine; I wasn't that much of a fantasist.

Wasn't much of a fantasist at all, in all honesty. I saw the world and my place in it pretty clearly, I thought; I'd had enough practice. I might yearn for things to be different, but I never really expected that they would be. Except occasionally, like when you've been two years away you can tell yourself that you've changed and sound fairly convincing . . .

"All right," I said. "You get her to marry you, and I'll be best man."

"Promise?"

"Safest promise I ever made. It'll never happen."

I said nothing about godfather to the baby, and neither did he. Barring disasters which even I couldn't wish for, the baby was a certainty; the need for a godfather less certain, but at least in Jamie's thoughts if not Laura's. We're an observant family, in our own sweet way. I couldn't do it, though. I couldn't pledge any kind of responsibility for this particular baby, and it would be nothing short of brutality if they asked me to. Laura would know that, if Jamie didn't; but I thought he probably did. He hadn't meant it as a serious proposal, only a way to batter at my defences, make me bleed a little more. He probably thought bleeding was healthy. *Better to bleed than fester*, he was probably saying to himself . . .

Whatever. We killed the bottle of Coke between us, and soon we were talking again: bikes and films, bad jokes and long involved stories, anything we could think of and nothing that could hurt. And it was all so like being teenage once again, thick-tongued and thin-skinned, it was easy; and

when the phone rang the first time it was afternoon already
and neither one of us had noticed.

Jamie answered, came back with a shrug.

"Laura says they've done the hospital, but all tests came
up negative. People are gossiping, but no one knows anything for sure even about Cousin Josie, it's all rumour; and
there's not a word about the hostages."

I nodded. No surprise. In honesty we were drawing a bow
at a venture here, and a pretty distant venture at that.

"They're going to have lunch now, before they try the
cops and the courts. You want lunch?"

"Sure." Not so very long since breakfast and breakfast
had been big, eating against the ravages of the night just
gone; but we were still playing teenagers, and adolescents
can always eat. "What is there?"

"Dunno, I'll go see . . ."

Sounds of fridge and cupboard doors opening and closing,
with increasing violence; then he appeared tossing a tin
fretfully in one hand.

"Bloody students, you'd think they were up for an award,
how cliché can you get?"

"Beans on toast, then?" Not a guess; I'd been a student and
a broke one myself, in this very flat yet. I could recognise
that particular label in the dark with my eyes closed and a
black cat sitting on my face.

"Beans on toast," he confirmed gloomily, retreating. I
couldn't keep from grinning. Poor Jamie, he was *not* used
to being poor. But then, anything more elaborate, I wasn't
sure he'd have been capable of cooking. Unless Laura had
been at him there too . . .

We ate off our knees in front of the TV news, and actually
Laura must have been at him, because what we ate was some
distance from Mr Heinz's original variety. Jamie had added
spices, mostly cumin and coriander, I thought, and a little

chilli; and he'd found some cheese also, to grate over the top. Tasted good.

There was nothing on either the national or the local news about Cousin Josie, but neither one of us had expected that there would be. Journalists still kept their noses out of family business, it seemed.

Jamie took the plates away, muttering about mugs of tea; I heard washing-up noises also and decided yes, Laura had definitely been at him.

Then the phone rang again. Jamie yelled something from the kitchen, went on clattering plates; my turn, I guessed. Maybe he thought it would be Janice this time, and I had some kind of lien on her conversation as he did on Laura's.

It wasn't Janice. I picked up the receiver and said hullo, and,

"Hi, is that Ben? This is Jonathan."

"Yeah, Jon, it's me. What gives?"

"There's someone here I think you ought to talk to," he said, all tension and TV dialogue, product of his age.

Behind his voice I could hear the yammer of a commentator, high on an undistinguishable sport. "Where's here?" I asked obligingly, though I thought I already knew.

"*Solara*, the tapas bar, remember?"

"Yes. Jon, I broke their big window for them, remember?"

"Oh. Yes. They've fixed it now . . ."

"But they might not be so keen on seeing my big ugly face in there again, you know?"

"Right. Okay. Um, how's about the station bar, then?"

Truth to tell, I wasn't so keen on showing my big ugly Macallan face anywhere in town, daylight or no; I didn't want to have to break any more windows. But he sounded urgent, he sounded wired. So, "Okay, we'll come. Twenty minutes all right?"

"Sure. See you . . ."

We hung up; I looked up from where I was sitting on the hall carpet, to find Jamie standing over me.

"Something?"

"Well, Jon thinks so. Station bar, we said. Are you fit?"

"I'll turn the kettle off."

He went to do that, then came back and claimed the phone, dialled a number.

"Me, sweets. Jonathan's got a bite, he thinks. We're meeting him at the station bar . . . Well, I'm not sure. Hang on."

He looked across at me. "Should the girls come too?"

"Um. I don't know. A crowd might spook the witness, whoever it is."

"Yeah." Into the phone again, "We think better not. We'll call you, okay? . . . Yeah, right, you do that. Listen for the phone. I love you . . ." And to me, "They're going on as planned. Hedge our bets, cover all bases, that sort of stuff."

"Right."

We put our feet into sun-dried, sun-warmed footwear on the step, pinched a couple of baseball caps from a hook in the hall to make up an elementary disguise, slammed the door with a prayer for no burglars today because this time I didn't have keys to Chubb up behind us, and set off down the hill.

The station was an edifice, almost a monument, lurking in the shadow of its massive Palladian portico. The bar was fake-Victorian, where the building was genuine: imitation oak-veneer everywhere, imitation crimson plush on all the seats, little shaded lamps on all the walls and the repro prints between them interspersed with odd gleaming fitments, the railway equivalents of horse-brasses.

It was awful, but it sold beer, and from a genuine

hand-pump yet; that was good. What was better, at a table in an alcove was Jon; and he was waving us over, and he was not alone.

Just a kid, the lad who was with him. Sixteen, maybe? Too young to buy a legal drink, at least; or he looked it, at least. That might have been part of his stock-in-trade, I thought, as pennies tumbled in my head.

He sat there sipping Coke, his dirt-blond hair in spikes and his shoulders hunched into a ripped leather jacket despite the sun, and he looked young and pretty and used in the bar's shadows, beaten and bruised when he turned into the light. Street for sure, a runaway run too far ever to go back: at first glance he looked homeless also, I almost looked around for his sleeping-bag and his dog on a string. But his fingers glittered with rings of gold, and his ears too; he'd a stud in his nose and another through his eyebrow, and a pile of notes and change on the table in front of him that suggested he'd paid for Jon's drink and his own, though most likely it was Jon fetched them from the bar.

Stock-in-trade, I thought, and *never trust a first impression*. Images can be so deceptive . . .

I slipped onto the bench seat beside Jon, patted his shoulder, said hullo.

"Hi. Ben, this is Charlie, he's a friend of mine, from before . . ."

"Before what?" I asked. Not that I didn't know. *Before I gave up renting*, obviously; but I was moved by what I guess you'd call a spirit of mean curiosity, I wanted to know which of them was going to say it first.

"Well, before I knew you, for a start," Jon said. *Chicken*, I thought. But in this context, 'chicken' had more than one meaning; and if Charlie was anywhere near as young as he looked now, and if he'd been doing what he clearly did even before I met Jonathan, he must have been scandalously young when he started, so much a chicken he was barely out of the egg . . .

"Jon used to look after me," he said. "When I first come here, when I didn't know the rules . . ."

He looked like a boy who knew all the rules intimately now, who bore even his bruises like an advertisement. But yes, I could see Jon doing the elder-brother bit and doing it well, if he found someone four, five years younger than him playing the same unchancy game.

"Uh-huh," I said. "So what about now?"

"Oh, now he just gets right up my fucking nose, doesn't he?" With a sideways scowl at Jonathan, who smiled easily back, and I thought that made sense too. No doubt Jon thought he still needed looking after, and no doubt Charlie violently disagreed . . .

Jamie came over with two pints in his hands; I introduced him to Charlie, who nodded brusquely. "Yeah, I know. Jamie Macallan, I seen you, loads of times. You too," to me, "before you went away. Heard you were back, though. Before Jon told us."

"Seen me where?" Jamie demanded.

"On the street, in the clubs – all over. You're *known*, mate." And if Charlie was nervous at meeting someone so well known and for such reasons, if he was at all faced down by the danger, he was determinedly not showing it.

Come on, catch up, Jamie, I thought impatiently. I took my pint from him, and slid along the bench to make room.

"Tell Ben what you told me," Jon said.

Too early, too precipitate; Charlie shook his head, one harsh hissing jerk of denial. "Not here. Christ, I *work* here! That's my pitch," to me, with a nod towards a video game ruining the counterfeit ambience in the opposite corner. "It's a good pitch, everyone knows me; I'm not blowing it for anyone. It's okay to talk here, if they don't think you're tricks they'll think you're missionaries, but I'm not saying anything that matters."

Fair enough. These alcoves weren't exactly soundproof, and you couldn't see who might be sitting in the next one over. I drank, gazed thoughtfully at the flickering lights of the game machine, had no trouble at all picturing Charlie of an evening: thumbing coins into the slot, sipping at a Coke balanced on the top, playing with a feverish concentration and looking every inch the lost lad adrift in a world too wide, scowling so hard at the screen because he didn't dare look over his shoulder. Image again, but pure seduction that would be, for the clients he wanted to attract. And once they'd known him a time or two, the wise ones would know the image for what it was, clever fakery and nothing more; but I was willing to bet they'd keep coming back. Charlie, I thought, was probably very good at what he did.

"So how come you ended up here?" I asked him. We were trapped by our drinks, we couldn't leave yet for somewhere he deemed safer; but if he wouldn't talk business, I thought he'd probably talk trade.

"I was thirteen," he said, "I was on the run, where's better than here? No one's going to follow me up, even down south people know what this place is like; and the local filth don't give a fuck as long as they get a share. Christ, they'd have paid my train fare in if I'd asked them, if I'd known . . ."

Likely they would. Rendered impotent by my family's malign influence, the police had turned malign themselves; after so many years of helpless inadequacy, they were now immeasurably corrupt, almost as much a burden on the town as we were. Or no, not that, because we were the major players; all that we left for them was the small stuff. As, for example, the rent boys working the station . . .

We sat and drank, and didn't once mention what we were there for, though it was a visible tension between us, an

urgency muted by awkward necessity; and as soon as all
our glasses were empty Jon turned to Charlie and said,
"Where, then?"

"Let's walk," he said.

So we walked, out of the station and down a long run
of old stone steps to the riverside. There at last he felt
comfortable, where he could see there was no one close
enough to overhear. Jamie and I had our caps pulled low
and I was making the air dance with light again around us,
the best we could manage for our own protection and his.

The tide was coming in, pushing against the river's flow;
Charlie watched the murky swirls in the water and said, "I
was in the cop shop three, four nights ago. That's where I
got this," touching his cheek, where a significant bruise was
yellowing. "They do that sometimes, take us in and knock
us about a bit, just to make sure we're not holding out on
them, you know?"

I think we all nodded. We all knew. Jon perhaps better
than the rest of us, he'd probably had personal experience,
but Jamie and I had grown up knowing how this town
worked.

"Well, they kept us in for the night, 'cos they know I
hate that. It's stupid, they lose as much as I do, but you
can't tell them. They think it keeps me sweet. Or that's
what they say. Anyway, come the morning, they got me
to carry breakfast to the other cells, and they had five or
six women locked up there. They never said a word, the
custody sergeant was with me and they were dead scared
of him, you could see; but it looked like they'd been in a
while. And I dunno who they were exactly, but they were
your blood," looking away from the river now, looking at
me and Jamie. "They had your faces, you know?"

"Jesus wept," Jamie whispered. "The *police?* I don't
believe it . . ."

"Don't you?" I did. Who better, to take and hide hostages?

They had the organisation and the facilities both, they had the temperament and the cause; oh, they'd love the chance to hit back at the family that had kept them down so long. Nor would they have any qualms about killing, some of them, if they only saw an excuse . . .

"Yeah," Jamie conceded, back on track with the way my thoughts were trekking. "All right. But— fuck, Ben, the *girls* . . .!"

Laura and Janice, gone to ask questions. *I've got friends at court*, Janice had said; but her friends might not prove so friendly, once they understood where the questions were leading.

"I've got to find a phone," Jamie said, and I could see him sweating in the sunlight, could feel the cold prickle of the same sweat on my skin.

"Here." Charlie had a mobile in his pocket, a tool of the trade, no doubt. "Just don't say my name, right?"

"Yeah, yeah." Jamie took it, turned it on, punched his own phone's number with fevered fingers. And stood listening, the embodiment of stillness; and then slowly, too slowly took the phone from his ear, gazed blankly down at it, said, "There's no answer, it's been switched off . . ."

I guess we all blanked for a moment, just like Jamie; then leapt to awful conclusions, just as Jamie so clearly had; and then some of us at least tried to scramble back from there, tried to find any other reason that would at least go halfway to making sense.

Jon did best, he almost sounded convincing. "Last time I was in a hospital," he said hesitantly, "there was a sign by the door asking people to turn their phones off. The frequencies interfered with some of the equipment, it said. Could be the same at a police station, couldn't it? All those computers and radios and stuff, it's bound to be a problem . . ."

Can't speak for everyone, but I at least watched Jamie and held my breath, waiting for Charlie to say yes, he'd seen a notice just like that, seen it often on his arrested evenings.

He let us down, though, he didn't say a word until Jamie asked him a question. And then actually it wasn't a word, it was a number the kid clearly carried graven into his skull; and Jamie pressed the buttons though I didn't think it was a very good idea at all, and when his call was answered he said,

"Hullo, could I have the desk sergeant, please? . . . Right, hi. I'm just trying to find some people, a couple of girls who said they'd be calling by the station to see someone there . . . No, I don't know who. The girls' names are Laura Grainger and Janice, Janice . . . ?"

"Mackay," said Jon.

"Janice Mackay, she's a law student here . . . Oh. You're sure? . . . Yes, of course. No, never mind. Thank you . . ."

And he switched the phone off and handed it back to Charlie, who took it gingerly, as though it were suddenly hot; and I thought it might be, if the police had a machine to tell them what number a mobile call was coming from. Most likely they did, and Charlie would pay a penalty for this. I could see him flinching already, in anticipation.

"He said the girls haven't been there," Jamie told us, though he really didn't need to. "Never heard of them, he said, no civilian visitors this day. And could he take my name, please? He was very keen on that. I think he was lying through his teeth, I think they've got them."

Of course he was lying, of course they'd got the girls. Two more hostages they'd got, and one who mattered more than any, to two of us; and us the most puissant perhaps of their opposition, and totally stymied now. Jamie needn't have withheld his name, they'd know it by now in any case. The least threat against Laura in her pregnancy, it was a safe bet that Janice would tell all. No point holding back small information against great risks . . .

At least I hoped, I prayed she'd see it like that, I prayed we'd been betrayed already.

Jamie was looking up, checking out the sky on my behalf, as he'd spent half a lifetime checking it out on his own. No danger of its clouding up, only fluffy little white things that couldn't block me for more than a few seconds at worst; my turn to track him, I knew what he was going to say before he said it.

"We're going round there. We're going to get her, them, back. You can do that for us, Ben . . ."

"No, I can't," I said. "Don't be thick, bro. Not a lot of windows, I bet, on the way down to the cells, are there, Charlie?"

Charlie shook his head.

"No. So we can't just run in, blast the doors off all the cells, find the girls and run out again. It'd have to be a demolition job, from outside. Take us a long time to find them, that way. Plenty of time for the cops to arrange another death in the family, and why the hell wouldn't they?"

Jamie glared at me for my good sense, then muttered, "If we, if we took hostages too, we could swap 'em . . ."

"I doubt it. Why would they? We couldn't kill ours without reprisals, we couldn't risk that, and a hostage you can't damage is no hostage at all." Besides, I'd had my fill of killing helpless policemen, I didn't want to do it any more.

"Well, what, then? What are you saying, that we just leave it? So next time your fucking father loses his rag, when we're all waiting to see who floats up on the tide this time, you and me are going to be down there beachcombing just in case it's Laura? One in six chance, I don't like the odds, Ben . . ."

"That's not what I'm saying. We need to be clever, is what I'm saying. Subtle. We know who they are," *and they know who we are,* "so we can outthink them. What we don't do is get into a fight, we're not the big battalions any more. Let's find a pub," always my prescription, a universal sedative, "have a drink and talk it through, okay?"

Wrap my hands around a pint glass so no one could see how they were sweating, hide in a shady corner not to have lights gleaming off my skin, cut myself off from dangerous sunlight like a man in terror locking up his weapons, for fear he should use them to his own destruction . . .

• EIGHT •

HOW TO GET AHEAD

Actually it was maybe not such a good idea in retrospect, in view of what fell out.

Finding a pub was not a problem, there were several to choose from; a shady corner was easy also, and we dropped into it. Sent Jon to the bar, not to have any difficulties with the landlord peering beneath our caps, mine and Jamie's, and soon we had the requisite pints in our hands and all the afternoon ahead of us to drink them.

But.

Pubs make good hiding-places, alcohol's a fine substitute for action; but . . .

But this was risk unrecognised, this bitter-sweet liquid; and Jamie and I, we couldn't get enough of it. Not enough, at least, to stop our minds from running on parallel tracks. *Laura's a prisoner, and she's pregnant. She's a hostage, and she's pregnant, and I love her . . .*

Every time our eyes met and I saw my pale face reflected in his, my harsh and jagged thoughts, fears, anticipations burn in his mind as brightly as my own; every time either one of us, any one of the four of us tried to talk sensibly about the thing; every time we all of us fell silent at the enormity, the impossibility of talking while the thing held true: each and every moment we were in there, is what it came down to, Jamie and I were gripped and torn and tortured by that single universal fact, that one more girl had been added to the list of the taken and this time we weren't just angry, or just afraid. We were crushed, overwhelmed, all but obliterated. Never mind that Janice had been taken too, never mind what I had minded so much before, that members of my family were taken. Laura – pregnant Laura, beloved Laura – eclipsed them all.

My life, both our lives seemed too light to offer in exchange, they didn't make the weight; but if we couldn't fight and we couldn't rescue then we had nothing else, no other response to give. If we'd believed that the girls, that only one of the girls would walk free as a consequence, I think Jamie and I would both have not walked but run to the police station right then; we'd have given ourselves over quite willingly to death or torture or long years of hostagery, we'd have turned Judas and betrayed every relative we had, we'd have led them all into a trap and laughed to do it, if only Laura could have her liberty in return.

And of course we had the right intermediary, Charlie was there with his contacts and his mobile phone, he'd set the deal up for us. Without a qualm, I thought. But no, we didn't trust the police, we didn't even need to discuss it. Just as well, given how mute we were, how despairing, how far from rational discussion.

We drank to fill the silence, to fill our bellies and our heads. Alcohol of course is a depressant, though we didn't need that; but it's also a relaxant and there at least it could help us and it did, working against what was drawing muscle-tissues and tendons so tight they might have snapped independently, like piano-strings in a sudden summer frost.

And maybe it relaxed something in our heads also, some early-warning system that might have bleated caution at us, *danger ahead* . . . There must be something of that, a gland of foretelling that science can't recognise; why else does instinct still rise up against rationality, prickling the scalp and the spine, being right too often for coincidence? If it is there and if it had done its job that day it might even have been listened to, we were so frightened for Laura; but alcohol suppressed it or incoherence overrode it or else it doesn't exist after all, because I felt nothing but anxious excitement when Jon said, out of the blue, "There might be a way to get at them, Ben. To get the girls out of there."

"Yeah? How?" I demanded, meaning *I don't believe it, let's hear it, you keep setting 'em up and I'll keep knocking 'em down, theories like pints, let's be having 'em* . . .

"Start a fire," he said. "In the station. Up on the top floors, nowhere near the cells, but they'd have to evacuate anyway, and once they bring everyone outside . . ."

I shook my head; it was Jamie who did the dashing with cold water. "We can't risk that, Jonathan. You know that, for Christ's sake, we can't risk *anything*."

"What's the risk?"

"They'd know it was us. Of course they would. We track 'em down and suddenly the station catches fire? Just like that? They're not stupid."

Neither stupid nor generous; they'd make us pay. Leave the girls in the cells, perhaps, let them smell the smoke; let 'em roast if the fire got that far. Or roast one of them as a warning, drag her up to the burning floors and set her alight, push her out of the window so that she fell like a signal flare, *this is stupid, boys* . . .

And it might be any one of the girls, the women; and it might very well be Laura.

Jon wasn't giving up, though, he was still talking. I tuned in again from the hissing, the crackling and roaring, the screaming in my head; and heard him say, "In daylight, though. It's different, if it happens in daylight."

"How?" Jamie demanded.

"The police may not be stupid, but they are conditioned. Like everyone in this town, you lot included. If the station catches fire before sunset, no one's going to think Macallan. Are they? Your magic only works at night, everyone knows that."

I took a breath and wondered, felt Jamie doing the same at my side. Was it true, was it still true, who knew about me? I couldn't answer that, neither could he; we glanced at Charlie, who was scowling.

"So how are you going to do that, then? Set it on fire in daylight?"

That was an answer, of sorts. If the word wasn't on the streets yet, neither two years after I'd first used my talent nor a full day after I'd most recently used it, then pretty much nobody knew. The police might, just might be an exception; but they were a leaky crew, what went in usually came out again. Usually via agents like Charlie, who would pick up gossip alongside their bruises . . .

"It's a talent," I said to him; and to Jamie, "I think I could make it look like a regular fire, too."

"You'd have to." Macallans traditionally have their own patent flame, that burns cold and destroys without consuming; like any true magic, it runs utterly counter to everything my physics teacher ever taught me. But in this as in everything, my own talent seemed to run counter: my dayfire was at least hot and it would set other things alight, though not itself go out when they turned their extinguishers on it.

Jamie was looking hopeful, *tell me you can do this, say it again, say it louder*; so I did. "I can. I'm sure I can."

It was the alcohol talking, maybe, as much as poor timorous Ben, false fleeting perjured Benedict; but it spoke well and convincingly, it caught us all, it led us hopefully through what was left in our glasses and so out of the pub.

Where Charlie stopped dead in the lead, turned to look at the three of us and said, "I'm not coming with you, mind."

"No, sure." No reason why he should; nothing he could do, no need to endanger civilians and friends. I wanted Jon absent too, though I didn't think I'd get that.

"I'm going back to my room," he said a little belligerently, "I'm packing my gear and I'm getting out. Moving on. If you're starting a war with the filth . . ."

"They started it," Jamie said; but Charlie was right, he was wise. He'd be best out of town.

"Where will you go?" I asked, good manners mixed with guilt, that we were driving him off an established patch and wrecking a lifestyle he seemed to have pretty well sussed, despite the bruises.

He shrugged. "North, south, depends on the trains . . ." Either he didn't know or he wasn't telling, which was fair either way; but he wasn't leaving us either, not immediately, he was still standing there, waiting for something.

I'm slow sometimes, but not that slow. Jon's face said he'd made Charlie a promise, *they'll see you right, for the information*; Charlie's face said it had all suddenly got more expensive.

I didn't even sigh, I just took out my purse and fished for what notes I had left. Jamie saw, clicked, produced his wallet; between the two of us, I think we made Charlie as happy as he could be in the circumstances. We covered the cost of his ticket at least, whichever way he went, however far.

Then he did leave us, after we'd said goodbye and thank you and good luck, after Jon had hugged him hard and kissed him sweetly on the cheek that wasn't marked; and we three headed off up the steps again and up the hill, to where the police station stood like a monument to Sixties graft, an edifice in concrete topped by a radio mast whose supporting wires were a roost for a thousand starlings.

It was those wires, I guess, that focused my idea. A place like that, humming with power, crackling with static – it's really not going to be a surprise if they have an elcctric fire. And all right, circumstances were unusual, the timing might be suspicious; but a place like that, humming with corruption, where every hand wore a knuckleduster and had fresh shit under its nails – they had so many enemies, any timing was going to be suspicious. There'd always be someone keen to set a little heat under their feet. My family would be prime suspect, to be sure, by definition; but as Jon had said, with any luck at all my family would be discounted, if we struck before the sun went down.

So I looked, saw the starlings cloud and wheel, saw the wires that ran *de haut en bas*, from the warm air to the cold guts of this building, this grey machine; and I thought *lightning*, wondered if I could imitate nature at her finest, making like the hand of God.

But no clouds, no prospect of storm, and that I couldn't summon up. No Prospero, me, despite the convenient aerial. Lightning without storm would bespeak Macallan despite the light; I couldn't chance it.

For a couple of minutes I just stood in the street there, looking. Birds, wires; concrete, glass.

Eventually Jamie nudged me, murmured, "Better move, Ben. We're going to look conspicuous, else . . ."

True enough. Lads hanging on street corners were not exactly an uncommon sight, but to a suspicious mind all people perhaps appear suspicious; and the police had reason enough to be watchful, and if they were watching we were a touch too old to be utterly convincing, minute by minute our caps would look less fashion and more disguise, my concentration too intense.

So we drifted down a side-street, trying to amble although I was still looking, still thinking *birds and wires, concrete and glass . . .*

Around the back of the station, a high wall with sheet-metal gates concealed and contained their motor pool; the gates were open, but that was no better a place to stand and stare. Cameras watched us like birds on steel poles, in steel boxes with steel spikes arrayed below, a new institution and all unpainted. Cheap and utilitarian, perhaps, but the effect went way beyond the budget. Whether they'd budgeted for that I couldn't guess, but those angular, galvanic structures encouraged an Orwellian paranoia, at least in me: the sense of someone watching and not trying to hide it, faceless but ever-present and wanting you to know it. Me, I thought that was hubris on the part of the police, unless it was an essential stroke to their much-damaged egos. Couldn't be easy being smart but not smart enough, strong but not strong enough, always second best: *Salieri meets Mozart*, I thought, and maybe he really had murdered the little bastard. Maybe murder was the only possible resolution, in the end . . .

Beyond the station wall the street went residential, or ex-residential: the houses here were a lot bigger than the average for this area, heavy semis with three or four storeys and large gardens, a Victorian comfort-zone. For 'comfort' a hundred years on, read 'expense': some, many, most of these houses were too costly now for families to afford. Or say rather that the families who could afford them would pay double or else settle for a home half the size, sooner than live this side of town.

A few had been in the same families' hands for generations, and still were; the majority though had been taken over by small business or charities, any company that was prepared to pay once for the property and once or twice more to keep the police sweet and my family smiling upon them.

Immediately behind the police station though was one
of the few, the very few exceptions, neither the one thing
nor the other, neither old money nor new. Theirs nor ours.
Big big house, entirely surrounded by garden which was
surrounded in its turn by its own high wall: a notice by
the ever-open gates, *The Sidings Project*, was uninforma-
tive unless you were in the know already, unnecessary if
you were.

The Shunt we'd always called it, no doubt kids called
it still. Both names worked off the same pun, that here
the tracks parted, here you left the main line. What it
was was a church-sponsored halfway house for druggies,
addicts who'd been through a rehab programme but still
bore watching, still needed more support than they'd get
in the moral dead zone that was this city. Getting skulled
was just too tempting here, if you were young and not
called Macallan: what the hell was there else to do? You
left one way, or you left another; and leaving by virtue of
pill or needle was easier. You didn't need to pack. Tickets
of course were mostly return, that was a disadvantage; but
you could always go again in a day or two, no sweat. Never
any shortage of gear.

Father Hamish ran the Shunt, which was why the place
paid nothing to us or to anyone. On the contrary, my
family actively supported it, visible charitable works were a
speciality of the house; and what we backed no one else was
going to bully. Hamish probably took his collecting-tin to the
police station also, he had *chutzpah* enough and to spare.

Though whether he'd be doing so well now, I suddenly
doubted. High-profile collaborators tended to suffer once
they lost their protection. I thought of Hamish chained to
a lamppost, stripped naked, tarred and feathered; and felt
nothing, no sympathy, no regret.

It wouldn't happen, though. He was too careful. He'd
be holing up with my uncle by daylight, cowering in the

priest-hole and celebrating Mass by candlelight only, and
only when Macallans turned up for surety.

Too bad, I thought, and here came that regret. I guess I
really, really didn't like Father Hamish . . .

Not a worry, three young men walking into the grounds
of the Shunt. People came and went all the time, looking
seedier and shiftier than we did. Anyone watching, acciden-
tally or otherwise, they weren't going to think twice.

Jamie and I had been regular visitors here, familiar faces
when we were teens, we knew our way around. We hadn't
come for rehab, of course, nor to help Hamish; we only
came to score. Someone would always have grass or dope
to sell, usually acid or speed if we wanted that, and this was
so much easier than finding it on the street. It was also easier
to persuade people here that we were not going to pay street
prices for our gear.

So – treading memories as much as paths, the soft stuff
of happening tramped down into hardcore – we circled the
house by way of the dense shrubbery in the garden, pushing
between rhododendron and holly, making gestures towards
being discreet.

Around the back was what we were looking for, as we
knew, the way to vantage: the fire escape, a classic staircase
of iron winding back and forth from one floor's windows
to the next. We led Jon up it fast, our feet shimmying on
gridwork, our eyes never glancing in for fear of finding
someone glancing out; and so past the last window and
on up, to where the roof was flat between peaks and not
overlooked by any of the dormers.

This used to be the smoking-spot, where we'd sit with
skinny kids and pass joints around, take more than our fair
share and feel nothing more than smug as we watched them
shiver and rub their arms and elbows, feeling the burn, the
constant prick of no needles.

Nice people we'd been once, Jamie and I. Whether we were so much improved even now, I wasn't certain.

Used to be the smoking-spot? Still was, judging by the dog-ends and the roaches. Did Hamish know, I wondered? Probably. I thought him more wicked than my family in many ways, weaker and more craven but not stupid, never that. Did he care? Probably not. Demonstrably not, if he knew. He'd never tried to stop us, and wasn't stopping them yet.

Still, we were not here to smoke, but to smoke out. If we could, if *I* could . . .

From up here, high, we could see easily over the police station's concealing wall. We could see the cars and vans parked neatly white in rows – *and I could set them all to burn, one touch of my mind, and mustn't* – and we could see the kennels, the pens of wire mesh with restless dogs contained.

For a moment then I could see nothing but Cousin Josie, with her face and hands and throat all bitten out. I wondered if it was one of these dogs did that, if the police had them trained that hard; or if it had been a confiscation, say, a pit bull from an unlawful fight that they'd decided to hang on to in case of need. Or simply for pleasure or profit, of course, perhaps they ran dogfights themselves. Perhaps they regularly threw a girl to the dogs, to keep them hot and ready . . .

But no, there'd been nothing regular about what they did to Josie. That was special, that was red-letter treatment for the message of it. Could still've been one of these dogs, though, or if not it could still have been here that the thing was done. Screams coming from the pigpen, no one was going to ask questions. Then wrap the body and dump it in a van, run it down to the river; the police had a boatyard down there, no doubt they had a Zodiac or two. In fact

I'd seen them, one day they were dredging the river for a body. Fellow-student that had been, love-affair turned bad and he vanished between one day's lectures and the next. Parents came up from down south, the police had to make at least a visible effort. They never found the body, as far as I remembered – halfway to Norway the boy's bones would be, most likely, unless he hadn't gone in the river at all – but the divers had operated from a couple of Zodiacs, that I remembered for sure . . .

And I wanted to burn all the dogs, just in case they'd tasted Josie; and it was harder to say no to that one, harder to keep a grip. *Remember Laura. And remember Janice, and remember the others too, all your pale helpless cousins . . .*

I remembered, and I set no fire to burn among those kennels; but *later*, I thought, *there's got to be a later. There's got to be a when-all-this-is-over; and when it is, oh, when it is . . .*

When it was, I thought, chances were there'd have been too much blood already, whichever way it fell out. I didn't honestly think I'd be hunting for dogs. But for now, I could pretend that was a promise; and however pretended, it was the promise that moved my eyes onward and upward.

Up the walls, the concrete layers of this multi-decker sandwich with its glass fillings; up to the top – to the mast, to the birds – and back down a slice or two. Not too far. The cells were below, I knew that even before Charlie told us, and heat rises; I wasn't putting a fire anywhere near the girls.

If I could put a fire anywhere at all. In the pub I'd thought I could, I'd said so; now I was starting to doubt. But I looked in through the windows and saw men and women working at desks, working at computers; and I thought about power running through cables, thought about cables breaking, sparks flying . . .

Closed my eyes to think better, to see more clearly; and felt my mind reach out across the breeze, felt it drift through immaterial concrete to find those cables that I knew were there.

And found them, or seemed to, like bright strings in the haze; and saw how the power flowed and burned within them, felt my own power rising to match it as the sun burned on the back of my neck. Reached out with my mind's fingers, thinking I could pluck them and play them like a musician, or break them like a thug—

And faltered, thinking this was only in my head, just a fantasy, what I wanted and not what I could. My eyes opened, and I lost it altogether; but when I glanced round – thinking that I'd find Jon ignorant and confident of me, Jamie knowing too much and deeply doubtful, thinking that I'd have to confess, *I can't do this, sorry* . . . – they were both gazing at me with the same expression, a sort of baffled expectation.

"What?" I demanded, glad of the excuse to say something, anything except *I can't do it*.

"You sort of – went away," Jon whispered.

I looked to Jamie for something more sensible, and all he said was, "I've never seen anything like it, Ben. What did you do?"

"I didn't do anything," I said, barely better than *I can't*. "What d'you think I did?"

"I thought your soul went walkies. I've seen, I've seen dead people," *I know you have*, I thought, *your brother, I was there* . . . "and it was like that, you know, how the face is just the same only it's empty, they aren't there any more? That's what happened to you, just for a couple of seconds. You were gone, bro. And I don't know what that is, but it ain't any talent I've seen before. No one shuts their fucking *eyes*, for God's sake, to use talent . . ."

True, they didn't. Talent came with light and we were all

of us utterly in the dark without it; no one would willingly close themselves off from its most sensitive touch, on their eyeballs.

But I shook my head, said, "I don't have anything else. I just reckon we haven't found half what we can do yet, if we try. That's the trouble with this family, it's been floundering around for generations, grabbing what was easy and thinking that was all. Even Uncle Allan," *whom I loved, whom God preserve in hell*, "I don't think he got close to seeing what we really had. Now shut up, will you, and let me concentrate . . ."

And I turned back towards the police station with confidence, certain of myself only because I truly knew nothing of what I did; and closed my eyes and reached again, found the insubstantial shadow that was the concrete wall and the vivid fiery strings that were the cables. I followed their bright pathways, tracked them to a node where many came together in a flaring matrix. I gripped that with a hand I didn't have; squeezed hard with too many fingers, one for each separate cable; and sent my own current flowing, racing, flooding into them like the sea at high tide floods its feeding rivers. Except that I was only a conduit, what I had I sucked from the sun and passed on, *bringing light to dark places* I thought and almost snickered at it.

The sun was inexhaustible, at least by me; but I was not, and I was trembling, sweating, close to falling when my knees folded. Close to falling a long way, close as I stood to the roof's edge; but someone's arms – *Jamie's arms*, I thought – caught me from behind, held me against a panting, straining chest. *Nice one, bro*.

But he couldn't hold me for long, though he'd swear that he could; I couldn't keep this up for much longer, nor should I need to. If it worked, it should be working now. One last touch, though: I yanked at all those luminescent strings and broke them, just like a thug. And saw their fire go out, or most of them, but saw how the matrix flowered into light too sharp, too cruel even for me with my eyes closed . . .

There was a bang came with that, back in the solid world. I turned my head away swiftly into Jamie's shoulder, into his hug. Hugged him back as strong as I could manage, which was not strong; opened my eyes and focused blurrily on his face, where he was staring back across my shoulder.

"What, what's happening?"

"Half their computers blew up," he said, "and the lights went out. Top three floors. Looks like you've got the fire too, middle floor. *Big* explosion there. Just perfect, man . . ."

Briefly, something shadowed the sun; I glanced up, saw a black mass of birds eddy and split and join again on the wind.

"Are you okay, Ben?"

That was Jon asking; Jamie was too engrossed. I nodded slowly, carefully, my head not feeling any too secure on my shoulders.

"Yeah, I'm okay. Thanks. Let me see, Jamie . . ."

He loosened his grip and I turned round, though I couldn't see a thing till I had rubbed at wet eyes with a wet hand, then dried it on my jeans and tried again.

Darkened windows, figures rushing to and fro; a couple of floors down the opposite of darkness, windows that flickered and danced with a hard light. No use their fire extinguishers on that. I could tell, I could feel it still inside me, it pulsed to my own heartbeat and I knew. A proper fire it was, real flame eating real oxygen, eating anything else it could find; but I was tied to it none the less, I knew its heat and its speed and its hunger. They'd not get near it, they'd never touch its core.

"You fit then, Ben?"

That was Jamie; I looked at him, puzzled. Just then I didn't think I fitted anything.

"We've got to get down there," he said patiently, his feet

dancing in the dog-ends to counterpoint his voice. "Stage two, yes? Rescuing the girls?"

Oh. Right. That was my job too, of course, no one else to do it. The question not did I fit, but was I fit; and the answer no, demonstrably I was not. My joints had rubberised, my bones felt like pasta cooked a long way past *al dente*; despite the light I thought I'd have a job lighting anything hotter than a cigarette for the rest of the day, and for that I'd need a match.

But.

The job was mine to do, and Laura's freedom, Laura's safety lay at the other end of it. Laura's and the others', all of them, Janice and my cousins too; but Laura's of course was paramount, how could it be anything else?

I was first to the fire-escape, despite Jonathan's gesture of protest – *what are you going to do, catch me should I fall? I don't think so, Jon-boy* – and first to ground also; first of us to join the swelling crowd in the street, Shunt residents and men in suits and kids with baby-buggies all gathering to watch the pigsty burn.

These people would know our faces, but no one was looking at them. Caps low and heads bowed we burrowed in from the edge, to where we'd be safe from any suspicious watchful Uncle Bob; and then we looked not at the fire but at the big gates and the motor pool beyond. If, no, when they brought their prisoners out, as they would have to, that's the way they'd come. Into a Black Maria – no longer black, of course, but the name still held: like steam-rollers, half a century on from the death of steam – and then into the street, under escort naturally and heading for the nearest jail at a guess. Didn't matter where they were heading, how many escorts in Escorts they had. Once they were out in the open, I could open them out; I could peel any van like a satsuma, winkle out the prisoners within. Be as obvious as I liked in my talent then, it wouldn't matter any more.

Police and civilian workers massed in the gateway, so that I couldn't see what was happening behind them. Someone called a list of names, started ticking them off; then the blare of sirens overrode his voice, as fire engines came racing up the hill.

There were three of them. Two parked on the main road, one came down towards us; and Jamie nudged me urgently, nodding to where a couple of police were heading over to herd our crowd away with the usual patent lies, *there's nothing to see, come on, move along now . . .* We slithered to the back but that wouldn't do it, it wouldn't guarantee our anonymity as the others dispersed. The kids from the Shunt were in a group, and as the police waved them off they trotted back across the road to where they'd come from, where they'd be on private property and immune to interference. None of us said a word, we didn't need to; we just tagged on behind them, faces averted.

In the garden were many trees, offering an easy route on to the wall that overlooked the station. The kids swarmed up and sat in a happy, chattering line; and again we followed, taking a necessary chance. We had to be able to see what happened.

For a while there was chaos down in the yard, police and firemen milling around, talking, shouting, giving contradictory orders. The firemen wanted to bring their tender in, but there wasn't room until some of the cars were driven out; I sat coughing in the swirling smoke, squinting to see, watching always for women being shepherded out of the station and into one of the vans.

Watching for it and not seeing it, seeing only strangers. Seeing men, a few men and teenage boys brought out in handcuffs or else simply gripped by the elbow, and yes, they were pushed into the back of a windowless van; but no, no women at all.

*   *   *

Time passed. Windows shattered, flames roared upward; retaining wires snapped in the heat, and the radio mast fell with a crash on to the flat roof. Firemen went into the smoke-filled building with breathing apparatus heavy on their backs, their faces masked; the tender was at last brought into the yard and hoses were connected up to follow the men inside; no one else came out.

At last, "They must have moved them," Jamie muttered beside me, once it was painfully, cruelly, obviously true. "They must have done it before, as soon as they knew we had them sussed."

As soon as he made that phone-call, most likely. He knew that, so did I. Neither of us said it. They'd taken the girls away, all our girls and women; and again we had no idea where, and again their lives were forfeit and we could only pray that no one would guess who had started this fire.

We thought, we hoped they'd be too busy, too distracted to pay any attention to the shadowed faces of the shadowed kids watching from the wall of the Shunt. At any rate – at whatever risk – we had to be certain; so we stayed until the last of the vehicles was gone from the yard, and definitely only the one had had any prisoners in it when it left. Then we slid down the wall and slipped away.

"Where now, then?" Jon asked, meaning *what now, what can we do, how can we get them back?*

"My place," Jamie said, with certainty.

"And if your dad's got people waiting for us?"

He just shrugged. "They can't take us. You by day and me by night, they can't touch us. And I want to talk to Dad anyway, see if he's got any ideas . . ."

Yes, I thought. We were that desperate, that devoid of ideas of our own.

We walked to the nearest taxi firm and took a cab across town, saying nothing; we wouldn't have talked anyway, with the driver listening in, but we had nothing to say to each other. We'd screwed things dreadfully, lost what we valued most; what was there to talk about?

There was no noticeable watch being kept on Jamie's flat. We let ourselves in and just slumped mutely, too low to think about eating or getting drunk or any other way to pass a little time, to keep our minds from dwelling on what we'd done. Jamie didn't even make a move towards his phone. Uncle James could wait, it seemed, as we were waiting.

For what, I wasn't clear. Just something to happen, I guess, looking back: something to take the burden of action from off our inadequate shoulders.

When it came, we all startled. Waiting or not, we weren't ready. There was a thunderous knocking on the door downstairs; even Jamie went pale, and Jon looked about fit to cry or maybe scream with the tension and the anxiety. Janice was his flatmate, I reminded myself sharply, and his friend; newly my friend also, and a good and uninvolved person, the most innocent victim in this. It was easy to lose sight of that, in my overriding, obsessive panic over Laura.

Panic doesn't have to be a mad hectic fight-or-flee response, all adrenalin and everything in motion; panic can be a stillness also, a stifling terror of making any choice or any voluntary movement, in the utmost certainty that it will be the wrong choice or the wrong movement and doom will come.

I've always known that; what I didn't know until that day was that even where there is no choice, panic can still hold you frozen. We knew we had to go to answer that knocking, but for a long minute none of us dared.

Oddly, it was me who moved in the end. Oddly, because I had no intention, I didn't make the choice; I guess it was just the situation made it for me, lifted me slowly and shakily to my feet, walked me across the carpet towards the landing and the stairs down.

The other two followed me with their eyes only, not a muscle else twitching to go with me.

Landing; stairs. One at a time I took them, old-man style, gripping the banister hard. There seemed no hurry in the world; the knocker had not knocked again, though I'd been an age getting even this far. Gone away, perhaps, given up and gone away? Perhaps, but I didn't believe it. Not so much urgent they'd sounded, as imperative: *you will answer this*. Not the sort of people to give up and go away. Just the sort of people to knock once and be satisfied with that, be certain they were heard and would be answered.

Sounded like my Uncle James, I thought; but this was daylight, and while he might venture out behind dark glass and a shield of lesser lights – indeed he had done to come fetch Josie's body, though his shield then had included rifles – I thought he wouldn't do so in person to come fetch an errant son. He'd just send the shield, or some part of it. With, perhaps, rifles. Not to point them at his boy, of course, good lord no: *for your protection, Jamie, that's all, we've got to look after the lad, that's what he said . . .*

Amazing, how your mind can fillet all the bones out of a situation in the space of a second or so, leave it soft and flabby, no threat at all. I knew, oh, I knew that was not what was happening here: I wasn't going to open the front door to find a couple of cousins there, come to take us home to Uncle James. I'd welcome them, I thought, I'd all but fall into their arms and say *yes please, take us home, make us safe; and fetch the girls too, you're grown-ups, you can do it . . .* But they wouldn't be there, it wasn't that kind of world. We'd tried to be grown-ups on our own and we'd cocked that appallingly; we weren't about to be rescued now, by family or any other tool of some capricious but ultimately merciful deity. No chance, that wasn't the way the bastard worked . . .

I opened the door, and there was no one there. Left, right,

across the road: no one at all. *Wrong again, Ben, they didn't wait. They didn't have the patience after all . . .*

What there was, I could hear the sound of a car cruising slowly down the hill and away. Could have been them, very likely was; I stepped forward to see if I could spot the car, if I could identify it. If I wanted to wave . . .

Stepped forward, and my foot nudged something on the step.

I looked down, the only direction I hadn't thought to check; and my eyes jerked away before they'd even registered what they were actually looking at. Something about the immediate image, glossy black criss-crossed with pale stripes, hinted at me strongly that I really, really didn't want to see.

I was sweating, even, as I stood there in restorative sunlight, in my element: sweating coldly once again, and that made more than once too often. I stared upwards into bright sky, forced my lungs to breathe slow and deep against a scared, asthmatic panting, and at last dragged my eyes back down.

A black bin-liner, that's what it was, wrapped around something about the size and shape of a football, and sealed with what looked like half a roll of parcel-tape.

Josie's body, that's what it reminded me of, wrapped in black plastic sheeting and sealed with waterproof tape, bound with rope, addressed and delivered on the tide right to our feet. As this was, right at my feet and saying *try me, weigh me, pick me up and carry me . . .*

Which I did, in the end, though it took a while. It was heavier than it looked, as heavy as I'd feared; and it weighed more in my mind even than in my hands as I bore it slowly back up the stairs.

I didn't want to take it in, to present it like a prize to Jamie and Jon, to play pass-the-parcel and make us all guess as I was having to. So in the end I didn't, I just sat on the top step and cradled it in my lap, trying not even to feel through the plastic to find the shape of whatever lay within.

I guess everyone's reactions were running at panic-slow pace, or else they'd been biting their tongues in there, not to ask for fear of being told; it took an age, it seemed to take forever before Jamie called through to me, "Who was it, Ben?"

However long it seemed it hadn't been long enough, or so it seemed; I couldn't answer him. Couldn't tell him, either. Not yet. I just stared at what I held between my hands, and finally, finally drew a section tight and worked my thumb through the plastic. Fair's fair, and he'd done it last time; and maybe I was trying to assert my rights here, just in case.

The other thumb went in, and tugged in opposition. I tore a hole in the bin-liner as small as I could make it, as slow as I could manage; just so I'd know first, so I could tell him if he came. When he came, if it was . . .

My thumbs touched something infinitely familiar, and I jerked them out with a gasp. The plastic settled slowly, and even in the dim light and through the small tear I'd made I could see hair, human hair, dirty-blond and boyish. Also the tip of an ear; and some of the hair was clotted dark and there were stains on the skin of the ear, and the copper-red metallic smell of clotted blood came wafting out and there must – of course there must – have been a mass of it, a mess of it, I'd never smelt it so strong.

I groaned; and God forgive me, there was more relief than anything else in that groan, and in the sob that followed it. I'd thought, feared, dreaded that I was holding Laura in my lap.

Shock at being right, or half right; horror and disgust; they all came after, they'd all had to wait. When they came, though, they came good, so that when at last Jamie came he found me huddled up tight against the wall, fœtal as I could achieve without an immersion tank and an inexhaustible supply of amniotic fluid.

I guess I'd put the package down. I didn't remember, didn't want to look. But I heard Jamie's gasp, his grunt; then – always braver than me, always willing to face what I only wanted to run from – I heard him crouch and breathe, and tear the plastic wider.

A slow hissing breath now, that didn't have much to do with lungs or an oxygen debt; something like a whimper, though again it came or seemed to come from somewhere other than his voice; a rustle as he wrapped it up again.

"It's Charlie," I said, largely into the crook of my elbow. "Isn't it?"

"Yeah." Pause, breathe a while, speak: "Guess the poor kid just couldn't run fast enough."

"No, right," I said bitterly. "He ran straight into us fucking Macallans, and got stopped dead."

NINE

WITH ONE POUND
THEY WERE FREE

I'd seen as little as I had to, as much as I could bear. Jamie had seen more, enough to be sure of a name; Jon had seen nothing at all, nor did any one of the three of us want him to.

Nor could any one or any two or all the three of us together stop him from seeing all there was, all that we'd been given.

Charlie was – had been – his friend; someone had to look after Charlie.

Jon stood in the doorway behind us, where we were sitting on the landing. Jamie had his arms hooked through the balusters; I was looking at him now because that was marginally better than closing my eyes and looking at Charlie disembodied, floating accusingly behind my lids.

"Charlie?" Jon whispered. Neither one of us turned round.

"I'm sorry, Jon." It was Jamie actually who was speaking, but it might have been either one of us. It didn't matter. "We really fucked this bad."

"Show me," though his thin voice was also saying *I don't want to see*, and for sure neither of us wanted to show him.

Jamie stood up and lifted the wrapped head as reverently

as he could, which wasn't very. It's hard to be reverent, with a torn bin-liner that in all honesty you absolutely don't want to touch.

But he carried it through into the living-room, Jon following his every movement with a bleached face and eyes that were sinking and bruising almost by the second. There was a coffee table in the middle of the floor, with nothing on it but a bowl of fruit and a box of Kleenex; Jamie set his burden down there, carried the fruit away into the kitchen. I heard the banging of cupboard doors, and for a moment thought he was going to come back with a plate to stand the head on, like a trophy or a chef's excess, *specialité de la maison.*

Should have known him better; he came back with a plain white linen tablecloth. He knelt down, spread that out, then looked up at Jonathan.

"Jon, are you sure? Ben and me, this isn't so new to us, we've both seen hard things before; and we didn't know Charlie, either. You don't have to be macho, it's not a challenge you lose cred for if you don't look . . ."

"Show him to me," Jon said.

So Jamie showed him, showed us both, showed us all. He still tried to mask the moment, getting his body between it and us as he ripped the plastic away and lifted the head onto the spread white cloth. I guess it was the raw stump he didn't want to share, the hacked meat and scabby wet red look of it, the hard lumps of bone and trailing stringy sinews: no neat headsman's axe had done this, just some bastard butcher with a blunted blade.

Jamie tried not to let us see that and failed, very much the order of the day; he placed the head carefully, sickeningly upright on its severed neck, and it toppled instantly over to give us a great view of its underside. So ill-cut, it was never going to balance; Jamie half-reached to try again anyway, glanced at us, shrugged and left it lie.

What he did do instead, he did close Charlie's dulled eyes for us, and that was a blessing. Then he flipped a corner of the cloth over the ruin of the neck, and I wanted to pretend it looked like he was only sleeping, like we saw him only in head-shot with a sheet drawn up to his chin.

Couldn't do it, it was too obscene, just the head of him on the table there; and there were streaks of dried blood all over his pretty, battered face and in his hair and his skin was as pale as Jon's, near as pale as the cloth he lay on for want of all that blood. Never mind the absence of his body, he couldn't have looked anything but dead.

Jon snorted, sucking snot, fighting tears uselessly; but he came forward and knelt down beside Jamie, and reached with shaking hands guided by half-blind eyes to take a handful of Kleenex and wipe away what blood he could shift, not much, and then to fold the cloth quite neatly over and around all that we had of Charlie.

"He's mine," he said, aggressively for him. "Okay?"

Okay, fine; we weren't about to dispute possession. But, "What will you do?" I asked. I couldn't imagine. He couldn't keep it, nor could he turn up at the crem with a head and no body to ask for a short service. They didn't come that short, I thought, hating myself for thinking it.

"I'll take him to some friends," he said, wiping his own face now with another wad of tissues from the box. "We'll try to find out what they've done with the, with the rest of him. Got to be somewhere, hasn't it?"

"Jonathan, be careful." If Charlie had died for talking to us – and there was no 'if' about that, it was as plain as the nose on Jamie's face or mine, the bloody nose on his own – then anyone identifying themselves as a friend of Charlie's was running a terrible risk.

"I will. Don't worry, we'll move in a pack. We can look after ourselves," he said, with a glance at the bundle that was all regret, *we couldn't look after our own.* "Have you got something I can, you know, carry him in?"

Not a carrier bag was the subtext there, and we both got it instantaneously. Jamie went off to rummage; I would have offered my rucksack, still sitting where I'd dumped it in the corner under my jacket and helmet, where I'd left them all when I'd run out on Laura, but that didn't seem appropriate either.

Nothing did, nothing could; but Jamie came back with a choice, a smaller backpack that Laura used to carry her schoolbooks around in and a coolbox for beers.

"Either of these do?" he asked diffidently. "Best I can manage . . ."

Jon nodded, and took the backpack. He put the wrapped head into it carefully, gently, as tenderly as seemed appropriate; then he stood up, slipped his arms through the straps and said, "Uh, I'll be off, then . . ."

"Right. Go well, Jon . . ."

Jamie hugged him, and so did I. He left us, walking gingerly out of the room, as if what he carried was heavier far than it ought to be; we stood listening as he made his slow way down the stairs and out of the door, closing it quietly behind him.

Then, "What's next?" I asked helplessly.

"I don't know, bro. It's their move, I guess."

"Yeah, right." We'd made ours, and it had gone horribly, unimaginably wrong. "You going to call your dad?"

"I guess." He didn't go to the phone, though. I think he felt as I did, like a puppet with its strings cut, no movement left in either one of us. "It's a funny thing," he said, "Jon didn't even seem angry, he never said a word about the people who'd done that to Charlie."

"He's not family," I said wearily. Indeed he was the opposite of family, he was cattle in my family's lovely phrase; he'd lived all his life under our hard rule, he likely expected monstrous things to happen to him and his, without any hope of payback. Never mind that this time it had come from another player in the game, he simply wasn't tuned to look for retribution.

"Well. It's something else added to the account," Jamie grunted, taking Jon's debts to lie alongside our own.

"I suppose." Me, I felt much like Jon, suddenly; I wanted this to end. I'd do anything to see Laura and the others safe, but I was more sickened than vengeful. It seemed odd, but I realised that I really, really didn't want any more killing.

And couldn't say so, not to Jamie, not just then. His loss, his fear was greater far than my own, or more cruelly grounded; he had what I only yearned for, and my doubts and qualms didn't amount to even a can of beans against his need. Laura's danger cut at us both, but the knife in my guts was a phantom conjured of my own obsessive dreaming. He'd had years of living with her, where all I'd had was wanting; now she carried his child inside her; in him that knife twisted deeper with every moment.

Engulfed by twin horrors, what had been done to Charlie coupled with what was threatened against Laura, against Janice and our cousins, I didn't in any case see how we could get out of this without more killing. Especially given the Macallan temper, honed by generations of kicking the weak. Anyone dares to kick back, you just kick the harder. Instinct or training, nature or nurture, it was there, it was imprinted; look at Uncle James. Even better, look at my dad. Knowing what would follow, he still couldn't control himself, and so Josie had died; and they'd want their revenge for that, and how long they could deny themselves a rampage was anybody's guess.

So yes, I expected more killing; I was just deeply uncertain now that my family would actually come out on top at the end. Wasn't sure that I wanted them to, either, wasn't sure what I wanted. Just not heads on spikes, that's all. No

more heads, no more sacrifices. Innocent or guilty, no
more deaths . . .

And as with everything else I'd ever wanted, I thought I
was only pissing into the wind, I never for a moment thought
I'd get it.

If we'd had ideas, I don't think either one of us would have
mentioned them to the other. Ideas were dangerous, ideas had
brought us to this. As it was, though, I don't think either one
of us was in any danger of being that creative, to find any
way to make this worse. Myself certainly not, I was battered
and numbed and beaten, and Jamie seemed no better. My
best thought in that time was to change my clothes: to lose
the shorts at last, and get into tough denim to face a tough
world clad for thorns.

When the phone rang, it was salvation or doom for sure,
it had to be. What we were waiting for, though we maybe
hadn't known that we were waiting. Not a wrong number, not
a telesales girl with her eyes double glazed and her voice well
insulated. God, even God couldn't be so cruel. Could he?

The phone rang, and we looked at each other. Bleak,
afraid, uncertain of God, knowing only a heap of broken
promises: which of us was going to answer?

It seemed that we both were, though it was Jamie who
moved. He could reach the phone from where he was sitting;
he didn't lift the receiver, though, he just pressed a button on
the base unit. The ringing cut off, and a voice said, "Hullo,
who's that?"

"Jamie Macallan." He didn't raise his voice, or even turn
his head towards the phone.

"Is your cousin Benedict there with you?"

"Yes."

"Well, then." The voice was male, smooth, assured. Unfa-
miliar, in tone as much as personality; people didn't gen-
erally sound so sure of themselves, speaking to Macallans.

Even from the other end of a telephone line. "You know that we have your women; you will be pleased to know that they are still . . . together."

Something about that little pause made me very unhappy indeed. He didn't, I thought, mean that they were locked up together; he meant that neither one of them had been separated in the way that young Charlie had.

Yet, was what he really meant . . .

"We think," he said, "that it was you two who set that fire in the police station. You know, of course, that it was a waste of time; it is however proving very inconvenient for us, and we'd appreciate the chance to discuss it with you. In person."

You wouldn't want us to separate your women. He was too cool to say that explicitly, but he didn't need to. He wanted us, he could have us.

"Let the girls go," Jamie said. "Straight swap. Okay?"

The man just laughed. "You misunderstand me. This is not a marketplace. I do not intend to bargain. Break a finger."

For a moment, we simply didn't understand. Then we heard a high breathy gasp, a sudden scream, a sob cut off abruptly; then we understood, all too well.

"*Laura?*" That was Jamie, his voice jerking as every muscle in his body had jerked. Me, I couldn't have spoken. Just as I couldn't have told whether it was Laura or Janice had screamed, nor was I sure yet. Nor was he, I thought, in all honesty.

Nor did the man tell us, nor give us the chance to talk to her, to learn.

"Come down to the quayside," he said, "to the pathway under the old bridge. Come now."

And then the phone's speaker clicked and went silent, as he hung up.

Jamie did pick up the phone after a while, his big Macallan

hands like trembling, misshapen claws, awkward on the buttons. I thought he was calling Uncle James, but no: he only hit four numbers. He listened for a moment, his face twisted, he put the receiver down again.

"What?"

"Didn't say where he was calling from. Doesn't matter. Let's go."

No need to ask where we were going. I picked up my jacket as he collected his, and we were halfway down the stairs before I said, "Don't you want to call your dad, tell him what's happening?"

"No. He'd only tell us not to go."

True enough, he would. I might have told him anyway, but it was Jamie's call and he was likely right. Safer, perhaps, fractionally safer if Uncle James didn't know. He might do something stupid, that would endanger the girls more. If that were possible.

Down the hill one more time we went, back down to where we'd come from: past the station and down the curving run of steps that was the shortest way to the river, chasing our own long shadows while the sun played on our shoulders, prelude to a farewell. That didn't matter, I reminded myself, once the sun had gone I'd still have Jamie. Night-time was his time, moonlight and starshine. And that didn't matter either, I reminded myself more hastily on the back of that thought; we were both of us helpless here, regardless of the light. We'd tried to make ourselves the protagonists, but we were only pawns after all and we'd been pinned so easily, we couldn't move at all, we couldn't risk it . . .

So we came down to the quayside, not speaking, not making plans. We were only here for the one thing, to give ourselves over into deadly hands; and that didn't need planning, and what else was there to say? I had only one truth in my head, *I love Laura*, and I didn't think I had much interest in the future so I only kept one wish for that, *I hope the girls will be okay in the end, Laura and Janice and all of them*, though even so much seemed greedy and unlikely of fulfilment. And Jamie knew the first full well and must have been sharing the second; so no point at all to talking, better to save all our breath for walking, as fast as we could manage. *Come now*, the man had said, and he had not sounded flexible or patient.

Turn to the right, river on our left; above our heads the high bridges, road and rail, a long drop to the water. Ahead was the old bridge: not all so old in truth, its span was as Victorian as the others, an arch of steel, though being so much lower it was designed to swivel on its central pier to allow ships to pass through to the upper reaches of the river. The mechanism was broken now, or else simply redundant; I'd never seen it working.

The abutments on either bank, though, they were old stone, the bones of an earlier bridge lost in a great flood. The pathway ahead of us was cut straight through the stonework in a narrow tunnel, dark and dank; and yes, if you wanted to meet Macallans in safety, this was as good as a cellar or a cinema or any place shielded from natural light. Even the westering sun was blocked now by buildings or the high bank, throwing only shadows into the tunnel's further mouth so that it showed grey and dim, no spark of light or promise.

I could see no one waiting for us on this side, nor make out any figures within.

"Straight in, then?" Jamie said; and,

"Yes," I said. What else? We were doing what we'd been told to do, what we had to do; fear for the girls had brought us this far, fear for ourselves couldn't stop us now. Though we were afraid, and rightly. I couldn't speak for Jamie, he had other terrors to drive him, but I carried Charlie's head on my back as surely as Jon had, and its weight was as great to me or greater.

It wasn't even a trap or an ambush, we knew too well what we were doing here; we walked into that tunnel's darkness as hostages already. I wanted to hold his hand, for whatever cousinly comfort I could draw from him, but he went ahead of me and all I could do was follow.

It was cold in there, cold in high summer, as cold as any work of man that never let the sun in; and damp also, the walls running with water that pooled blackly beneath our feet. So used to the tingle that daylight gave it, my skin prickled now with shivers that were something utterly else, wrought of chill and a building panic I had to fight hard to contain.

We went in ten or fifteen paces, halfway through to the pale arch of light that marked the end; then Jamie stopped, and I stopped behind him. No point in going further. This was where we'd been told to come, and here we were.

We could I suppose have stood there looking at each other, at the faintly darker shadows that we made in that darkness. Our eyes would work eventually against the dimness, seize every stray particle of much-reflected light, till at last perhaps we would see each other's faces; but each would only be a reflection of the other, a thumb-smudge of fear and nothing more. I didn't want to see myself, or any semblance of me.

So we looked at each other no more than we looked back; only forward, trying to see more than a literal light at the end of the tunnel.

For five minutes, maybe ten, we were still and silent and scared, huddled into our jackets, into ourselves. Then abruptly there was more to see, there was a silhouette, a figure, a man walking slowly towards us. Light flared from his hand, dazed us, left us blinking at a burning after-image as it laid a bright path for his feet to walk upon; but that was nothing, only a torch, no use at all.

Noises behind us, footsteps, our shadows thrown distorted and dancing on the walls that closed us in so tightly; a glance over our shoulders showed us two men there with a torch each. They weren't coming any closer, only blocking the entrance; and besides, two of them and only one of him. No question which counted for more. We turned back to face the singleton, the cool one, the one still coming.

Torchlight from him, directed generously downwards, not to blind us; torchlight from them, spilling past us. It wasn't easy to fix anything for certain, the way the beams jerked and the shadows shifted, but at least we could see, of a sort.

We saw a man of middle height and middle years, smartly dressed, dark suit and tie. His hair was combed, his expression almost benign. I didn't know him, except that I would have laid money that he'd been the voice on the phone and was also very much the man in charge, here and elsewhere. Jamie, I knew, wanted to kill him and couldn't; I wanted the killing to stop, but if you'd pressed me I thought I might have made an exception in his case.

When he was two, three metres away he stopped, gazed at us, smiled slightly unless that was the way his mouth fell naturally; then he lifted the hand that didn't hold the torch. It held something else, a dark plastic tube that fitted comfortably into his palm. Looked something like an asthma inhaler, only it seemed to me he was holding it upside down, nozzle at the top.

"*Carpe diem*," he said, and yes, he was definitely smiling, he was enjoying this.

"What?" I didn't understand, didn't particularly want to; the question was automatic, the voice it found was hoarse and strained.

"cs the day," he said, and did.

He pressed or squeezed the top of his little tube; and not a fine spray to keep asthmatics breathing, no, what came was a lance in the light, a jet of liquid speared at our eyes, Jamie's and then mine. I had time to close them but no more, my shielding hands were far too late.

First a prickling on my eyelids, on all the skin of my face and then my palms, where the liquid ran; then an acid burning, I thought my skin was being etched to rags and slime; and then pain such as I had never felt before, had only ever seen in other cousins' dreadful deaths under my Uncle Allan's culling ministrations. I heard Jamie moan and sob beside me, his shoulder pressed against mine and I shared his agony as he shared mine. We both of us dropped down onto the wet floor of the tunnel, crouching and rolling, gasping, not breath enough to scream with and every breath making it infinitely worse as the stuff was sucked inside to set our throats and lungs aflame; and dimly, distantly I heard the man laugh. Heard him say, "They'll do now, lads. Come on, nothing to be afraid of here."

Rough hands on us, grabbing our own hands that were already pulling away from our faces, too scared to rub for fear they'd rub the pain deeper, or else rub flesh from bone. Pulling them behind our backs with no resistance from us, shackling them with handcuffs; and then those hands in our armpits pulling us up again, forcing us to stand against the wall. Hoods of cloth being dropped over our heads, and even the light weight of them making the burning worse wherever they touched. Then we were turned and pushed into walking, hands gripping our arms to guide us; and we were taken out of the tunnel and eventually into sunlight, I felt it warm on my agonised fingers and was hurting too badly to use it even if I'd dared.

At last my shins banged against something hard and sharp, a voice close by my ear said, "Up," and I fumbled my foot onto a step. My other found a floor above it, my head cracked against a low roof, the man who held me laughed and shoved me into shadow, out of the sun. I banged into a wall of metal and slid down it, thought vaguely that I was in a van; felt

Jamie come in behind me, felt him trip over my feet and fall; heard the doors slammed and locked behind us, and then thought only of the cruel, crippling pain that was eating at my weeping eyes, thought I was blinded, thought I'd never see Laura or Janice or anyone, anything ever again.

It was a long time even before I thought or remembered that it really didn't matter, that pain from these people's hands was only a prelude to death, that I couldn't seriously expect to survive this.

Slowly, slowly the worst of the pain ebbed away as we drove quickly, quickly through the streets. It wasn't like a tide retreating, so much as lava cooling: less fierce, but still very much there. Bubbled and blackened my skin must be after that chemical washing, hideously scarred. For what short time I got to go on wearing it . . .

At first I was only aware of our speed in that it threw me around the van somewhat, rocked me and rolled me, banged my face against the walls and made me use my hands as best I could: made things worse, in other words, made the fire flare up with every hard contact.

But then things didn't hurt so much, and I was still being tossed and turned; and *still going fast*, I thought as I scrabbled and slid. No sound of siren overhead, though; if this was a police van, they weren't using their best toy. Likely it wasn't, though. Why draw attention? Probably just one more scruffy van with dodgy lights and a dodgy MOT, being driven by some dodgy freak with a heavy right foot. The only way anyone would notice would be if it didn't run the lights at amber, if it didn't rev hard at every junction, if it didn't blast its horn at any delay.

Fetching up in a corner, I wedged myself there as best I could, with my feet on the wheel-arch and my back against the door. Shortly after there was a soft thump of bone against my shoulder, and that was Jamie, searching or slipping I couldn't tell, but finding me none the less. He pressed up against me, and we shared that corner and wedged each other for company.

Eventually the van slowed, almost to a crawl it felt like, though it was hard to tell speed with no visuals to mark it off against. First gear it was in, at any rate, we could hear that; hear the horn too, blasting and blasting. *Traffic jam*, I thought, and *still keeping in character, acting like a dickhead . . .*

But then the engine cut, we went from crawl to stillness to silence to other sounds, the banging of doors while the van shifted beneath us, rising on its suspension as it lost all its passengers but us.

Still they left us a long time in our own private darknesses, in the darkness of the van. My face and hands still felt cruelly tender to the touch – not that I would have dared touch even if my hands had been free for it, but the hood touched my brow and cheeks and nose and the metal door unkindly touched my hands behind my back – but nothing was actually hurting any more, by the time the doors jerked and opened, and I nearly toppled straight out.

Saved myself with an effort of back and stomach that nearly gave me a rupture; and I needn't have bothered anyway, because someone grabbed my shoulders and pulled me backwards, and I did topple out.

It wasn't a long fall, only two or three feet, but blind and tied it was a paralysing shock, and the ground when it hit me hit me hard.

Jamie landed half on top of me half a second later, and I hope he was grateful for the cushioning.

They dragged him off, hauled me up and propelled us as before, grip and shove and steer from the rear. We couldn't go cautious, we weren't allowed; my mind juddered at every hurried, awkward step, expecting door or wall or staircase any moment, meeting none of them.

The ground changed, from gravel to wood; I lost another brief, useless tingle of sunlight; I figured we'd come from outside in.

Inside what I couldn't try to guess, I wasn't even certain I was right. At first our footsteps sounded hollow, like walking on a bridge except louder, echoing, contained. And then there was a doorway, a narrow one, I banged both shoulders as they pushed me through; and on the other side of that it was like the boards were laid on concrete, there was no noise and no resilience. Only it couldn't be concrete because the floor was uneven suddenly, rising and falling unexpectedly, illogically . . .

A little of that and then they pulled us to a halt, they held us still; directly in front of me I heard metallic sounds: keys in locks, clatter of hasps, squeak of hinges. Wooden thud, as of door banged back against wall.

"This going to hold them, then?" a voice asked, male, heavy, anxious. "Straight up?"

"Safe as houses," my own guide and tormentor assured him. "Look at it, what are they going to do in there? Besides, we've got their girls. A piece of fucking string would hold them. They came, didn't they? They're being good boys."

And then unexpectedly I got a vicious kick in the solar plexus, and a rabbit-punch in the kidneys as I doubled over. Wrapped in another kind of pain, learning a lot here, I was only vaguely conscious of it as they stripped everything out of my pockets and then unlocked the cuffs, stripped the watch off my wrist and hauled me up onto my feet again; I was only starting to recover when a sudden shove in the back thrust me forward. I went through another doorway blindly staggering, then slipping on wet stone and falling and cracking my head on a wall as I fell so that I wasn't really conscious at all when they threw Jamie on top of me. Again.

*   *   *

If I was really out, though, it can't have been for long. Mostly I just lay there feeling damp and dizzy and bright-headed, watching sparks fly in my skull and not trying to figure it out at all, neither what made the sparks fly nor what was the weight across my back that was making breathing so hard a thing to do.

Until the weight moved, until it rolled off to lie beside me and groan. Groaning made connections in my reeling head, groaning made sense. I groaned myself. And then I had it figured, that the lights in my skull weren't fireworks, they were damage; and I was damp because I was lying in a puddle; and the weight had been Jamie, and he sounded pretty much as damaged as I was except that he'd had a softer, dryer landing and might not have caught his head such a crack.

Jamie's job to be the tough one, then, up to Jamie to get us sorted. I waited for him to move, and marked him as he did: as he pushed himself up onto his elbows and then his arse, as he fumbled with the hood over his head, as he pulled it off and sat there for a minute, gulping air.

Funny, I could almost see him in my mind. My eyes were useless, my ears were muffled by my own hood, but still I knew every move he made. Hearing and touch, both amplified by this stretching darkness, perhaps; general closeness of body and spirit both, twenty-five years of being his bro; I don't know what exactly was giving me what I had, but I took it as a gift.

I even knew just what he was doing as he lifted tender, trembling fingers to his cheeks and eyes, trying to find how much of his face was gone; and I heard, felt, knew his surprise when he found flesh and skin unscarred, eyelids and eyelashes and his eyes unmelted behind them. Shared his rush of relief, begrudged him not a moment of his momentary slumping then, before he remembered me.

His hands on my body, gently helping me up, resting me

against what felt like a wall of rock, jagged and unaccommodating; his hands on my head, lifting off the hood and throwing it aside.

His hands invisible to me even now, everything was black still though the cloth was gone.

"It's all right, Ben," he murmured, his fingertips like feathers against my face, touching to reassure us both. His touch tingled, but little more than that. No pain now, nothing to measure against what had gone before; I thought maybe I would never feel pain again, now that I knew what true pain felt like. "Look, you're fine, we both are."

I couldn't look, and I didn't feel fine; I breathed deeply as he had, though the cold air bit at my nose and the back of my throat, and tried my voice to see if I still had one. "What was that?"

"CS gas, I guess. The police have had it for a year or two. Though, I dunno, no one ever said it was that bad. I don't think it can be, the everyday stuff they carry on the streets. I reckon this was something extra. The four-star de luxe variety they keep for special occasions. But it just goes for the nerves, hurts like shit but it doesn't leave a mark . . ."

"So how come I can't see, then?" I demanded fretfully.

"Because there isn't any light in here, moron."

Oh. "Where are we?"

"Somewhere dark. Moron." And then he kissed me on the cheek; and then he swore, and spat, and dragged the back of his hand across his mouth and swore again.

"Christ! Don't suck your thumb, Ben. Burns like fuck still . . ."

Like chilli-juice, I guessed, it hung around longer than you'd think. *Don't rub your eyes, Ben.*

So I didn't, though my hands were itching to. My hands were itching anyway, but it wasn't all chemical reaction. I wanted to touch and press and worry at all the bits that had

hurt most, to find where the pain was hiding; I wanted to see
if squeezing my eyeballs would make them work better, or at
all. Not sensible, but instinct doesn't operate from a platform
of sense, in any meaning.

I wanted to probe my skull as well where it was aching,
to find out if it was bleeding also; but I thought about
CS-residues in an open wound and didn't want to find out
how that felt. So I just took Jamie's word for it that the flesh
wasn't running off my face, and sat on my hands to stop their
wandering independent of my brain.

"Okay," I said, softly, slowly, letting my lungs and voice-
box take their time over the words and the breath needed to
power them. "Where do you think we are?"

"Haven't a clue. Hang on, don't you move . . ."

Took him a little while to get moving himself, but I sat
virtuously still and patient, no hurry anywhere in my soul,
and when he did finally push himself to his feet I tracked him
around our cell with ears and sensitised skin, feeling almost
that I walked the walls with him.

It wasn't a long walk. He went off to my right and came
back to my left, feeling his way; the only moment of interest
in that brief peregrination was when his foot kicked against
something that clanged and rolled.

"What was that?"

He stooped, groped for it, said, "Bucket." I heard him set
it upright, and then he added, "Honey-bucket, I guess."

"Sweet."

"Yeah. Still, better than not having one."

He went on, came back, slid down the wall to sit beside
me, his leg and shoulder touching mine. And said, "The wall
with the door is all wood, the rest is rock. Floor, walls and
ceiling. Any ideas?"

"No."

"Me neither." We both dwelt on that, and then he added,
"Did you know, the Eskimos empty out their honey-buckets

for the huskies to eat? Lots of protein still, in human shit."

"I told you that, bro. Got it out of a book. But you're supposed to call them Inuit, these days."

"Not in any book I ever read."

"You never read books."

"Don't you start, I get enough of that from Laura," and I could hear the grin in his voice and somehow managed to match it for a moment, before the enormity of the situation rose up to swamp my courage. Be bloody lucky if either of us ever saw Laura again. Lucky if we ever saw anything again, except perhaps the man who came to kill us . . .

"What about that door, then, think we could batter our way out? With the bucket, maybe?" Before we filled it . . .

"Doubt it. Feels rock-solid. Have a go, though?"

"Sure . . ."

I think we both knew it was futile, waste of effort; but hell, we had nothing else to do. He went first, banging and clattering, making noise just a couple of metres from me; his energy gave me the will to move, and I crawled slowly and methodically across the uneven floor, doing my best impression of a fingertip search and coming up with absolutely nothing. Wherever this was, whatever it was for, there was nix, *nada, rien* to be found inside it except the two of us and our bucket.

Our bent bucket, as I discovered when at last I stood up, found him, took it from him. I found the door also, and the few gouges he'd made in it with the bucket's base; I added a few more for form's sake, then desisted before our only tool, our toilet was buckled beyond possibility of use.

Jamie was sitting down again; I joined him again, pressing close, temporarily warm from the exercise but conscious of the extreme cold of our prison, walls and floor and all. If we were kept in here any length of time, it was going to be no fun.

If we were kept in here any length of time it would be a miracle, something I was well past hoping for . . .

"I've measured it from side to side," I said, "'tis three of me long and two of me wide," on a giggle that was only a little hysterical. Actually, I was suddenly on the up again, oddly cheerful; it seemed my courage could be swamped but not sunk, it would rise regardless. Stupid, but welcome. And I'd always said, I'd always known that despite everything, if I had to face death I'd sooner do it with family at my side; and barring Laura – and that after all was the point of this, to bar Laura from any closer acquaintance with death – then Jamie was as he had always been, closest and best of family. For Laura's sake, perhaps I should have protected him also or tried to, given myself up alone; but if you can't be selfish when you're dying, even, what the hell is the point of it all? And I was sorry to be hurting her by taking him with me, but gladder to have him there at the end. Presumptive end. Not much we could do, but the baddies might yet cock this up. Though they'd shown precious little tendency to error, thus far . . .

"Unh?" said Jamie.

"Wordsworth. Early. Forgivable, some say; but I say he was older than us, he should've known better. We would've known better. Wouldn't we?"

"Ben . . . How's your head?"

"Sore." I sighed, against his shoulder. "All right. You did the walls, I've done the floor. Inch by inch."

"What did you find?"

"Naught for your comfort."

"*Ben . . .*"

"All right. There ain't nobody here but us chickens, and that there tin pail. They haven't left us a hairgrip, even, to pick the lock with. Not that you'd expect to find a hairgrip, I guess, in a cave, but . . ."

I'd only been rambling for my own amusement, maybe a

little for his; but suddenly I was listening to myself, and this wasn't funny any more.

"Jamie, we're in a cave!"

"I know that. I *told* you that."

"Yes, but how many caves are there? In a, what, twenty-minute drive? Half an hour, max?" Hard to tell, in our pain and isolation from the world, but it certainly hadn't been a long drive. Not long enough to take us out of the area we knew so intimately well.

"A few," he said slowly.

"Caves that have been blocked off like this, turned into storerooms? They didn't put that wall up for us, it's been there years."

"Okay," he said. "We're on the Island. So what? It doesn't change anything."

In the immediate external situation, us locked in and helpless, no, it didn't; but my internal landscape had shifted massively. Knowledge is power; I hated being in the dark.

Closed my eyes, to forget how much I literally was in the dark, and sorted this through in my head. The police weren't acting alone, they might be prime movers but there was a genuine conspiracy here, and the family that owned the Island must be major players also. They'd needed somewhere to hold us, that was dark and safe and private; so they'd cleared out a storeroom, a converted cave somewhere behind the bright tawdry face of the attractions. Nothing darker, nothing safer than a cave with no windows and one strong door. Nowhere more private, either. Just a few metres away, no further than a good shout, there must be hundreds of people milling; but no point in shouting, they'd never hear.

So. This place had been specifically chosen, prepared for us, swept clean; but when they'd moved the girls out of the police station, they hadn't had the same kind of notice. Would they have brought them here also? If we tunnelled – if we had a jackhammer, for example, and a compressor

to power it and a generator to power that, and a good flow
of air to keep us from choking ourselves to death and plenty
of time above all, and endless strength and patience – maybe
we'd come to another cave and find them, and tunnel on to
safety, maybe . . .

But maybe there wasn't another, or it wouldn't have
been ready for them; maybe they'd have been locked into
a building somewhere, there were always attractions closing
down, going bust or running foul of health and safety regs.
Maybe someone would have seen half a dozen women being
herded against their will, maybe the rumour would reach
Uncle James, maybe we might have done some good after
all. Sure, our own lives would be forfeit if he mounted a
rescue bid for the other hostages, but that was so anyway,
I thought we were already forfeited past redemption; and
my life for theirs, mine and Jamie's both, that was a trade
I'd make without hesitation.

And maybe I was grasping at straws here, but they'd left
us precious little else to grasp at, bar each other.

We did that too, the long dreary bitter time that we were in
there. We hugged one another literally for warmth, metaphorically for reassurance. Even those periods where one of
us would get a desperate rush on and have to walk it off – up
and down, seven paces each way and don't knock your head
where the roof sinks at the back there – while the other only
wanted to sit in semi-transcendent stillness, closest either
of us had ever come to an isolation tank, there was still
a mental hug going on. Better than two minds tracking as
one, closer and more sharing, halfway to the telepathic link
I'd shared with my late lamented sister and infinitely more
comfortable, that I think was what kept us rooted to the
world. If they'd split us up, if they'd had two handy caves
to store us separately, God knows how either one of us would
have coped. It was hard enough in any case: we might both

jabber and grin, but there was a terrible tension underlying all, and a looming terror held back by thin, thin walls.

We talked a lot, jabber-and-grin nonsense and easy nostalgia, telling old stories and old lies, nudging each other's memories, branching into fantasy on a sudden whim. Our throats grew sore and our voices husky, an impossible drink of water became the thing we yearned for most, though we quickly put a ban on saying so; we both used the bucket when we had to, and something else I put my own private ban on was even a mention that Pandit Nehru used to drink a glass of his own urine first thing every morning.

Time passed, we had to assume that, though we had no way of checking. We even dozed a little, though seldom at the same time, at intervals between the talking and the pacing and the mental drift. We couldn't keep from speculating, was it still the middle of the night or had we talked and slept, paced and drifted enough, was it morning yet? And if so was this a good thing, a sunrise devoutly to be wished, or were we better trying to hold it back, hoping we weren't there yet, did dawn spell dawning disaster?

Something else I learned, as we slowly ran out of things to say: it would never have occurred to me until I'd lived it, but life on death row can be deadly, infinitely boring.

It had to come at last, of course, and we'd been waiting long enough or far too long, but still neither one of us was ready when it did come. Maybe no one ever is ready, or ever ought to be. Maybe that's the unforgivable sin, to be prepared for an inevitable but useless death . . .

It announced itself with the faintest possible murmur of voices through the wall, that we only heard or thought we heard because both of us had sunk at last into a dreadful, snaring silence; it confirmed its arrival with a clattering of metal against the wooden door, and then a pause, and then great wrenching, tugging sounds that shook the wall and us where we were leaning on it, finding it warmer than the rock if only barely.

We jerked to our feet and backed away, seven paces and an automatic stop; his hand found mine and I was wired so tight I couldn't even find the space to feel grateful.

The door banged open, there was a fierce glare of light that all but blinded us after so long in the dark, we had to squint to see; and what we saw was a figure, a silhouette framed and shaped by light, tall and black and terrifying, doom made flesh . . .

Until a voice said, "*Ben . . . ?*"

The voice was female, young, bewildered and exultant both; faintly accented and surely familiar, but I didn't have time to grope for any understanding before she'd run those seven paces in three strides and grabbed me, the momentum of her pushing me back one extra lethal step so that my head did crack against the cave's roof and my skull sang once more with a dance of light.

"Oh, God. I'm sorry . . ." Her hand rubbed my head, but she was laughing against my neck as she did it; and then she said, "But what the hell are you two doing here, anyway?"

"Being rescued, I think," Jamie said quietly beside me. It was his hands that drew us apart, his eyes and mind that were seeing clear enough to name her. "Janice, what's happened?"

"Uh. We, we found a way out, and we were trying to get away only there were these, these blokes, they would have seen us and they had guns, so . . ."

Her turn to slip into silence, as a heavy metal bar slipped from her hand and clattered to the ground, barking my ankle *en passant*. I looked down at it, she looked down at it, I don't know what she saw but I saw how the end of it was darkly wet, staining the rock.

I didn't ask what had happened to the blokes, I thought I

knew. Thought I knew how she was feeling, also. This time it was me who reached to hold her, she who didn't resist. Jamie was twitching, skittering behind her shoulder, only one thing on his mind but afraid to ask for it, just in case. He was my bro; I did it for him.

"Janice, Jan – where's Laura?"

"Outside," she said, and her eyes gestured towards the door. It was easier to look that way now, our eyes were adjusting and besides there was a small crowd of people clustered there, cutting down the shine. I could still see more shadow than skin, but they were all women, that I was sure of, and all kin also. Even at this distance, even with women in indirect daylight, there were enough of them close enough together to raise a bit of a buzz.

No Laura there: but not my job to enquire further, certainly not my job to go and find her. Jamie was gone already, pushing, almost elbowing through the press of pale family that stood between him and his beloved.

Also between me and mine, of course; but I stood there noble and self-sacrificial in my own mind at least, watching him go, letting him go, trying to let them both go; and I held on to Janice for comfort, for a substitute, for the most ignoble reasons I could imagine. If she knew, if she understood or guessed, if she saw where my eyes had gone and figured my mind was gone with them, she didn't seem to mind.

And she was doing pretty well, actually, at the substitution business. My attention wasn't long gone, my imagination was only briefly focused on Jamie and Laura before she called it back to the here and now, to her. She leaned into me, a long slim body of contrasts: whippy and hard but soft and yielding also, so many textures contained under not very much acreage of skin; trembling where I touched her but her own hands gripping tight and strong, both bringing and seeking reassurance, *it's okay now, tell me it's okay* . . . She smelled sour and her skin was greasy, a long day and a night of fear not washed away; but also she smelled as she had the night before, warmly female, smoky, all the scents of promise and welcome.

And then she lifted her head a little, only a little, nice I thought that she didn't have to stretch to kiss me; and I could tell how long it was since she'd had a cigarette, the tobacco-taste was stale and fading, and I thought, *Bastards, they didn't have to take her baccy . . .*

And giggled into the kiss, almost choking on it, weariness and relief combining to bring me to that bubble-touch of hysteria again. She pulled away, staring at me. "What?"

"Nothing, nothing." I drew her back, just to hold this time because it felt good just to hold, when I'd thought never again to hold anyone but Jamie, and him not for long at all. "So tell us, then, how come you busted in here? You weren't looking for us . . ."

"No. We didn't know they'd got you. How did they get you?"

"Later." *We gave ourselves up because they'd got you* – romantic, perhaps, but not heroic. The girls were the heroes here. "You first."

"They were scared," she said slowly, picking up the story just after the bit she didn't want to think about, "and I was curious. They said there might be more men, they wanted to get out of sight, so they crowded into the big room outside. I thought that was stupid, we either got away or gave ourselves up again, but I did want to know how come they'd left us unwatched but they still had two men guarding this place. With rifles. So I left them jabbering in a corner," and she was trying to control it for my sake but oh, she was undisguisably contemptuous of my relatives, and would never know how sweet that was to hear, "and I bust open the door to see what was inside. That's all. I think I was hoping for more guns or something, though God knows why. We couldn't really have a shoot-out, not with this crew . . ."

"No." Laura would chance it, and I thought probably one of my cousins also; but the others not, they'd be useless.

"Your turn now," she said, but I shook my head.

"Not yet. They left you unguarded, you said, but you must've been locked in," and stripped of anything useful as I had been, keys and penknives, purses, credit cards. "You found a way out, you said, but how?"

"Oh." She smiled slightly, a touch of happy memory, what I'd been working for. Pleased with herself, she was; very pleased she would be later, when the rest had a little faded and this shone out. "They had us in the cells to start with, yeah? I just asked the wrong guy the wrong question, I suppose. I never thought the police might be involved . . . They locked us up with the others, me and Laura. But then they took us out of there in a hurry, brought us here and just shoved us into this arcade, it must have been the first place they could think of. They barred the doors on us and there weren't any windows, of course, those places, it was like being locked into a safe. But all the lights were on and the machines were running, there were dumpers in the ashtrays, they'd only just cleared the people out before we came, it was that sudden. All I really wanted to do was smoke those dumpers right down to the filter, I was desperate for a fag; but no one had a light, they'd taken everything off us. So I was going round almost on my hands and knees, looking for a live match someone might have dropped; and the other thing I did, every slot machine I came to, I dipped my hand into the tray. Well, I do, I'm Scottish, yes? And I found a quid, you almost always do. Stuck it in my jeans and forgot it, and went on looking for a light.

"But when they moved us, after the Island had closed up for the night, they put us in some kind of breezeblock office over the way. And it had windows, little ones with these big metal bars over them," glancing down at her big metal bar with its speaking stain on it, "but the bars were on the inside, our side, and they were bolted into the walls, and the bolts had these great big screw heads on them, and the pound fitted the slot? So me and one of the others, Serena, we took turns all night and half the morning, and we got two bars off in the end. And then we broke the window, and nobody came; so I slithered out and had a look, and there weren't any guards, so I jemmied the door open and let the others out. And then . . ."

And then she faltered, but I knew the rest. A couple of guards, a couple of girls with iron bars and desperation on their side.

"Show me," I said; and she thought I meant the quid, she dug it out and showed me a buckled, scarred piece of shrapnel the Queen would not have recognised as coin of her realm. But I took her hands and turned them, and saw the damage to her nails and fingertips and knuckles; and just as I was wincing in sympathy with that, I couldn't help it, I remembered *break a finger* and a girl's scream. Janice's fingers weren't in prime condition, but none of them was broken. And she hadn't mentioned Laura in her list of martyr-heroines, and Laura wasn't the girl to sit idly by and let others work her rescue for her . . .

Janice gasped, and I realised just how tightly I was squeezing her poor hurt hands.

"Shit, sorry," I muttered, blushing for other reasons entirely. "Come on, can we get out of here now?"

"Mm," she said, eyeing me thoughtfully and then leading me by the hand, not allowing me to let go. "You'll want to see Laura, see how she is . . ."

TEN

BEN BEHAVING MADLY

How Laura was, was busy. Focused.

And distressed, and in pain, and anxious, and infinitely relieved; and dealing with all of those by stepping aside from them, leaving them lie for later. Focusing hard.

Not quite hard enough, I thought; Jamie was beside her and just a little behind – where I thought he'd been told to stand: *don't get in my light*, I thought she'd said, or something like it – and she couldn't forget, couldn't ignore him, couldn't focus him out. Kept turning her head to check before she turned back, focused in.

What she was focusing on, of course – this was after all Laura, medic Laura, wannabe doc and mother-to-be Laura, little-friend-of-all-the-world Laura who disapproved of any pain on principle, except perhaps my own – what she was kneeling over was the fallen body of our foe. One of our foes. Not the man who made puns in tunnels, just a heavy: who looked particularly heavy now, sprawled face-down in the dust and sand and garbage that covered the road. Who looked dead indeed, his flesh slumping flaccidly on its cage of bone and his head seeming bent out of true at the back, a mess of hair and blood and I thought broken bone.

Give it up, Laura, I wanted to tell her, *let his ghost go*.

She was groping awkwardly one-handed, left-handed –
she who was so determinedly dextrous – for any pulse she
could find at his wrist or at his neck, and then and not for
the first time feeling with already-blooded fingers at the soft
giving spot on his skull which shouldn't have given so much
even when he was a baby.

At last she did give it up. She twisted her head aside and
tried to stand, pushing at the ground with her one hand while
she kept the other cradled against her stomach; and couldn't
do it, and reached instead up and behind, for Jamie's instant
aid. He helped her to her feet, turned her gently towards him,
wrapped his arms around her and kissed her mucky hair. Not
enough, I thought, he couldn't kiss away her failure; but then
Janice at my side made a sound, a soft and guilty choke in
her throat, and it was my turn to focus, to hold and hug and
try to give impossible comfort.

I thought vaguely that there was an irony here, I who had
wanted no more killing seeking to succour someone who had
just killed for the first and worst time, even though she'd had
better reason for it than ever I'd had; but she didn't give me
time or space to pursue the thought, burrowing her face into
my neck, demanding the attention of more than my body.
Her shoulders shook under my hands, I felt her tears trickle
down under the collar of my shirt, and I did what little I
could, working my fingers into tense muscles, pressing my
cheek against her hair and murmuring platitudes, "It's all
right, Jan, it's okay, you did what you had to, it was just
self-defence," and really, really didn't want to lift my head
even for a moment, to spy on my coz where he was doing
much the same thing for his beloved, my beloved Laura.

There were questions and more than questions, there were
urgencies clamouring at the fringes of my mind, beating
dark wings at my windows; but they had no more impact
than a butterfly's wings. If they were stirring up a storm it

would come later, I could deal with it later. Right now it was easy just to turn right in on Jan, engulf her the best I could, be her shell against the world for a while.

And so I was, till she chose to open us up: and that came only after she'd sniffed, snorted, knocked her forehead meaningfully against my ear for whatever meaning I could extract from that, shuffled a few inches over to rub her face dry against my other shoulder and then glanced up and taken another kiss from me, that I was by no means loth to give her.

"You know, it's a funny thing," she said, eye to eye with me, nose to nose, other eye to other eye and holding my head tipped down at the requisite angle with both hands dug well into my hair, "I've been shut up with four of your relatives for the best part of a day and a night, and that just made me feel queasy and ill; and now here I am with you, and whatever it is it's much stronger with you, you're absolutely crackling, and it makes me feel better. How is that?"

The question startled me, more ways than one. Macallan women didn't usually upset anyone very much, even *en masse*. Maybe Janice was hypersensitive to whatever it was, the aura, the disturbance in the ether that hung about us like a curse, like a blessing, actually only another fact of life to be endured or enjoyed in whatever measures came along. *Maybe she's been hypersensitised*, a dry thought whispered in the back of my head. Maybe too-close exposure could do that to a girl, maybe the friction of mucous membranes could leave her with more than one legacy to remember a Macallan man by. I'd have to ask my mother. Or Laura, of course, I could ask Laura, she should know . . .

But Janice wanted me answering her question, not sliding off into a private and tedious morbidity. She gave my head a wee shake, to remind me; and, "Patterns of interference," I said, traditionally. "Pack a lot of us together and everyone's out of synch, everything clashes. Like an orchestra where no one's in tune with any of their neighbours, yes? Get one of us solo, especially a bloke, and it's just a buzz on a single frequency. Like a TENS machine, some people kind of like it. Gets louder in the light, too. Like now," for me, I could feel myself crackling as she'd said; and I was pleased that it helped her, because it made me feel wonderful.

"Hmm," she said, as if she wasn't entirely persuaded or satisfied by that bog-standard answer. But she didn't chase it any further, or not just then. She turned to face the road and so did I, though I was very aware of her also: how her eyes were drawn back instantly to that still, abandoned weight of flesh that lay in the dust, that had been a man before she changed it, made it what it was.

She gazed at it, and I felt the shiver of it in her yet; but then she turned her head firmly away to find Laura, nothing morbid in her, and I thought *good, great, you're going to be okay, girl* . . .

Which was actually not a surprise, I'd have been surprised if she'd been anything other than okay, ultimately.

Laura also was looking better than she had, much improved by my cousin's closeness; but though she still held his with her left, her right hand she still held painfully pressed against her.

Was I following Janice across the road towards them, or was I leading her? And which would it look like, and did it matter to anyone except me? No time to figure out an answer, any answers; here we were.

Janice detached herself from me, where I hadn't actually noticed that we were still attached. I noticed the loss of her, though, and so it seemed did Jamie, I saw his eyebrows twitch; but that was peripheral, I was watching the girls.

Janice touched Laura lightly, carefully on the shoulder, like a message, *thanks for trying, sweetheart, and I'm sorry I didn't leave you the chance to do better*. Laura gave her a fragile smile in return, and then passed it on to me.

"Ben, how are you, did they give you a hard time?" *This bastard won't tell me*, her eyes were saying, and her fit hand squeezing his.

How was I? I was hungry, murderously thirsty, exhausted and still shaky with reprieve; but, "No, I'm fine," I said, not to betray whatever lying reassurance Jamie had been giving her. Besides, it was true, I felt terrific in despite of all my troubles; and in any case they seemed trivial, they were trivial next to what she'd been through. I'd heard her pain down the phone, and that had been bad enough. Not a random victim, worse than random: her suffering had been for us, in place of us, as a demonstration to us, which had made it weigh in any case far more grievously on us than our own hurts did. And now it wasn't digits coming down the line, or pictures in my head. Now I was seeing it, seeing the lines of it drawn on her face and in every angle of her body; seeing the cause of it on her hand there, where her two middle fingers were bound together with strips of cloth, the one doing its best to splint the other; seeing it and being weak as ever, thinking *I can't stand this*, wanting to run away.

Responsibility always takes me that way. I want to get right out of its reach, where no one can point a finger and say 'Guilty, guilty . . .'

Wanted to run and couldn't run, not until we all ran together; so I did the next best chicken thing. Just the one moment of staring, what I had done to Laura – or the latest thing that I had done to Laura, perhaps, I couldn't claim to be innocent or uninvolved in other minor matters: like Jamie, her pregnancy, everything that was her life now I had brought to pass, and none of it my intent and most of it far, so far from my desire – just long enough of looking to brand it forever in my memory, and then I closed my eyes.

And saw it still, burning, ineradicable, that long slender

hand with the crude cloth splint; and under the cloth I thought I could see the flesh of her, swollen and torn and tender, and inside that misshapen flesh there was the bone and I thought I could see that too, snapped cruelly against the joint . . .

Yeah, sure, Ben. Since when have your eyes had x-ray vision?

Well, since the afternoon of the previous day, sort of. Potentially for years, perhaps, since I'd learned what to do, begun to learn how much I could do with sunlight . . .

Not serious, I wasn't being serious. Nothing healthy, nothing positive ever came from any kind of talent. But . . .

But I had done that, seen through concrete with my mind's eye and found the bloodbeat of power, the throb of the building's circulation within it . . .

Electricity, Ben, not blood. Cables, not broken bones and tendons.

But I had been brutally beaten up by my father just a few days ago, and the following morning I'd lain in bed in sunlight and felt so much better so quickly; and had told myself it was coincidence or the cat that worked the magic, or truly that I hadn't been so much hurt after all, nothing more to it than that . . .

And neither there was. Who did the x-rays that time, who told you about the broken ribs?

I hadn't needed telling, I'd felt them, damn it, tried to breathe inside them . . .

Yeah yeah, sure. And how many times have you been dying from heart attacks or strokes, how many times has a cough been pneumonia or worse, when did you stop believing that those flickery spots in front of your eyes sometimes are the first symptom of a brain tumour?

Well, all right. I exaggerate sometimes, privately; I live with more interior foolishness than I'm prepared to admit to my friends. But mostly those times I know I'm being foolish.

And I could remember vividly the pain, the vivid pain of my ribs and I thought that had not just been bruising; and what cuts and bruises I'd shown had gone so fast, too fast. Though I'd performed no mental x-rays, no deliberate bone-knitting operations on myself, I thought that maybe sunlight could work that magic on its own, on or inside my own body; where maybe for anyone else it needed direction from me, it needed intent and positive, affirmative action.

Or maybe I was dreaming here, pissing into the wind once more, half-delirious after a long time of terror in the dark, hungry and crazy-thirsty and pushed somewhere beyond rationality. Loco, cuckoo, seeing things . . .

But I could see those things, so long as I kept my eyes shut, and seeing is pretty much believing. I could see Laura's hand shift out of focus, out of view almost, and I could figure quickly what was happening, that she was twisting or being drawn into Jamie again, into the comforting shelter of his body against the world's hard winds. Didn't even need to open my eyes to find her; hell, I could find Laura in a cellar in a blackout, just by inbuilt private radar; or I liked to think that I could, or I needed to believe it. I just reached out and gripped her shoulders, where I knew her shoulders had to be, without lifting my blinded eyes to see them; reached and gripped and turned her back towards me, ignoring her "Ben, what, what are you *doing?*"

Eyes and mind held in a fierce focus: I thought I was only a lens, nothing more than that, a device to seize all the sunlight my skin could reach and channel, retune it to a wavelength somewhere far beyond sight, make it hard and tight as a drill-bit and pierce through dull cloth and flesh till it found that savaged, splintered bone. And then to refract it, to scatter it through and through, penetrating every fibre; and then to draw all tight again, to weave in a different pattern a multitude of bright threads to make a

coherent whole which not cuts off like a light extinguished
but slips and slithers free, is reeled in, releases . . .

Fuck. All of that, so subtle and so new; I made it up or else
it came to me, I held it there in my mind like an inspiration
and then it was gone, frayed to nothing and gone, and I was
so shaken I wanted to lie down right there on the road, to
feel gritty sand under my palms and tarmac beneath my
shoulders.

First, though – first I had to open my eyes. And that was
hard, because I knew something at least of what I'd see, other
people's eyes staring at me. But I did it, and yes, there they
were. Staring, gaping. Friends and family, and I wondered
what they were seeing, if they could give it a name, if that
name would have 'friend' or 'family' anywhere attached.

Didn't matter, either way. I'd done what I'd done, what
I'd had it in me to do and so must. If I'd done anything at
all beyond make an arse of myself, standing eyes-closed and
scowling in the middle of the street, doing nothing . . .

I was holding something, I realised, in my hands; and of
all the staring faces Laura's was the closest, way closer than
anyone's else; and her eyes were widest, her skin was sweaty
but her jaw was slack. She knew what the others didn't, she
knew what I'd done or tried to do; and that was the moment
that I knew too, that I had at least done something.

It was her hand, I saw, that I was holding. And Jamie, I
saw, had also seen that much, that I was gripping her poor
maimed fingers between my own; his face was just beyond
her shoulder, glaring not staring, and he was reaching around
her now to shove me away. I shook my head at him hard,
looked down and pulled off that crude bandage, confident
suddenly because I had to be. The alternative – that I'd
crunched her broken finger to no effect, that her slack
staring was pain-induced and nothing more – was too awful,
not possible, please not possible . . .

"Try it now," I whispered, trying it for her, stroking gently all the length of pale flesh and bone, knuckle and nail, "see if that feels better . . ."

"Ben . . ." She took her hand from me and worked the fingers slowly, like a guitarist without her instrument, playing the air. "Ben, what did you *do?*"

"Christ, love, I don't know . . ."

Nor did I; but I wanted to jubilate regardless, I wanted to dance and frolic in the street there, for all that my body wanted only to slump bonelessly and weep. No swelling to be seen in her finger, no awkwardness in its motion; better yet no pain in her, only a dawning wonder.

Jamie took her from me, stilled her hand with a hesitant touch, did his own gaping now, at last. I felt myself grinning fatuously, hurting not at all; looked around for somewhere to sit as my treacherous legs began to fail and saw nothing like that, only Janice stepping to my side. So I hung on to her instead, felt the willowy strength of her stiffening against my weight and thought that would do, that was enough.

Enough for me and substantially better than sitting, actually, the living warmth of her and not too much stare in her eyes, she didn't really understand. Maybe only Jamie really understood, maybe it was only he who was truly shaken to the roots. Or he and I both, because I thought my own roots might rip out now. At last.

Enough for me, to stand and be held up; too much for Janice, too soon for me. She grunted after a minute or so, said, "Hey. You're too heavy, I'm too light. Whatever. Can we find somewhere to sit?"

"I don't know," I said, glancing up and down the road. Locked and shuttered storefronts, litter-bins, lampposts. No seats. "Can we?"

"Come on."

*   *   *

She nudged me into moving, though I wobbled like an old 'un and sighed softly at every step, every time my hollowed bones had to take the weight of flesh and weariness that comprised me.

Over to the wall of the shooting-range, one of the shooting-ranges: electronic guns these days and electronic targets, and no doubt it was as fiddled electronically as it always used to be with simple mechanics. Tip-up metal targets they were when Jamie and I used to come often, and you had to be super-accurate to make them tip, there was just this one spot you had to hit to get them to go all the way over; and of course, of *course* the guns didn't shoot straight. We never expected them to. That was the challenge, discovering any particular rifle's bias and learning to compensate, aiming to miss.

It sounded like a précis, I thought, an abstract of my life: low expectations, try to compensate, aim to miss. The trick, of course, was to get the compensation right, point fallible equipment in an appropriate direction so that luck or judgement can bring you back on course. Doesn't matter which. Luck flips the target over, you still claim the plaudits as your due. And the prizes, of course, never forget the prizes . . .

Me, I'd made a speciality it seemed of compensating wrong. All the way, one-eighty degrees wrong. Aim low and miss by a mile, every time. Call it stubbornness or stupidity, again it didn't really matter. The result's the same.

Whatever. This electronic shoot-'em-up gallery was as solid, as unvirtual as its predecessor. We sat on the ground and set our backs against it, where the sun had warmed the painted breeze-block gaudy wall. Janice kept her arm around my neck, so that my head felt flesh and bone instead of concrete when it toppled backwards. Nice.

"What was that, then," she murmured, "miracle healing?"

"Something like." Then, more honestly, feeling the weary residues of it all through me, "Not a miracle, no. Just the ol' family magic . . ." Unless Jesus had been just a talented lad like me, good with sunshine? Maybe so. But he'd ended up crucified. I shivered in the warm there, into the warmth of her, and her arm tightened a little.

"So why are they all so gobsmacked, then?" she demanded. "They're family, they must have seen it all before."

"Well. Not quite like that. Even I didn't know I could do that." Nor did I want to talk about it, just then. I opened my eyes, looking for a change of subject, and found one easily. "Why's this place so empty, do you know?" It should have been teeming; the sun said it was midday or close to, and the Island hardly closed in summer. There should have been crowds, like there had been— Christ, was it only two days ago? How time crawls, when you're having a really, really bad time . . .

She shrugged, against my side. "I suppose they closed it, aye?"

"Suppose so. Someone should go see, though."

Not Jamie, he was being private with Laura, heads together, hands together. One of the women, then: they were standing in a group, doing nothing, only gazing at her, at him, at me . . .

Not hard to catch someone's eye, though it was harder to hold it. I had to raise my voice in the end, call her over; even shouting was difficult, took more energy than I could spare.

"Serena! Come here a sec . . ."

She came, a little reluctantly, I thought. Good choice, though: somewhere in her thirties, solid and sensible, a lot less feeble than my female relations tended to be after years, after generations of repression by the male line.

"Serena, do us a favour. Go down to the causeway, see if you can figure out why there's no one here?"

"Okay, yeah." She nodded, then hesitated, went on after a second, "Is there anything else you want, Ben? You look wasted."

Wasted was how I felt, all my life a waste except perhaps for this moment, when I'd finally done something inarguably useful. I found a smile for her, and said, "I'd love a drink, if you can ask one of the girls to find one. Water, anything . . ."

Another nod, "I'll tell them," and off she went. I closed my eyes again, let my head slide sideways into Janice's supportive shoulder.

"Sorry," she said softly against my ear. "I should've thought. Didn't they even give you water?"

I shook my head, meaning *no* and also *nothing for you to feel sorry for*. Her hand turned my face a little, her lips touched mine gently, moist and generous; I breathed her air gratefully and felt the soft pressure of her tongue against my dryness, not intruding, just sharing what she had.

Might have been five minutes later, might have been ten or more; I was well past counting, but eventually a breathy voice said, "Ben?"

I opened my eyes, lifted my head from where I was still nuzzling at Janice like a sleepy child, found my young cousin Christa standing in front of me, blocking out the sun. Her arms were hugging half a dozen cans against her chest.

"We broke open a machine," she said, almost on a giggle, *how's that for being bad girls?* "We've got Coke, Fanta, Irn Bru . . ."

"Coke," I said. "Please . . ."

She held a can down to me; I lifted one hand with an effort, gripped it tight. God, it felt cold, beaded with its own chill, it felt wonderfully good just to hold it.

After a moment Christa offered one to Janice also, but she

said no. "It's okay, we'll share. Give one to Jamie, though, he'll need it."

Christa looked doubtful, scared almost at the thought of approaching so powerful a cousin who was – yes, still, a flick of my eyes confirmed – so engrossed with his girl. But a nod of my head and, "Go on, do it," and she went.

I didn't watch her progress; I watched my own hands instead, the other rising to force a finger through the ring and crack the Coke open. Hiss fizz but no foam, no wastage. I lifted it slowly, took a sip, a swig, a long long guzzle; the icy bite of it filled my throat and belly.

I glanced aside at Janice, said, "Call her back, if you want. There may not be much left to share."

"No, it's all right. Take what you want, take it all. I've been drinking water all night. What I really want's a fag . . ."

So call her back, send her to bust another machine, she'll thank you for it . . . I was going to say that, right after I'd had another drink; but suddenly everyone I could see was turning to stare down the road a way, and all their talk was failing, and in the silence I could hear someone running, coming closer.

I sat up to see, and it was Serena in a major hurry, she probably hadn't run so fast in twenty years.

Not me she ran to, but Jamie, who was standing can in one hand and Laura in the other. I could hear what she said, though, what she gasped and stammered.

"The causeway's closed off, there are gates locked and a notice, says it's shut today. Same on the far side, on the shore, they've pulled a chain across the road; but there are cars and a van parked there, waiting. I don't, I don't think they're punters, they were unlocking the chain. They can't cross yet, the causeway's underwater, but I think the tide's going out . . ."

"Did they see you?"

"I don't know. They could have done. It's a fair way but I wasn't, you know, I wasn't *hiding*, I'd gone right up to the gates to see what the notice said. I saw them, and I wasn't looking for them . . ."

"Right. Okay, we'll assume they did. Any idea how long we've got, before the causeway's clear?"

"No, I couldn't tell. I just remember the tide seems to rush out, it's so flat all around here."

"Yeah. Thanks, Serena . . ." Jamie looked around, found me, came across with Laura in his wake. "You fit, bro?"

No. "For what?"

"Well," he said judiciously, "I suppose we've got rifles, a couple," *from those guys the girls ruined.* "But I don't much fancy a shooting-match, we couldn't win it in the long run; and anyway, it's your call. You're big chief in daylight, and the cavalry's coming." We'd always been the Injuns, the robbers, the pirates in childhood games. We felt it showed proper family feeling. The cavalry was always, by definition, the enemy.

And he was right, it was my call; and *I don't want any more killing* was once more the loudest call in my head, despite the body that was still lying in the dust not so far away. Or maybe because of the body. Bodies, plural, it ought to be, they'd said there'd been another man on watch; I wondered briefly where he lay and how he'd got there, never doubted he was dead but who had made him so? Serena perhaps, best guess, she'd be up for that. No mercy in her, I thought, no hesitation after seeing or hearing or knowing her cousins dead, taken away one by one and killed, no mercy, no hesitation . . .

Me, I might not be merciful exactly, you couldn't call it mercy; but I was deeply hesitant. It wasn't only that I didn't want to kill again, I really, really didn't want anyone else dead, whosever hands their blood might lie on.

So hesitant I was, I nearly cried off altogether. *I can't,*

I nearly said, *I'm too exhausted, look, I can't even stand without help, I haven't got the strength to light a candle* . . . He might even have believed me. Ordinary use of talent didn't leave you in this state, but what I'd done to Laura was very far from ordinary.

Except that without me, if I bottled it, they had no one; all they could do else was hide. No other way off the Island. Plenty of hiding places, to be sure, but patient search would find them all. And I who wanted no more killing would die knowing how much, how very much more there was to come, all my cousins by daylight and my enemies – or perhaps my other enemies, my cousins were also cavalry – by night, Ossa heaped on Pelion where Ossa is a mountain of bones . . .

"Give us a hand up, Jan?" I said. After a second she nodded – working it out, I thought, pretty much as I had, that this was best of a bad range of choices – and lithely stood, reached down to grip my wrists and hauled me smoothly, almost casually to my feet.

Jamie whistled appreciatively. "You've done that before."

"Ah, it's just balance. Let your weight do the work. Pick 'em up, knock 'em down – I like to play with the big boys."

Laura twitched an eyebrow at her, across Jamie's shoulder; I deliberately didn't look to see what face Janice made in response, but it had Laura's mouth twitching also, fighting a smile down.

Anything that could make Laura smile just then was fine by me. Ritual humiliation? Sure, no sweat . . .

I even took Janice's arm when she offered it, and genuinely leaned on it too, needing more than the gesture of support.

Jamie was frowning as we headed off at the best pace I could manage, which was not fast.

"What's *wrong* with you, Ben? Okay, you're knackered,

but we both are; and okay, you just did something amazing, but talent doesn't take it out of you like that . . ."

"Did, though." Sunlight was putting it back in again, but slowly, so slowly, a trickle of honey down the empty pipework of my bones. "I don't know, Jamie, this is all new to me too," and we didn't have an expert in the family any more since Laura and I between us had put Uncle Allan out of the picture. No wisdom to draw on, we had to work this out for ourselves.

"Unh." He looked at me with something more than gratitude, something uncomfortably close to respect. "You want to tell me how you did that, with Laura's hand?"

It was the hand he was holding, I noticed, though he held it loosely, not trusting his strength against her fresh-healed bones.

"Later," I said. "One thing at a time. Oh, and Jamie?"

"Yeah?"

"Leave the rifles."

The pace of any march is militated by the pace of the slowest; which made this no march at all, if a march has any briskness to it. It was an effort to me just to walk; before we reached the point where the Island's only road ran down between rocky promontories to become the causeway, Jamie had taken my other arm against the urgency of the moment and he and Janice were all but carrying me along.

We came there at last, though, and found the high steel-mesh gates closed against us, as Serena had said. When we were kids in winter, we used to climb them, quite unfazed; no chance of that today, not for me at least, but no need either. The sun was doing its stuff, dosing me, drowning me in power. I couldn't use it for physical things like walking or climbing, but that mattered not at all. The gates were fastened with a chain, and the padlock was on the other side, but again, no matter. I reclaimed my hands, wrapped them around the chain and channelled light through my prickling skin and into the warm steel links.

Pulled lightly, no pressure; the links stretched and snapped like soft warm toffee. I dropped the chain, put my hands against the gates and pushed them open.

Twenty metres ahead, the sea was still lapping across the road but only gently, visibly retreating. At the far side, on the mainland I could see vehicles queueing up, impatient to get at us; the first was a 4 x 4, and that was already edging down into the water, high on its tyres and confident of crossing. We'd done the same in Jamie's jeep, I remembered. Take it slow, and the bow-wave you made would keep the engine from flooding.

Slow was crucial; we had time, I had time, then, but not much of it. A couple of minutes, no more. After that, we were back into killing-mode again.

Well, hell. Stopping them was all I was after, just now; never mind the long view, react to the immediate. Do the thing that's nearest. Nearest to me was our end of the causeway, like a broad black ribbon dropping down into the water, glistening wet; and I'd seen Jamie rip a road up in his rage . . .

This needed to be bigger, though, this had to stop them back at their end, where they couldn't wade and scramble on to our rocky shore. Even at low tide, no one would be fool enough to try to cross other than by the road; there was quicksand on either side of the causeway, and innocent-seeming stretches of still water that might look like they wouldn't wet your wheel-nuts but actually hid pools deep enough to swallow your car with you inside it.

So. First things first: get them off the road. Stop that car . . .

Half a dozen ways I could have done it, probably, with little or no danger to the occupants; but I suddenly found in myself what I'd never suspected before, an instinct for showmanship, a taste for the dramatic moment. A lust for power, a critic might have called it – though I never yet met anyone more critical of me than I am: 'low self-esteem' just doesn't begin to cover even the pedestal of my monumental contempt for Benedict Macallan – or else the ill-discipline to use the power I had with no discrimination.

Certainly I felt powerful, more so than I was used to. Drained of my normal workaday human strength and then flooded with sunlight, it seemed as though I had been overfilled with talent. Not only my skin but all my body was fizzing with it; I could feel the pulse of every artery and vein as they wrapped around the resonance of bone.

And I stood on the causeway's sandy wet descent and looked at the water, the last of the tide that lapped it and the deeper surge of wave and current that was drawing back on either side; and I played King Canute in reverse. No throne to sit on, but I thrust my hands into my pockets to look as casual for my friends as maybe he'd tried to look for his court, and I stopped the tide; I held it; I impelled it forward, against the moon's suck and all its habits and inclinations.

Well, actually I didn't. If the sun itself can't do it, can't out-pull the moon, what chance for me? All I did, I set my will and talent against the water I could see, and pushed at it. Just as a child might use his hand to scoop the retreating sea into a scraped trench, I used my mind to net as much as I could and to shove it as hard as I could along the slow-revealing line of the causeway's road.

Or put it another way: I made a tidal wave. Not such a big one, in all truth, not a tsunami, Hiroshige would never have bothered with making a print of it; but it looked pretty good to me all the same, the way the sea sank down and reared up and rushed away, leaving the road and the stony way it stood on and the sands beside looking oddly exposed, almost bereft for a few seconds until fresh waters broke in behind that rushing wave to cover all again.

The wave rolled on, sweet breaker, the kind of wave our local surfing lads would kill for but almost never saw; on this coast they surfed in dry suits against the cold, wore masks and hung banners on their cars against the sewage and chemical pollution, then headed south and west as soon as they could manage.

Actually I'd never meant to make such a wave, would never have imagined I could drive such a weight of water. Didn't know my own strength, obviously; or the sun's strength, rather, I'd never felt more transparent. All I'd wanted was a wavelet, like a last freak of the tide, a sudden rise of water to break through that driver's bow-wave and swamp his engine, stop him dead.

Suddenly I was afraid that I might stop him truly dead, I who wanted no more killing; but the water was running, and I had no time to change my mind even if I could have thought of a way to break that wave apart and disperse all the water in it.

Wave met car and broke apart seemingly of its own volition, at that jarring consummation. It broke against the windscreen, not quite roof-high on such a high vehicle; but that was only the curling frothy top of it. The great mass of water thrust underneath and lifted, carried the car like a bottle, like a message, finally threw it back and dropped it on its side some twenty metres behind the chain-posts that marked a point higher than the highest flood tide had ever reached on this shore.

Reaching so far, the wave also surged and kicked among the other vehicles queued up and waiting. Didn't have the strength now to lift those or overturn them; but a few more engines I thought were getting flooded, a few men more I thought would panic, would not want to set foot or tyre on that suddenly-inimical causeway.

I watched the tumbled 4 x 4, and it was harder now to be casual, to be cool even in seeming; but the two passenger doors opened – upwards – and two men clambered out and jumped to ground, followed by two others. *Lovely*, I thought. All alive, no one badly damaged, but oh they must have been shaken up in there, dice in a rattler, and all piled on top of each other at the end. I couldn't have asked for better.

"That was neat," Jamie said behind me.

"But?" It had been a compliment with a serrated edge; his voice carried doubt slathered all over it.

"Well, are you sure it's enough? Is that going to hold them? And even if it does, how are we going to get off, as long as they're waiting for us over there?"

There aren't enough bodies, he was saying, *you've got to send them screaming to their mothers with all their childhood nightmares turned real, turned gory, acted out in wet flesh right under their noses . . .*

"It'll hold them for a while," I said, though maybe not all day. Maybe not even all the turn of the tide. I couldn't make a wave without water. "But I'm not finished yet, that was just putting them on hold. You watch."

The causeway was the only way off for us, but the reverse didn't apply to them; they had boats, we knew that, they had at least one Zodiac inflatable that they could make a landing from, anywhere on the Island. That wouldn't have mattered – *let them come*, some less civilised voice inside me was muttering, *they've seen what I can do with water, now let them see what I can do with flesh* – except that we knew they had guns also, and a couple of men sneaking round with rifles could even up the odds in no time. They'd just need to see us first, or come at us from two sides at once, so that while I was busy with one of them the other would be busy with me . . .

What I needed to do, then, I had to put a total stopper on them now, so that they wouldn't even think of launching a commando raid around our rear. So that if someone else thought of it, say their ultimate boss – the

man with the gas, perhaps – if he gave them orders, they'd
still say no.

So after the tsunami came the earthquake. Wrong way
round, seismologically speaking, but I never was a purist
even in love, so who cares?

Technically speaking, of course – for the purist – it wasn't an
earthquake either, or anywhere near. No continental plates
rasping together, even I couldn't manage that, even on that
day; even my blindsight couldn't look all that way down into
the earth's crust to find a fault, nor could I have made one.
But if any poor unlucky fool with experience of earthquakes
had been splashing down the causeway just then, I'd have
defied them to tell the difference.

When Jamie ripped a road up two years earlier he'd been
in haste and in rage, and he'd just torn the tarmac apart.
Effective, but superficial. Me, this day, I'd bought myself
time enough to do it properly; and I had the need also,
I had to be certain that nothing could get across when I
was done.

I closed my eyes and did use my blindsight one more
time, to look down through the water and the road. The
water was a shifting mist and the road lay in strata beneath
it, tarmac and concrete, grey layers I could see through like
murky transparencies. Beneath them, and hardly more solid-
seeming, were the rocks and shaped stones that had made
the original causeway, when there had been a monastery on
the Island – well, just an island it was then, presumably,
hadn't acquired capital status yet – and the monks had built
themselves a permanent way across, using whatever came
to hand. The stones had likely been salvaged from some
Roman ruin, there'd been enough of those around.

I looked, concentrated, tensed – and heaved. To my
closed eyes they might seem vague and nebulous, but to

my stretched senses, to my mental grip they felt impossibly massy, too deeply embedded in a millennium of silt and held too fast by the road above, I'd never shift them. I couldn't even shake them; doubt shook me instead.

Only that I had to, for Laura's sake, for Janice's, for Jamie's. Everyone I cared for, it seemed to me suddenly, was here on the Island, and very much at risk. It was for me to save them, or nobody could.

I stripped off jacket and T-shirt, to have more sunlight on my bare skin; whether that would really help I wasn't sure at all, but maybe it just might, and I needed all the confidence I could snatch at. Never mind looking cool or casual now. Then I reached and gripped and heaved again, all my energy— no, I didn't have any, but all the sun's energy that I could gather focused through me onto one pale shadow of rock, deep down beneath the road.

I heaved, and it seemed to stir, a little. I pushed and pulled at it, and was sure that it had rocked. Do the thing that's nearest, don't think about the hundreds of others; once move one and the rest would be easier, the seal of centuries would be broken and the seawater would help, rushing in among them with its own power.

Rock of ages, lift for me . . . I wrenched at it and it came, it burst up and out, I didn't open my eyes but to my strange otherworldly sight it seemed to me as though all God's work had been undone in a moment and chaos had come back to the earth.

Dimly, I thought I heard it rip up through the surface of the road, and then splash back into the sea; I thought I heard shouts of startlement behind me. I thought perhaps I'd shouted too, some wordless cry of effort and exaltation mixed.

One was good, but nothing like enough; I didn't even look to see what that had done to the road. I turned my attention back below again and found the next stone, turned it and twisted it into the hole the first had left. It rolled and fell, and another fell with it; and after that, yes, it was easy. Like dominoes: one goes and they'll all go, though these needed my help still and I was in there among them, pushing and yanking amid the tumble and rush, rocks and water and the fall of great slabs from above . . .

I was feverish, I guess, I was crazed with a terrible excitement; it took Jamie to stop me, seizing my shoulders and shaking me hard, yelling "Enough!" into my ear.

That made me open my eyes, at least, so I could catch the last tremors of what I'd done. The road was broken and gone, ten metres ahead of where I stood; where the sea had been licking lightly over tarmac, bidding farewell, now it was rushing back, seething and bubbling into a trench. There was no tarmac, except for the odd slab tilted at a strange angle, shifting and sliding in the tug of new currents, losing its perilous hold on the rocks beneath and slipping away out of sight.

How far had my internal avalanche run? Undersea and inside I couldn't have told, I couldn't judge distance at all; standing looking with my normal vision, I figured it was a hundred and fifty, maybe two hundred metres to where two stilt-legs and a crazy-tilted platform stood sentinel over a jagged end of road, answering my question decisively. That was all that remained of the shelter that had offered protection to the ignorant or lusty; I'd gone a neat halfway with my destruction. Beyond, the truncated causeway ran back to shore like a pier. There were men there, I saw, little men running; running onto what remained, running towards us, which I thought was foolish of them . . .

"Fuck," Jamie breathed, still hugging me close. "You mad bloody bastard, how are we going to get off now?"

"Worry about that later," I gasped, not worried at all.

"They can't get on now, except by boat. We can watch for a boat . . ."

"Sure we can. Better *pray* for a bloody boat, I don't fancy the swim." He let go of me then, stepped back a pace and rumpled my hair, grinning but still shaking his head; his rough touch felt oddly cool against my scalp until I shook him off with an affected scowl, lifted my own hand to smooth my hair again and found it sodden with sweat.

I picked up my T-shirt and used it like a towel, then slung my jacket on over bare skin and turned back to where the girls were watching from beyond the open gates.

Something *spanged!* off the steel fence; a moment later there was a thin cracking sound from the shore, like the snap of something brittle, like my mind, like my resolution . . .

I twisted round again, even as Jamie ploughed past me yelling, "Get down, they're shooting! Laura, fuck's sake, get *down* . . .!"

Shooting they were; a couple of men were down on one knee on the causeway, rifles at their shoulders. Why hadn't I seen their rifles before? I'd *known* they had guns, for God's sake, I should've been looking for guns . . .

Blaming myself, furious with myself but the more furious with them, I raged against the road's end where they were crouching, tore it apart, ripped off great chunks of tarmac and concrete and hurled them hither and yon. The men scrambled to their feet and went sprinting back towards the shore and some supposed safety; I wrenched up another rock and followed them with it, my own patent guided missile, while my mind shrieked *Janice*, shrieked *Laura, Jamie, their baby* . . .

Somehow a whisper cut through that shrieking, just as I was poised to deliver my rock like a meteorite, like God's justice my own. *I don't want any more killing*, the whisper said; and God help me, it still seemed true. I still let the rock fall, no, I still *threw* that bloody rock;

but I threw it at the only place I knew was safe, was empty.

Dunno how much that smart 4 x 4 had cost its owner, but there wasn't much left of it after the fire that followed the explosion that followed the rock plunging to earth through its engine-space . . .

ELEVEN

KISSING COZENS

They threw bullets, I threw rocks, they stopped with the bullets already.

We retreated, none the less. They might start up again with the bullets already, and all of them aiming at me; nor did I think I was immune. I thought I might have done something of an unconscious healing job on myself, lying in sunlight under Fizzy's purring weight my first day back; not the cat but the sunlight working miracles, I thought maybe, I'd felt so much better so fast. But I didn't think I could patch up a bullet's rampant passage through flesh and bone and such. Not that fast, not that good. Hubris could keep . . .

The Island's only road curled all around it, snake-style, climbing the while; the attractions lined the road, clung to it, fed from it like parasites sucking at a vein; where it petered out into rocks and sand and scrub, no more remotely-flat land to build on, the developers had given up.

Not so the monks. *Nearer my God to Thee* must have been their driving philosophy, or else – lacking the inspiration of Victorian hymns – they'd taken their cue from the barons and dukes who'd built castles on the highest promontories that mediaeval technology and sweat could aspire to. Whatever, the monastery had gone up and eventually fallen down on the very peak of the island, a beacon of holiness amid rocks like devil's fangs, God's tongue lodged behind Satan's teeth, or else a monument to a sensible founding abbot's defensive priorities on a coast vulnerable to raiders. Post-religious, the same site had acted as beacon again in a more earthly sense, *no monks to save now so let's save the mariners*; those hymn-singing Victorians had built a lighthouse among the tumbled ruins of the monastery's walls.

That still stood, it stood still as it was always meant to with the old keepers' house beside it, though no light burned within its lantern now. Something of a museum it had become, preserved and adorned with prints of ancient wrecks along this coast, open for tourists and school parties to trudge up its hundred and twenty steps and admire the view from the top. Seeking our own safety from our own more mundane enemies – neither the devil nor the deep blue sea – we climbed the path that led between rocks and carven stones, we came to the heavy wooden door that was locked against us, I blasted the lock and let us in.

On the stone-flagged floor were a few display cases, *mementos mori* if that's the plural; around the round wall rose the whitewashed steps that would take us up to the lantern. I'd already climbed half a dozen before I checked, looked back, saw Jan just behind me and Laura and Jamie hand in hand behind her, the others all grouped at the foot ready to follow . . .

Ah, the responsibilities of leadership.

"Look," I said, "this isn't going to need all of us up there. Not all at once. And I'm *hungry* . . ."

I paused; they waited. *Brutus, you should be living at this hour* . . .

"Okay," I said, on a sigh. "They've converted the house next door into a cafe, there must be a freezer and a

microwave in there, there's got to be food. And coffee.
What we need is a rota, people to watch from the top in
case anyone comes at us in boats, while someone else does
kitchen duty. It'll be more comfy in the cafe anyway, a better
place to wait. Maybe I should come and open the door for
you . . ."

"No, don't worry, Ben." That was Serena, taking charge
at last. "We'll manage," to the accompaniment of nods from
my other female cousins, identifying something they could
do, something they were used to, providing comforts for the
menfolk.

Laura was murmuring to Jamie; he grinned up at me,
said, "She's hungry too. Hungry for two, she says," and
his hand patted her belly protectively, possessively, *hungry
for three*, it said. "You go on up, take the first watch; I'll
organise things down here."

Which made our female cousins even happier, by the look
of them, to have a man to organise their providing. I nodded,
turned my eyes upward, climbed the steps.

Took me a while to register other footfalls tracking
mine, the sound of another's breath at my back. *Slow,
Ben, slow* . .

I didn't look back; acknowledging that she was there
would have been an acknowledgement also that she'd once
again taken me by surprise. I've got my pride.

I was slow on the stairs as well as in my understanding,
and getting slower all the time. Adrenalin disguises exhaustion, but not for long; it had carried me from the causeway
this far, but no further. The rest I had to do by myself . . .

Except that I didn't; a quick scurry of light feet and Janice
was there beside me, slipping her arm through mine, once
again offering a support that I needed, that I'd never have
asked for.

"What is this," I hissed leakily on the outbreaths, "Succour-
a-Wounded-Warrior Week?"

She shook her head. "I used to work for Moncrieff the butcher every holiday. All that blood and bashing, miles better than a paper round."

"So?"

"So I'm used to hauling sides of beef," she said, slipping her lithe arm around me now, dragging my slack arm across her shoulders and hanging onto the wrist thereof, hauling me up the last few steps into the lantern.

"More like beef dripping," I grunted, sliding down a wall of glass and stone to sit on cool wood boards. "Chicken bones. Pork scratchings . . ."

Janice laughed and settled herself beside me. Like the shooting gallery, but different: the sun came in over our heads here, made angles of light against machinery and gleaming crystal, made the dust dance but left us in shadow, left me alone. And we were hidden here also from friends' eyes, relatives' eyes, as they were hidden from us, no targets to shoot at. Jamie could snog Laura all he liked, if that was what he was doing; couldn't touch me, up here, turned away. They could both of them poke and worry at her burgeoning soon-to-be-bell-shaped belly, a toll of things to come, but what I didn't see the hurt couldn't give me grief over, not now, not today . . .

Actually, I thought I was just too dog-weary to be snarling-dog, dog-in-the-manger jealous in my usual urbane and charming fashion. *All passion spent* was how I felt, overdrawn indeed at the angst-bank, sapped and sucked dry; frankly, I couldn't be bothered to care.

"Aren't we supposed to be watching?" Janice murmured after a minute, though she made no move to do it.

Me, I couldn't be bothered to care about that either. "Nah, that was just an excuse to get you alone," I said, eyes closed not to watch anything, not needing to look at her.

"Yeah, right," and now she did move, up and away from

me in one swift movement. "What are we watching for, exactly?"

"Boats," I said. "A Zodiac in particular, they've got one of those at least."

"What's a Zodiac?"

"Oh. Flat black rubber thing. Like a ring doughnut with a bottom to it, and filled with pricks. Penis on the half-shell. Pork, you'd know about that. Long pig, for roasting," though I didn't want to roast anyone ever again, not even another cop, I'd cooked too many already. And couldn't think of any other way to keep them off, bar roasting or boiling or simply popping their rubber bubble and letting them sink or swim for as long as anyone could swim in the wicked currents around the Island; and didn't want to think about that at all, only that she was making me do it.

"Be serious, Ben. We aren't all magic-users, you know."

"You don't all need to be. I'm here, aren't I?" In all my reluctance and exhaustion, a most unreliable guard. "And then it'll get dark," *soon, please God, before anything happens*, "and then it's Jamie's turn, his call, his turn to play God. He can get us all off . . ."

"Can he? How? He doesn't think so."

"Playing God. I *said*. Parting of the Red Sea. Walking on the water. Miracle-workers one and all . . ."

"Ben," she said, crouching, touching my eyes to make me open them and then staring in from not very far away at all, close enough to see all the way through to the Zodiacs in my head, "what's the *matter* with you? You sound drunk, and I know you're not."

I knew that also, and regretted it. I'd have liked to be drunk, just then. "Defence mechanism," I said. "Clever prattle, it's a gear that kicks in sometimes. When I'm tired, when I've been wound up and I'm running down, when it feels like my springs have broken." Or when I'm nervous, but that I surely wasn't, why would I be? We weren't in any danger now. We could see trouble coming if it came, and I really, really didn't think it would. I thought my little exhibition-piece down at the causeway would have given them all cause to pause, to keep their side of the water.

"All right, love. You sit there and prattle all you like, I'll stand watch. Black boats like doughnuts. Anything else?"

"Oh, any boat that comes close. Or helicopter, I suppose, they've got a helicopter," but I couldn't see them using it, except to spy out the ground, perhaps. Zodiacs were loud enough, unless they paddled in; what were they going to do with a helicopter, not to attract attention? Paddle that? Or dress it up as a cloud, perhaps, with its own internal hailstorm, *clatter clatter* that somehow never made it down to earth?

Besides, there was nowhere on the Island that I could think of, flat enough to bring a chopper down on. Nor did I think any of their heroes was going to dangle his way down on a rope, only a thread's thickness from falling and me below. No, I was not expecting trouble.

Nor was I expecting to sleep, knackered though I was. But that crept up on me as I sat, had me nodding and jerking my heavy head up again, forcing my eyes wide against its lure, not to embarrass myself while Janice paced and gazed all around me; and a minute later I was nodding again, nod and jerk until the jerk was too much to achieve and never mind how much a jerk she thought me, it was so much easier just to let it all slip, to slide down under this cool shadow I sat in, to tumble into darker shadows still . . .

No dreams down there, or none that I remembered; nothing at all until there were voices I seemed to be listening to without understanding, girls' voices in a void. And then a touch, a hand on my cheek and my name spoken, drawing me up again.

Slow memory, where I was and who was with me, or who'd been with me when I left her, when I went away. I opened my eyes and she was there still, Janice smiling at me, close enough to blur; and my head was skewed awkwardly sideways on my shoulder and my mouth was open and the stubble on my chin felt wet where it pressed against my jacket, where I must have been dribbling in my sleep.

Brilliant, Ben. Even the hypersmart prattle would have been preferable to this, drooling and probably snoring also, while she did what was needful. God, what a picture I must have made for her to gaze upon, no wonder she was smiling . . .

I eased my head up against a stab of pain in my twisted neck, grunted, dragged a hand across my chin. "Sorry. Sorry, Jan, I . . ."

"It's all right. We've got doughnuts."

"What?" I tried to scramble up, dizzy and stupid still; she laughed, and her hands on my shoulders had no trouble holding me down.

"Not black ones. Doughnuts with jam in. Coffee too, and burgers . . ."

I stared round wildly, uncomprehending; and saw little cousin Christa standing in the doorway with a tray in her hands, steam rising about her.

Ordinarily I hate eating just after I've woken up. Dunno how far back that actually goes – way back to baby maybe, something my mother did to me, a good yawn interrupted by a vast choking leaking nipple, who knows? – but I can date it certainly to a well-established antipathy ten years ago. Sunday afternoons, Dad would come banging in from the pub yelling for his lunch; Mum would have everything ready; she'd send Hazel upstairs to fetch me.

Who would be still in bed, still sleeping, hiding from the grisly twin realities of family life and a Sunday teenage hangover. Who would be thumped awake by my darling twin; stood over while I clambered into Saturday night's drinking clothes, the first my bleary eyes could find on the bedroom floor; dragged down to face roasted meats and boiled vegetables in insistent profusion while my mouth still felt as slimed and foul as if I'd been licking fresh cowpats all night, while my head throbbed to the beat of a mistimed diesel and my brain spasmed and flinched inside my skull, while my stomach lurched in counterpoint and sent burning acid reminders up to my gullet. Every Sunday, this; and was it any wonder if I'd picked up a wee phobia about food and the proper times for ingesting it? I liked half an hour at least between dream and diet, though double that was better. And I had to have clean teeth and a dirty towel, I had to have scrubbed off the clagginess of sleeping, inside and out . . .

And that applied to a midday doze as much as a night's virtuous slumber, but it didn't apply today. Janice woke me, showed me food; and oh I was starving, I was there and able for it, I'd have jumped up and snatched the tray from little scared Christa if Jan hadn't been holding me down still.

"You stay there," she said, "I'll pass you."

And did: a skinny mean burger in a soggy white bun, lashings of ketchup that wasn't Heinz by a distance, not even a copy of a copy, but did she, did either of those girls hear me complaining? They did not. All they'd have heard if they'd been listening was the tearing and gulping sounds of a predator not equipped for chewing. Christa was listening, maybe, at any rate she seemed to be watching; Janice was attending to her own appetite. She might have been, oh, say half as hungry as me? Which made her ravenous, lupine, slow only in comparison . . .

Christa might have borne the tray aloft, but Jamie had seen to the loading of it; on that I would have laid whatever fortune I could lay my hands upon. Three burgers each, a pile of doughnuts for afters, chocolate bars and biscuits and a pint of coffee per person. Amazing that wee skinny Christa could even carry so much . . .

Often I'm slow, just then I was slower in everything but eating; it took me a shocking time to register that there was something odd going on here, that Christa having brought the trough to the pigsty should still be standing there, tray in hands, watching us consume. Waiting for the empties, perhaps? What, cardboard plates and polystyrene beakers? I didn't think so.

She hadn't said a word since I'd woken, and whenever I looked at her she darted her eyes away; but by definition that meant that whenever I *wasn't* looking, she was looking at me. And checking back, the first thing I'd thought about her, I'd thought she looked scared; and I did still think so.

Not scared of me, surely, not that? Because she'd seen me tear the causeway up? Nah, she'd been around Macallan men all her life. Unless she was scared of us all, constantly, permanently . . .

But I didn't believe that either, I'd seen her happy enough. As good as it gets, at least, for the female of this particular sub-species.

"Chrissie?"

She jumped, stiffened, somehow seemed to glance up at me even though I was sitting a metre below her eyeline, almost seemed to salute. "Yes, Ben?"

"You lot all right down there, are you? Nice and comfy, lots of food?"

"Yes, we, we're fine, Ben. Benedict . . ."

"Just Ben, pet. No worries, then, eh?"

"No, no. No worries. We've got Jamie, anyway. Only . . ."

Only Jamie's no use to you, is he? Not in daylight. Good for reassurance, sure, sure; he was a man, he was competent, confident, allowed no worries in himself. But that wasn't enough, demonstrably. Not for little Chrissie, maybe not

for the others either. I remembered suddenly how scared I'd
been last night, how certain of facing death this morning;
and these girls hadn't had just the one night of it, they'd
had days and nights and weeks. Amazing that any of them
could function at all, in the circs; no blame at all if they got
antsy when their prime protection wasn't right there among
them. And Christa couldn't possibly be eighteen yet, she'd
likely never faced anything more dangerous than a smoking
joint or ever been out of a male relation's ambit, and she'd
always been a shy wee thing who jumped at shadows if she
didn't have a dependable hand to hold . . .

"What's going to *happen*, Ben?" That was the closest she
could get, seemingly, to *I'm shit-scared, Ben, I have been
for a terrible long time now and I'm not going to stop just yet,
not till I'm home with all my teddy-bears around me* . . .

"I'll tell you what's going to happen, pet lamb. We're
going to sit around all afternoon, it'll be boring as shit but
never mind, eh? We can talk – you talk to Jamie, he's a
good listener," *you can hold his hand and feel better for it,
he's not been painted half as black as I have; and Laura'll
be there too, she can talk to you, she'll know what to say
where he doesn't* " – and no one's going to hurt us any more,
no one's going to come near. And after it gets dark, we yell
for help and Jamie leads us home. All right?"

She nodded doubtfully. "I suppose . . ." *If you say so* was
the underlying burden, as it must have been all her life, so
used she was to serving Macallan men.

"Trust me, love. Better yet, trust Jamie," *trust Laura,
she's a doctor*. "We're fine now. Cancel red alert, resume
stations. Real life picks up again tomorrow. You seeing
anyone at the moment?"

She hesitated, nodded, blushed a little.

"Good. Well, sit down and work out just how many dates
he owes you, and just how special the first one needs to be
to make up for all of this." I wasn't going to ask who he

was; a cousin for sure, she'd never have the nerve to date outside the family. And she was just the sort of girl most of my cousins would go for: pretty enough and quiet, willing, submissive with it. The sort of girl who'd say 'obey' and really truly mean it, really want to . . .

She smiled faintly, shook her head.

"No, I mean it. You deserve a treat."

"Tell him that means he owes you one," Janice chimed in. "They fall for that, every time."

Took a little more cajoling, but at last Christa went away not looking scared so much as interested. Big improvement; I thought we deserved applause. Janice thought all the males of my family deserved shooting. Jamie included, and very possibly me too.

"I mean, look at her! That poor wee watery broth of a girl – and they're all like that, except Serena, maybe. They're so *passive* . . ."

"They were scared, Jan. They've been scared a long time."

"Aye, all their goddamn lives," she said, eerily echoing my own thought that I'd so deliberately dismissed. "And it's your fault, all of you."

Not me, but I didn't say so, I thought she might not recognise the distinction. "They're bred that way," I said instead, *mea culpa, mea maxima culpa*. I tried to think of the plural of that, not to take generations of guilt onto my own inadequate – though accustomed – and reasonably innocent shoulders, but I couldn't remember enough Latin. Father Hamish would have been ashamed. "*Inter*bred that way. Selected for subservience."

"It's disgusting."

Of course it was disgusting, it was Macallan at its purest. What could I say? Too late to work backwards, to shuffle genes and reschedule the training to produce bright, vivacious, determined girls, sisters and cousins who could

meet the world on its own terms and tell their menfolk to
go hang.

Instead I pushed myself to my feet, found them steadier
than they had been and my legs willing to bear my weight
once more. Walked across to where she stood, gazing out
but not I thought keeping watch just now, not seeing the
wide and empty sea; put my arms around her waist, nudged
her ear with my chin, murmured, "I'm sorry . . ."

She snorted. "Not me you should be apologising to,
boy." But the wrath ebbed away from her, I could feel
her slowly relaxing, her body leaning into me, some kind of
forgiveness; then her head toppled back against my shoulder,
her mouth twisted into a wry smile, and she said, "You're
feeling better, aye?"

"Aye."

"That's good."

Good that I was feeling better, she might have meant, no
more than that; but maybe she was meaning also the way my
hands were moving, gently over her stomach, finding ridges
of firm muscle to belie how flat and soft it seemed to the eye.
Not a surprise, that, I knew it already from our one night
together, just a couple of nights ago. And by imputation from
things that had happened since, how she'd hauled me about
in my weakness. The confirmation, though, the rediscovery
now in this moment of ease, that surely felt good to me.

Nice to learn that there were advantages, there were
positive results to be had from butchery. Me, I'd only ever
seen the other side . . .

And me, I was snorting suddenly, choking on a shame-
ful giggle; and she was frowning suspiciously, saying,
"What?"

"Nothing. Cheap puns, doesn't matter."

"*What?*" she repeated, demanded, turning in my arms to
skewer me with a glare.

"Only, I'm grateful to your Mr Moncrieff . . ."

And I could say no more, just bury my foolish mouth in her hair and hug her hard; and that of course was how bloody Jamie found us as he came running light and fast up the stairs and into the lantern before either one of us could find the wit or the will to break away.

"Unh . . . Oh, hi, Jamie . . ."

"Hel-*lo!* Sorry to bust in like that," though he looked not sorry at all, he looked bright and delighted to have bust in like that, "only I just thought you two might like a break from all this grand-old-Andy stuff."

"Unh?" God, I was being so articulate; but it's hard to articulate when all the blood you have is in your skin, so that your jaw- and tongue-moving muscles are suffering severe oxygen-deprivation, like every muscle else, like your lungs and your brain also so that you haven't the breath to talk proper even if you had the control, even if you had the mind-power to figure out what to say . . .

"Duke of York," he said, beaming. "Marching up and down. Doing sentry-go. Shepherds, guarding their flock. You've done your share, do you want me to spell you?"

"Well . . ."

"No," Janice said, flat and emphatic. Janice's arm, I noticed, was still or again around my waist, under my jacket, against my bare skin; must have been just me, doing the pulling-away-too-late bit. "No, it's okay, thanks, Jamie. We're fine."

"Yeah, right. Laura said you'd probably rather not be disturbed; I just thought I'd check." *Check up on what she was telling me*, I thought he meant, and felt the blood rise one more time. "Here, Jan, she sent these up for you . . ."

And he pulled a miracle from his pocket, or what I deduced to be a miracle from Janice's gasping, grasping glee: a pack of Regal King-Size.

"There's a machine, in the cafe," he said smugly, watching her tear into it. "Laura smashed it open. All for you. Plenty more down there if you need them, but you have to fetch them yourself, I'm not running those stairs again."

I laughed, or tried to, tried to sound casual and sarky after my finest manner. "Come on, Jamie, even Jan's not going to smoke her way through twenty in an afternoon . . ."

"Sixteen," she corrected me. "They short-change you, in machines. And I wouldn't bet on it, bro."

That brought me up short: no one but Jamie ever called me that. Before I could think it through, though – idle picking-up of what one boy called another or something more definite, a message, meaning what? meaning it as Jamie did, or literally, or more? – she had a cigarette in her mouth and was waving her hands dramatically. "Someone got a light, then?"

Jamie's jaw dropped, his hand lifted to his lips, his eyes swivelled involuntarily behind him, to that endless circle of steps. Grand old Duke indeed: *down and up again*, his face was saying, *and then down one more bloody time . . .*

Janice was groaning with a throaty desperation, to hold the gates of heaven in her hand and have no key. I chuckled; he was doing it awfully well, but I knew this boy of old. Sweet joy it was, to spoil his charade. "Here," I said, and clicked my fingers in the refracted sunlight as though I sparked a Zippo. A pale little flame danced in the air between finger and thumb; I held it out towards her, and it took her only a moment of bulging eyes and sagging cigarette to get control, to stoop, to swallow her slightly-manic giggle at the way the obedient flame bent and stretched to meet her, and to light her fag.

Jamie nodded sober approval towards her, winked cheerfully at me, and I wondered if maybe I had misread his charade after all and not spoiled it in the slightest. But when he did the see-you-later bit, followed by the turning-to-go bit, I still snapped my fingers at him – without fire this time, nothing to light but Jan's laughter which didn't need a flame, only the joke of one – and said, "No, you don't. Come on, hand them over. What if the sun goes in?"

He stood still, sighed loudly, didn't look back. "It's all just wool off a sheep's back with you, isn't it, Ben? Pull it over someone else's eyes, then . . ."

And he lobbed a small rattling thing high over his shoulder, and I caught it as he trotted off, down and out of sight.

And I grinned at Janice and said, "That boy never forgot a box of matches in his life, love."

She grunted, glared down through obscuring floorboards to drop a mute malediction on his head, then inhaled deeply, cocked her head to one side and gazed at me, breathing out, letting a slow veil of smoke cloud the little distance between us.

"Why don't you hate him, Ben?"

One pace of sharp mental retreat, before I caught my balance or anything like it; then, "Oh, I do," I said lightly.

"Yeah, right. Sure you do. But come on: he steals this girl you adore, he gets her pregnant, she worships the water he walks on – and so do you. How come?"

"Habit, I suppose. He always did get everything I wanted, and you sort of get used to that in the end. It's not his *fault*, he's just glossier, shinier, sexier than I am . . ."

"Well, his nose is smaller," she said consideringly, "I'll give you that. And he dresses better."

"He can afford to." Could afford to once, on Uncle James' money; could still, I supposed, on the profit from his redundant cars, if Laura would only let him. At the moment he was likely wearing the Armani out, with no promise of anything but Levi to follow.

"So?"

"So what?"

"Money, looks, charisma. You say he got it, you didn't. He certainly got the girl. Why don't you hate him?"

"Oh. I did, actually," often and often, through childhood and teenage and since, with very different degrees of raging passion. "But I can't keep it up. I love him too, I always have. He's – he's *Jamie*, that's all. He's my coz, my bro, my blood brother, my best mate . . ." And I was inarticulate again, pinned like a pawn, floundering like a flounder on the floor. "Is that what you want to hear? 'Cos I can't do any better, that's it. He's Jamie, I'm Benedict, I don't hate him except sometimes, when I really really do."

"No," she said, stepping closer, "that's not what I want to hear. Never mind, though. We'll try it again later."

Later it would have to be; she apparently had totally other plans for now. Like one hand on the back of my neck to hold me, one on my cheek to guide me, and just that little hint of stretching up to kiss me.

Okay, we'd kissed before, and more; we'd danced in the dark fantastic. I used to think – back when I was a kid, ten or eleven, when my older cousins had done their familial duty and enlightened me a laughing little about some interesting few of the facts of life – I used to think that kissing was an essential part of the act of love, that you couldn't actually do one without the other: that you had to be kissing while you bonked. I remember a long dispute I had with Jamie about it; he'd got hooked on another aspect entirely and maintained that doggy-style was the only sensible, maybe the only possible way the wondrous but peculiar thing could be achieved, on account of the absolute necessity of keeping one's hands on the girl's breasts throughout. I of course insisted that what he proposed was simply out of the question, because her mouth would be in the pillow; we fought like Lilliputians, Big-Enders versus Little-Enders, for weeks before a raid on his brother's room produced magazines and

The Joy of Sex to prove us both wrong. Gobsmacked we were after that, the pair of us; I can't speak for him but my own night-time fantasies took some very bewildering turns for a while, before individual investments in our own picture-libraries and judicious swapping of material settled things down for the traditional long wait, the certainties of pubescent and impatient boys who have yet to discover how anything really feels or happens or results.

Janice and I had kissed, but only fleetingly, *en passant*, in pursuit of something greater. Just now kissing was all there was; we weren't going to tug each other's clothes off and do the whole show right there, make the beast with two backs on the dusty lantern floor. At least I wasn't, and this time I was determined not to be overruled; no lock on the door, and too much chance of someone else pattering up the steps with drinks or news or questions. God, just think if it were Laura . . .

So we kissed, with no physical goal beyond the kissing; and that made it slow and deep and patient, exploratory, promissory, revelatory. Her tobacco tongue posed questions; mine proposed answers, which she seemed to find acccpt- able. I wondered if she tasted tobacco also; but I thought probably not, her taste-buds would be numb or inured to it, or her brain would tune it out. She probably just tasted me, or a version of me: like colours seen through coloured shades, some skewed untrue but most clinging hard to what they were.

We kissed, and at last we stopped kissing. Stopped at that level, at least, when lockjaw threatened. Fell back on whisper-kisses, soft touches, teasing nibbles; and she mur- mured, "Still want to know why you don't hate Jamie, then?"

"Go on, then. Tell us."

"Later . . ."

*   *   *

As it happened, it *was* Laura who came next up the stairs, climbing for two: climbing for curiosity mainly, I thought, checking out Jamie's report for accuracy or us for staying-power. Luckily, by the time she got so far, we had exhausted all the obvious possibilities of kissing in isolation, and I was still being firm – not to say rigid – about breaking that quarantine; it was kissing or nothing, and at last the kissing had had to stop. I was down on the ground again, she'd got me that far, sitting wedged once more like an angle iron between floor and wall; Janice was no longer kneeling athwart me, straddling my hips, her folded arms a pillow for my head and all her body there within my ambit and accessible, brutally tempting in defiance of my resolution . . .

She'd moved from there to sitting side by side with me, shoulder to shoulder, skin to skin; but then a sudden post-noncoital hunger had sent her crawling over to where she'd left her cigarettes, and when she'd come back she'd settled a couple of feet away, consideration for the non-smoker or some other motive keeping her just at hand-holding distance.

Which is what we were doing when Laura came in, we were holding hands, our fingers loosely, passively inter-linked, no intent in the world.

So quite why I scrambled so hastily, so awkwardly, so blushingly, so *guiltily* to my feet is not a question I care to think about overmuch, even now; it's prone to have me doing my madness-in-public act: kicking at the air, muttering, shaking my head hard, anything to dislodge the memory and stop me dwelling there.

At the time I just babbled inside my furious skin, all too aware that I had amused and superior female eyes watching me from both sides, though I was trying to twist away from all of them, talking to the windows, to the walls, to the foetus: "Laura, hi, what are you doing, all the way up here, should you be doing that stuff with, with the, you know, the baby coming?"

"It's not coming yet, Ben. Exercise is good for me. Good for us both. Actually, I thought maybe you'd both appreciate a pee-break . . . ?"

Actually, she was right. The moment she'd said it, I was bursting. I glanced at Janice; my first reaction was on the tip of my tongue already, *I'll go first, okay? You stay, talk to Laura,* and was blocked only by the sudden panicked thought that maybe I really didn't want her talking to Laura, not just now, not with that wicked smiling light in her eyes . . .

Didn't matter anyway what I wanted, what I might or might not have suggested. Janice held out both her hands towards me, *help me up*; I gripped her wrists and pulled unhurriedly, she swayed to her feet and swapped our hands around somehow so that it was she holding me, tugging me gently towards the door, saying, "Thanks, Laura, you're a pet. Won't be long . . ."

And then there were the steps down, and her hand on the back of my neck, scratching, not lightly; and her saying, "You know your trouble, Ben lad? You don't *think*, you just panic all the time, do what you always have done, run in circles with a wing trailing . . ."

Oh, was that my trouble, was it? Right now I thought my trouble was beside me, raising welts; or above me, doing sentry-go more dutifully than we had and still giggling the while, no doubt about that. Or both, a man can have more trouble than one. Born to it, but I did think that this was more than my inheritance as the steps led us downward.

Halfway down, we encountered Jamie coming up, and received a severe change of plan.

He had cans of Coke in one hand, chocolate bars in the other. "Don't hurry back," he said. "Sorry, but I've had all

I can take of the wet relatives. And it's our turn up there, I reckon."

Not for the duty, he meant, for the privacy: for kissing in isolation, or doing whatever more their greater nerve could encompass. Or their greater need, perhaps. They had so much more to lose than I did, if either one of them lost the other, which both must have been certain of last night. For sure they deserved some time alone.

Who knows, maybe an objective voice would say that I deserved or even needed a little of what I got in the cafe, in Jamie's place. Janice wouldn't, but she was no more objective than I was.

We went out of the lighthouse and around its curving bulk, following a brick-laid footpath; came to the little house behind and paused to tut disingenuously at the broken door, where someone – probably Jamie, though it might have been Serena insisting on her prior right, my permission – had forced the lock, with a lump of rock by the battered look of it.

Just inside were the toilets, where we both got what we really did urgently need, a comfort-break, a long and steaming piss. I was out first, and waited for her; then we went on through another door into the cafe proper.

My female cousins were grouped, almost huddled together by a window, keeping watch over the grey sea more diligently than we had from our far better vantage. Feeling abandoned by the nervy look of them, by the eager way they jumped up to welcome us, or rather me.

"Benedict! . . . Ben, come and sit down . . . Sit here . . . Would you like a coffee? Christa, fetch Ben a coffee, how do you like it? Black, Chrissie, and some biscuits too . . ."

Oh, it was strange, it was rare to be greeted so effusively by my family, to whom I had only ever been first an adjunct and then a misfit, always something less than I should have been, a weakling and a failure in a tribe that had no time for either.

Briefly, I enjoyed it. Milked it, even. Took the seat they beckoned me towards, and left Janice to drag up another for herself; nibbled a biscuit, sipped a coffee, basked a little in the general relief my womenfolk were showing, simply to have me with them.

The unaccustomed pleasure paled quickly, though. Not quickly enough for sceptical Janice, who'd had to fetch her own coffee also and radiated a silent but scathing discontent at my side, which I felt sure would find lyrical expression later; but I guess I'm not cut out for adulation, especially when it's cut by that same wariness that Christa had shown earlier, that borders on simple fear.

It made me uncomfortable, restless under their eyes. Janice actually broke first, lost all patience with their tongue-tied gladness, their admiration; but when she stirred beside me, when she thrust herself to her feet and said, "There's nothing doing here. I'm going for a walk," it was the work of a moment to follow.

"Hang on, Jan, I'll come with you."

She checked, and seemed on the verge of saying no, of saying, "No, I don't want you," which would have been a hard thing to handle for more reasons than the one, the being left behind with my new fan club. She only shrugged, though, pushed her way through the door and left me to catch it on the rebound.

Behind me I could hear soft moans of disappointment, of returning anxiety, *he's our shield and defender and he's leaving us*, but I thought they could live with the disappointment. They didn't really need me, they only thought they did.

I was expecting excoriation from Janice, but again I thought I'd live through it, if uncomfortably.

In fact, after she'd stormed and scrabbled her way down the hill – straight down, not troubling to follow the road around – with me trailing puppy-style in her wake, she stopped and waited for me, breathing hard; and when I reached her she slipped her arm through mine and said, "Never mind, eh? I was adored once, too."

I shook my head, wanting to say no, it wasn't that, it was only that they felt safe with me there and scared without, and fussing was the only way they knew to say so. But I didn't have much spare breath myself, it had been a steep and tricky scramble; and by the time my lungs had caught up with me my brain was way ahead and wondering, thinking that she wasn't just talking about the girls in the cafe. And before I could work my way up to asking her – *how do you mean, what are you saying here, something about Laura and me?* – she was tugging on my elbow, wanting to be moving again.

I glanced around to get my bearings, then said, "No, this way. I'll show you something, a special place of ours . . ."

I took her round the ragged rock that we called Greenbeard, to the smooth-worn boulder where Jamie and I had always liked to sit and talk and watch the sea, where we'd brought fish and chips and griefs just days before, where I'd never brought and never thought to bring anyone else.

This was the far side from the causeway, where the Island's rocky flanks plunged into unplumbed depths of churning water. Unplumbed by us, at least; drop pebbles and kraken-waking chunks of stone into it as we could, as we did, as we had all our lives, we'd still never heard an echo coming up from when they settled on the sea-bed.

"They'll not be coming now," Janice said, scanning the bare horizon. Then, "Will they?" with a touch of uncertainty.

"No." Not with the sun already westering somewhere

behind us, below the peak of the Island already, casting its shadow out across the sea. Not time enough left for a game of hide-and-seek through the attractions, even if they'd worked themselves up to face me again after my little touch of temper at the causeway. Come nightfall, there'd be Jamie, and for all they knew there'd be all the family massing on the shore. They wouldn't come now. "I didn't bring us here to watch."

"What, then?"

"Just to sit, I guess," I said, and did; and so did she beside me, grunting with pleased surprise when she found the boulder still warm beneath us.

Only I couldn't sit here without talking, without being serious. Even without Jamie, the habit was too ingrained. "You know," I said slowly, watching how the spray flung up beneath our feet, "I used to think . . ."

"Did you? So why did you stop, then, too much strain on the old brain cell, was it?"

I just looked at her. She grinned, hugged herself against my arm, said, "No, go on, then. What did you use to think?"

I used to think that I was born to run, that this wide horizon was a fence made to close me out, to keep me from ever coming home; but I was back now and I was looking at her, and the second of those two states was the greater surprise. I felt suddenly that I owed her something, more than I actually had it in my gift to bestow; so I did what I could, I gave her what I had, I lied to her.

"I used to think I'd bring Laura here," I said, though in fact I'd never got that far, I'd learned too soon that Laura would never grant me that right, to bring her to my special places.

"Uh-huh," she said, and her grin had a wholly different quality suddenly. "Starting to figure it out now, are you?"

"What?"

"Why you don't hate Jamie, fool . . ."

· TWELVE ·

TRANSFIGURED LIGHT

A bit before dusk, we made our way back to the road, and so up the hill to the lighthouse. *Before the light fails*, I'd said, meaning it two different ways. I didn't fancy that scramble over weed-wet rocks in the crepuscule; and my shift was over anyway, my time was passing, I had to hand the baton on to Jamie.

Which I did with a flourish, albeit only verbal.

He and Laura were already down from their vigil or their solitude, whatever they'd actually been doing up there; one day, I thought, I might ask, see if they really were bolder than I was. We found them in the cafe, sipping coffee, seemingly undisturbed by the ongoing anxieties around them. The cousins were at the windows still, watching the sun, silently urging it on down; after my abandonment, they were obviously desperate for the dark, to be under his protective aegis.

I detached my hand from Jan's, purely to clap it loudly onto his shoulder; and never mind that Jan instantly put her arm round my waist instead, and never mind that Laura smiled privately at the sight of that, I had my own pleasure to exact.

"Sun's going," I said, loud enough for everyone to hear,

though I knew damn well that everyone was well aware
already. "It's your turn now."

"To do what?" he demanded.

"Get us off, of course."

"Yeah, right. How do I do that?"

"Well, first," I said cheerfully, having it all planned out
in my head, "you let the family know where we are."

"How, Ben? We don't have the phone any more. They
took it off Laura at the station. This one's dead," with a jerk
of his head towards the payphone in the corner of the cafe.
"Either they've cut the lines or you did, when you ripped
up the causeway . . ."

"Yeah, I'd expected that. But it's okay," it was all part
of the plan. "You just set a beacon, something the family
can't miss. They'll come. Then we'll know it's safe to cross
back, no one's going to be watching for us with a rifle after
a fleet of Macallans turns up."

"Unh." He thought about that for a moment, nodded
slowly, then went on, just as I'd hoped. "But how do we
get across? They're not going to turn up in boats . . ."

"Don't need them to. We'll walk. I'll show you. But we
need the beacon first, soon as it gets dark enough . . ."

I was teasing and mysterious, he grumbled and glared
at me; but he came outside, with all the others following. To the east the sky was fading to purple, and the
moon was up as though she'd known we'd need her;
I grinned contentedly, and pointed at the black bulk of
the lighthouse like a finger shadowed against the falling sun.

"Beacon," I said. "That's what it's *for*, right?"

"Right . . ."

There was respect in Jamie's acknowledgement, as well
as confusion and some irritation: just the combination I'd
been working for. Sheer ego, but I wanted to show my

clever cousin, all my cousins just who was still in charge here, even after my light was gone.

We waited, not for long and I at least was not impatient at the waiting; the sunset was gorgeous and I enjoyed every moment of it, leaning on Jan's shoulder and talking quietly about the colours, about other sunsets I'd seen on my travels, high in mountains or down on the coast. I didn't get much back from her but grunts and frowns, but that was okay. I was riding shamefully high on my own self-satisfaction, and refusing to be ashamed about it.

At last the sun was gone, we were left only the moon and stars to play with, no trace of a tingle on my skin except when I touched Jamie's. I touched him, and he turned his eyes up towards the lantern of the lighthouse, dead these many years but due to live again tonight, though it would die a lasting death in the process. More obedient than inspired, Jamie reached out with his talent, and set the lantern suddenly ablaze with nightfire.

Cold blue light, flickering and flaming, guttering in no wind that we could feel; we had stark shifting shadows at our feet now, and it was easy to see the path down to the road below. All part of the plan . . .

"Let's go down to the causeway," I suggested, knowing that my suggestions were orders tonight. "By the time we get there, something may be happening."

What was due to happen duly did. There were plenty of houses along the coast here, plenty of people to see the light; some if not most would know what it was, what it portended; one at least of those some was sure to have a contact in the family, sure to let them know. The Macallans have few friends, but who needs friends when the bulk of your enemies are cowed and subservient, and have learned major lessons in greed and acquisitiveness from you?

We took our time, going the long, slow way all around

the Island for reasons of comfort and safety, for a total
lack of hurry now. We watched and worried over each
other's footing at the top, where the path might be clear
to see in the ice-blue light but jumping shadows made every
step uncertain; Jamie took the steepest section backwards,
risking a fall himself to hold Laura's hands and guide her
feet directly. Jan and I, we linked tight together and took
it side by side, risking each other, both for one and one for
both and "Stop *giggling*, girl, we'll slip . . .!"

The downspiralling road took us out of the immediate
glare, the lightfall from the lighthouse, though it still flared
its *look at me!* message to a hopefully-watching world. Jamie
could have made torches or fireworks or wills-o'-the-wisp if
they'd been needed, but the moon gave us light enough to
walk by.

Light enough to romance by, also. Janice's feet lagged,
unaccountably to me; when even shy backmarker Christa
had overtaken us, I murmured, "What's the matter, is it
all catching up with you? Not far to go now, love, and it's
over . . ."

"It's not, you know," she said certainly. "It's hardly
started yet." And then she stopped dead, which meant per-
force that I stopped too; and she said, "Nothing's the matter,
actually, I just wanted to be sure you weren't staring at Laura
over my shoulder," and then she kissed me. Again.

I didn't even think to look, to see if Laura was gazing back
to find us. I didn't think much at all, until I registered her
hand inside my jeans, her fingers cool against my heat. Then
I broke away, rough enough to make her gasp; but even then
I was only thinking, *Later* . . .

And said it, had to say it, not to have her think that I was
thinking *Laura* . . .

"Later," I said, aware that I was gasping also. "Not now,
not yet, that's all . . ."

"Raincheck, then?" she said softly, to be sure of me. "You're not raining on my parade?"

"I wouldn't dare. Even the bloody weather wouldn't dare."

That drew a chuckle from her, her hand into my back pocket and her head to my shoulder, where it best fitted. We set off so, she matched her pace to mine and we soon caught up with Christa. Janice's free arm dropped around her shoulders and we went on as a threesome with Jan making casual girl-talk about the relative density of the English male, purely I thought – I hoped – to win a smile from my shy and edgy cousin.

The others were grouped by the open gates when we eventually caught up, gazing in silence at dark and seething water. The tide had come in and gone out again – *all part of the plan, Mr Macallan* – but there was still no chance of a dry way over, where I had broken the causeway.

Jamie had gone through on his own to stand where I'd stood before, only a few metres from where the tarmac turned to rubble and nothing, where the sea pecked at its crumbled edges. I detached myself from Janice and went to join him, the smug pleasure of the latter almost, almost overriding the reluctance of what came before.

He didn't turn round, though he must have heard me and known me from my step or his deduction or else something deeper, something instinctual, blood calling to blood.

He lifted his head a little from his contemplation of the waves, and just said, "How?"

"Later," I said, one more time. "Wait."

"For what?"

"For that," I said, and pointed past his shoulder, so that he would see.

*   *   *

Over on the mainland, on the Military Road a car's head-lights were cutting at the night, their beams dipping and rising, turning as the road turned, flashing full-frontal in our eyes and turning again.

We watched it come, watched it turn into the car park and sit still, its lights still burning like another kind of beacon. No other traffic was moving; I thought I could hear its engine, grumbling across the water.

"So? It's Lover's Lie-in, over there."

"Not tonight, it isn't. Look."

Here came another, on the track of the first; and a third and a fourth along the coast, that must have thought the dual carriageway to be a faster route from town.

Jamie was persuaded by then, but we waited a while longer, till there were a dozen cars in that car park and more than a dozen men out on their feet, standing in a loose group and staring towards us. Seeing little, I guessed, against the black unlit bulk of the Island, certainly seeing less than we were. No matter. Jamie suggested giving them a sign, but I said no. Let them wait a little, as we had waited.

"What are we waiting for now?"

"Just you," I said, smirking slightly. "Come on, part the waves for us. Let's walk on the water."

"Listen, hyperbrain," and oh, did he sound fed up, and did I rejoice at it, "I can't, I've been thinking and I can't, I just can't see *how* . . ."

"Clue?" I suggested guilelessly.

"Benedict . . ."

He was growling now. I grinned, and said, "Think about sand. Soft sand, how you'd make a good path to walk on through it."

"I am not," he said, "*stamping* into that," with a gesture at the sea's chaos before us.

"Don't stamp, no. Press." And then, relenting, "You ripped a road up, remember? Didn't think twice about that.

So you can do the opposite. If you can pull things up, you can press them down. Squeeze it, good and hard."

"Ben, man, that's water out there. It's a liquid, it doesn't bloody press. It doesn't *squeeze*."

"Glass is a liquid," I reminded him. "Technically." We'd picked that up at school once, in a physics lesson, and loved the concept of it. "Remember? It flows, if you just leave it long enough."

"So?"

"So you can walk on glass."

"If you have to. If it's strong enough . . ."

He was weakening, I could hear it in him; he was getting interested. "Good and hard, Jamie. That's all it takes."

"Have you, have you done this, then?"

"Me? No. I only thought of it this afternoon. Thought I'd leave it for you."

And then I stepped back a pace, no more jokes now. It was his to do if he could, if he could meet the challenge of it; and if not, hell, we'd just have to yell over and tell them to find a boat. Not a problem really, but I did want Jamie to do this for me, for all of us. To lead us Moses-like, dry-shod across the sea . . .

He stood stock-still, rock-still, working on it in his mind. I'd been light and teasing, but it was no easy task in truth. Two hundred metres or so he had to run his road, to a point we could barely see in moonlight; and he was going to trust Laura to it, he had to be sure.

Then he lifted one hand, just a little, just to waist height. I watched the water, and saw a line of light sparkle across the surge, blue phosphorescence, nightfire dancing on the waves.

On the stilling waves . . .

Attaboy. The word was on my tongue but I didn't even breathe it, not to break his concentration.

The nightfire was a by-product here, only fallout but I was well glad of it, for the light it gave to see by. I saw a path make itself through the sea, only two paces wide but that was wide enough; I saw it flatten, depress, sink down maybe half a metre so that walls of water built up on either side. Walls that held, that only spray came over.

I stepped up beside Jamie again, heard how hard he was breathing.

"That it?" I asked softly.

He licked his lips, while his eyes stared fixedly. "Dunno," he whispered. "I think that's all I can do. This, this ain't easy, bro. Is it enough?"

"Well, let's see."

I strolled forward, as unconcerned as I could make it look, not for his sake but for the girls' behind us. The drop at the causeway's edge was a metre or more, down into a trough where blue light glittered and ran over black stillness, broken only where the odd edge of rock thrust upward. Too far to stretch a toe down, to try it. This was my payback, I supposed, his revenge. Nothing to do but take a leap of faith . . .

I breathed deeply, once, and jumped.

And skidded when I landed, lost my feet completely, landed joltingly on my butt. Yelped from the shock of it and then laughed, couldn't help it, from the surprise and the relief and the sheer delight of being proved wrong. I'd almost been expecting to bounce, on water jellied under the pressure of Jamie's talent; I'd forgotten the chill of nightfire, hadn't thought that what had seemed only a side-effect would be so effective, to freeze the surface of the sea.

Pulled myself to my feet still giggling, and so up and out again, over to the gates, no idling now. How long Jamie could hold this together was a question I didn't want to ask, more particularly didn't want to learn an answer to.

"Come on, then," I said briskly. "Snap it up. We're walking home, kids. It's slippy down there, mind, but solid as rock . . ."

Snap it up they didn't but edged, rather, sidled forward with many a sidelong glance at me, at Jamie, at each other. Everyone seemed to have found a hand to hold; not to be left out, I found Janice's.

I ushered them straight past Jamie, right down to the water, to that weird conjunction between man's work and magic's. When I saw them staring, shuddering, trying to back away I said urgently, "Don't think about it. It's there, it's to use, that's all. Look."

I jumped down again, more carefully this time; stood firm on solid ice – *how deep? Don't think about it* – and reached up, both arms to help with the jumping. "Who's going first?"

Pause. Silence.

Then Janice, "We're all going together."

Well, not quite, but I didn't say so. I just took her hands, took her weight as she leaped lightly down beside me; squeezed her fingers gratefully for showing them a lead, and turned back for the next.

To my surprise, it was Christa who was at the front. I gripped her waist and lifted her easily down, she seemed to weigh almost nothing; gave her a grin and a kiss on the cheek, "Good girl," and nudged her on to Jan.

Serena had to bully the others a little, but they all came down, all the cousins. Just Laura left now; when I reached to help her, she shook her head.

"I'm not going. Not without Jamie."

Fuck it! This was not good; but, "You bloody are," came from behind her, from the man himself, in a harsh groan. "Who do you think I'm doing this for? Go on, go! *Now . . .!*"

"I'm not leaving you on your own." There was less

certainty in her voice this time, though, and she was looking
at me even as she spoke to him.

"Of course you're not," I said, reaching for that light and
easy tone again, almost making it work. "I'm staying till
you're all over, then us two are coming across together."

"So why can't we all go at once?"

*Because neither one of us knows if he can do that,
stupid* . . .

She wasn't stupid, of course, she'd worked that out for
herself; but her hesitation was upsetting some of the others.
I tried to blast that into her head with a telepathic glare, as
I said, "Why do some parents always take separate flights?
Because they're neurotic, pet, that's all." And I gripped her
waist and lifted her down too, to stop her thinking that
one through to the obvious implications; and she weighed
plenty, did Laura, with their baby inside her, but I managed
not to fall or even stagger, and I kissed her cheek also.
"Go on, now. Quicker you are, quicker we'll both be with
you . . ."

And then I clambered out again, and by the time I'd
turned around Janice was leading them off, bless her, in
a long crocodile, each of them holding hands fore and aft.

"Back up, Ben. I can't see 'em . . ."

I backed up all the way, to stand beside him once more;
and we watched our women slither across the sea, and at last
saw them reach the rubble on the further side and scramble
up. To be met by men, Macallan men I was sure, I was
certain, I hoped to God . . .

"*Christ . . .!*"

"Don't let go yet, Jamie," and I was suddenly urgent, now
I could afford to be. "There's still us."

Technically, we didn't matter so much; our safety was
inherent in the girls', we could wait for a boat if we had to.
Only, I wanted to be over there. More than this would be
happening tonight, and I wanted my say in the rest. And I

wanted to see Jamie safe with Laura and me with Janice not
to see either of them stranded among Macallans, and also I
wanted to meet that promise, *later . . .*

Jamie turned his head slowly to look at me. His skin
glistened unhealthily, his hair was dank with sweat, his
breath came in hard painful gasps, and he was grinning
like a moon-happy fool.

"What are you doing?" I asked him.

"Checking if it's still there, when I don't look at it.
It'll need to be." He blinked a couple of times, then
said, "Is it?"

"You know it is." Didn't look any different, any less solid
to me; it still lay like an impossible frozen ford through
the water, holding hard against the sea's suck and all the
imperatives of nature.

"You fit, then?"

"Fit as I'll ever be." It was him that looked bad, that didn't
look up to this; I was just praying his exultant mood would
carry us over.

"You want to fly?" he suggested, with a thin cackle. "We
could try flying, see if that works too . . ."

"No, Jamie, I don't want to fly. What would I tell Laura,
if it didn't work? I can't give you back to her all broken.
Come on, we're going to walk it. Heads high, feet dry."

I hoped . . .

Side by side, we stood on the edge; one last glance at each
other, which was both a betrayal and a declaration of confidence – *I have my doubts about this, bro, and you're the only
one I can admit it to* – and then side by side we jumped.

Jumped and skidded, clutching at each other for balance;
and started walking, good steady pace, heads up and eyes
forward. Like walking past a rottweiler on the loose, I
thought; *don't look round, don't let it see you're afraid.
Don't let it smell your doubts. Don't run.*

Ahead everything looked normal, if the word 'normal' can exist in the same universe as a corridor of seawater iced solid and running with light, while the sea unleashed swirled and hissed just a few scant inches behind walls of chill, only intangible will to hold it; I didn't want to see or know what was happening behind us. Whether Jamie could hold those walls together at our backs, while he himself walked between them. I thought it just might be too much like trying to haul yourself up by your own bootstraps, the laws of physics and magic both ought to be against it . . .

Halfway and all seemed well or well enough, except that my feet were bitter cold now and Jamie's grip on my elbow was getting tighter, tingle turning to a hot pulse as he urged me on.

"Better hurry, coz, I think I'm losing it . . ."

Don't run. "You're not losing it, Jamie man," I said, even as my treacherous feet picked up speed to deny me. It was all in his head; if he thought it was gone, then was gone. And we were too far, far too far from safety for him to lose it yet . . .

"Look," I said, stooping to thump the wall of the walk, about knee-high to me. How deep the water was that we walked above, I didn't like to think. Not so deep, actually, this was the causeway's route and its rubble was still down there, sometimes rising to trip us and never more than a metre beneath our feet; but a man could drown in very little water, and the sea would be vengeful if it caught us now, would hurry us away from here I thought and hold us a long time in its privy halls . . .

"Look," I said, stooping to thump, meaning to show him how stiff and solid he was holding it; but the wall seemed to crack, seemed to break and spring a leak so that my hand came up running wet. "Shit," I said. And then, hastily, "Spray," I said, "just spray, I'm soaked all over from the spray . . ."

Which was pretty much true, but irrelevant. What we walked on felt not so solid suddenly, and Jamie wasn't grinning any more. When I saw his head turn to look back, I knew he was right. He was losing it.

"Fuck," he gasped, eyes front again, stiff and staring, measuring how far we had to go. "Think we'd better run for it, mate. I can't do this . . ."

"Yes, you can. Sure you can, and we're not running anywhere," just walking very, very fast now, slipping and sliding like kids on an icy pavement. I could see the walls bowing, bending inward, and my feet were wet now as well as cold. More than spray was splashing over the edges, making puddles.

Twenty metres. Five long skidding strides, and it was only fifteen. Even with my eyes glued to the sunken path we walked, trying to add my useless to Jamie's faltering will, I was aware of figures stood in safety at the end there, waiting for us, pale faces above dark clothes and voices calling, encouraging, urging us on.

Three further strides, and there could only be a dozen left; and a surge of water came from behind us, lapping and tugging at my ankles, making me stagger. And then I did look back, we both did; and Jamie said, "Oh, fuck," and I swear I could smell his fear, unless it was my own.

Never mind the protocol, sound advice and confidence-boosting wasn't going to help us now. Water can't crumble, but that was how it looked in the dark there as the nightfire faded, a long glowing line of light dying from sight as the walls crumbled and fell in atop it . . .

We grabbed at each other, and ran.

Ran through water that was ankle-deep and then calf-deep and getting deeper; ran on a surface that ran itself, that seemed to melt beneath us; ran, waded, plunged, floundered towards where the voices were, seeing nothing now but the water that swirled and surged and tried to claim us for its own as there was nothing left to run on, nothing to push against, only each other to cling to . . .

How we covered those last few metres, I honestly don't know. You couldn't say we swam, not with our arms tight around each other and our bodies bucking and twisting in the rampant sea. We just kicked, I guess: kicked against the world and its monstrous sense of irony, kicked against all the shit and all the glory and somehow just had momentum enough to carry us through, to where strong cousinly hands could haul us out.

We lay on sand-gritty tarmac, sodden and shaking, gasping and spitting up salt, colder than the water and God knew that had been cold enough. I had water in my eyes, in my ears, it felt like I had water in my skull; I could neither see nor hear nor think. I was only dimly aware of anxious female voices, being overriden by men; it was male hands certainly that came down hard on my back, squeezing what little air there was out of my lungs. Just checking, I supposed, making sure they didn't squeeze out water. Took a massive effort to push myself up against that pressure, to bend my head around and whisper, "Don't, I'm okay . . ."

Cousin Conor it was, kneeling astraddle me with his big hands ready to squeeze again. He didn't take my word for it, that there wasn't the need; he looked aside, presumably for someone else's nod. And presumably got it, because he gave me a grin and thrust himself upward, out of my line of sight. I sighed, breathed as deeply as I could manage, coughed and spat and dropped my head down again, on to the pillow of my folded arms.

With my head turned sideways I could see Jamie, prone beside me, his clothes oozing water and his face strikingly pale, his eyes just pits of shadow. Open pits, though:

somehow he managed a smile. No words, but none were
needed. *We made it*, his smile was saying, *we're home
free.*

Not true, I thought, certainly not the whole truth, but it
was enough for now. I sighed one more time and let my
eyes do what they most wanted, let them fall shut while I
concentrated on breathing and listening to the pound and
surge of my blood, of my heart, a counterpoint to the
defeated sea.

They let us lie for a while, not for long enough. I heard a
voice say, "Jamie? Your dad wants to go now, if you're
ready," and figured that for my own summons too.

So. Hands flat to the road, and pushing cautiously upward;
I made it onto all fours and thence awkwardly, wobblingly
to my feet. Jamie was no better, beside me. Chill and
exhaustion after panic and frantic effort had drained us
both; we couldn't even cling to each other, had nothing
left to share.

Conor was there, though, sturdy and reliable and willing.
Impressed, it seemed; proud of us both. That was rare— no,
that was something totally new for me. I wondered how hard
he was finding it, or how strange, given my reputation in the
family.

Someone else, another cousin was looking after Jamie;
it was too much trouble to squint through the darkness, to
look past the classic Macallan features for whatever touch
of individuality would tell me who. I just leaned on Conor's
shoulder and let him steer my shaky legs, along what was
left of the causeway to the cars.

Jamie was following; I was more aware of him than
anything else, tuned in to his faltering footsteps, the sound
of his strained breathing, both only echoes of my own.

It was his voice called me back into an effortful focus
on the world, on the night. I hadn't found my voice yet,

beyond that first croaked whisper; certainly hadn't thought to ask a question. If anything I'd been glad of the chance not to question, just to let things happen to me for a bit.

But Jamie said, "Where's Laura?"— and abruptly I was back, my weakness only a hindrance now as I stared around the car park. He was right. No Laura, and no Janice; nor Serena, Christa, none of the girls we'd gone to rescue, who'd really rescued us.

"The women have gone ahead." A cold, blunt, gravelly voice from a static figure standing in the shadow beyond the cars: Jamie's dad, my Uncle James. My least favourite person, probably, in the whole wide world, and the man who was making the decisions here. He'd likely done that deliberately, separating the girls from us. Not using them as hostages, exactly, only as security, a guarantee that this time we'd do as he wanted.

It worked. Jamie perhaps gave him a stare, across the car roofs. I didn't even do so much, I just slumped through the door that Conor opened and sat wetly shivering, waiting to be taken wherever Uncle James had decreed. I did my seatbelt up, only because Macallans as a class did not; my head dropped forward, I wrapped my arms around my chest and closed my eyes again, vaguely hoping that seawater would stain the fabric of the seat. Not that this was Uncle James' car, I didn't rate that highly. Not in my current state.

We didn't even get to travel in the same car, Jamie and I. His dad was taking no chances, it seemed, after our last rebellion. Needless precaution, belt and braces on shrink-fit jeans; I was going where Janice had gone and nowhere else, and Jamie I knew would be frantic to catch up with Laura, picturing her frantic at being taken away from him.

It was a brief drive, maybe ten minutes, maybe less. When Conor killed the engine I lifted my head, wiped the condensation off the window – whoops, that was all

my moisture, *sorry, Conor* – and saw that we'd come to a
minor cousin's house on the waterside, just where the river
met the sea. Convenient, I guessed. Equipped with warm
towels, I was sure, and a gas fire, and a change of clothes
that might come somewhere near fitting me. Equipped also
with Janice, of course, who would sit behind me on the
hearth and rub my hair dry, and comb it through with her
fingers as the warmth seeped into my bones and hard-edged
exhaustion mellowed towards a sleepy drift . . .

Cousin Diarmuid's house had been a working building once,
a shipping warehouse on the ground floor – still with its
heavy wooden gallows-beam jutting out over the water,
which we used to dare each other to walk as teenagers,
leaving and collecting trophies on the pulley at the end
to be sure that no one cheated – and the pilots' offices
above. There was a little wooden tower on the flat roof,
where they used to watch for ships coming in; Diarmuid
watched the stars from there on clear nights. He might
have been watching tonight, I thought, it might even have
been him who spotted Jamie's nightfire beacon and alerted
the family.

Maybe I'd ask him later, if I remembered. If I didn't fall
asleep on his floor, in front of his fire, soothed by gentle
fingers. That was the new plan: get dry, get warm, get
comfy, get to sleep. The last had worked out pretty well,
no reason why this one shouldn't also.

Except that when Conor ushered me into the house,
into the big living room, there were no women there.
Not Janice, not Laura, none of the freed hostages. Uncle
James was there, of course, and other men of the family,
but no one else.

Diarmuid came in behind me, tutting when he saw me
drip on to his polished oak floor.

"Upstairs with you, lad," he said, a firm hand on my

shoulder setting my skin to jumping even as it turned me back towards the door. "Jamie's there already, drying off and raiding my wardrobes. You're much of a size, I'm sure we can find something to fit you too . . ."

I was also sure of that, though Diarmuid was shorter and considerably fatter than either of us. But I twisted free of his hold, just for a moment, to glance back and ask, "Uncle James, where are the girls?"

"I sent them back to my house," he said dismissively. "Lucy will look after them. We don't need them here."

He was wrong. I needed them, or one of them; so would Jamie. But that was a need Uncle James would only see as weakness, and he'd allowed us no chance to argue. I trudged wearily up the stairs in Diarmuid's wake, wondering how soon he'd decide he didn't need us either, how quickly we could follow. If we were lucky, we could persuade Conor or another cousin to drive us; I didn't want to wait for a lift from my uncle . . .

As we walked across the landing, it occurred to me to wonder just why Uncle James thought he needed us at all.

Debriefing, I thought, more perhaps in hope than expectation, *that's all, he just wants a report on what happened, and then he'll let us go . . .*

Diarmuid opened the door of his dressing-room and we caught Jamie debriefing early, standing amid a pile of discarded clothing and just wriggling out of his wet underpants. He threw me a thin-lipped look when really he ought to have been winking, we should have been sharing a grin at his giving Diarmuid such a visual treat. I gathered that he too had already inquired after the girls.

He hooked a towel up off the floor, and knotted it around his waist; Diarmuid fussed around his feet, picking up all his saturated gear.

"You could have left these in the bathroom, Jamie, and spared my carpets."

"Sorry. I didn't fancy the dash, butt-naked." Not much trace of apology in his voice; Jamie, I thought, was steaming angry. Me, I didn't have the energy to steam.

"There are bathrobes, you know. That's what they're for. Benedict, come with me . . ."

I undressed dutifully in the plush bathroom, dumped my clothes where Diarmuid told me to with a pang of regret for my sodden, spoiled jacket, and took the chance of a quick hot shower while I was there. Towelled off quickly, wrapped myself in a floor-length hooded robe that I'd have stolen without a qualm if there'd only been a way to smuggle it out of the house unseen, decided against any of the startling array of slippers lined up against one wall and went barefoot back to the dressing-room.

Where I found Jamie little further on in his dressing, wearing only a pair of Calvin Klein short johns, with the towel around his neck now. As I came in he gave his hair a desultory rub with one corner and I thought *Janice* with a pang I thought he was sharing, only with a different name attached.

It was a surprise to find him still there; I'd have expected his father to send for him sharpish if he lingered. Maybe Uncle James wanted us both together, and was allowing him the leeway to let me catch up . . .

"You all right?" I asked him.

"Yeah. Knackered, mostly. Still shaking, look," and he held up a hand to show me.

I laid my palm against his to match him, tremble for tremble. Adrenalin, I guessed; kicks in fast, takes a while to get absorbed through the system. "Well, we made it," I said, for what comfort that supplied. "You were brilliant. And the girls are okay . . ."

"Not here, though."

"No." Again we matched, grimace for resentful grimace.

Nothing more to be said, except, "We'll chase them, right? Soon as he lets us."

"Right." Then Jamie did grin, at last, though it looked a little forced; he indicated the room with a jerk of his head and said, "Been in here before?"

"No, never." We'd had the run of the house on our occasional visits as kids, but a dressing-room had held no attractions, once we'd established that the name did explain its entire function. A dressing-up room it was not, or not for children.

"It's amazing, have a browse. Kex are in those drawers there . . ."

Not hard to see why Jamie had got bogged down in his selection, knickers and nothing more. The room was crammed with wardrobes, chests and tallboys, barely enough floorspace free to change in; and there were clothes enough in there to keep a trendy menswear shop supplied through the Christmas rush and after. Cousin Diarmuid might dress his boyfriends up to the nines of fickle fashion, but he must strip them bare when they left him.

I rummaged through the plentiful supply of underwear, where Jamie had directed me, and finally settled on a pair of black Brass Monkey briefs. We both added plain top-quality T-shirts, black for me and white for him; then we burned up a sudden rush of nervous energy in a giggling, stupid half-hour of chucking suits at each other, "Here, try that, hon, you'll look stunning . . ."

Armani, Jasper Conran, Nicole Farhi in both sharp and casual moods: how could we choose? Everything we laid hands on seemed to fit, we must have matched Diarmuid's ideal as closely as we matched each other; everything felt wonderful as we paraded the narrow aisles, twirling and posing like idiots.

Me, I'd have chickened at the last, I'd have settled for

jeans — designer jeans, *natürlich* — if Jamie had allowed me.

He wouldn't, though. "If I'm going down there grand, then so are you," he said, "and I am. Laura'd never forgive me, else. She's going to want to see this . . ."

See it and keep it, I reckoned; Cousin Diarmuid would have a job reclaiming this gear, if he ever tried.

Jamie fixed on Ralph Lauren, in the end. I found a two-piece in charcoal grey that must have been made to measure some unknown but lusty lad; it was too smart even to be labelled. But it wasn't that which grabbed me, though it might have been measured exactly for me. It was the red silk lining, flaring unexpectedly when I swung the jacket open. I loved it, and Jamie wouldn't let me take it off.

Sober dark socks of heavy silk, that felt amazing on my feet; and then we raided the shoe-cupboard and rebelled just a little against the implicit formality of our suits, each of us picking a serious pair of boots, Docs for him and Cats for me.

Half an hour at least we'd taken in there, likely more, and still Uncle James hadn't despatched anyone to fetch us down. That was strange, it was unnerving, it made me wonder again why the hell he'd had us brought here. Jamie was getting fidgety also, once we'd stamped around a bit to check the boots out; fun-time was over, we both knew that, though we did drag it out a little longer, to raid a drawerful of watches and a few other essentials from the jewellery-box. Jamie took a couple of matching gold rings, I noticed, one too small for his wedding-finger. He didn't wear the other, though it was a perfect fit; he just slipped them both into a pocket and turned away, conspicuously avoiding my eye. I found a pair of earrings, tiny jade buddhas that went into my own breast pocket as I struggled to remember whether Janice had pierced ears. If not I could always buy her the holes as an extra present, if she'd only sit still for it . . .

*   *   *

That was that, though. One last survey of our finely clad
and discreetly-glittering selves in the full-length mirror that
made the door so heavy; one last grin at each other that
mutually faded; and we pulled that heavy door open, his
fingers above mine on the handle so that neither one of
us was doing this to the other, and we walked out and
down and in.

Into a room of murmuring man-talk, smells of whisky
and good cigars, an air of quiet triumph and patient waiting.
That last the most unexpected, though I hadn't counted on
any of this: my family was hardly famous for its patience,
and I couldn't think what they were all so visibly waiting for.

Uncle James was in positively expansive mood, for him;
he acknowledged our arrival with a nod that held no dis-
approval for the time we'd taken, a twitch of the eyebrow
to register our sartorial eloquence, and a generous wave
of the hand towards Cousin Diarmuid's sideboard, where
spirits were.

I thought probably I ought to eat, we both ought, it
had been a long time since the burgers; but there were
nuts and olives to chew on, and I had no appetite for
anything more.

Macallan for me, Laphroaig for him, the cool bugger, and
a bottle of Bud each – the Czech stuff, the proper stuff, no
American derivatives for Diarmuid – as a chaser; we retired
into a corner, with no more information to mull over than
a murmured, "Just wait, you'll see," from Conor when we
tried to interrogate him.

We waited, we speculated in shrugs and whispers, we
checked the time constantly on our brand-new watches;
good practice, that, for shooting our brand-new cuffs. And
we picked specks of lint off each other's sleeves and
wondered where on God's good earth lint came from,

because no one ever actually used it for anything except bandages, you never saw it around and yet it was always there, in specks, waiting to cling to any particularly smart suiting that happened to wander past . . .

We were bored as hell, in other words. And bone-weary, spoiling the cut of our clothes by sagging at every joint; and we'd run totally out of things to say to each other and wouldn't talk to anyone else, because no one would tell us the one thing, the only thing we really, really wanted to know.

We did think briefly about a getaway, slipping out and calling a taxi, going after the girls without an exeat from Uncle James. But something big was happening or due to happen, there was unfinished business still; and if even Jamie's dad thought we ought to be there, I was reluctantly inclined to agree.

At last, something did happen. At precisely 2:05 (I checked), Diarmuid's telephone rang.

Uncle James answered it, without even a glance at his host for permission. He spoke, listened, spoke again; then hung up, swept a glance around the suddenly-silent room to be sure he had everyone's attention, and nodded towards the door.

Still no one was talking, or not to us. They muttered to each other, too low to overhear, and began to file out. We went with Conor when he beckoned, but he wouldn't answer questions; he just smiled with a grim satisfaction, and told us again to hold our horses, we'd see when we got there.

Into the cars once more, this time both of us in Conor's, and off we all went in convoy: up onto the dual carriageway and along the route of the river till we came to the first bridge over. We crossed there and headed back east, towards the coast again; and then south, leaving the main road and following a tourist trail that led nowhere except to a pub on the high cliffs with a famous cave beneath, that they'd done out as a restaurant.

We parked by the pub, which was dark of course and all locked up, this time of night. The moon was sinking now, but still bright enough to throw our shadows over the edge as we trekked in silence and single file along a footpath above the cliff.

Soon we could see lights ahead of us, bright lights where no buildings were. No roads either, but those were a car's headlamps for sure, dipped to shine on the turf. Doors were open, interior lights were on too, showing us the high boxy shape of the car: Uncle James' Range Rover it was, well up to the bouncing ride over rough ground it must have had to get itself here.

There were figures too, silhouetted against the light, standing waiting for us. Slowly, my tired mind was working this out. The rough hand of Macallan justice was in action tonight; Uncle James was in vengeful mood, and he'd chosen a spectacular theatre to hold his private circus in.

A couple of hundred feet below us, the sea crashed and thundered unseen. Just here, more than the cliff defied it; a limestone spur ten or twelve metres wide thrust out maybe another fifty metres, though the unstinting work of water swirling at its base had hollowed it into a great arch, a landmark for sightseers and sailors both.

They were cousins, of course, at the car, more male scions of my wide-branching family. With them was one man else, standing tall and still, all too clearly a captive although no one's hand was on him. None needed to be, Macallans don't hold or bind their prisoners.

Nor was the man a stranger. Despite the strange glaring light and the black shadows it cast – or maybe not despite, maybe because of – I knew him instantly. Knew him from another place of shadows and glare, difficult seeing. The tunnel under the bridge, the man with a torch in one hand and a tube in the other, a teasing joke on his tongue as he cs'd us for his pleasure . . .

"Who *is* he?" I hissed, barely above a whisper. Meaning the question for Jamie, perhaps for Conor, not seriously expecting an answer; and receiving one unexpectedly from an unexpected source, from Uncle James himself, some few paces distant.

"He is," he said with a slow satisfaction, "the Assistant Chief Constable with special responsibility for this city. He is a man with whom this family has had an understanding, for many years. His family owns and runs Pirate's Island, by special dispensation. He is also the man responsible for all the recent outrages against us – but I think you know that already, do you not?"

Well, yes, I did; I just hadn't realised that my uncle was on to him too.

"I began to suspect," he went on, "when the police station burned down yesterday. It was reported to me that the fire seemed . . . unnatural. Unlikely. When I attempted to contact this man," whom it seemed he wouldn't even dignify with a name, "I was told he was unavailable. Unavailable to me! So I made enquiries elsewhere, and learned that a number of women had been held in the police station for some time; also that they had been removed shortly before the fire. I presume that was your doing, by the way, Benedict? The fire?"

I was about to confess it, but Jamie stepped between us. "Mine as well, father. They had our girls too, they had Laura; and we thought we could rescue them . . ."

Instead of being rescued by them, but that I was not going to say.

"You should have come to me." He fixed us both with

a portentous frown, his displeasure equally divided. "However, events have turned out well, despite your meddling. When the women came across the water this evening – and that was well managed, Jamie," with a nod, all the approval it seemed he would allow his son for the minor miracle he'd worked, "they confirmed to me that they had been in the hands of the police. That meant that this man was responsible, beyond question. He had already left the district in a hurry, this afternoon; but I had had him watched and followed, in case my earlier suspicions proved justified. Collecting him tonight was not a problem."

And oh, he was pleased with himself, my uncle. Problem solved, normal service to be resumed immediately. Or immediately following tonight's extraordinary general meeting . . .

"What are you going to do with him?" I asked, though I thought I could guess.

"He will take a walk," said Uncle James, with an unpleasant little chuckle and a glance at the rough rock outcrop. No accident, I realised, that the car was parked just so, where its lights threw a beam all along the arch.

That was my uncle's special talent, to make people do what they didn't want, to work their bodies against their struggling will. Once, he'd used it on me; I could still remember the terror as my muscles jerked to his command, my mind a helpless prisoner, unable even to raise a scream of protest. And all he'd done to me was sit me in a car I didn't want to sit in . . .

Turning my head away from the memory, I saw tonight's intended victim standing alone among his enemies, knowing for sure that he was due to die, though probably not knowing how. I thought of him taking that brief and cruel walk, pirates and planks, I thought, *a long walk off a short pier*; and I knew how it would feel, every step his unwilling legs would stumble over the rock under my uncle's unrelenting gaze until they took a step too far, a step off rock and into air.

And I grabbed Jamie's arm and pulled him away from his father, away from all our indifferent cousins; and I said to him urgently, "Jamie, I don't, I don't want any more killing."

"What?" He seemed honestly surprised, almost bewildered. "For God's sake, Ben. This is the bastard who had Josie killed, and Karen. And that kid Charlie, delivered his bloody *head*, remember?"

Yes, I did remember, I was not about to forget. Nor forgive, but even so, "I just don't want anyone else to die," I repeated. "It's got to stop sometime, it's got to stop *now* or it never will," and I meant more than just the killing, I meant everything my uncle and my father and all my family did in this town. "And I can't stop him, Jamie, it's got to be you." *For Laura's sake*, I thought about adding, and didn't. *For your own sake, for both of you and the kid too; she won't stay with you else, she's too decent to tolerate this* – but no, let him work that out for himself.

Which he did, perhaps; at any rate, he nodded roughly and turned back towards his father.

"Dad, no."

"What? What do you mean, no?"

"I mean you can't do this." He was speaking loudly enough for everyone to hear; deliberately so, I guessed. Committing himself, making a public stand, leaving himself no back door to scuttle out of. Laura would have been proud. "There's been too much killing already. Karen and Josie, they're dead, they're out of it; but so are two of theirs, and the rest of us are safe. This isn't justice, it's cold murder, and I won't let you do it."

Uncle James stared, and then he laughed, loud above the muttering that surrounded him. He didn't even bother to answer Jamie; he turned his head and gazed almost benignly at his captive, and the man began to walk.

Began to sweat, too, for all his determined, silent pride. Christ, I was with him all the way, remembered panic sweating my own skin as I relived the few moments I'd felt Uncle James' hand in my head, tugging my strings. I wanted to scream for him, because I knew he couldn't scream for himself; I wanted to sob, I wanted to look away, I wanted to run away; above all I wanted to stop him, to hurl myself on him bodily if that was what it took to halt that inexorable march.

And didn't, did none of those things. Bodily hurling was as futile as screaming, I'd only be bodily dragged off again; running away would help me no more than it helped him. At the least I had to be there for him, I felt an imperative urge to watch, to share what I could; but more than that, maybe far more than that, I had to be there for Jamie. I could do nothing here, but Jamie could. Not only the best of my many cousins, he was also the strongest in his talent; maybe my will could stiffen his, help him stand up to his father with more than words . . .

Whether he needed my help just then, I don't know; whether he felt even a shadow of my mute urging, *do it, Jamie, hold the guy back, break your father's concentration, anything, but do something. Please . . . ?*

Whether he needed me, whether he felt me or not, Jamie did indeed do something. Jamie did something wild, extravagant, fantastic.

Jamie threw down Falston Arch.

Or blew it up, perhaps. Shattered it, scattered it, crumbled and splattered it. Whichever.

He'd learned a lesson from me, I think, each time we'd stood at the causeway to work magic. The second time, I'd taught him that talent runs wider than any of us can imagine, that it's limited only by our imaginations; the first, that we're stronger even than we think we are.

Tell him a week before this that he could and would seize a span of limestone as broad and deep as a good-size house, that he'd grip it and squeeze it and break it into shards and gravel and dust, he'd have laughed like a bampot and given you a hangover cure. But he'd seen me do it to the road, and now he did it to the arch.

Like me, he didn't do it all at once, he had to feel his way into it; unlike me, he didn't have any time spare for experiment or failure.

Standing behind him, I saw his fists clench spasmodically; I heard three or four sharp cracks like a rifle firing, somewhere close. Several of my cousins ducked and swivelled, looking for trouble, never thinking to look among their company.

Stone cracks in sudden heat or sudden cold, or under tremendous pressure. The more straticulate the stone is, the more fault lines there are already, the sooner it happens and the more catastrophically.

Plenty of strata in a limestone crop, plenty of faults in this one: the snapping, crackling noises were the sounds of faults running through the traumatised rock as fast and free as the tear in a balloon when it pops.

Jamie I think was the only one of us who didn't react at all, he just went on traumatising. Even Uncle James startled, he jerked and glanced about him, and the one man who'd been moving before stood still now, abandoned like an animator's model, inanimate in himself.

Push comes to shove, squeeze comes to crush, everything comes to the crunch. Too many faults come to total failure.

Total failure came to the arch as we stood and watched, as we stared in the dark. There was a halo of nightfire above and about it, dancing on the grass before us, sparkling in the air;

there was a sudden ripping sound, a hundred or a thousand buried fault lines pulling themselves apart at once; the top surface of the arch's span, all that we could see, began to tip and tilt, this way and that, great slabs of limestone sliding and grinding and tumbling free.

Grind turned to roar, the ground we stood on trembled and shook, a great cloud of dust rose up in front of us. The wind off the sea blew it back into our faces like a smokescreen; the last sight I had of my cousins, most of them were running.

My eyes were full of grit, watering, stinging; I fumbled my way like a blind man in a hurry, squinting and seeing nothing, hands stretched out to feel.

At last, just when I thought I'd missed him, my fingers found cloth and flesh, found a man standing and shivering, his hands over his face. I pulled them down roughly, peered closely at him to be sure. My uncle's sacrifice, his enemy and mine.

I turned him round, away from the car's lights and the path that had brought us here. Turned his back to the swirling dust and pushed him, screamed in his ear, yelled, "Run, you fool! Run like fuck . . .!"

Gave him another shove to get him started, waited till I was sure he was moving under his own strength, the impetus of survival; then I turned again, groping more cautiously towards where I thought I'd left Jamie.

The wind blew the worst of the dust away, tears washed my eyes clear. When I could see again, it was Jamie I saw first, standing just where he had been and gazing in awe and wonder at what he'd achieved, what the sea had failed over centuries to achieve on its own account. Falston Arch had become something else, Falston Stack I supposed, a massive limestone pillar separated by twenty or thirty metres from the mainland now.

There were half a dozen men left on the height here, where there had been dozens; others were coming back in ones and twos, but none of them concerned me. Only a couple truly mattered, Jamie and his father.

Uncle James of course had not run, he too was still where I had seen him last; and all the power of his will, all his furious intent was fixed on Jamie.

As I watched, helpless in moonlight, my uncle unleashed that fury on his son. As he had once – at least once – before, when I was his victim, he broke the cardinal rule and used his talent against his own family, his own flesh; and this time it was to crush no minor rebellion, not merely to move a reluctant boy to where he wanted him.

Did he mean it, was it conscious choice or only the rage in him blindly reacting? I couldn't say, and still can't. Maybe a man of Uncle James' stamp, defied once too often and too publicly, made to look small and weak in the eyes of those who look to him for power and command – maybe such a man on such a night could do such a thing coldly and deliberately. Maybe he did.

At any rate, he did it. His eyes glittered, he reached out with his mind and seized Jamie's, took control of it all; and he marched Jamie swiftly and silently to where the cliff was crumbling and broken, where the arch was gone. Thus far, and one step further. Without a word or a glance around at the rest of us, he marched his son, his only surviving child over the edge.

Jamie, who'd been so ecstatic earlier he'd wanted to fly, or try it: Jamie didn't fly, he fell. He fell and was gone in a moment, and briefly I thought I heard the sound of his body breaking on the broken rocks beneath us.

Everyone was frozen, everyone was staring at Uncle James; they all knew what he'd done, and none of them believed it.

I moved first, I think, a few faltering and useless steps

towards the edge, where Jamie wasn't. I checked before I
got there, turned back, gazed wildly at the cousins where
they stood bewildered, found Conor among them and ran to
him.

Grabbed him by the shoulders, shook him hard, shook
him out of his stupor; then I spoke to him, forcing the
words out on hard little breaths through a throat clamped
tight with shock.

"Conor. Listen to me. Take the car, drive to his house.
Take him with you," with a jerk of my head towards my
impervious uncle. "Just do it, right? Take him, leave him
there, bring Laura back. Not here, bring her down there,"
another jerk, he'd get the idea, "to the beach. Tell her Jamie's
hurt, understand? Just that, tell her he's hurt . . ."

I waited for his nod, and got it; then before he could start
having doubts or asking questions, I pushed myself away
from him and ran.

Back along the path, but not as far as the pub where we'd
left the cars. There was a way down from there, I knew, to
the narrow strand beneath the cliff, but I was too urgent to
take so long. There was a nearer place where the cliff had
partly collapsed, where generations of scrambling kids had
reduced it further, to a steep scree slope.

Surfing the scree was a game we all used to play, despite
fences and warning signs and our parents' loud and frequent
prohibitions. It was a stupid and dangerous game even in
daylight, even with friends around you; by night, alone and
with the moon's shadow turning the whole face black, it
was potentially lethal.

Nor was there really so much hurry. Jamie was dead or
dying; what could I do? Zilch, was what. Or near zilch. I
could hold his hand, I could talk him on his way; perhaps
that seemed urgent enough, to get me there before he was
utterly gone.

Though I don't remember thinking so clearly. All I knew
was the urgency, the appalling rush that was on me; and I
don't remember a moment's hesitation at the fence, where
the cliff fell away into darkness just a metre or so beyond.

I vaulted the fence and stepped out almost as blindly,
almost as driven as Jamie, though it was my own mind
driving me.

Stepped out, and down. My heel found gravel, that shifted
and settled a little before it took my weight; I heard the
scutter of loose stuff sliding already.

My other foot now, my hands thrust out for balance and
my mind striving to remember how to play this. *Keep on
your feet* was the crucial rule. *Bend your knees like a skier,
lean into the slope and go with it when it goes, don't try to
fight it. Never, never try to stop . . .*

A few stuttering, uncertain steps down and then I almost
didn't need to step again, the whole surface was moving
beneath me, slipping away like an avalanche of rock and
I had to ride it, I had to stay on top. If I fell it would roll
me over and roll over me, and there might be two bodies
on that beach come morning.

Truly an escalator, the cliff carried me down, faster
and faster; I had to move fast to stay with it, because
you can't stand still or it steals your feet from under
you. There's a seriously smart trick where you can run
backwards to go slow, but you need to be expert for that,
and well in practice. I hadn't done this for ten years or
so, and besides, slow was not on my mind. I leaped, made
skidding, careering contact with the sliding scree and leapt
again, going down through the dark in a series of crazy
bounds.

And hit the hard stuff at the bottom without warning,
without being able to see. My foot turned on a boulder that
didn't shift, and then I did fall, I rolled and tumbled ten or
twenty feet over jagged rocks and came to rest at last with

a bone-bruising thump that knocked out of me what little breath I had left.

Lay where I was for a brief time, fighting for air while the last scatter of scree pattered down around me and torn horribly between the desperate need to move and the need not to move at all just now, the absolute imperative of stillness.

Slowly, various bits and pieces began to hurt, quite badly; it dawned on me that if I didn't go with the desperation and get myself up right now, they might hurt so much that moving became impossible. So I did move, just fingers and feet to start with, just to check that I could. Nothing was broken, seemingly; I put my hands down on rock-strewn sand and pushed myself awkwardly up onto my knees. Breathed deeply and ran what internal checks I could, finding sharp twisting pains and soreness but nothing worse; and then external, patting lightly over my head and what skin I could get to. Rips in my smart suit I found, skinned knees and knuckles and a few cuts, one swelling already forming under my hair where my head had cracked against a rock.

I felt a little dizzy but not disoriented, not I thought concussed, though it was hard to be sure of that. I tried to count fingers, but couldn't see even a hand's span in front of my eyes; I had to wait a minute longer before they adjusted to the starlight.

Decided I was okay then, that I could make out just the three fingers I knew I was holding up. Okay to walk, at least; so I scrambled cautiously to my feet and set off. The tide was coming back in again by now, waves hissing over sand, leaving me only a couple of metres'-width of beach between water and tumbled rock at the cliff's foot. That panicked me again, as I glanced up at the dark mass of the cliff and thought of Jamie's long fall down; even if he'd survived it he must surely have fallen into water, he must be drowning if he wasn't dead already. And either way, dead or dying, the sea must be sucking at him, pulling him in deeper, pulling him away from us who loved him . . .

That had me running again as best I could, stumbling through the hurt of a yanked ankle and much-abused muscles. And as I ran, even through the jolting pain of every step my traitor mind was thinking, *dead or dying, Jamie's lost to Laura* . . .

She would be free and needful, oh, so very much in need; I thought I could claim her now, I could step into my cousin's shoes and take care of her, her and her baby both. I could take them and love them, take them away from here. We could build a new life together, the three of us and any more kids that came along; I could be her substitute Macallan, it's what Jamie surely would have wanted for her. I could hear his voice in my head, his dying words urging me to do it; I could see his final movement, fingers fumbling weakly in his jacket pocket to find those rings, then pressing them into my hand as a token, *these are my future, yours now, take and wear them with my blessing, in memory of me* . . . Even if he was past speech, past movement as surely he must be, surely I'd be right to do that thing . . . ?

Thinking so, I pounded along the strand hearing nothing but my own thoughts and my own blood pounding in my ears, my own aching gasps of pain and lack of breath; and at last I came to where the great pillar stood swirled by wild water, its fallen arch standing proud like a boulder dam between it and the cliff, with the sea washing against both flanks.

That's where I found Jamie, though it took me some time to do it. I checked this side and then the other, scrambling on hands and knees across the shifting rock to do it; I couldn't see him on either side, and thought he must be gone already, utterly gone, carried away by tide and current to God alone knew where, what watery grave he would lie in. I walked the

ridge of rock for the height it gave me, scanning, scanning;
and almost trod on him then, almost tripped over his body
and fell again.

Caught myself with an effort, staring down. There he was,
lying sprawled and still at my feet, just meat and bone, I
thought, flesh emptied of what was truly Jamie. I squatted
beside him, reached to touch and found him cool already,
spray-soaked and blood-soaked too, I thought, and not a
twitch in his skin where my fingers lay against it.

No hurry now. I settled myself awkwardly on the sharp
rocks, lifted the weight of him into my arms, cradled his
wet head against my shoulder and didn't cry, didn't scream
against the brutality of the world or my uncle or any world
that could have my uncle in it; only sat and held him, rocked
him a little maybe, clutched him against me and waited for
the world to catch up with us.

Which it did, though it seemed to take forever. The cold
crept from him to me, I passed through shivering into an
icy stillness that matched his own, and at some timeless
point during that endless wait I became conscious of more
than my own pulse beating between us, he had some faint
threadbare pulse of his own.

Nothing I could do about it. I held him in an echo of his
silence, watched for dawn.

Short northern summer nights: the day came blessedly
fast, though it seemed eternally slow to me. The sky shifted
from black through purple to blue, with a skim of clouds in
cerise; then the first flare of light on the horizon, *here comes
the sun* and it was my time again.

My head still swirled and shuddered around the single
terrible thought, *he's gone or going and Laura's free*; my
imagination was still feeding me glimpses of the future:
Laura and I, Laura and I with the child, two and three
of us cosy together, shaping a brave new world with all

horrors put behind us. Telling the kid about its father, of course, giving it a handsome hero of a dead dad, *never forget him but don't grieve either, you've another father now*. The kid content and Laura above all, Laura grieving as she must but coming through it, learning to love again and this time learning what she'd totally failed to learn before, learning to love me . . .

And the sun came up and touched me, my bruised and brutalised skin danced in response, I turned my eyes on Jamie's waxen face and closed them not to hide it from me, not to hide behind but only to see more clearly.

Blindsight took me in, took me under his skin and through his flesh and bones to find that spark of life that I could feel; showed me how weak it was, how pale a flicker within the mass of him. I knew no way to feed it, to share my strength with him. But I could see the damage too, all the breaks and tears and blockages that were so slowly killing him, that saw no hurry in it. And what I could see wrong, I could by definition see where it should be put right; and I knew already that I could do that, I'd had the practice on Laura's hand . . .

When the girls came, Laura and Janice running as I had run along the sand with Conor in their wake, I wasn't aware of them. I was far gone, lost somewhere deep in Jamie's blood and bone; I didn't even hear their voices call my name. They couldn't come close to touch me, they told me later, couldn't pull me back by main force into my own body. They couldn't get near; I was on fire, they told me, pale flames leaping on every inch of my exposed skin and Jamie's too, and a radiance of heat about us making our smart ruined suits smoke and char, all but making the air glow and the cracked rocks crack again.

Nothing they could do but stand and wait in a torment,

they told me, in a fever of anxiety; and it was a long wait, and not relieved when at last the flames faded and died away and I slumped suddenly down like something boneless, like something quite burned out at the core, as seemingly dead as Jamie.

THIRTEEN

BEN AND THE ART OF MOTORCYCLE MAINTENANCE

Glorious lassitude: this I thought must run close to a true definition of heaven. Never mind the *foie gras*, never mind the trumpets; I was content, better than content with sipping lassi on a Tudor lawn.

Well, mock-Tudor, actually. But that was the house, and it was behind me. Before me, if I chose to lift my head and look – which I must do every now and then, to sip – was wooded valley with bone-bare hills beyond, under a sky baked white. I was clad in my Spanish swim-shorts and the rest of me was all skin, all absorption, practising photosynthesis without benefit of chlorophyll. Even my eyelids were doing their bit.

Someone opened a window, and music crept by me on the grass. Sounded good to me, but I still hadn't caught up with all the new British bands despite days of this intensive-care programme, masses of food and nourishing drinks, all the sleep I could squeeze in and as much sun as I was allowed, which was almost as much as I wanted. In all truth I could have listened to the radio every hour I was conscious, I could have reeducated myself, Christ knew I was doing nothing else. Even listening felt like too much work, though, when not listening was so much easier, not being tied even to the weak thread of a DJ's playlist so much of a relief.

I turned my head, or at least let it drop sideways, onto a cushion of bruised grass. Intense aroma, sweet and astringent both: smells were so potent suddenly. I hadn't remembered the world so washed with scents.

Opened my eyes and there he was as he had been all day and every day of this slow convalescence, promoted from coz to bro to twin, Thai twin perhaps, invisibly linked to me. Every time I turned my head, I found him. Even at night: they had us in a twin-bedded room, while the girls shared the double next door. I must ask about that, when we were going to change around, now we were near fit again. Only that actually I didn't want to change. Not yet. I still had my moments, and a sight of Jamie was the best medicine we'd found thus far.

Even now, the sight of him made me smile. Dressed much as I was, just in the Calvin cyclers, he was lying on his belly with his face hidden in the crook of his elbow. His skin glistened lightly in the light; even his sweat I thought was having to sweat it, fighting through the Factor Millennial that Laura made us wear to wreck our tans with.

The image of golden youth he seemed just then: smooth and supple and unmarked, unscarred, the perfectibility of man.

"Jamie?"

I meant to ask him who the band was, that I could hear; but he just grunted, his bones seemed to settle a fraction further inside his skin, if he wasn't actually asleep he was as near as made no difference.

Fine, let it be. It didn't matter. I could always ask Jan, she loved being shocked by my ignorance; only I wouldn't, probably wouldn't, probably wouldn't remember . . .

I remembered nothing clearly about the day that followed the

night the arch came down. Nothing after the sunrise, after I
plunged all my consciousness into a final, desperate attempt
to save Jamie. Only a blur, a mess of mists and colours, my
body nothing but a conduit to channel light and a sense of
form, my self a speck of flame fighting to bring some order
into chaos.

I got lost, I think, within that alien place: lost all touch
with who I was or where to find myself, couldn't discover
a way back. There was terror, I think, a growing panic, the
knowledge of Benedict as someone separate from Jamie
slipping away from me; and at the last a feeling of surrender, of giving myself up almost willingly if only I could
restore him.

I didn't actually heal Jamie, or not then. There was just
too much that needed mending, and I didn't have the time or
the strength. All I could do, all I did was hold him together,
keep the spirit in the shell, fix enough of the damage to
ensure that his heart was still beating and his lungs taking
air. Beyond that, the suck of his need was greater than
my own sense of self-preservation; I would have drained
myself and damned us both, I think, if the weather hadn't
intervened.

It was those clouds I'd seen that saved us. They massed
up and covered the sun, barred my access to its light; that's
when I fell away from Jamie, when the girls could finally
get to us.

That's also what interrupted my reluctant sacrifice, barely
in time. Cut off while I still had a thread of self-awareness,
something in my subconscious must have reeled that thread
in before it snapped, before my flame could fail altogether.

At any rate, they tell me that I opened my own eyes in
my own body, somewhere on the beach there where Janice
was struggling to carry me on her own, all along the shore
to where they'd had to leave the car. Conor had gone ahead,
they say, with Jamie; neither one would let Laura help to

haul us, not in her condition, she'd risked too much already
with all that running.

It was Laura, apparently, who saw me wake. She told
Janice, who promptly dropped me on the sand. And dropped
down herself a moment later, Laura says, onto her knees and
crying.

I don't remember, but they say I was quite rational for a
moment there. They told me they were taking me to hospital,
as soon as they could get me to the car; and it seems that I
said no, don't do that, hospitals can't help. Wait for the sun,
I said, and I'll sort it . . .

Then I passed out again. Conor came back, and helped
the girls with me; and being a true Macallan, trusting talent,
he overcame their doubts. He brought us all to his house,
on a new estate outside the city. The sun was out again by
then, and burning brightly; I was awake and fretful, I'm told,
insistent. Dreadfully pale and weak, Jan says, but they did
what I told them, regardless. They helped me pull off the
scorched rags I was wearing, to get more sun on my skin;
whether I needed that I don't know, but it felt good, I said.
They tell me. Then I had them strip Jamie too and lay him
out beside me on the lawn, though Laura had a phone in her
hand all the time, ready to call an ambulance the moment
she decided that I'd failed.

I put my hands on Jamie, and again we flamed together,
we burned a great black patch in the grass; but it seems I'd
learned from the last time, because I pulled away of my own
will after ten minutes or so. Jamie seemed better, they say,
he was less pale and breathing more easily. It was me that
worried them more, losing what colour Jamie had gained,
slumping almost into unconsciousness again.

But I roused myself after lying in the sunlight for a
while, and then I did it again. And so the day wore on,
brief passages of treatment interspersed with longer spells
of recovery; and each time Jamie looked more healthy,

his visible cuts closing and bruises fading, along with the
dark swellings that spoke of broken bones or other internal
wreckage.

Towards evening, it was his turn to open his eyes. He
asked for water, they tell me; which was Laura's cue, her
turn to break down in tears after a day of stubborn denial.
They put her to bed, Jan says, even before the two of us.

That's all that I know of the day, all that they've told me;
for myself, I retain nothing of it. My first true memory is
waking sometime in the night, desperately thirsty on my
own account; felt myself in a single bed, opened my eyes
to a room I didn't recognise that was filled with shifting
shadows, glanced round wildly – and found Janice in a chair
beside me, ruining her eyes with reading by a nightlight.
She looked up as I shifted, and smiled magically in the
gloom.

I remember asking what the book was, of all stupid questions; I've never managed to forget the answer. *Criminal
Law*, it was, by Smith & Hogan. A classic text, apparently,
for law students to digest.

By then, I'd noticed that mine was not the only bed in
the room, nor was the other unoccupied.

"Is that . . . ?"

"Yes," she said, and the smile was in her voice also. "He's
going to be fine, we reckon. Laura still says he's got to see a
doctor tomorrow, but he's all right. How are you feeling?"

Knackered was largely how I felt, scooped out to the
bones of me; but wonderful also, utterly content to be lying
in a warm bed and warmly smiled at. Thirsty was all I told
her, though. She passed me a glass of water, I drained it, I
lay back on the pillow and thought it might be nice to hold
her hand until I fell asleep again, but I fell asleep before I
could suggest it.

*   *   *

"Hey."

"Mmm?"

"Look."

"Do I have to?"

"Yes," and her toe worked its way firmly into my ribs, forcing my eyes open.

She stood above me, smelling of petrol, her oily hands wrapped around something that gleamed metallically in the light.

"I just want to know if I've put this together right."

I reached out and took a grip on her leg, used that to pull against, to draw myself up. Her knees folded, trapping my hand as she sank down beside me; I made no attempt to recover it. We grinned at each other, and she stole a quick kiss before she showed me the carburettor.

This was the way, I thought, to self-service a motorbike: have a neophyte do the work while you soak up the sun and advise occasionally, criticise and comment. I approved wholeheartedly of learning-curves, the steeper the better.

"Looks okay to me," I said, turning the carburettor over in my one hand, reclaiming the other to test its solidity. "Does it work?"

"Wouldn't know, would I?"

"Well," I suggested, "why don't you put it back in and try it?"

She looked uncertain for a moment, then, "Can I?"

I just smiled, lay back in the grass and closed my eyes again. After a moment, I heard her stand and walk away; the smell of petrol faded, except for what was on my hands now. I liked that, that residues remained. Lovers' bodies should smell of each other, and ours were getting little enough chance.

Some brief time later, I heard the throaty roar of a big bike starting up come down at me from the road. It revved and faded, revved again, settled to a muted grumble and then picked up again and this time didn't die, it only moved away.

I smiled privately, checked that Jamie was sleeping still, and joined him.

It was Conor who'd collected both bikes from the flat and driven them out here one by one; we were neither of us capable yet, even if we'd had the resolution to go so far.

That same day, Janice had vanished for a couple of hours without warning, giving me worries I didn't need. She came back before I was frantic, though, before my imagination could persuade me that it all had to be done again, that she was hostage or worse.

She came back with a bag of clothes from her flat, and news of little comfort.

Fizzy sent his love, she told me, weaving her fingers in between mine, stroking the hairs on my forearm, giving us both a tingle; Jon didn't. She told me that too, just to be clear.

"How is Jon?"

She sighed, shrugged; said, "Static." Said, "He was just sitting. Didn't move at all, all the time I was packing. He just sat there, stroking Fizz."

"Cats are good," I said slowly. "When you're grieving."

"Yeah. I guess Fizzy's not my cat any more. That's not my flat now, either. He said a friend of his is pretty much living there, and he sort of made it obvious that he'd rather I wasn't. I'll fetch the rest of my stuff when I can organise a car, I haven't got much. Conor won't mind, will he?"

"Shouldn't think so."

"I'll find somewhere else, it's not hard."

"No." What was hard was Jon, Charlie, the damage we'd done. But, "He'll be okay, love," I said. "If his friends are looking after him. It just takes time, that's all."

"Sure." Neither of us looked at each other, for the better avoidance of doubt.

Jamie and I, we'd only left Conor's house once so far. In his car one evening, the two of us sitting together in the back while he drove us to a predetermined destination.

Conor had been a revelation, at least to me – or he'd had a revelation, rather, that night on the cliff-top. Nor was he the only one, from what he'd said to us. Uncle James had made a fatal error in trying to kill his own, his only son; the cousins had been deeply traumatised, seeing family turn against itself. Even the hardest of them, the ones who had never stopped to question a Macallan's innate rights and privileges, even they were full of questions now. Conor was a convert, a rebel, one with us.

So he drove us to a meeting he'd arranged on the roof of a multi-storey car park, that was meant to be just us and Uncle James; but my uncle came with protection, or he thought so. Although it was night-time, his time, at his insistence, he still brought my father with him. And my father brought a gun.

For what good that did him, which was not a lot. Jamie was still appallingly weak, not fit really to be out of bed let alone facing this kind of confrontation; but Jamie leaned out of the car's window, leaned into moonlight and just twitched the rifle out of my father's grasp, sent it flying through the air and bent its barrel double before it fell with a clatter onto the concrete.

My father swore horribly, rubbed his wrung hands together, glared at him, at me. Not a problem.

Uncle James wasn't much of a problem either, when it came to it. I guess Conor hadn't told him his son was still alive; he stared in at Jamie, his mouth working like a fish out of water, all confidence ripped from him.

Me, I got slowly out of the car, rested against the roof

only hoping that that just looked cool and not needful, and said, "Uncle James, I'll keep this short. I haven't got much to say to you anyway, only that it's over, really. Do you understand?"

"No. What? What are you talking about?" His eyes were still on his silent son, not on me. I hoped to change that, with what I said next.

"I'm talking about you, and this city. The blackmail, the violence, all of it. It's finished. I'm holding you to account for everything our family does hereafter. This time, you're the hostage. You can't touch me in daylight but I can touch you, I can do what I like to you; and I wouldn't like it, but I would do it. If I had to. And if you come after us at night, well, we've got Jamie," and he'd just been reminded what Jamie could do, that his talent was stronger than anyone's in the new generation. Stronger and broader far now, under my tutelage. "And Conor, and others too," taking doubts for certainties, which I figured I could afford to do. "We're the police now," I told him. "Only you can't buy us off or bully us, or threaten anything against us. We're stronger than you are, we make the rules. So you just stop, right? I'll know, if you don't. I've got friends, I've got contacts. And we will stop you, if you make a move on anyone again. That's a promise."

My uncle blustered, of course, he stepped forward, imposing in his sheer bulk; and he came to an abrupt halt as Jamie pushed against him with just a whisker's-width of talent. And then he walked backwards, straining and struggling all the way, his eyes bulging as he fought uselessly at the air, as he had his own first taste of what he'd spent so many years administering to others.

No chance he had to use his own talent, nor my father either. Jamie had learned this from me, he'd fogged the air before their eyes so that they couldn't see to get a mental grip.

He forced Uncle James right up against the parapet and then pushed just a tad harder, bending him backwards over the edge, giving him a taste of terror, just a hint, an echo of the other night. Not as dangerous a gesture as it seemed; if Uncle James should overbalance, I knew Jamie could catch him by the feet and pull him back. And I was sure – fairly sure – that he would.

If I was a mite uncertain, though, my uncle was craven with doubt. His hands flailed, his voice broke a couple of octaves higher than usual, I couldn't hear the words but there was pleading in his frantic yell.

"Let him up, Jamie," I said. Jamie did; I looked at my sweating, gasping uncle and thought he seemed shrunken, suddenly, bereft of the power that had always made him loom so large.

"That's it, uncle," I said. "No more pay-offs, no more protection. Your hand is off this town, as of now and permanently. Us to answer to, if you don't listen."

I didn't wait for his response, or to exact a promise. He wouldn't respect that. I just told him; then I slipped back inside the car, slammed the door, and Conor drove us home.

"Ben?"

"Uh-huh."

"You conscious?"

"You want to call it that, I'm conscious."

"Yeah, right. Why does it feel so good, to feel so fucked?"

Because we're still breathing, bro. But he didn't need telling that, so, "Always feels good, to be fucked."

"Yeah, that's a point. Why aren't we being fucked, damn it? We deserve it. And I'm up for it, if she's gentle. Why aren't the girls all over us?"

He knew the answer to that one too, I could hear him

smiling through the complaint, even while he tried to sound peevish. In fact we were still all over each other, and there wasn't room for the girls. Sometimes I had nightmares, waking or sleeping, when I was suddenly back in his bones and lost again, spinning slowly in broken colours, pulled by the ebb of his blood; then I needed to open my eyes and see not Janice but him, to hear his breathing out of synch with mine.

"Maybe they just get off on playing nurses," I said.

He snorted. "Good nurses get into bed with their patients. That's my definition of a miracle cure . . ."

"You want to tell them?"

"I already did. I was in the bath. Janice shoved the soap in my mouth, and Laura pushed me under."

I laughed. Bathtimes were the best times, the only fun we were allowed, but even there we never got just the one girl at once. They were scrupulous about that; being careful, I guess, not quite trusting themselves to keep this pact they must have made, not to come between us till we were ready.

Other things, other people had come briefly between us, when the girls really couldn't keep them out. Jamie's mother had come, my Aunt Lucy, slipping away from the icy fury of her husband in his stymie, where we had laid him. Jamie had held her hands and talked to her for an hour, down the far end of the garden; he'd been quiet for a long time after, only shaking his head at me and at Laura when we'd asked him questions. I didn't fancy his chances long-term, Laura could out-stubborn a mountain given time, but time was what we silently, mutually determined to give him.

Another time, my own mother came. My turn to be private with a pale and fretful parent, down where the garden fell away into a wild dene; and my turn still to be private after, scowling at interrogations. To be frank I didn't much fancy my chances either, Janice had a steely look in her eye when at last she gave over with the questions already; but for now, no, I didn't want to rehearse the words I'd said or she had. He's a shit, I'd said *inter alia*, you should leave him. She'd only shaken her head, *no, I couldn't do that* or maybe *no, I'm not listening, you mustn't say such things*. Whichever, it was too personal, none of it bore repeating even among so small and close a public. And it did me good to find one secret I could keep from Jamie, it defined another difference between us. Or I could pretend that it did, that what I'd said to my mother was not only an echo of what he'd said to his. So long as we didn't tell, we could both of us pretend we didn't know.

"Seriously, Ben. What are you going to do, have you decided?"

"Oh. Yes," I said. Had to tell him sometime. "I'm going away."

"You're bloody not."

"I bloody am."

"Ben, you can't!"

"Try and stop me."

"I will, and all. I'll trash your bike, mate. I mean it. I'm up for that. You can't go. Not again. I thought you had it sussed now, I thought that's why you came back. You can't just keep running away . . ."

Distantly, I heard the cue that said it was time to relent, time to stop teasing. "I'm not," I said. "Not this time. I'll be back. I have to be, term starts in September."

"Unh? So what?"

With the roar of the bike's returning loud in my ears, I had to raise my voice to confess. "So I'm not exactly going alone."

The bike's engine cut abruptly, nicely timed to match his own silence. Me, I held my breath also, grinning broadly as I waited for the storm to break.